THE BEST THING THAT CAN HAPPEN TO A CROISSANT

THE BEST THING THAT CAN HAPPEN TO A CROISSANT

Pablo Tusset

Translated from the Spanish
by KRISTINA CORDERO

CANONGATE
Edinburgh · London

First published in Spanish in 2001
by Ediciones Lengua de Trapo

First published in English in 2005
by Canongate Books, 14 High Street, Edinburgh EH1 1TE
This edition published in 2005

British Library Cataloguing-in-Publication Data
A catalogue record for this book is available
on request from the British Library

ISBN 978 1 841956 89 3

Typeset by Palimpsest Book Production Limited,
Polmont, Stirlingshire

Printed and bound in Great Britain by
Clays Ltd, St Ives plc

www.canongate.tv

TABLE OF CONTENTS

Look for the bare necessities
The simple bare necessities
Forget about your worries and your strife
I mean the bare necessities,
Are Mother Nature's recipes
That bring the bare necessities of life

—Baloo's Song
Terry Gilkyson

THE BROTHERHOOD OF LIGHT

The best thing that can happen to a croissant is to get spread with butter: this is what I remember thinking as I split one down the middle and smeared it with discount margarine spread. I also remember how I was about to sink my teeth into it when the telephone rang.

I picked it up, even though I knew I'd have to answer with my mouth full.

'Yeeeees . . .'

'Are you there?'

'No, I've stepped out. Please leave a message after the tone and leave me alone. Beeeeep.'

'Cut the comedy routine, will you? And what is that you're chewing on?'

'I am eating breakfast.'

'At one o'clock in the afternoon?'

'I woke up early today. What do you want?'

'Come by the office. I've got news.'

'Go to hell, I'm not into guessing games.'

'Well, I'm not into talking on the phone. There's money involved. I can wait for exactly half an hour. No more.'

I hung up and worked on the croissant for a bit, deliberating between showering, shaving, and sitting down to smoke my first Ducados of the day. I decided to have a smoke while shaving. Provided that nobody came too close to me the shower could wait, whereas my three-day-old stubble had to go – made me look like a deadbeat from a mile off. The day was not starting out brilliantly. I was out of coffee and clean shirts, and I had to turn the entire living room upside down before I found my keys. Then, just as I opened the downstairs door the sun hit me right between the eyes. But I hung tough, and managed to make it over to Luigi's bar.

I walked in like I owned the place. Just in case.

'Luigi, how about a coffee? And maybe you could save me a couple of leftover croissants – I just finished my last one. Speaking of which, what do you do, make them lift weights or something? If you could get your dick as hard as those things maybe you'd smile a little more.'

'Listen, if you want same-day croissants, you can pay the regular price. If not, fuck off and eat the ones I give you out of the goodness of my heart. Get it?'

'Hmmm . . . no, I'm not sure that I do. When I come back later to pay for the coffee you can explain it to me, more slowly. Oh . . . and I'll take a pack of Ducados, too, if you don't mind.'

'Why don't I just tell you to get the fuck out of here right now?'

'Because when I've got cash you know I'm liable to drop a nice wad of cash in this rat hole of yours.'

'And when you don't I have to let you run a tab even for cigarettes. Oh, before I forget: Fina came around yesterday looking for you, she said to call her. So are you screwing her or what? She's got some pair of tits . . .'

'You're gonna go straight to hell for your adulterous ways, you know that?'

The intense sunlight in the bar was getting unbearable, and everyone in there seemed about ready to go stark raving mad from the heat, so I made my escape, sticking to the shady side of the street for the last two blocks until I reached the entrance to my brother's office. Thirty something stairs later I found myself at the door to Miralles & Miralles, Financial Advisors. For the record, I am the second of the two Miralles; the firstborn son was no doubt already inside, showered, shaved and dressed up in suit and tie since seven in the morning. As I walked in I called out a general team 'hello', and then greeted Maria with a more personalised 'Hey, how are you?' to which I was reciprocated with a 'battling the phones, darling, you know . . . my God, you're huge.'

'I take care of myself. You know, like, I try to eat a lot of fat and not move around too much.' At the far end of the offices I could see they were dealing with clients, a pair of young couples, and so I decided to keep the banter to a minimum. Only Pumares, who was weaving through the desks, looked up and lifted his eyebrows in a silent greeting. I returned the gesture and went straight to the office of Miralles the First.

He had already caught sight of me heading toward him through the glass partitions. Not an easy man to catch off-guard.

'You might want to turn on the air conditioner, your people are roasting out there,' I said as I walked in, just in case my Magnificent Brother had some kind of rude greeting already prepared.

'It must be that hangover, giving you the shakes.'

'No, no. I would have one, though, if you didn't fuck me over so bad in the balance sheets.'

'It's just as well. I've got a job for you.'

'I thought you were into fending for yourself.'

'I am, but someone's got to take out the trash. That's always been your strong suit.'

'Let me guess: you're getting divorced. No: you're moving out . . .'

'Could we save the jokes for later, if you don't mind? I need you to look into something for me.'

'Well, let's see . . . why don't you give me a lead of some sort – like, is that "something" related in any way to the colour blue?'

'I'm trying to locate the owner of a certain property . . . an old house in Les Corts. Five hundred euros are yours if you can find out before Monday.'

One thing was for sure: if one little name was worth that kind of cash to The First, it had to mean that the information would be used to cut a deal worth millions. I doubted it was anything illegal – The First would *never* do anything illegal – but I could smell it a mile off. He was probably going to put the squeeze on some poor sucker – either some old guy on a fixed income, or an orphan, or the last endangered flipper seal in the Mediterranean. Or something of the sort.

I tried to hit him up for a little more dough – after all, a guilty conscience doesn't come cheap.

'Well, you know, I am kind of booked up these days . . .'

'Don't give me that. Five hundred euros for a first name and a surname. Not one bit more. Yes or no?'

The same offer, twice in the space of a half hour. Some fucking life.

'Well . . . I'll need an advance.'

'I paid you your earnings on the tenth: don't tell me you've drunk your way through three thousand euros already . . .'

'I also bought the newspaper and a tube of toothpaste. I want half the payment up front.'

'I'll give you twenty-five per cent.'

Shit. I shrugged in grudging agreement. He scooted back in his little swivel chair and took a metal cash box out of his desk drawer. A wallet full of surprise cash was much more than I had expected to earn at the start of the day, and I began to weigh my options as to how I might best invest the money while Miralles the First counted out payment number one in coins. Despite his well-tended physique, chiselled at the local gym-of-the-moment, and his tailor-made suit, he was still the living image of Dickensian avarice.

I walked around to his side of the desk and scooped up the coins.

'Thanks, kid,' I said, enunciating as best I could, which I do quite well.

'I've told you a thousand times, I don't appreciate you calling me kid.'

'You think I like it? I only do it to annoy you.'

With a disgusted look on his face, he handed me a Post-It with the address in question.

'You might want to take a shower. You stink.' I waited until I was closer to the door to respond.

'It's the stench of the Miralles clan, kid: you've got it too.'

I exited as fast as I could, so as to leave him seething beneath his Hugo Boss. I thought I heard him say something, but I had already turned to leave.

One-nothing, my advantage. Plus a tidy sum of cash in my pocket.

My next move was to head to the supermarket to stock up on a few things. I was feeling like bathing myself in a mountain of spaghetti smothered in heavy cream sauce, nice 'n' wet, and of course I would also purchase a slab of real butter to spread on Luigi's croissants. All this could be had for loose change, and for a bit more dinero I could fire up some potatoes, eggs, clembuterol-injected pork, and spongiformed veal's brains. I'd drop some more dough at Luigi's that night. Subtracting what I already owed him, I could only drink about thirty euros' worth of booze, but getting drunk in Luigi's bar on a limited budget is far more feasible than going to any other joint in the neighbourhood, where I would easily blow through three times as much. This, of course, takes into account the fact that with Luigi you can always run a tab for the last few. The rest of the money, then, would go toward securing some hashish – I had gone at least forty-eight hours since smoking the last of my stash.

After a quick evaluation of priorities I decided to rectify the medication issue first, and headed for the park on Calle Ondina to see if Nico was around. Luckily I found him in his usual spot – no easy feat in the morning hours. Mainly because mornings are not my forte. But there he was, sitting atop a park bench, his clunky boots resting on the seat part. Next to him I recognised a friend of his, a guy who looks like he just escaped from Mauthausen. The human race knows no middle ground: it's either Marks & Spencer *pret-a-porter* or shit-stained fake Nike jogging suits.

'What do you want, chief?'

'An eighth.'

After a pause that made me suspect he was caught in some sort of autistic trance thing, he wandered aimlessly toward the edge of the park, leaving me alone with the Mauthausen guy, who was not looking particularly lucid himself.

'So, like, do you think the price of an eighth has gone up, you know, because of the euro?' I asked, more than anything just to see if the guy was still alive.

'What do I know, man: it's all the same shit . . .'

That about summed up his interest level, though I was genuinely concerned with the answer. If a thousand pesetas equals six euros, then five thousand would be thirty. Rounding down, of course. No doubt Nico had figured out a way to take advantage of the scheme and raise his prices. The little guy, meanwhile, seemed to have entered a kind of personal-reflection moment which I thought best not to interrupt, so I lit a Ducados and sat down on the bench for a smoke. One great thing about stoners is that you can sit down next to them and smoke in total silence for half an hour and it's no big deal. They can entertain themselves. Thirty seconds in a lift with a Registered Windows User, on the other hand, is enough to give you migraines. Of course, there are plenty of things for which stoners are hopeless: their conversation stinks, you can't ever borrow money from them, things like that. And then the stoners who go straight and become traffic cops or logic professors end up creating pure chaos out of things like roundabouts and counterfact conditional equations. At that point, I reached into my pocket and produced the Post-It that The First had given me, to see if I was anywhere near the address he had written 'Jaume Guillamet 15', it said, in his superb penmanship. For a few moments I focused on trying to place the location in my head. I know the street well enough: number fifteen had to be at the upper end, and so I mentally walked up Guillamet and tried to picture the buildings on either side of the street, but anyone who attempts such an exercise will inevitably prove one of my more original hypotheses – erroneously attributed to Parmenides – which states that reality is a circumstance filled with voids and holes. In the middle of all this Nico returned with the hash so that was the end of my astral trip. I said goodbye to him and the friend, with that facsimile of courtesy one adopts when speaking to one's principal drug supplier, and I left via the south end of the park. A day of joints, food, and booze now lay before me. The only thing that sullied my horizon somewhat was the prospect of bumping into Fina. It is common knowledge that women, too, are like black holes, capable of absorbing all the attention that one lavish upon on them. Obviously, this excludes women who charge in cash for their services, and unfortunately Fina did not charge, at least not in the money sense.

So I took off, and on the way to the supermarket I made a detour to check out the building numbers on Jaume Guillamet.

Turning off Santa Clara, the first number I spotted was fifty-seven; all I had to do was backtrack a few yards. Even from a distance I quickly located the building that The First was interested in. I had walked by it so many times that I had never really noticed it, but now it seemed like a rather incongruous structure given the context: a turn-of-the-century cottage, with a little garden enclosed by a brick wall from which two tall trees rose up. It was kind of hard to understand how the hell that little shack, with its boarded-up windows and a sprawling yard that took up the entire width of the sidewalk, had managed to survive amid the line-up of eight- and nine-story apartment buildings. That one single structure turned the entire stretch of Guillamet into something out of a painting by Delvaux or Magritte: ruins, statues, train stations with neither trains nor passengers. It was a kind of absence, an eerie stillness, a portrait of something that was missing. Naturally I wasn't about to ring the doorbell – that is, if there even *was* a doorbell. The very small amount of reason I possessed advised me not to take that step until I showered, put on some clean clothes, and thought up a good excuse for whoever might open the front door. But I did stop to look for a second or two as I walked past. The wall was about two yards high, and the abundant ivy that covered it seemed healthy, indicating that the building was not entirely abandoned. I walked round the perimeter of the garden in search of a door, a sign, or a bell of some sort, and in the heat of my investigation I stepped directly into a pile of dog shit as I rounded the first corner. Serious dog shit, the kind you practically never see anymore now that everyone goes around scooping up the turds of their euro-pets with little Marks & Spencer bags. I tried to wipe off the mess by rubbing my shoe back and forth on the curb, but the crap had gotten wedged in the little corner between the sole and the heel and so I had to take off the shoe. I looked around for a piece of paper or something to wipe it off with, and next to a lamppost by the wall I found one of those little red rags that you hang from the back of your car to signal that you're driving with a heavy load. I was not fully convinced that I wouldn't stink of designer dog shit by the time I reached the supermarket, but I had to abort the effort once the rag was rendered untouchable.

Given the high stress level of this kind of detective work, I deemed it was time to finish up for the day. So I tossed the rag on the ground (I always enjoy reminding myself that I live in Barcelona instead of Copenhagen) and I made a break for the supermarket before it closed.

I don't know why but at Dia, the discount supermarket, it always feels as though someone's filming a movie about Vietnam. But it is cheaper than Caprabo at the Illa shopping centre, where you half-expect to find Fred Astaire and Ginger Rogers come out dancing a polka in the frozen food section. To my aforementioned purchases I added a bunch of idiotic impulse buys that I found along the aisles, a veritable obstacle course of giant unopened cardboard boxes that looked as though a Hercules had just airvac'd them down in a parachute. On the endless cashier's line I double-checked that my selections did not exceed my original budget, and paid. Then, in a stroke of brilliant foresight, I remembered to stop at the tobacco shop and buy a pack of Fortunas for my hash joints.

When I returned home I demonstrated remarkable restraint and waited to roll my first joint until after showering (by then, even I had begun to notice that I smelled like a sweaty dancing bear). But as soon as I got out of the shower, like a triumphant baby dolphin, I didn't even bother drying off: I went straight to the sofa and got to work on the hash. I rolled a hefty little reefer, and given my two days of abstinence it wasn't long before that nice little pleasure tickle began to take effect. It was a shame that the general state of the living room did not match the immaculate condition of my freshly cleaned and deodorised body. My bourgeois weaknesses always come out after a shower – maybe that's why I shower as little as possible – and so I sat there staring at the blank television screen hoping that by contemplating the nothingness before me, I would overcome the sudden urge I felt to get up and start cleaning house. It's incredible how illuminating a turned-off television set can be: it reflects you, looking back at you, right in front of it. Fuck.

The sound of the telephone ringing was the one thing that delivered me back to Planet Earth.

'Yeees . . .'

'Good afternoon. I'm calling from the Centre for Statistical Studies. We're conducting a standard media audience survey, and I was wondering if I might be able to take a few seconds of your time.'

It was one of those telemarketing girls, with one of those extremely sweet voices that is nevertheless incapable of hiding the underlying hostility of someone who genuinely hates her job. The annoying part, of course, was that the survey bit sounded like an excuse to try and sell me something, and that got on my nerves.

I decided to put her to work.

'A survey? How grand, I *love* surveys.'

'Oh, do you? Well, then you're in luck . . . Could you give me your name, please?'

'Juan.'

'Juan what?'

'Juan Tosockmi.'

'Wonderful, Juan, wonderful. Now tell me, how old are you?'

'Seventy-two.'

'Your field of work?'

'Pastry chef.'

'Pas-try . . . chef. Perfect. Do you like music, Juan?'

'Oh yeah, I'm wild about music.'

'Really? What kind, specifically?'

'Oh . . . Handel's *Messiah*, *La Cucaracha*. In that order.'

The girl was starting to hesitate, but she wasn't about to give up. She went on to ask if I listened to the radio, if I watched television, if I read newspapers and if so which ones. After she went through her little routine, she hit me with the big question:

'Very good, Juan . . . Now, as a way of thanking you for helping us out, and given your taste in classical music, we're going to award you three CDs – or cassettes or records, your choice. The only payment involved is for shipping and handling, it comes out to about ten-fifty, does that sound good to you?'

'Ooh, I'm so sorry, but I'd have to check with my husband for something like that . . .'

My voice is unmistakably male, caveman male, which clearly unglued her. That was precisely the moment to stick it to her.

'Oh, I'm sorry. I hope you're not alarmed or anything, it's that we're gay, common-law marriage, you know. We've been living together ever since we got out of rehab and opened the sweet shop – we're going on six months now. And as luck had it, we have this customer – he's gay too – who comes in to buy our chocolate-covered cream puffs – if I might say so myself, we make *incredible* cream puffs – and anyway, he introduced us to the Society of the Brotherhood of Light . . . you *are* familiar with the Brotherhood, I suppose?'

'Well . . . uh, no . . .'

'Oh, well, you'll have to get to know us. We'd absolutely love it. In the mornings, when I stay at the sweet shop, he presides over the services at the Brotherhood. And then we switch in the afternoons . . . So you say you haven't seen the Light yet?'

'No . . . no . . .'

'No? Well, don't worry, we can set you up in no time. Let's see, what's your name?'

The girl had lost it by now.

'No, no, you see . . .'

'Wait – better yet just give me your address and I can come by today and we can have a chat, how would that suit you?'

'No, no, I'm sorry, it's just . . . they don't allow us to give out our address . . .'

'They don't what? Well, that's no problem: I can locate your telephone call on my computer and I can send out one of our Lesbian Big Sisters to talk with your supervisor. Wait, wait, the number's coming up on my screen right now. Let's see . . . you're calling from Barcelona, right? If you can wait just a few seconds your address should come up . . .'

That was about as much as she could take. Almost immediately I heard the click of the telephone on the other end.

Mission accomplished. I took a long drag off the joint and in a splendid mood I went to the kitchen to put on the water for the spaghetti. At that moment I had no idea what was going down at Miralles & Miralles; nor did I have any idea of the predicament I was about to get myself into.

TOP-HEAVY FRONTAL LOAD

An inordinately loud clap of thunder roused me from my nap: brrrrrrrrrrrrm, just as I was dreaming about a bunch of treacherous creatures that possessed the singular ability to sink their little legs into the earth, take root there and survive indefinitely in vegetable form. They even had a name: borzogs, a strange hybrid between nettle and elf. You could walk among them and not suspect a thing and then suddenly – bam! – they would come alive, rip their roots out of the ground and become legs once again, and the little motherfuckers would take hungry bites out of your legs.

It was after seven in the evening and raining buckets, a real springtime thunderstorm, short but fierce, and my head cleared as I gazed out at the sheets of water coming down outside my window. Barcelona is pretty cool when it rains: the trees become bright green, the postboxes bright yellow, and the bus roofs bright red, all washed clean by the pouring rain. I don't know what the hell is wrong with the buses in Barcelona, but from up above they always look like they're full of shit. Except when it rains hard and everything becomes green, blue, and red – primary colours against a gloomy grey, turning the city into a giant toyland – a massive Scalextric or a Legoland. I put some coffee on to face my second wake-up of the day, much more relaxed at this late afternoon hour, and I turned on the radio.

Something slow was playing, a melodious black voice accompanied by long drags on a saxophone. Afterwards, I turned on my computer and as it booted up I lit a joint and poured myself a coffee. I settled down in front of the monitor and connected to my server. Hmm.

Twelve messages. Three of them junk mail. The other nine had a little more sizzle. I did a superficial scan for prioritising purposes. John from Dublin: 'hey, how are you, here are some Primary Sentences I've been working on,' etc. The people at the General Patent Office: 'unfortunately we cannot provide you with the information you requested.' Blah, blah, blah. Lerilyn from Virginia: 'I can't stand my American scene, I miss Barcelona so bad . . .' Her note was signed with kisses (*besos* spelled with a v) and an *hasta luego* (minus the h). I lingered a little longer on a message from the Boston Philosophy College, inviting me to give a lecture during their summer session. Naturally I had no intention of going, but I entertained myself with that email for a few minutes, for the ego boost it provided. In the street, I may be a nobody, but on the Web I do have something of a name for myself and I do still have a shred of vanity – another one of my bourgeois weaknesses. The other six messages were from the Metaphysical Club mail server which I downloaded before logging off so that I could read them at my leisure. From what I could tell, everyone was talking about my latest instalment. 'If every word introduces a new concept, the simple phrase "all that which does not exist" is sufficient to make everything that does not exist, exist.' This was the message from a guy named Martin Ayakati, in an attempt to refute my most recent Metaphysical Club effort. A slightly insignificant, though not entirely meaningless comment. But inferior to my own, in any event.

I decided to be organised about this, and respond to my messages one by one as I read them. I hit the 'reply' button and began to write, in Spanish:

'To say "all that which does not exist" is to introduce, effectively, a new concept, but it does not bring into existence anything more than that very concept which it introduces. That is, a certain entity about which we know nothing except that it bears the name of "all that which does not exist." I should point out that in the same fashion, a woman may call herself "Rose" and that does not mean that she is full of thorns . . .'

I was just getting warmed up when the telephone rang. It was becoming clear that this was to be a day of telephonic interruptions.

'Yeeeesss . . .'

'I've been calling you for half an hour, but I kept getting a busy signal.'

It was The First. He must have called while I was checking my email.

'What the hell do you want now? We agreed to meet on Monday, didn't we?'

'Not anymore. Drop it.'

'Whaat . . . ?'

'Drop the whole thing. I'm not interested in the information any more.'

'Oh, no? Well, I, for one, am still interested in those five hundred euros.'

'I have no doubt that you haven't even begun to do what I asked you.'

'Well, I have, in fact. It has taken up a considerable amount of my mental space. And anyway, a deal is a deal. You owe me that money.'

'Fine. Keep the advance I gave you.'

Now that was definitely weird. I had to take advantage of the opportunity to hit him up for more.

'I don't have the advance any more, and I turned down another offer because I was counting on the balance that you were going to pay me next Friday. You do the math.'

'All right, all right. Don't start in with me. Come by tomorrow and I'll give you the rest. But forget about the whole thing, all right? Forget it.'

Interesting: The First was giving me a whole five hundred euros, free and clear: without arguing, without bargaining, without getting all hot and bothered. Something major was going down, I was sure of it. Or at least that was what I inferred from the vehemence in his voice, the 'drop it', that odd imperative, 'drop it.' Now that I think about it, there was definitely a note of alarm in his voice, although at the time I perceived it as impatience, an impatience that was just what I needed to put an end to the conversation before he had a chance to have misgivings about the money.

'All right, I'll come by tomorrow. Listen, I'm kind of busy right now . . . And if you need to call again, try not to ring so loud next time, all right?'

'Wait, there's something else.'

'What's wrong?'

'It's Dad. He broke his leg.'

'His leg . . . what for?'

It wasn't a joke; I was just shocked by the news. My Father's Highness never does anything without sufficient motive to justify his actions.

'There's been an accident, he got hit by a car. He called me from the hospital and I went over to pick him up. Mom is a bit hysterical. She hasn't called you yet?'

'No . . . Is it serious?'

'No, he's all right. He's in a plaster cast up to his knee, and he'll be stuck with it for a little more than a month. He's in a bad mood now because their plan was to go to Llavaneras this weekend and stay there for the rest of the summer. Please, do me a favour and go visit them, they're pretty shaken up.'

That was the very first time my Magnificent Brother had ever asked something like that of me. But the truly weird, even alarming aspect of this was the 'please' bit. Maybe our father's accident had unnerved him – or who knows, maybe there was still a heart somewhere beneath that Hugo Boss suit. In any event, it was still highly unorthodox for him to have unloaded all that cash without a fight.

I picked up the telephone again and punched the number of the Miralles headquarters. I don't know what got into me – all this must have given me some kind of filial adrenaline rush.

My Mother's Highness actually answered the telephone, another unusual turn of events. After a brief exchange I could tell that the initial shock of the accident had subsided, but she was still quite out of sorts. I asked her why she hadn't called me as soon as she'd found out about the accident, more than anything to show a little interest.

'What do you think, Pablo José? That after all this, I've lost my mind, too? Of course I tried calling but you weren't there, and then what with everything, I forgot. Your brother went to pick him up at the hospital.'

'Is Dad there? Can you put him on for a second?'

'No, no, he needs to rest now. He's in bed. And I should warn you, he's in a foul mood. I suppose you'll be coming by to see him?'

I don't know why, but I said yes.

'All right, sure, I'll come over for a few minutes sometime tomorrow morning. I have to go to Sebastian's office so I can stop on the way.'

'Fine. Come by at around one and we can have a drink and then eat together.'

Suddenly, somehow, this had turned into a lunch obligation. But, well . . . it was just for one day.

After hanging up I fixed myself another joint and poured some more coffee, hoping to return to my messages, but I couldn't concentrate. In reality it wasn't that big a deal: my father had gotten his leg all smashed up and The First had had a moment of weakness. Nothing terrifically out of the ordinary. But my mind has, as they say, a mind of its own, and when it doesn't want to concentrate there's nothing I can do about it. I got up from my chair and wandered over to the window. The rain had stopped, something by El Último de la Fila was playing on the radio, with that voice that can turn the stupidest song into a transcendental symphony, and I started to get all sad as I surveyed my living room, a veritable trash pit stretching out before my eyes. In that indoor jungle I half-expected a borzog to sprout up and start nipping away at my calves. The mere idea put me in such a negative mood that I indulged my bourgeois weaknesses and decided it was time to clean house. I started with the bedroom, the room that has come to be the eye of my domestic storm. Beneath a pile of underwear that had started to grow roots at the foot of my bed I found a copy of *El País* from a few weeks earlier, and I stood there fixating on it, trying to remember why the hell I had saved it. Thanks to this subtle distraction manoeuvre, my urge to clean gradually subsided, and I was able to put the pile of underwear back where it was and head for the kitchen in search of something edible. I had a major craving for a couple of fried eggs and a plateful of chips smothered in mayonnaise, something that my newly-stocked refrigerator could most certainly offer.

I was already getting to work on this when, for the fourth time that day, the telephone rang – just as the potatoes were getting nice and brown in the big skillet and the oil for the eggs had begun to crackle and spit smoke in the small one.

'Hello?'

'Heeeey, how aaare you . . . ?'

I can't stand people who don't identify themselves on the phone. It's like, everyone assumes that their voice is instantly recognisable, even when spoken through some piece of shit telephone receiver. This voice, however, was unmistakable. The voice of Fina.

'Hey. You got me. I'm just about to fry a couple of eggs.'

'Yeah, so? What's going on with you these days . . . ?'

I also have a strong aversion to people who call and expect me to direct the conversation. As far as I see it, the one who initiates the call is driving the bus. But Fina evidently doesn't feel that way.

'Nothing. I just told you: frying eggs.'

'At this hour?'

'Well, so what? Is there some kind of no-eggs-after-dark law I haven't heard of?'

Giggles. If there's one thing I like about Fina, apart from her tits, it's that she laughs at my stupid jokes. That's what saves her.

'Listen, my potatoes are starting to burn . . .'

'Wasn't it eggs?'

'Eggs with potatoes. Fried. In oil. Olive oil.'

This time she responded with a fake laugh and finally got to the point.

'Do you want to meet up later?'

'What time?'

'I don't know . . . in a little while, like nine maybe. At Luigi's?'

By now the chips were burnt, but they weren't any worse for the wear. I smeared them with mayonnaise and snarfed them down, using them as shovels for the eggs. Then I flopped out on the sofa. Suddenly a wave of lethargy came over me; all I wanted to do was settle in, watch TV and ventilate a bag of peanuts as soon as hunger struck again. I've always felt that I watch far too little TV. Somehow I always end up watching TV late at night, when my only options are an Ab Flex infomercial or a masterpiece of classic cinema. Naturally I always opt for the Ab Flex, but by the third zap, I start yearning for a good, primetime Telecinco show and those sets decked out with curving staircases and trampolines. That's always how I imagined heaven would be – the heaven that the Marist Brothers always promised would be ours if only we would stop jerking off in chapel. Anyway. I got up from the sofa, very grudgingly, and went hunting in my closet for something clean to wear. I found an old polo shirt and put it on, but when I raised my arms the tail popped out from my pantwaist and dangled just below my belly button. Then I remembered that I have a mirror, and I went over to check myself out. A 1.80-metre sausage stuffed into a *Starsky and Hutch*-esque Fred Perry shirt. I rummaged around a bit more until I located a shirt large enough for my dimensions. It was slightly frayed at the neck from stubble abrasions, but who the hell would bother noticing the neckline of my shirt? Well, Fina would, but Fina and I are pretty tight; she could care less about things like the state of my shirt collar. The real drag was that I was starting to feel all heavy from the eggs, the mayonnaise, the expense of energy, what with all that getting up and down from the couch to dig through my closet . . . Luckily I was able to lay a long, noisy fart that unleashed about a quart of intestinal volume, which gave my gut some breathing space.

It was almost nine-thirty by the time I turned up at the bar, but Fina usually arrives even later than I do, so I was cool. It was doggie hour: after dinner, all the neighbourhood social outcasts emerge from their apartments with the excuse of walking the pup, and afterwards they all find their way over to Luigi's bar, which ends up looking like some kind of a dog show. Luigi and Roberto, the night waiter, were behind the bar. About Roberto, there's not much to tell – he can pretty much be summed up in one adjective: Mexican. This is something that you would only notice when he talks, because his talent for singing *corridos* is pretty much nil. I ordered a beer and leaned against the bar. The remake of *The Fly* was playing on the TV up above, and at a table nearby, a man and a woman sharing a plate of octopus made faces of disgust. I downed my beer practically in one gulp and then ordered another. Both Luigi and Roberto were busy taking orders from the tables, and so for lack of better entertainment I just sat there staring at the telly. The main guy was already pretty bugged-out, as they say, his face covered with boils about to explode and his body plagued with insect bites: 'I'm saying . . . I'll hurt you if you stay,' the fly-man said to his girlfriend as the spit dribbled from his face. I finished off the second beer and started in on the third. If there's one thing I can't stand it's when my life becomes some kind of interior dialogue, so I kept my eye on the TV monitor until the movie ended and struck up a casual flirtation with a boxer puppy while his owner sunk his day's pay in a slot machine. I had almost forgotten that I was waiting for someone by the time Fina showed up. Although, to be precise, she did far more than just show up – her entrance into the bar was most definitely an arrival. A grand arrival in a sweater dress that showed off every last curve from her tits down to about fifteen centimetres below her crotch. A pair of diamond-patterned fishnets took over from there down to a pair sadomasochist-housewife boots. In addition to this, she had dyed her hair orange, very short, buzzed at the back, and she had made up her face taking special care to outline her lips. A long pendant hung from her neck, swinging back and forth and pointing suggestively toward her plunging neckline, just in case anyone hadn't noticed it. The guy at the slot machine missed a Triple Bonus, the man eating the octopus with his girlfriend dribbled oil all over his shirt, and Luigi almost had a choking fit before jumping up to greet her. She approached the far end of the bar to solicit a hello kiss and then Luigi, with a sick sweetness he did little to hide, whispered something in her ear – 'it's been so long since you last came around,' or something of the sort. Everyone had to wait for the little ceremony to conclude before any more beer could be ordered. Then, finally, we settled in to the table in the back.

'I was waxing my legs,' Fina said as she sat down. That was her excuse for arriving two hours late. She said it shyly, but that was a well-practised tactic on her part.

'How's your husband?'

'He's in Toledo. A Hewlett-Packard product demonstration.'

'Why didn't you go with him?'

'I didn't feel like it. Anyway, he's better off going alone

on those things. That way at night he can go to a topless joint with the competition and get wasted while discussing inkjet versus laser printers. If I go, I ruin the topless bit and they end up having to talk business in a regular bar.'

'That dress is a knockout.'

It had to be said, what the fuck, why else had she spent two hours getting all dolled up?

'You like it? It's been in my closet forever, I just never wear it.'

'Well, it's not only the dress; it's you. You're not looking too shabby.'

'Oh . . . I can't remember the last time you said such sweet things to me.'

'I can't remember the last time I saw your body looking like that.'

'Only because you haven't tried . . .'

Touché. The only way out of that one was a stupid joke. I assumed the face of a fly-man wracked with bodily spasms.

'I'm saying . . . I'll hurt you if you stay.'

'Huh?'

Fina hadn't seen the flick. I tried again, this time with a bright-eyed-American-youngster look on my face singing in the corresponding accent.

'Que seraaaa, seraaaa, whatever will be, will be . . .'

She laughed out loud this time, raising her hand to cover her mouth. When the fit subsided, she asked me to make the face again.

'Please, please, please,' she begged me. I said no. She insisted. I started to get nervous. She laughed even more at the idea of making me nervous . . . Luckily, Luigi appeared with our beers. He pulled a chair over and sat down next to Fina.

'And your husband . . . ?'

'In Toleeedo.'

'Toledo? What the hell is he doing in Toledo with a wife like you here?'

I intervened on behalf of poor José María.

'And what the hell are you doing bothering us here with a wife like yours at home?'

'Well, the wife I've got isn't half as hot as this little lady.'

'Next time I see her, I'll let her know you said that.'

'Bah. You think she doesn't know already? So,' he said, turning back to Fina, 'in Toledo, huh? Well, I'm right here, you know? At your disposal for whatever you might need.'

That was when Fina decided to play the intriguing-female act.

'Oh, really? And what sort of services are you offering?'

'Full service. No charge.'

'God, if that isn't the last thing on earth anyone needs . . .'

'Don't be so sure. Men like me are in high demand.'

'Right. For making livestock feed, for example.'

'You stay out of this. I was talking to the young miss here.'

'Young Mrs, if you don't mind. I'm a married woman.'

'Yeah, but with a husband in Toledo, that's like having an uncle in Alcalá.'

'He's back on Friday, you know.'

'That gives us two days . . .'

Seeing as how Luigi had his work cut out for him, I went over to the bar to get cigarettes and finish my beer. By now I was about eight or ten in and I was starting to get drunk, but the night was still very young. From the look of things, the next two hours would be occupied by Fina's usual round of heartfelt confessions and Luigi's subsequently lewd comments. Yes, we were in for it: Luigi was liable to come and sit at our table every chance he got between serving up sandwiches and beers. Roberto, on the other hand, always exercises a bit more restraint: he'll come to the back occasionally to smoke a cigarette, or to answer a call on the mobile hanging from his belt, but he doesn't make a habit of sitting down with the clientele. More regulars entered the bar and approached our table; we would then exchange a few trivialities, and if the conversation wasn't lurid enough, they'd eventually move on. The only time Fina and I were alone was in between these interruptions, which wasn't necessarily a bad thing, because conversation interruptions can sometimes actually help you keep track of whatever you're discussing – e.g. the hen that moves forward along a white line, etc. And after all, Fina is a woman – e.g. a black hole – which means that if you don't cling to the edge of things you're likely to disappear forever, swallowed up by the abyss. Two-thirty in the morning had come and gone by the time we left in search of another watering hole, and that was only after the obligatory vodka shot and the comical farewell scene between Fina and Roberto and Luigi. I was actually able to pay for everything, including what I owed him from that morning, but the night-caps at the Bikini were going to have to be Fina's treat. This was, as always, the moment when Fina would use me for support, and she hung from my arm, resting her cheek against my shoulder as we walked up Jaume Guillamet. The result of this manoeuvre is a slow, zig-zagging advance which is very easily mistaken for the aimless reverie of two people in love.

'You're so cosy,' she said, grabbing my deltoids with the full force of her palm.

'Right. That's because I'm fat. If you weren't so fixated on losing weight you'd be cosy, too.'

'Oh, no. I still have ten pounds to lose yet.'

'Don't be silly: ten pounds of tits and arse degraded by the heat that contributes to the universal entropy . . .'

'The what?'

'Do you have any idea how long it has taken nature to bestow you with those knockers you so despise? You don't mess with the cosmic order, sweetheart.'

'That's only because you like fat chicks. Anyway, weren't you the one who said I was looking so cute?'

'Yeah. But before, you were unbelievably fucking cute. The unbelievably fucking is exactly what you lost.'

That night I very purposefully guided our steps toward Jaume Guillamet, crossing diagonally to save the extra walk around to the traffic light at Travessera. Inevitably, of course, I focused my attention on the house at number fifteen, with its brick wall and its little garden, and as we passed in front of it I noticed something.

'Wait a second,' I said to Fina, as I tried to disentangle myself. I circled round the car that was parked in front of the entrance and as I separated the tall grass in front, I looked at the lamp post that rose up alongside it. Once again, there was a red rag tied to the post, only this time it was fully clean, as if it were brand-new.

I don't know what possessed me at that moment – alcohol-fuelled humour, I suppose – but I untied the rag from the post and tied it around Fina's neck, and we continued to walk up the street.

'Danger: top-heavy frontal load,' I joked, in a Magilla Gorilla voice.

Fina laughed her head off. I did too, but not that much, really, because there's a limit to how much you can believe in chance occurrences like that red-rag thing. Of course, looking back now, it wasn't until the following day that the real paranoia set in.

VENISON LIVER PATÉ

My alarm rang. It had to be my alarm: what else could make such a horrendously cacophonous bleeping noise? My operating system, however, is calibrated so as not to wake up quite so easily. I am filming a saga of slumberous events: onscreen is a vast meadow of white, an infinitely long sheet of white paper. Tiny lightning rays that are somehow more like little baby tornadoes fall slowly down upon the paper ground, perforating it. At first they come down weakly and are widely-spaced, a slight annoyance that forces me to move forward carefully so as not to sink my foot into a hole. But the rain continues its attack, and the floor grows more and more pockmarked, making my advance more and more difficult.

Total anxiety. I slam down on the alarm clock.

I was lying in bed, uncovered, with my shirt still on and my pants only halfway down. At least I had made it into the bed, the beginning and end of all my travels. But I had actually managed to set the alarm clock. Now I faced a truly desolate bedroom panorama. Brutal hangover. Headache. Burning in the stomach. And many holes, including Fina, the blackest of them all. Then there were all those borzogs that perforated the ground with their bionic legs; and then the thunder of a million drills being drilled into my head. Finally I made it to another hole – the drain in the sink, to whose spout I clung with desperate thirst. Twelve o'clock.

The best thing that can happen to a hunk of butter is to get spread on a croissant. But there were no croissants to be had. There's always something missing. Thursday June 18, the International Day of Non-Existence. My only consolation was the thought that I was about to collect the rest of that money from my brother and so I shaved, drank some coffee, smoked a joint, put on the previous night's clothes and walked out into the street in an attempt to adjust my life to something that might seem something like a movie script: action, dialogue, and as little brain-wasting as possible.

Luigi was already up and ready for action.

'Up at the crack of dawn, eh?'

'No talking. Please. A coffee, if you don't mind.'

'What time did you get to bed?'

'No idea.'

'So you didn't get any action . . .'

'Don't fuck with me today, Luigi, I've got to go to my parents' house and I have to get in the mood, you know?'

'You really must be low on cash, huh.'

'No, it's my father. He broke his leg. So listen, I got to go, have to stop by the office to settle an account. I'll pay you later, OK?'

Luckily it wasn't too sunny and I was able to arrive at Miralles & Miralles without having to jump around looking for the shady side of the street. But as I climbed the staircase, each step I took pounded away at my temples. At the reception desk, as always, was Maria.

'Is my brother visible?'

I looked up toward the glass wall in front of his office. I couldn't see him through the metal blinds; the light wasn't even on in there.

'He didn't come in this morning. It looks like today is absence day for everyone . . .'

'He hasn't come in at all?'

The news came as such a shock that I didn't register the 'absence day' bit, so very parallel to my International Day of Non-Existence and the proliferation of giant holes everywhere around me.

'Your sister-in-law called in. He's sick. Flu, or something like that. She said he had a high fever, couldn't even get out of bed. He must be pretty bad.'

'And how do you all plan to get by without His Excellence?'

'Who knows? Everything here has to pass through his office. For the moment, Pumares is stalling everything he can. And to complicate matters, your brother's secretary hasn't turned up, either. Didn't even call in.'

I left Maria with her telephones and left the office in a foul mood. All I had left in my pocket was a bit of loose change and so, not knowing exactly where to go, I took a walk around the block. After briefly weighing my options, I decided to go to my parents' house first and then pay the obligatory visit to my Poor Sick Brother afterward. I knew he had to have money at home – he always has a fairly healthy wad of bills in his wallet, not to mention his Magnificent Credit Card. For the moment, I couldn't face the prospect of either my Father's Highness or my Mother's Highness – much less the two of them together, the double attack – and so I detoured at my apartment just long enough to fire up a joint and shake some of the hangover out of my system. I sat on the couch and as I smoked I prepared another joint in anticipation of the ten-minute martyrdom that lay between me and my parents' house.

The main residence of my illustrious parents rises up above the western fringes of the Diagonal and takes up the two top floors of one of the poshest buildings in the neighbourhood.

You'd have to get to the heart of Pedralbes to find something comparable in attitude and status. The doorman wears a uniform with a silver cap, to give you an idea of things. Mariano Altaba is his name – that is, Mr Altaba according to my father's standards for addressing staff: always in the formal, always with utmost respect. I guess this is what makes him feel less guilty when they hand-deliver him his mail and carry out his trash in exchange for a salary that barely amounts to his subscription to *Hunting & Fishing* magazine. My father is one of those people who feels guilty for having money, but not so guilty to want to give it up.

Mariano (or rather Mr Altaba) was not alone. His companion was a massive uniformed security guard who gave me a good once-over; it appeared he wasn't quite sure what to make of me. Clearly the building's Distinguished Residents' Committee had resolved that their geo-stationary satellite alarm system was not enough to protect themselves against the great unwashed. Luck was on my side, though: Mariano made the appropriate gestures indicating that he knew me and the jury set me free.

'Pablo, boy, what kind of rumpus are you concocting these days?'

He didn't even bother putting on the little silver cap that he takes off when nobody's there. I only lived with my parents in that flat for a couple of years, from age sixteen to eighteen, but Mariano surely still remembers the situations I would cook up in the summertime, when the old folks would decamp to Llavaneras with Beba and their Magnificent Oldest Child, leaving me in peace and in charge of their winter residence. I responded to his greeting with a cordial pleasantry and went upstairs in one of those lifts that leave your balls hanging suspended in mid-air every time the brake starts to kick in. I remember one especially insane night when we went behind the Barsa football stadium in search of a hooker willing to jerk Quico off in that supersonic vertical vehicle. We ended up having to hire two girls because nobody was willing to go off alone with three guys. Our brilliant idea was that Quico would come just as the lift lurched to a halt. We made three attempts in half an hour and finally hit bingo on the third try. The negative, though, was that everything got all gunked up and we had to spray the mirror with Windex to clean it all off. The very same mirror in which I now found myself reflected, fifteen years older, sixty pounds chubbier and perhaps, after all is said and done, a bit wiser.

I reached the fourteenth and final floor, got out and rang the service bell. I knew Beba would answer it anyway, so I figured I would save her the trip to the front door. She was having a bit of trouble with her legs lately.

'Pablito!'

'Beba!'

'Ohh, look how tubby you've gotten!'

'Only to keep up with you, Pussycat. Gimme a hug.'

I grabbed her and even tried to pick her up and give her a little spin, though without success. I got her about halfway up, an effort which made her giggle.

'Pablo! You're going to drop me!'

I let go. She grabbed my hand and brought it to her lap – Beba has a lap, even when she's standing up – and dragged me into the kitchen. As I walked past the ironing room I recognised the maid of the moment – it was the same girl who was there the last time I came around, which surprised me. About twenty years old. Still holding on to me, Beba pulled out two chairs and we sat there face to face, hand-width apart.

'Now, when was the last time you came to see us, stranger?'

'I think I came by at Christmas.'

'What? And it's already the end of June. Bad, bad boy. You came to see your father?'

'Yeah. Well, to see everyone. But they told me that my old man got pretty banged up.'

'Mmmm . . . don't be difficult, he's in one of his moods . . .'

'And Mom?'

'The same as always. Seems she's taken up French lessons.'

'Wasn't she doing some furniture restoration thing?'

'She dropped it. She couldn't take the smell of the varnish. Said it gave her migraines. I mean, migraines, for God's sake. She's gone mad, totally mad. Now she's doing French. She bought a computer with disks that talk and so now the one who's gone mad is your father. Don't go telling him I said that, but . . .'

She laughed with that big old face of hers, but quickly recovered upon hearing the voice of my Mother's Highness, approaching through the door to the dining room.

'Eusebia, I do hope you haven't forgotten to place the order for the venison liver paté . . . Pablo José! How on earth did you get up here?'

'Hello, Mom. Through the back entrance. You can't hear it from the other end of the flat.'

'Good heavens, you look like a truck driver. Let me get a look at you.'

She took my face in her hands, kissed my cheeks and stood there observing me.

'You are fatter than ever, my dear. And that shirt you're wearing? Don't you have anything else to put on?'

'I forgot to do the wash . . .'

'Well, call the dry cleaners. Most of them do deliver, you know . . . Well, now. Let's go outside. Eusebia: would you please tell Loli that she can serve us our aperitifs out on the terrace? And take out the white wine at the very last minute – otherwise it will get warm, and that would be terribly boring.'

The general colour scheme of the living room had changed since the last time I'd been there: what had been orange at Christmas was now pale yellow, including the recliners and the rug beneath the piano. Grand piano, of course.

'Well now, what's new with you?' my mother asked, to stir up the conversation. The journey to the terrace is a long one, requiring slight navigation through the antiques.

'I'm all right. Same as usual. And you?'

'Awful, darling, perfectly awful. Everything's simply upside down, what with your father. You can't imagine what he's been like. You can't even imagine.'

She stopped for a moment before walking through the glass door and onto the terrace. She turned toward me and asked me the usual question, in the usual tone of voice.

'I don't suppose you have a new girlfriend that we might like to meet?'

'You'll be the first to know . . .'

'You need a proper girlfriend, dear. A woman always helps a man get focused, you know. Just the other day, as a matter of fact, we met Jesús Blasco's daughter. A lovely girl. Love-ly. Twenty-seven years old. And I thought to myself: this girl would be so perfect for Pablo José. She's a bit hippy, you know? I think you'd get on so well.'

'But I'm not a hippy, Mom. Not in the least.'

'Well, what I meant to say was bohemian . . . I think

she left the Conservatory to play jazz music. She has . . . artistic inclinations, just like you.'

'I don't remember ever having had artistic inclinations.'

'Pablo José, darling, you are so difficult. You remind me so much of your father whenever you get like that, when you decide not to understand what I'm trying to say.'

Ah. My Father's Highness. The main course, so to speak, of my visit. And there he was, stretched out on a chaise longue under the awning, scanning the newspaper through his reading glasses, with a non-alcoholic bitters at his side.

'Pablo! I thought you were coming by before one.'

I shrugged my shoulders as I leaned down to give him the customary double-kiss.

'Well, you know my time zone is a little bit behind that of the Peninsula.'

'What Peninsula?'

FH never gets my jokes. He's the only person in the world with whom I have no choice but to talk seriously.

'Sorry. I got distracted on the way over.'

He didn't stop his charade of reading the newspaper – FH doesn't really read the newspaper, he skims – as I sat down next to him.

'I don't understand it, you're always getting distracted. I can't imagine what you find so distracting out there. I walk down the street and I don't get distracted by anything.'

'Well, I'm a little absentminded, you know.'

'Absentminded? Absentminded people don't get distracted, they may occasionally get lost . . .'

That's another thing. With FH, you have to search and search until you hit on the exact word that, according to him, is appropriate to the situation at hand.

'Maybe I'm a little scattered, too.'

'Well, scattered is not a good thing to be, son. You have to concentrate on what you're doing.'

My Mother's Highness, sensing an imminent Ode to Proper Conduct, decided to make herself scarce. Murmuring something about having to help Beba and the maid, she summarily vanished from the terrace. At that precise moment I knew I was in for an attack, full force, because FH had set the paper down, sat up in the chaise, and lit one of those cigars that often imply the imminent delivery of a momentous speech.

'If I had been "scattered" when I was your age, I would never have gotten where I am today.'

'You mean in that chair, with your leg in a cast?'

'Don't be funny, damn it. I'm serious.'

'I'm being serious, too. I just don't know what you mean with that "I would never have gotten where I am today." It's an ambiguous statement, frankly.'

'Well, I think it's perfectly clear: you're going to be forty and you live like a seventeen-year-old.'

'I'm going to be thirty-five.'

'Well, you're going to be forty some day too, aren't you? In any event, that's irrelevant. You're at an age in which you should be living another kind of life. By the time I reached your age, I had two degrees under my belt, I had passed my Notary examination, I had founded my own business, and borne two children. And I had a proper wife and a decent home to live in.'

No fewer than three possible responses occurred to me. For example: yes, but you were a failure when it came to your younger son's education, who will soon turn thirty-five but lives like a seventeen-year-old. But instead I just said, rather grudgingly, 'And that's admirable, Dad. You are a great man.' He took this literally, in keeping with the obstinate fart that he is.

'I don't know if I am a great man, but I am a man. A solid, upstanding, self-made man.'

'Oh, really? And what am I supposed to do? Try to be just like you and truly search for my own destiny, or try to be unlike you and end up a sad copy of a self-made businessman?'

'What you need to do is live a life that is worthy of your name. Look at yourself: you look like a . . . I don't know what you look like, in point of fact. You're fat, you're a perfect disaster, you don't have a profession to speak of, nor do you have a job, a house, a wife or a family. Pray tell: if it weren't for your brother how on earth would you survive?'

'My brother?'

'Yes, your brother.'

That was a low blow.

'Look, Dad. I came to see you today because they told me you had an accident. This means that I am willing to chat with you for a while, in an amicable tone, but that does not mean, under any circumstances, that I am willing to offer some kind of defence of my way of life. I live off the income that comes in from the business that you founded. That is true. And I use my earnings in the manner which I find most opportune, just as Sebastian does with his. He does it his way and I do it mine. But if you regret having given me a piece of your cake, I will gladly give it all back to you, down to the very last cent of my inheritance. I'd be perfectly willing to pay the rent that you would charge someone else for the flat that I live in. And if I can't pay you I will move to another, less expensive one.'

'I'm not asking you to give me anything back, that's not what I mean.'

In the bottom of his heart he's a softie. A sentimental softie. There was a time when he drove me insane, but I've got his number. I took advantage of the lighter moment and the subsequent lull to redirect the conversation.

'So what was it like?'

'What?'

'The accident.'

'That was no accident.'

'Oh, really?'

'Really. Those people hit me on purpose. Now I don't want you mentioning this in front of your mother. We got into an argument over this point.'

'That they hit you on purpose?'

Silence. A sip of bitters. That meant he didn't want to discuss it, at least not right then.

My Mother's Highness then arrived bearing plates some godforsaken shade of yellow, and the maid trailed her with what very well might have been venison liver paté, despite thc suspicious absence of any antlers. MH approached me and inquired as to whether I would like a drink. I asked for a beer. She, on the other hand, offered me bitters, vermouth, white wine, champagne, Coca-Cola, anything that would be more appropriate as an appetite opener to be sipped on a garden terrace on the fourteenth floor of a building high above the Diagonal, where Her Royal Highness the Princess Cristina and her husband, Iñaki Urdangarín, take their daily stroll. She finally conceded to my request for a beer when I suggested a vodka with Vichy water, which she regarded as even less acceptable. FH hid behind the newspaper and I took advantage of his evasion tactic to look down onto the street between a crack in the trees. From there you can see a substantial stretch of the Diagonal, from the Hotel Juan Carlos down to Calvo Sotelo, the La Caixa towers and a fair-sized chunk of the city all the way down to the sea. It was slightly overcast, but visibility was good, and in the distance you could clearly spot the two skyscrapers in the Olympic Port that look remarkably like a twin set of lipsticks. My eyes worked their way back to our neighbourhood. From there, you could almost read the label on the satellite dish at the top of my building, which is entirely owned by my Father's Highness: right there, on the left. And just a bit further up you could make out Jaume Guillamet street where, caught in some kind of idea-association vortex I couldn't help trying to locate the house at number fifteen.

'You can come to the table now.'

Those were MH's orders. FH tried to stand up with the aid of crutches and I offered my assistance.

'I'm going to get dressed now,' he announced.

My father's very idiosyncratic sense of etiquette prohibits him from sitting down at the table in shorts, and so my mother begged my pardon ('You'll excuse us for a moment, won't you, Pablo?') and they went off together, I assume, to get him into a pair of long pants, something that can't be terrifically easy if you are pushing seventy, your leg's in a plaster cast and you weigh about a hundred kilos. I sat by the table, just off to the side. Total apathy. My beer was there, but it wasn't normal beer, it was some faggy imported thing, with a hermetic seal on the top, like the kind on those old-fashioned soda bottles. I sipped. Eh: kinda warm. I had no appetite, but I told myself that I couldn't pass up the chance to eat well and attacked a prawn in the hope of whetting my appetite. Not too tough. The beer cut the sweet taste of the coffee I had swigged at Luigi's bar and the prawn stimulated my dormant taste buds. I followed up with some steamed cockles and some delicious canapés of artichoke hearts, and then a couple of anchovies in brine. This was home sweet home, at the end of the day.

Beba appeared carrying a bottle of white wine coated in a fine layer of frost.

'So how are you doing?'

'It's tough going. But I'll make it through.'

'Patience. And try the venison liver paté, it's good. It's the dark one.'

'Listen, Beba. What do you know about my father's accident?'

'Well . . . they say he was coming out of the park and a car jumped the curb and rammed into him.'

'And the driver?'

'He got away, they say. A couple of tramps who saw the whole thing from a bar got out and helped your father into a cab. Your brother picked him up at the hospital afterwards.'

'And you haven't heard anything else?'

'Anything else like what?'

'I don't know . . . didn't Sebastian tell you anything?'

'Sebastian was acting strange yesterday. I mean, I know he's strange in general but yesterday he was weirder than usual. He came into the kitchen to say hello but that was it between us.'

Beba has an excellent radar, but you always have to wait a while before she verbalises anything concrete. In any event, my snooping mission had to be aborted because my hosts returned to the terrace just then. FH had changed out of his Burberry shorts and into a pair of grey wool Dacron pants with a slit near the bottom that allowed him to slip his cast through. He was still wearing one tennis shoe on his good foot, and the same scotch plaid shirt that had matched the shorts, so the resulting look was slightly eccentric – he looked remarkably like a tramp who'd been clothed by the charitable donations of this wealthy neighbourhood. MH maintained her appearance as per her official bylaws governing informal events: white jeans and an ample blue tunic bordered with golden birds, Bengal tigers and peonies, all of them set around in a mandala motif. Ever since she discovered Lobsang Rampa she's had this yen for all things oriental. Some couple I had sitting before me. I tried not to draw too much attention to myself by consciously reducing my brain waves to the very barest minimum, but it was useless. MH opened fire, though pretending to speak exclusively to FH.

'I was just telling Pablo José that we met the Blascos' daughter the other day.'

'Mmmm.'

FH was focused on peeling a prawn without touching it too much, as if it were a repugnant thing, and so he didn't pay much attention to what my mother was saying. But it takes a lot more than a sluggish mumble to discourage my Mother's Highness.

'Carmela, that's her name. An exceptional young lady. Ex-cep-tional. An only child. Did I mention that she studied jazz, just like you?'

'Mom: I've never studied jazz in my life.'

'Oh, no . . . ? Well, you did play guitar, didn't you? Anyway, the point is, Carmela made quite a magnificent impression. Mag-nificent. A real modern girl. You'll love her, I know it.'

I was about to mention that every day I walk past hundreds of people I'm sure I'd love if I met them. The problem is, they're never the people I actually end up meeting. But in the interest of restraint, I simply assumed an expression that indicated I was deeply engrossed in my chewing. Not worth getting involved.

'Well, for the San Juan holiday I believe the Blascos are organising a garden party in Llavaneras. I'm sure Carmela will be there, and I should warn you, I showed her a picture of you. She seemed quite interested.'

For once in his life, my father saved me from having to try and get out of that one.

'Don't get too worked up. We're not going to be in Llavaneras for San Juan.'

'Oh, but why not? It's not for another week yet, and Dr Caudet himself said . . .'

'We've already had this discussion, Mercedes.'

My mother now turned to me for support.

'Would you believe how ridiculous he is being? Your father doesn't want to leave the house because he thinks those people meant to hit him.'

'Mercedes, we've already had this discussion.'

'We haven't had any such discussion, and you know something else? I'm beginning to think that you're paranoid. That's right. Paranoid. For the record.'

'Mercedes, please. Enough.'

My father said it: enough. He left the prawn half-peeled, and for effect, ran his napkin over his lips – which were still immaculate – and then threw the napkin onto the tablecloth and began the complicated manoeuvre of standing up, fumbling with his crutches. The aperitif was over. A shame, because the venison liver paté wasn't so bad. Fortunately, after his temper tantrum we ate more or less in silence, at least for the beginning, which allowed me to fully concentrate on the food at hand. Beba still hadn't lost her touch in the kitchen, and in my honour she had prepared one of her specialities: steak in wine-and-mushroom sauce. My Mother's

Highness, of course, barely even picked at the dish, opting instead for a lettuce salad, chewing no less than twenty times per mouthful. According to her, her personal trainer had recommended this as a saliva-whetting exercise, according to some kind of proper nutritional-assimilation theory. This was preceded by the ingestion of an endless sequence of microscopic homeopathic pellets especially prescribed for the reinforcement of sulphuric – or sulphurous, or hydrosulphuric – tendencies. I don't remember that last bit very clearly.

We had to wait until dessert before my mother retired to the kitchen, where she busied herself with the coffee, the one thing she insists on making and serving herself. This, of course, left me alone with my father.

Start:

'All right. Explain.'

'What do you want me to explain?'

'The thing about them trying to hit you.'

'They didn't try. They succeeded.'

Pause. Me, with a vaguely sceptical look on my face. My father, with a Father's Highness look on his face.

'Now why would anyone want to try and hit you?'

'I don't know. All I know is that they could have killed me if they had wanted to. But they didn't.'

Time out for an information-gathering digression.

'How many of them were there in the car?'

'Two.'

'Did you recognise either of them?'

'Pablo, dear, are you stupid? If I knew who they were I would have done something by now.'

'And the car?'

'I don't know. It was red. Small.'

'Number plate?'

'I didn't have time to look.'

'Did you report it to the police?'

'What do you want me to report? That a small red car hit me on purpose? The people at the hospital filed a report with the police. That was it.'

By now I was starting to feel like Colombo.

'Witnesses?'

'A couple of construction workers. They were having lunch at the bar on Numancia and they came running out when they heard me scream and hit the hood of the car, but by the time they reached me the car had already taken off. In any event, I doubt they would want to get mixed up in declarations and such. They helped me right away, they even hailed a cab and offered to take me to the hospital, but I told them not to worry.'

'What do you think the men in the car wanted? To nick something from you?'

'I don't know. I doubt that.'

'What then? A couple of madmen who get their kicks running over pedestrians?'

'They didn't seem the type.'

'What type did they seem, then?'

'Thirty or forty years old, average clothes . . . they could have passed for office workers. I think they were paid hit-men. They did the work without blinking an eye and then they left the scene.'

'All right, Dad. What kind of trouble have you've gotten mixed up with?'

'Me? I haven't gotten into any kind of trouble.'

'What then?'

'I don't know.'

Game over, insert coins. He wasn't going to budge on that one, but I still hadn't sorted out the basic issue. All right, let's see.

'Dad: would you mind explaining why you've bothered to tell me all this?'

Very pregnant silence. He made little knots with his napkin as he responded.

'Because I wanted you to know.'

'Does the security guard downstairs have something to do with this?'

'I hired him yesterday.'

VERONICA AND THE MONSTERS

At five in the afternoon I awoke from a dreamless sleep. Not dreaming pisses me off. I am quite accustomed to remembering my dreams every time I wake up, just like a man who is accustomed to taking a crap every morning: if one day you wake up and you don't crap it's because something funny is going on inside you. Plus, it's extremely useful to remember your dreams. And I'm not talking about Sigmund Freud's Greatest Hits. I'm talking about the kind of dreams that function like little oracles, a dimension of dreaming that is only within reach of the person who understands that enlightened reason is often the most farfetched esoteric fantasy, the most baroque of religions.

I flicked on the radio. Coffee. Joint. A state of mind most conducive to reconnecting with my Metaphysical Club emails. It even felt like a good moment to read John's Primary Sentences, which tend to be dense and concentrated. But first things first. I had to resolve the cash issue. Otherwise there would be no joints, no beer, no butter for my croissants.

Step one: I dialled The First's private number, so as to prepare the terrain and not just barge into his office out of nowhere. One of The First's Adorable Children picked up the phone – specifically the more adorable of the two, the one who always insists on calling me 'Uncle Pablo' no matter how much I glare. I think it was the older kid – it was the bigger one, at least that much I know. I also think it was a female that picked up, but I wasn't too sure because she sounded pretty much exactly like her mother.

'Is your father there, sweetheart?'

'Who may I say is calling?'

'Pablo. Pablo Miralles.'

I heard her shout, 'Mommy, it's Uncle Pablo, he wants to talk to Daddy. I think he's drunk, he didn't even recognise my voice!'

The mother got on the line. My Adorable Sister-in-law.

'Pablo?'

'Yes, that's me.'

Role reversal. I was the one calling, but she was the one asking for me. She sounded tense.

'I need to talk to you,' she said, without a trace of the slightly superior tone which I had always detected on the few occasions we had spoken in the past.

'Fuck, everything's such a big mystery these days.'

'What makes you say that?'

'Nothing. What's wrong?'

'Nothing serious, not for the moment at least. But I need you to come to the house as soon as you can. I need to discuss something with you.'

'I was planning on coming over now anyway. I need to see Sebastian. Can you get him on the line?'

'No, no. He can't come right now,' she said, hesitating for a moment. 'He isn't here.'

'But at his office they told me he was in bed, with a fever and everything . . . did he go in to work this afternoon?'

'No. Come over and I'll explain. I can't go out. I'd go out to meet you, but I can't get away just now.'

At this point in the plot, I realised that I was going to

have to get used to expecting the unexpected – these hiccups in the normal routine of things were beginning to grow more and more frequent, and weren't showing signs of letting up. I had exchanged a total of thirty-seven words with Lady First since the faraway day she had married my Magnificent Brother. Yet now, all of a sudden, she was asking me to come over so she could spill some kind of secret. Strange, very strange. But ever since the First had started giving away free money, saying things like please and stopped going to the office because of some alleged indisposition, well, anything was possible. Skirt-chasing was the first thing that crossed my mind. It all fit, including the simultaneous absence of both The First and his secretary. It all fit. Minus me, of course. What the hell did I have to do with The First's marital crises? I should admit, though, that by then I had begun to get curious, perhaps indiscreetly so, about what exactly was going down.

'All right. I'll be over in a little bit.'

'Not a word of this to your parents, all right? If they ask you, just tell them Sebastian is sick. It will only be for a few days. And the same goes for anyone else who asks questions.'

The request had a bit of the imperative in it.

'Are you asking me to lie?'

'Look Pablo, this isn't a time for games. You and I have never gotten along, so if I am swallowing my pride and asking a favour of you it is because I have a very good reason to do so.'

Frank and direct. I wasn't familiar with this side of Lady First. But her request for discretion did seem to confirm my skirt-chasing hypothesis. A hypothesis which, I must confess, I relished: The First, starring in his very own sex scandal, shacked up with his secretary. What an embarrassment. Or better yet: with a hot young, black percussionist recently arrived from Havana. Or even better: caught up in a zoophilia-and-necrophilia cult affair. He would end up on every last newspaper in the galaxy for that one, cover photo and all: the congregation convening at night-time in the Montjüic cemetery, honourable citizens all dressed up as drag queens, teetering atop massive platform boots, eyeliner running down their faces, and him, perfectly positioned to kiss the arsehole of a baby goat . . . Anyway. I probably shouldn't get my hopes up, I told myself. The bit about the secretary was highly improbable. She seemed like a very sensible girl, and in addition to being a terrific office ornament, I'm sure she was the kind of secretary who used her work-hours well, making Excel currency exchange spreadsheets and such. Before getting into bed with my brother, she would have tried to get an honest job, or at least would have gone elsewhere to prostitute herself decently.

But all this inevitably brought me back to the three hundred and seventy-five euros I was expecting. The idea of paying yet another courtesy call upon my parents so soon after the last one to casually suggest that they slip me a few bills to pay for my blue-zone parking spot was out – that one would definitely not fly with my FH, who always tends to suspect ulterior motives whenever I make some heartfelt gesture of filial piety. And anyway, I don't have a car, and it was possible that my father would catch on to the ruse. I decided to weigh my alternatives. Skimming dough off Lady First would have all the sizzle of a first-time hit: after all, I was a member of the family, and it was time they treated me like one. I could also surreptitiously sidle my way into the bedroom of one of her Adorable Children and root around – though at the risk of setting off one of their anti-theft alarms. Even at their tender age they were no doubt well-versed in the more rudimentary methods of private-property protection.

So, for the moment, I got dressed and set out for The First's family home.

My Magnificent Brother still has yet to achieve the status of a real Father's Highness, which means he had to settle for buying the typical attic flat on Numancia, just to the south of the Diagonal psychologists' neighbourhood, and bide his time until cashing in on the rest of his paternal inheritance which will eventually permit him to establish his winter residence wherever the fuck he wants. Even so he sure did use the 150 square-metre penthouse to full advantage – he'd even managed to fit in a jacuzzi and matching piano. Of course, we're talking about a cabinet piano, which doesn't take up all that much space. The one down side is that Debussy simply doesn't sound quite the same as on a grand piano, but my Magnificent Brother is a patient man, and he knows full well that there is a time for a cabinet piano and a BMW, and a time for a grand piano and a Jaguar Sovereign.

The entrance hall of his building has sofas as well as a doorman – a slicked-back dude with an electric blue lab-coat that works as his uniform – but the lifts aren't half as fun as the ones in my parents' building. They just take you up to the penthouse without much antigravitational excitement.

Doorbell.

Lady First opened the door. We double-kissed on the cheeks. She was looking better than I remembered. She invited me to come in. In the hallway another one of The First's Adorable Children crossed our path – this one was much shrimpier than the firstborn, and most probably a male, judging from the absence of earrings and ribbons.

The thing walked in front of us, executing a rather complex movement that recalled the locomotion of the quadruped, specifically that of the crocodile and other reptiles, resting its knees – rather than paws or the inferior homologous extremities – on the floor, and of course, lacking the charm that a long, zigzagging tail lends such scaly beasts. A relatively rudimentary system, no matter how you look at it: they make one think of the degeneration of the species that Jean Rostand feared. But the surprises didn't end there: suddenly the thing stopped cold, rested back on its voluminously padded butt, looked up toward the sky and made a face that was mysteriously reminiscent of a human smile.

Horrors. It had no teeth.

Ill from the apprehension, I tried to ignore the creature by stepping over it with a wide leap. My sister-in-law, on the other hand, was clearly accustomed to this, and without exhibiting any visible signs of disgust she bent down and scooped up the little creature, who revealed his clearly limited intelligence by accompanying his babble with a few – as far as I can tell – utterly unjustified claps of the hands.

'Veronica, could you please look after Victor for a moment?' Lady First called out toward some remote zone of the hallway.

Given that we were alone in the living room, I deduced that "Victor" had to be the name of the little creature, which confirmed my suspicion that he was a boy. It didn't seem possible: he didn't even have teeth yet and yet he had a gender. Veronica, who turned out to be an obese teenager with a Greenpeace t-shirt and a pair of lavender-coloured elastic pants, appeared on the double. I liked the look of her and I offered a friendly hello. I have a soft spot for people who are so obviously fat, even if they are earthy-crunchy types. The little creature went from one set of arms to the other, continuing all the while with his delirious gesticulations. Veronica toted him down the hall, far from my presence, a most welcome gesture which only reinforced the positive feelings she had already inspired in me. I don't want to come off as racist or anything, but those human puppies sure do stink, especially in the early stages: they give off the raunchiest stench, a combination of sweet perfume, butt creams, baby formula . . . a repugnant halo that sinks into everything with which they enter into intimate contact.

'Sit down, make yourself comfortable. Would you like a drink?'

'Do you have beer?'

'I don't think so.'

'Vodka?'

'Absolutely.'

'Vichy?'

'Sparkling water, I think.'

'Then I'll have a Vichoff: tall glass, ice, fill it halfway with icy vodka and juice of half a lemon, and then top it off with some fizzy water if you don't have any Vichy. And don't use a cocktail shaker; the water loses bubbles that way.'

'Um, how about just making do with a whisky?'

I looked over towards the bar and spotted a bottle of Havana 7. In general I prefer Havana 3, which is less sweet, but fucking The First always buys the most expensive. He's that kind of guy: if they made a more exclusive version of air, he'd breathe it.

'I'll take that bottle of rum. Do you mind if I drink straight from the bottle?'

'Whatever suits you.'

Lady First had poured herself a few drops of whisky in a short glass. She grasped the bottle of rum, as if to pour it, but with her thumb pointing down, as if she were transporting it some very long distance. She handed it to me. Then she sat down on the enormous four-seater sofa that faced the one I sat on. This was not the woman I knew: the little bottle gesture, the indifferent way she sat down, tucking her leg beneath her, the hesitant sips of whisky . . . Plus, she wasn't half as repulsive as I remembered. Maybe because most of the times I had ever seen her she had been pregnant, and pregnant women always make me anxious somehow – I don't know what it is, but they seem like alien eggs about to expel little monsters. Looking a little closer, she actually seemed to bear a slight resemblance to Greta Garbo. Maybe it was the hairdo. A pair of green eyes finished off her look just so.

I decided to get comfortable. I unscrewed the bottle, held it high, and placed the cascading spout just above my mouth and filled it to the brim. Then I lowered my elbow and swallowed. Lady First took her first shot. Point blank.

'So what did you think when you found out that Sebastian wasn't at home?'

Fine. I was perfectly willing to play the game, as long as it involved free rum.

'You want me to be straight with you?'

'Please.'

'I assumed he was mixed up with his secretary and that they spent the night together. Something unexpected came up and they couldn't make it to the office this morning, and that was why they played sick.'

'But I was the one who called in to say that Sebastian was indisposed.'

'That could still fit the theory.'

'All right then, fit it.'

'Option A: Sebastian called you and told you some kind

of believable lie, convincing enough to justify his no-show but inappropriate enough to make you want to keep it from his employees, and so he asked you to call his office and say that he was sick. You believed him and have followed his instructions like a good wife.'

'And option B?'

'Option B: you know perfectly well that your husband is shagging his secretary and this pisses you off no end, or maybe not. That part doesn't matter. The main thing is that you don't want a scandal and so you make sure to cover it up.'

'Option C?'

'I was just getting to that. My poor brother Sebastian and his lover have been abducted by extraterrestrials right before your very eyes, but you refrain from telling anyone for fear that people will think you have gone mad.'

I took advantage of her slight discomfort to steer the conversation in another direction.

'Yet now I ask myself: how do you know that Sebastian's secretary didn't show up for work?'

She resisted losing the serve.

'How do you know that I know?'

I let her have that one.

'Because you didn't act surprised when I mentioned it.'

'Maria might have told me when I called the office.'

'Might have done. Did she?'

'Yes.'

'Still, that doesn't fully answer the question. Maybe you already knew when she told you.'

'Not bad. You're clever.'

'Clever enough to mistrust my own wits as well as your flattery. You know something that I don't and you're playing some kind of game with me.'

'You misinterpret me.'

'Possibly. It's just that I'm not into mind reading.'

She took another sip of whisky, so I tipped the bottle back again. My prudent first swig had had little effect, and so I tried another, waiting for the cascade to fill my mouth to the brim, so that I could just barely close and gulp it down. I was then suddenly taken with the illusion of brandishing a sword and climbing aboard the first galleon that might appear before my eyes.

Lady First, however, was firmly planted on solid ground.

'Well, for someone who doesn't like mind reading you've done quite a good job of guessing. The situation is, in fact, a combination of the three situations you propose.'

'Including the extraterrestrial abduction?'

'Not exactly. Or well, I don't know, to tell you the truth. I am beginning to suspect that anything is possible at this point.'

She paused for a Marlboro Super Extra Light. The whisky, I assume, had done its job, and she was ready to come clean. I was all ears.

'Sebastian has been seeing his secretary for the past two years. You were absolutely right about that. I know and he knows that I know, among other reasons because we've discussed it a thousand times. Are you surprised? Don't be. Our marriage has never worked. Or, in other words: it has always worked perfectly because it is based on mutual convenience. He sleeps with whomever he wishes but he always keeps up his appearance as a family man, and I can spend my time doing absolutely nothing if I wish, with the excuse of being completely dedicated to my husband and children. There is nothing worse than having an ambition and feeling unable to fight for it. Have you ever tried to write, for example?'

'I think I once wrote something about some vacation I took, but when I discovered *Penthouse* magazine I started getting more interested in photography.'

She smiled.

'Any excuse is good enough if you really want to give up. I got some things published, you know? But then, when everyone begins to think of you as the great talent of the future and you don't feel you can meet their expectations, that's when it starts to get bad. And that's when you begin to look for excuses.'

Now that she mentioned it, I did seem to remember hearing something from my family about the literary merits of my Magnificent Brother's Brilliant Fiancée, but that was a topic that had definitely not come up in years.

'There's more. The best thing about our marriage is that your brother's freedom relieves me from the obligation of sleeping with him, something that any other husband would have insisted upon. Sexually speaking, men have never interested me very much . . . Why are you looking at me like that?'

'Listen, honey, honestly, this is a little out of the blue . . .'

I took another swig of the rum. Shit, with Lady First.

'I'm only giving you the background on this because I don't want you to misinterpret things: your brother and I love each other, but more importantly we . . . we understand each other. He is the only important person in my life who doesn't pressure me. If I didn't love him I wouldn't bother to explain all of this to you now. And if you think I'm telling you this because I need some kind of confessional catharsis, think again. I would be far better off hiring a bleeding-heart lady psychologist. That way, at least, I would avoid getting rum stains on the sofa upholstery.'

'But she'd charge you more than it would cost to clean the sofa.'

I tried to hold my ground, but I did acknowledge the admonition and so I placed the bottle on the side table, stood up and went over to the little bar cart for a glass. Then I assumed a voice that made like I took all this very seriously.

'All right, sis, so now I've got the back story: you're not into shagging men and my brother looks for action with secretaries. What else?'

'Bring the whisky over, if you don't mind.'

Role reversal. Now I was the one who offered the bottle to her. She seemed to be lingering in a bout of rhetorical recollection.

'Maria Eulalia Robles. Lali.'

'Huh?'

'Executive secretary. Degree in Business and Economics, a Master in Business Administration, English, French, advanced computer skills . . . We went to school together.'

'And now your husband takes advantage of her talents. What a small world.'

'Not so small. I was the one who introduced her to your brother, and I was the one who recommended that he hire her as his personal secretary when your father retired. She's Sebastian's type. She looks a little like me . . . And I knew that Sebastian was Lali's type, too . . . So I put them in touch to facilitate things a bit for your brother. When your lover also happens to be your secretary, you can walk down the street together with no problem, you can even eat in a restaurant where they know you, especially if they've seen you with your lover and your wife at the same time. Do I make myself clear?'

'As a bell. But this is a lot of information all at once.

Kind of an overload, in fact. Excuse the question, but now that the issue's on the table, what is there between you and Lali, exactly?'

'Nothing worthy of a pornographic movie, so don't get excited. In any event, that's not important right now. I have shared a few private details with you because I want you to understand that I am perfectly aware of Sebastian's double life, and that I even play a role in it to a certain extent. Very often he doesn't return home until five or six in the morning. Normally he tells me in advance, and if not he'll call me as he's leaving the office. As far as the nanny is concerned, he's working. The neighbours never see him come in, but if they did, they would see him with his briefcase. The important thing, however, is that everyone sees him leave here in the morning.'

'Very crafty.'

'He didn't call last night. And this morning he wasn't in his bed. His alarm didn't go off – oddly, that was what woke me up. I phoned Lali's house right away but all I got was her answering machine. I haven't heard anything from either of them since noon yesterday.'

I assumed that the information update was complete, because after that last bit she downed the rest of her whisky in one go, placed the glass on the table and just sat there staring at me.

'I spoke with him yesterday afternoon,' I offered.

'Where?'

'On the phone.'

'Did he say where he was calling from?'

'No, but I got the impression that he was in his office.'

'Oh, really? Why?'

'I don't know,' I said, thinking aloud. 'If he had called from a phone booth or from his mobile I would have noticed it. But maybe that's just because I assumed he would be working at that hour.'

'You didn't hear voices in the background, or the sound of a photocopier or anything?'

'I don't think so. But his office is pretty soundproof, and over the phone I don't think you can usually hear any extraneous noise. Can you remember ever having heard background noise when he's called you from there?'

'No. But I tend to talk to him after normal office hours.'

'Well, it doesn't matter. The point is, in the middle of the afternoon he was fine. He called to give me some news from the office and to tell me that my father had broken his leg.'

As I said this, I remembered perfectly well that The First's attitude over the phone had not been normal, not in the least bit, but for the moment I decided to refrain from mentioning that part. Right then I wanted to find out exactly what Lady First wanted from me. Because evidently, just as she herself had indicated, she wasn't telling me all this just to unload her emotions on me.

'Have you tried to find out what might have gone down?' I asked, to get some information out of her. She shrugged her shoulders, tired.

'I called the hospitals, the City Guard information line . . . Nothing. I didn't expect much, though. If he had had an accident I would have known, someone would have gotten in touch with me. And I've been ringing Lali's house all day but all I keep getting is her answering machine. I don't know what else to do. I'm worried. And not just because he's been gone for over twenty-four hours, but because yesterday, around noon, he called me to ask for something rather strange.'

'What?'

Her eyebrows went up at this one, as if she were trying to be succinct but precise.

'He told me to go into the room that he uses as his office here, and to look for a certain file in an envelope and to send it by certified mail to our address.'

'The address of this building?'

'Yes.'

'And what was in those papers?'

'I don't know, exactly, I only opened the file for a second, and leafed through three or four loose sheets of papers. They looked like typed reports on some kind of companies. I read one or two paragraphs, it was all very confusing, names in initials, legal terminology, that sort of thing. And so I just put them in an envelope, wrote out the address and brought it to the post office before it closed.'

'And you didn't find it odd that he would ask such a strange thing of you?'

'Well, of course I did, that's why I'm telling you about it now. But I don't understand anything about his business, he just told me it was extremely important to receive a large envelope postmarked by I don't know what date, and so I believed him. I figured it was some scheme of his, you know how he is. He did seem nervous, though. And after everything that's happened, I'm ready to suspect just about anything. I've been turning this whole thing upside down all day now.'

'Why don't you report the disappearance to the police?'

'It's not worth it. Not yet, at least. It's only been twenty-four hours. And the first thing they'll think of when they start to investigate is that he ran off with his secretary and that the two of them will reappear in a few days. And if not, they still wouldn't think it terribly strange.'

'But if you tell them everything you just told me . . .' I

said, though immediately realised that that wouldn't be such a good idea.

'Right. So what are you going to do?' I asked.

'I don't know, but for the moment I don't want your parents finding out about this. It would bring to light a number of things that neither your brother nor I are interested in them knowing about. It's information that won't do them a bit of good. And in any event, there's nothing they can do to help. But I need your help to keep them at bay. If I hadn't told you the whole story, I would have been taking a serious risk. That you would inadvertently blow the lid off all this. And now that I necessarily have to count on you, it turns out that you are the only person who knows enough to help me look for him. Anyway, you couldn't be in a more ideal position to help me.'

'Me?' I have travelled five continents, but if there's one place I've never been it's an 'ideal position.'

'Well, you are, after all, a fifty per cent partner in your brother's business . . . the business belongs to both of you. You could, very discreetly, try to get some information out of the staff. They know you well enough, and I understand you've done some research for them, isn't that right? In your brother's absence, you're the owner and free to go there and poke through the office without anyone getting in your way.'

'I wouldn't be so sure about that. No, maybe they wouldn't try to stop me from doing anything, but they would probably find it pretty strange if I were to suddenly start hunting through desk drawers. I mean, we're talking about years and years of indifference here. In general they send me the balance sheets, I pretend to understand them and they give me whatever money they want to give me. And as for those little information-gathering projects, I always deal directly with my brother.'

'You could go at night . . .'

The mere thought of entering Miralles & Miralles at night sent a wave of nausea through my body. That would be like breaking into a church through a side window to ransack the tabernacle, with the Father and Son bearing witness to the desecration of their House.

'At night-time it will be slightly difficult to get information out of the staff,' I said.

I could tell she was starting to get exasperated by my escape attempts, so she tried again with a shortcut.

'All right then. Now you're going to tell me that you think I'm a paranoid who fantasises about kidnappings every time her husband sows his wild oats, aren't you? Or else you're just going to tell me that you could not give a damn about everything I've just told you and that you're not going to do a thing about it. Is that it?'

'Lady, if you gave me a few more options I could tell you something else.'

'Such as . . . ?'

'That I'll do what I can. Don't ask me what. But I'll do something.'

Mistake. Deep down I'm a sentimental softie. I simply can't help it, though it is definitely a mistake to let people in on that. It must have been the half-bottle of rum that got my tongue wagging. I don't usually drink hard booze before sundown.

Just then the chubster babysitter re-entered the living room, interrupting us. In her arms was the boy creature, and the Adorable Girl Child was tagging behind on foot.

'Excuse me . . . Merche wants to know if she can watch the telly for a bit.'

Lady First turned to the Girl Child.

'Have you finished your homework?'

'Yes.'

Apparently, the boy creature was still in his domestication phase. I leaned back in the chair and extracted the glass from my left hand, just in case. If the right don't get you / Then the left one will. So they say.

'It's half past eight, there's no children's television on at this hour,' declared Lady First, consulting her watch.

'We videotaped the cartoons,' the Girl Child replied, with surprising acuity.

'Which cartoons? The Japanese ones?'

'No. Walt Disney.'

I was relieved. Apparently, any initiation in the ways of martial arts was expressly off-limits, and this relaxed me somewhat.

'All right then, you can watch them until dinnertime. But first say a proper hello to your Uncle Pablo.'

Good Lord.

She advanced toward me like a mythical beast. I was about to stiffen up to protect myself when suddenly she stopped and said 'Hello, Uncle Pablo.' Then she brought her disproportionate head close to mine, and with her brows obscenely knitted together, actually tried to plant a smacker right on my lips. Everyone was watching, including the small toothless creature, and so I had no choice but to hold my breath and subject myself to the abuse without flinching. Fortunately, Veronica and the monsters disappeared almost immediately to back back to wherever they had come from, but all I could think about was getting out of there as fast as I could, even if that meant leaving the rum bottle unfinished.

Lady First staved off my retreat by grabbing hold of my arm.

'Pablo. I'm counting on you. Call me, whenever, if

anything at all occurs to you, no matter how silly it might seem.'

I, meanwhile, had something else on my mind.

'Hey, how did you find out about my father's accident? You didn't look surprised when I mentioned that, either.'

'Sebastian told me when he called about the envelope. He told me that a car had jumped the curb and hit him, that it wasn't serious but that they had to put his leg in a plaster cast. He left for the hospital after that. Now that I think of it, it wouldn't be such a bad idea to ask your father if he knows where Sebastian went after dropping him off at home.'

'Right. Hmm. Listen, uh, sis. I forgot your name . . .'

She took it as a joke.

'Gloria.'

'Pleasure to meet you, Gloria. Do you always drink three whiskies before dinner?'

'In general I don't drink anything before putting the children down. And you? Do you always drink rum straight from the bottle?'

'Only when extraterrestrials abduct my brother and my sister-in-law asks me to investigate the case.'

It wasn't even nine and I was already drunk. Bad scene. As I left the flat I tried to take a walk to assimilate the information I had just been given, but I couldn't think in any coherent fashion. And so I went straight home and fell asleep, with my head feeling something like a pyrotechnics warehouse.

QUIVERING SHELLFISH

Kiko Ledgard, the old host of Three Two One, is wearing an elegant white smoking jacket. The set is a Chicago street scene from the 1930s: Buick parked along the sidewalk, Jazz Club alley, barber shop, liquor store, Salvation Army mission. Four character actors stand around looking bored, each one with his or her accessory of choice: the hooker swings her bag, the policeman swings his club, a grizzled drunk swings his bottle, and the detective, his felt hat. I look over at Lady First, inquisitively. She's leaning toward the drunk, while I favour the detective. We argue. Kiko Ledgard tries to confuse us even further: if we go with the detective we have to play a game; we are told we can opt for the Buick instead if we want – it's a guaranteed winner and definitely not the booby prize. But Lady First and I decide to take our chances and we accept the detective's game. Applause. At the back of the set a door is flung open, and out come four secretaries dressed up as Betty Boop, hugging a giant amusement-park slide with a huge fake croissant at the top. Kiko reads the little note that comes with the contraption: 'To be a good detective, you have to follow the clues to the very end.' He stops. Once again, he tempts us with the Buick. The public shouts out all sorts of contradictory answers; we ask Kiko to keep on reading. Objective of the game: to reach the gigantic croissant by clambering up the slide. The ascent is divided into various stages, identified by vertical markers with red flags attached to each one. They will give us 100,000 croissants for each little flag we knock down, upwards to a total of 1,000,000 croissants if we reach the top. Piece of cake: I remove my jacket, roll up my sleeves and attack the contraption. Lady First insists that we should have gone with the drunk. She's drunk now, too. She kisses me on the lips and stands there looking at me with her vapid eyes. The audience roars, but they are not encouraging roars; these people are out for blood. Kiko Ledgard has disappeared and in his place now stands his female counterpart Mayra Gómez Kemp, in fishnet stockings, boots that belong on the feet of an evil girls' school warden, and very short, dyed-orange hair. She cracks her whip: 'All right, you motherfucking drunk, move your arse!' Until this moment, I had not recognised myself in this dream, but now I understand that the drunk on the set is me, and that all this has been nothing but a cruel farce. I try to climb, but I weigh too much. Plus, I'm drunk, and the slide is coated in a thick coat of butter that oozes through my fingers and prevents me from securing a solid position from which to advance. I look up, hoping that the sight of the prize will infuse me with the strength I need to forge ahead, but there is no longer a giant croissant at the top of the slide. All I can see in the semi-darkness is my Adorable Niece, throwing tiny ninja stars that she kisses lovingly before hurling them down.

I woke up with a start. This time, I was grateful for the vista of my obstacle-course bedroom. God bless every last pair of dirty underpants, I thought. According to the alarm clock it was one in the morning. Hangover. The best cure for a hangover is to immediately start boozing again. But that would be impossible unless I ate something first: blackout risk. So I took a quick shower and swallowed four egg yolks which I washed down with a couple of glasses of milk, a good working method for filling the gut with something nutritious when in a rush. And I was in a rush because the bars would close if I didn't step on it.

I left my flat and walked down to Luigi's bar, stopping first at the light to let a motorcycle by. Then I began to cross the street, but before I got halfway through the zebra crossing when I heard a thunderous boom, which made me cover my head instinctively. Just in case. Various cling-clangs followed.

I looked up the street: the motorcycle that had just whizzed by me was now affixed to the side of a massive garbage truck that lumbered down the street with its blinkers on. The people sitting at the outdoor tables in front of the bar rushed over to the motorcycle and, after a moment of indecision, I did the same. But by the time I'd walked the fifty-or-so metres to the scene of the accident a small group had already formed: four garbage collectors, a cab driver that was double-parked nearby, the owner of the outdoor bar, plus a few other rubberneckers. Ten or twelve people at this point. The motorcycle rider was sprawled on the street, minus his helmet, which now rolled around on the asphalt like a Chubbies doll. The remains of the BMW – big and red, like an insect in heat – looked like a neoistic artistic experiment destined to end up in the Bilbao Guggenheim alongside some kind of provocative title like 'The Twilight of the Gods' or 'The Woman who Gave Birth to Newton.' He coulda been killed. Shit. Given that there was already a fairly large group of charitable souls waiting to tend the wounded, I was all ready to turn around when a gap suddenly opened up in the crowd and allowed me to catch a glimpse of the accident victim's face: Gerardo Berrocal, sixth form, Marist Brothers. Berri, now with grey hair and no more glasses. But it was Berri, no doubt about it.

Shit.

I was that close to busting through the throng of concerned citizens and saying hello – 'Man, Berri, it's been a long time, can I call you an ambulance?' – but I stopped myself. Still, the coincidence changed my interest level considerably. Someone had already called an ambulance from a mobile phone and I decided to stay there until it arrived, even though Roadrunner and Coyote, the unfortunate nickname of the police duo that generally refuels at Luigi's bar, were already on the scene. The ambulance turned up a few minutes later: two men dressed in white opened the back door, went over to Berri to check him out and in a flash had a stretcher at his side. Before moving him they placed a stiff brace around his neck just in case something major had happened to his neck. When they closed the back door of the ambulance, I raised my thumb, as a reflex, and a 'Hang tough, Berri' escaped my lips. Luckily I was the only one who heard that.

I resumed my journey to Luigi's bar, profoundly affected by the whole thing.

'Roberto. Pull out that bottle of whisky from the freezer, will you?'

Roberto whistled hard.

'Starting heavy, huh, man?'

'I just saw my old school chum smashed against a garbage truck.'

'The accident out there? They came looking for Coyote and Roadrunner. Was it serious?'

'I don't think so . . . But I've had kind of an off day, and that was about as much as I could take. Come on, out with the bottle.'

He went toward the kitchen for the booze, but halfway in his mobile rang and he stopped to answer the call. The bar was still pretty packed; they had brought the outside tables in, but there was still a healthy crowd inside, as well: a couple, two taxi drivers going at the slot machine, etc. The clock on the wall read two-thirty. I waited for Roberto to finish up his phone chat and return with the Moskoskaya.

'Shot of fire water for the gentleman,' he said, serving me an icy dram. I downed it in one go.

'Hit me again.'

Down the hatch.

'Again.'

I even had a fourth and then asked for a beer to chase it down, as well as a newspaper – for appearance's sake – and then I went over to a table. MTV was on the telly, with that Jamiroquai video they always play, and so I turned to the front page of the paper: the minister of godknowswhat had issued a warning about something related to whoknowswhat. On the editorial pages, eloquent odes to the Truest Truths and bitter denunciations of Mediocre Mediocrity. I had done a damn good thing withdrawing from the real world. But the real world has a way of coming down around your ears whether you like it or not. Either the money in your wallet runs dry or a garbage truck appears out of nowhere in the middle of the street and bashes into your childhood schoolmate. My Magnificent Brother had mysteriously disappeared and my Father's Highness had gotten his leg smashed up. *No et fiis mai de la calma.* Not the calmness around you, not anything, and most of all not Lady First. She, I said to myself, is not to be trusted. You can't trust someone just because one day they don't seem half-bad. If you start thinking someone is all right, that's when you're really in for it. It's best to project all your positive energy upon those who have the least involvement in your life: a regular at the bar or a hooker in the red-light district, that sort of thing. But never, I repeat, never allow your sister-in-law Gloria to seem 'all right.' You shouldn't even call her *Gloria*; she is Lady First, a potential enemy.

'Roberto, gimme another beer.'

'Right.'

'Hey, Roberto. You think I'm an all right kind of a guy?'

'Well, that depends . . .'

'Oh, yeah? On what?'

'On what is convenient given the situation.'

More beer. I was already drunk. Again. Drunk and brooding. Thinking for long periods of time isn't very cinematic, is it? Ellipses. That's what I need, ellipses. Show the clock on the wall, the star with his newspaper and beer, fade to black, back to the clock, the ashtray, the collection of empty beer bottles. Unfortunately real life requires a lot more work than the movies, plus you actually have to live it, in real time. But then again, you get a lot more done in real life, too. As such, by the time the clock read three-thirty I had already drafted an initial plan of action for tackling The First's case. Once I had completed this homework, I sat around thinking about how the hell I was going to spend the rest of the night. You only get out of life what you pump into it, I thought to myself. But I was broke and Luigi, my only potential money-lender at that hour, was nowhere near the bar. Sometimes he goes home and leaves Roberto to close up, but sometimes he just stays and hangs out, chasing cats on the patio or meddling in the private affairs of some regular customer. I asked Roberto.

'He's inside, doing the books.'

I got up, walked over to the door at the back and tapped lightly. Luigi was sitting at his desk in the back room, in total accounting-chaos mode: a bank book, piles of bills and a tiny metal box overflowing with bills and hand-written notes.

'Hey, Luigi. I need to ask a favour.'

'As long as it isn't money . . .'

'I always pay you back, don't I?'

'Yeah, but I don't see you until you do, and when I don't see you, you're not spending money here. Bad for business.'

'I'll pay you back tomorrow, I swear. Tomorrow morning I'm gonna get paid a bundle.'

'Is it my imagination or have I heard that one before?'

'Come on, Luigi. When have I ever lied to you?'

'Every chance you get.'

'OK, but never when money's involved. I need seventy-five euros. Seventy-five. That's all.'

He was starting to soften. This was made apparent by his head, bent down in deep concentration as he studied a bunch of supermarket receipts from Caprabo.

'And I suppose you want to owe me for tonight, too, right?'

'Well, tomorrow I can give you half, I promise. Instalments.'

'What do I look like, a La Caixa cash machine? Tomorrow you will pay me the full amount. No more, no less. And I'm serious about that. Tomorrow, understood?'

I got it, and got out of there as fast as I could, heading up Jaume Guillamet. You could barely even tell that there had been an accident at all – all that remained were some tiny slivers of glass that twinkled under the streetlights and a pile of those round salty bits that had been sprinkled on the ground to soak up the blood. I continued walking up the street until I reached number fifteen. For a moment, I crouched down in front of the entrance to the garden, as if I were tying my shoe, and surveyed the lamppost. I was not at all surprised this time to see a red rag tied to the top. In fact, I was glad to see my expectations fulfilled. I had that astute, crafty, somewhat self-satisfied feeling that sometimes comes from the ingestion of alcohol: the world was, once again, an ordered system. After duly noting this minor detail, I continued up Travessera to Numancia and then began to walk down toward Plaza España. I arrived at the bar on Parallel with a half-hour's worth of hunger. I tapped on the closed blinds. Light behind the peephole. I gave them the sign and they let me in through the side door. I ordered an *esqueixada*, octopus tapas, meatballs, and a giant spicy croquette otherwise known as a *bomba*. I ate slowly, savouring every bite, and little by little I began to feel better. The only thing left for full satisfaction was a good crap. The toilet was, however, every bit as filthy as one would expect from a semi-clandestine bar on the Parallel that was open all night for any random person that wanted to eat. I improvised a hygienic seat cover with a few bits of toilet paper, taking care that the tip of my prick didn't touch the seat. When I finished, I performed a quick jerk-off against the sink, mentally conjuring up the image of a certain TV hostess with a truly commendable pair of tits; it wasn't that I was desperate or anything, but I needed a little bodily discharge so as not to come prematurely later on. Then I scrupulously washed myself clean and took a sniff of the armpits: *no problemo*. By the time I hit the street I wasn't even drunk anymore, and filling up my stomach had helped erase the acrid taste of vodka and beer in my mouth.

The dawn light was still very weak, the traffic on the

streets sparse. I like that hour of the day, around five-thirty, six in the morning. Around seven shit starts getting ugly again and the best thing you can do is let the day shift get to work, let the world continue to spin on its axis while you get some sleep. I walked for a while, smoking a cigarette, and then hailed a cab. This one smelled like La Toja shaving cream. Early-morning news on the radio. Friday, 20th of July, World Cup game in France, the Spain team having their pre-game meeting somewhere, blah, blah, blah. It was a pleasant-enough background drone, and mixed nicely with the breeze coming in through the open window and the noise of the diesel engine. I got out at the Boquería market and allowed myself a stroll amid the various stalls, so that I might admire some or other well-stacked lady fishmonger sitting high on her icy throne, like a Queen of the Seas amid gifts of lemon and clove and the aroma of live, quivering shellfish. I then directed my walking tour down various winding streets, paying little attention to the route I took and far more to the light-hearted glee that was now causing a strain on my zipper. Inevitably I arrived at the plaza with the hotel, almost without realising it. It always happens that way. What I saw lurking about on the streets was not terrifically stimulating and so I ducked in to one of the bars in the hope of finding something better inside. The owner was busy rummaging through the freezers behind the bar. He was a bald fellow, his forehead eaten away by psoriasis. The coffee machine was plugged in and seemed disposed to fulfil its electricity-related tasks. I ordered a coffee. Now, anyone who is unfamiliar with the hooker scene in this area should know that this is just about the exact opposite of Amsterdam. That is: the client waits behind the window of a bar, showing himself off as it were, and the hookers walk around in a sort of invisible carousel ride around the plaza. When you spot one that you like, you signal to her and then she enters to sort out the details. At this hour, the night shift had already turned in. The girls on duty now were the ones who generally catered to the men that have just gotten off their shifts supplying the stalls at the market. The pickings are generally better at the saunas in the Eixample, which is the territory of exorbitantly-priced female philology students who drink skim milk and say things like 'fellatio.' Anyway. The scene there that morning was pretty dodgy: only three chicks chirping and none of them was my type. The oldest of the three looked frightfully past her sixtieth birthday and stood there in front of the window, insisting and gesticulating to me as I shook my head no over and over again, trying nonetheless to retain an amiable expression on my face. My efforts, however, were not nearly insistent enough for her, because she came into the bar for me.

'Hey, sweetheart. Wanna come with me for a bit?'

'Another day.'

'Come on, I'll suck your balls nice and long.'

'Thanks – but as it turns out I've already had them sucked – before I went out tonight.'

She laughed at that one.

'What a joker. Oh, we'll have a good time, you and me. Come on, come to my room and you can heat up what I've got cooking.'

She vaguely reminded me of Mrs Mitjans, one of the regulars at my mother's canasta games, and this rendered her absolutely unserviceable. Naturally I had to say no about fifteen times before she finally gave up. I invited her to a drink and she ordered a coffee with milk and a croissant. As she breakfasted I tried to sidle away from her so that the girls on the street would see that I was still free, but it was tough going. As soon as she finished the croissant, she resumed her insistent attack, this time with caresses, the kind of caresses that only a hooker or a woman in love know how to administer – as if they're dying to touch you, stroke you, feel you. It's not easy to resist that kind of avid manhandling. Hookers know it and they push hard, touching and whispering all the while. After some time, this one eventually threw in the towel and returned to the plaza, though she continued to make little faces at me through the window. By now a new girl had joined the carousel, and she was pretty tasty-looking, at least from where I was standing. I waited for her to move a little closer so that I could check her out better. Thirtysomething, maybe even in her forties. She was all woman, with short hair, dark, nice ass, smallish tits, serene face. Serious. Very serious. I looked her in the eye. She didn't make any faces, just walked in and over to the bar.

'What's up?'

'Hi. You still working?'

'I just started. What do you want?'

'A fuck. Typical. Hard.'

'Thirty. Extra if you want a room.'

'Well, I was thinking around forty, but that includes the extra fifteen for a room over at the corner. It's clean . . .'

She didn't have to think twice.

'All right. Forty if we go to the hotel.'

We entered the joint, her walking a few paces ahead of me. There's something about hookers that reminds me of drug dealers: in public they both always act as if they have absolutely nothing to do with you, and it's mutual. At the counter a kid with a face full of hardcore acne memories gave her a keychain with the number thrity-seven and charged me the hourly rate. Lift. Taking a cheap hooker into a by-the-hour hotel lift almost always means she's gonna start sniffing your zipper to gain time on the way up, but this one didn't seem keen on that, she just nibbled at her thumb a bit.

'What's your name?'

'Pablo. You?'

'Gloria.'

Shit.

The room was beige, I think I had been in there once before but it's hard to say; they all look more or less the same. Gloria lowered the bedspread to reveal the whitest of sheets with crisp hospital corners, an extremely hygienic touch that had a rather soothing effect. She extracted a pair of condoms from her jeans pocket and left them on the bedside table. Then she sat down at the foot of the bed, undressed, and walked over to the tiny sink, with a sniff of disdain directed toward the bidet. She raised her leg and rested her thigh against the basin, positioning herself so that her cunt was just within reach of the water, and then she began to douse herself with little scoopfuls of water from the tap. The rite of ablution. That moment, when they wash their nether regions, has always seemed so sordid to me, but this time there was something unexpectedly lovely in that scene, bathed in the oblique early-morning light that filtered in through the window: her tiny tits with their conical nipples reflected in the mirror; her wide, full arse filling up the washbasin; the chap-chap of the water slapping against her protruding vulva. *Venus at her Bath*, or better yet, *Maiden Watering her Flower*. A good oil painting of that scene would have been worthy of some hall in the Louvre, and a good photograph would have most definitely been worthy of presiding over some mechanic's garage. I undressed quickly, uncomfortable from the insistent erection trapped inside my pants, and I approached my Venus, who was now gently rubbing the space between her thighs with a pastel-pink towel. She had left the sky-blue one for me, in tacit acceptance of the gender-inspired colour conventions suggested by the hotel linen service. I approached her from behind and embraced her, slipping my hands under her arms in search of her breasts, which I took in my hands as two cornucopias of sheer abundance.

'Wait . . . wash up first and then we'll go to the bed,' she said, extricating herself. I then approached the wash-basin to fulfil the baptismal rite. First I placed my prick, hard as a cucumber, under the stream of water that flowed from the tap and then carelessly dried it off. The cold water and subsequent contact with the rough towel succeeded in relieving, if only partially, the tension that had built up in my cock. She, in the meantime, had flung herself onto the right side of the bed and waited for me there, watching me all the while, never once altering that serious expression on her face.

'Move over to the other side, if you don't mind,' I said. She moved over and I stretched out on the bed, breathing harder now from the arousal.

'Let me take it from here. Can I kiss you?' I asked.

'Anywhere but my lips.' I began on her neck, briefly, and then quickly descended to her breasts. I entertained myself there for a while, savouring that smooth, creamy delight, and my pleasure grew as I began to feel her nipples grow hard, that puckering of the skin around her areolas. My cock, once again, was back in full force.

'Are you comfortable?' I asked. She nodded yes, as serious and focused as before, observing my journey across her breasts with a kind of relaxed curiosity. I slid my right hand down toward the centre of her sex. She separated her right leg, which was resting on her foot, allowing me to extend the full length of my finger across her mound, cold and damp from the prophylactic rinse she had just given herself. Little by little, my mouth still playing games with her spiky nipples, I tilted my index finger to the side and pressed deeper, hoping to shift open her lips. That was when I began to feel a much warmer mound, a delicious swelling down below. I selected one of the condoms on the night table at random, put it on (not without a certain predictable difficulty, which is overcome by ignoring the enclosed instructions) and began to mount her, rocking back and forth as she adjusted her position to accommodate me. I could feel my heart beating at the base of my prick and I tried to keep it from plunging directly into the crevice between her legs by raising up a bit and situating my balls in her little nest, simply enjoying the moment, the feeling of just being there, between her open legs. At moments like these I often feel an overwhelming urge to declare unconditional love, but I contained myself and kissed everything within reach of my lips – everything except the mouth, the mouth of a hooker who doesn't want to get kissed by just anyone but who will have sucked at least five other cocks by the time her shift is over. Hooker issues. When I couldn't hold back any longer and decided to award myself with the anticipated prize, I separated my thigh a bit with my hand and I moved forward, pressing hard with the tip of my cock, rudderless, until I felt myself hit it. I pressed on some more and felt that feeling, as if I had just passed through a silken scrim, and then I felt it once again, even more intensely, when I buried the full length of my little earthly representative inside her, and once I was in place I positioned myself firmly on my elbows, so that she could breathe beneath my 120 kilos. I would have stayed there forever, but that wouldn't be possible – I knew that – and so I had to perform a repeated enter-and-exit motion to fool myself into feeling that I had been inside of her for ages. She let me do my thing, not bothering to put on any special effects show. From her side of the scene, all I heard her do was release one very controlled breath each time I lunged into her. I did this slowly but with increasing pressure, which forced her to tighten her muscles to resist the compression that I was subjecting her to with my shoulders. When I felt the imminence of orgasm I let her go, put my hands where my elbows were, so as not to hurt her in the final thrusts, and I came long and slow, with that Wookie-esque roar that comes out whenever I'm really satisfied. Next came that soft, slow, wet sensation and then my prick resumed its normal dimensions, all the more ridiculous-looking beneath that miniature raincoat, swimming in a puddle of white goo.

I lay face up for a bit and once my breathing stabilised I asked her if she minded spending five more minutes in bed, just enough time to smoke a cigarette. She said all right and asked me for a cigarette, a light cigarette if I had one. I rummaged through my pants, found the pack of Fortunas, handed her one and lit it for her. Then I lit a Ducados and returned to the bed.

'Happy?' she asked.

'Like a king. If we wait a little, I'll do it again.'

'Right. That'll be another twenty-five.'

'Another twenty-five? Come on, we're already here – you're better off negotiating a good price and repeating with me than going out to the street and looking for someone else.' She lay there for a moment, staring up at the ceiling. Then she took a drag off the Fortuna.

'All right. I'll leave it at twenty.'

'But all I've got left is fifteen. And I have to catch a cab home after.'

'Well, if you want, put on a condom and I'll suck you off for ten.'

'I don't like getting sucked off.'

'Really? That's kind of weird . . .'

'Yeah, I guess I'm sort of a pervert. Come on: another fuck for ten?'

'Forget it: twenty. You can take the metro home. If you don't have enough I'll give you some loose change for the ride.'

'I haven't taken the metro in years. It depresses me.'

'Don't start and try to take advantage of me now . . . I'm not a sister of charity, you know? I already gave you a discount before, and now I'm doing it again.'

Ah, who cared. A ride on the metro can't be that bad if you're riding well-fucked. I accepted the second round for twenty. We finished the cigarette, I hugged her, she hugged me, she rested her cheek against my chest, we rubbed up against each other for a bit and repeated. Almost exactly the same as before, although this time it was much more relaxed, now that I had been liberated of the intense urgency to ejaculate. We smoked another cigarette after it was over. Less than half an hour had gone by, but it was still enough time to lazily surrender to the post-coitus ritual. This time around she used the bidet, soaping up her cunt from her pubis down to her arsehole, keeping her back to me the whole time. I had to light another cigarette and look away from her so as not to start getting hard all over again. Then, as she got dressed, I went back to the sink for another little spray of water. She waited for me to finish and then I paid – that was when I realised that she hadn't asked for the money up front, which is standard operating procedure in this kind of encounter. With that, we left the hotel together.

We said our goodbyes outside the hotel.

'Well. If you come around again, now you know. Gloria. Ask around for me, I'm usually about at this time of night.'

'It's a shame you caught me so low on cash . . . I'll definitely come back to see you sometime,' I said, even though I knew I never would – the next time around I'd most likely avoid her, in fact. Not a good idea to fuck the same woman twice: the libido has a shocking propensity for developing fixations.

I suppressed my desire to kiss her, even just on the cheek. So I just gave her a goodbye wink and went on my way up the Ramblas, in a vastly improved mood. I was already making my way to the Atarazanas metro stop when I realised that it had to be after seven: I could take a cab to the office and ask for the fare at the reception desk. Maria controls the cash box, and Maria is always on my side.

I used the cab ride to formulate a plan. First, before going to bed, I would load the washing machine and get it cranking. If the auction with Kiko Ledgard and Lady First was going to be the next day, I would need some clean clothes. Then, I'd call the telephone company wake-up service to ensure that I would be awake early enough to set my plan into action. And then I would have to get some sleep: something told me I had a long battle ahead of me. Of course, there was no way I could have known that right then, as I rode back home, happy as a newborn pup after fulfilling his fertility rites, someone was beating my Magnificent Brother to a pulp.

THE BLACK BEAST

I woke up without a hangover, to the sound of the telephone ringing. 'Twelve o'clock, one minute, ten seconds . . .' I heard when I picked up the receiver. For having scarcely slept four hours, I felt pretty well-rested, far better than I expected to feel. The only thing I remembered from my last dream was a mere replay of my episode in the bar with the hooker, although in the dream my hotel companion was a lovely lady fishmonger from the Boquería market. It appeared that for some time I had been trying to penetrate my mattress, without success. This is a very frustrating experience, one which I don't think women can quite understand; it's something like trying to get your arm into a jacket sleeve and not being able to. Just take out the arm and replace it with a prick, which is far more delicate and ends up getting hard as a red pepper what with the rough friction of the fabric. Those mattress manufacturers ought to be a little more sensitive to this issue – the puncture-resistance of their products could do some severe damage to someone's orthodontial work. In any event, the dream left a nice taste in my mouth, and I was in a fine mood what with the scent of summer in the air, mixed in with the sound of the traffic down below, transporting me back to the days when twelve noon meant something else entirely, when it was the heart and soul of a day that began so very much earlier.

The washing machine had long since finished its cycle. Before doing anything else, I hung the clothes so that they would have as much time as possible to dry. Then I had a breakfast of coffee and milk – no croissants, no butter – and smoked my first joint of the day in the living room. I took the second one with me into the toilet, and I smoked the third one as I drank my coffee, back in the living room. Once I felt I had a grip on my plan for the day, I looked in my wallet for The First's phone number and punched it in.

'Gloria? It's Pablo. Any news?'

'No. I've been standing by the phone all day but no, nothing.'

'Can I come and see you?'

'Yes, of course. Why, is something wrong?'

'I've got a few ideas. Do you have any money in the house?'

'Well . . . I don't know. Yes, I suppose I have some. If not I can send Veronica out to the cash machine.'

'Right. What time can we meet?'

'Whenever you want, I'm not going anywhere. Merche isn't going to school today and I've called Veronica to help me out.'

My bourgeois weaknesses breathed a sigh of relief: my Adorable Niece and Nephew were safe and sound at home. We agreed that I would stop by before lunch. As I hung up the phone I tried to think up some old wives' trick for drying shirts, and wondered how long it could take. What if I stuck it in the oven? I decided to shelve the problem for later and instead punched my parents' phone number without thinking much. Sometimes a bit of improvisation helps to sharpen one's lying abilities.

Beba answered the phone.

'Look who's calling! Don't tell me you're missing us already . . .'

'I always miss you, hot stuff. Is my mother around there somewhere?'

'Yes, she's at the computer working on her French. Should I tell her it's you?'

'Please.'

I waited a bit and after a few seconds my Mother's Highness got on the line. She seemed to be in a good mood.

'Bon zhour, com on talley-vou?'

'Hi, Mom.'

'Mercee bo koo. Zhe swee tre contant pas ku etu dee le fransais.'

'*Etudie*, Mom, in this case you would say that you like to study, in present continuous.'

'But didn't you learn Canadian French? You have such a ghastly accent. Let's see: say "ronard."'

'Ronard.'

'Don't you see: that's very Canadian. You talk as if you had a bubble in your mouth. You should never have spent so much time in . . . where was it that you went?'

'I don't know, Mom. I was in a lot of places. Listen, how is Dad doing?'

'Don't remind me. I actually managed to forget about him for a while.'

'What's up . . .'

'What do you mean, what's up? What's up is that Mr Miralles is in a horrible mood. Hor-ri-ble. You can't imagine how unbelievably stubborn he can be . . . well, of course you know, but today he's really outdone himself. For two days now he's had me locked up in this house. Says that if I so much as cross the threshold he will stop speaking to me, just like that. Those are his exact words. Oh, and that's not all: he refuses to let Eusebia out as well.'

'Well, be a little patient, all right?'

'Hostages. That's what we are: hos-tages. I had to send the kitchen maid out to do my shopping. But rest assured, I plan on going out this afternoon, no matter what he says. And if he stops speaking to me, that's just fine. Really. Lately he has been acting simply ludicrous . . .'

'Don't worry . . .'

'Lud-i-crous. Would you believe that this morning I caught him in the library fiddling with his rifle? That clever man tried to hide it behind his back, like a little boy caught with his hand in the cookie jar. Can you just picture it? Your father, in his pyjamas, trying to balance a crutch in one hand while hiding a two-and-a-half-metre rifle behind his back? Pathetic. What with all of this, of course, I had to call Doctor Caudet, who tells me this is normal – I mean, really. Normal. He said that if your father gets too nervous I should give him a Valium and take one myself, too.'

'So, fine. Let him take one and then . . .'

'Oh, no, no. I already tried that. But he refuses. I brought a pill and a glass of water to the library, and you wouldn't believe how disgusting he was. You know, the old "what's that you've got there" with that bulldog face of his, and me, "well, what do you think, Valentín? A Valium and a bit of mineral water." "Well, I absolutely won't take it," he said, "so you can just take it right back to the kitchen." I mean, the *kitchen*, for heaven's sake . . .'

'All right, all right, don't go flying off the handle. Dr Caudet already told you this was normal. What you need to do is just try not to get him worked up. And if he doesn't want you to leave the house, be a little understanding and stay in. I know it's a drag, but it'll only be for a few days. All right?'

'Pablo José. What on earth has gotten into you? Are

you in on this, too? Don't tell me you're taking this paranoia seriously?'

'No, but . . .'

'Oh, no? And since when have you ever found it useful or interesting to obey your father's wishes?'

'Mom, just listen . . .'

'Right, right. Of course, it's a *good* idea to indulge your father's flights of lunacy just because he's sprained his ankle and refuses to admit that he was completely distracted as he walked down the street . . .'

'Mo-om . . .'

' . . . because I'm sure that's what happened. He didn't see the car that was manoeuvring around and he walked straight into it, as if he meant to. Do you know that lately I've caught him trying to sneak little peeks at the young ladies that pass him by on the street? Yes, I kid you not. Last Sunday as we were coming back from Mass he practically walked into a lamppost. It pains me to say it, Pablo José, but your father is turning into a dirty old man. A dirty old man. But, of course, no: Mr Valentín Miralles refuses to admit that he got distracted while inspecting some young lady's décolletage. No, no – Valentín Miralles, distracted? No, that couldn't be! If *he* got hit by a car it had to be because someone *meant* to hit him.'

'Mom. Wait, wait a second. There's something you don't know.'

That sure stopped her in her tracks. My mother always wants to be in on everything.

'Oh, really? And pray tell, just what is it that I know nothing about?'

I hesitated a moment, as if I didn't know quite what to say.

'I can't tell you.'

'Pablo José: I order you to tell me what is going on here, immediately, or I am going to have a fit! Eusebia,' she called out, 'bring me a Valium and a bit of water please. Quickly, or else I might faint. Now Pablo José,' she said, turning her attention back me, 'please do me the favour of an explanation. Right now.'

'It's nothing, Mom, really. I don't want you to get nervous . . .'

'Oh, no? Well, if it's nothing, then why won't you tell me? Answer me that.'

'Because I can't. I don't want Dad to know I told you.'

'When have I ever told your father anything?'

'All right. Okay . . . Is he around here somewhere?'

'No. He's in the library. You can talk.'

This was where I began to improvise upon the plan in my head.

'You'll understand when I explain, it has to do with something from way back. Do you remember a company called Fincas Ibarra?'

'No.'

That didn't surprise me. I had just spotted the name on a jar of mayonnaise that I had left on top of my refrigerator the other day. I could just barely make out the label from where I was in the living room. Good thing I didn't buy Kraft.

'As you may recall, Fincas Ibarra is a small real estate outfit. Remember when Dad began to invest in apartment buildings?'

'Pablo, I have no idea. Your father invests in absolutely everything, don't confuse me with details.'

'Well, the point is that Ibarra took him to court, several times. You don't remember any of those proceedings?'

'Remember? For ten years the entire world tried to take

us to court, I can't imagine what was going on – all I remember is that we were getting calls from lawyers at every hour of the day and night.'

'Well, the Ibarra people tried to sue Dad. And at the end of the day they lost. Apparently Dad rented apartments through third parties in a number of Ibarra buildings that seemed to be in particularly bad shape. He hired a technical team to go over them with a fine-tooth comb and once they had sufficient evidence, he sued the owners for not complying with all the regulations and codes for residential buildings. The Ibarra company was declared guilty, couldn't appeal the verdict, and auctioned off the majority of their buildings at rock-bottom prices, and eventually folded with a pile of unpaid bills to boot. Naturally Dad bought the majority of those buildings and ended up making money off the deal. Don't ask me how, but he earned back all the money he'd invested in his technical research and made a hefty profit when he sold them off, for way more money than he'd paid.'

'Don't even tell me . . . I don't know how on earth your father always manages to make money with his schemes. Juan Sebastian takes after him that way. You, on the other hand, resemble him much more physically. And you're just as stubborn, too . . . although, well, in that respect, all three of you are exactly the same. Now, perhaps you can tell me what all of that has to do with not letting me and Eusebia out of the house?'

My little introduction had worked perfectly, for it calmed her down with all those confusing details. I should note that they were not all inventions, strictly speaking: I had once heard FH spouting off about some pretty similar deals, and so it wasn't all that hard to come up with a story that was somewhat based in reality. All I had to do now was finish it off, but that was no problem, I had warmed up pretty well by then.

'So you see, Ibarra ended up in jail. And after Dad aired all his dirty laundry, even more of his shady deals came to light: extortion, Social Security fraud, and who knows what else. They gave him ten years. He only served two, and in a low-security jail at that, but he took it pretty hard and blamed Dad for everything he went through. He swore he'd get Dad back as soon as he could, and as it turns out, he was released about five years ago. Now he has several different companies, all in his wife's name. You're following me?'

'Yes, I follow you, but that rude man's business dealings are of no interest to me, frankly.'

If my Mother's Highness considered Ibarra rude, it meant she had swallowed the bait. For MH, cheating the Social Security system is terribly unseemly. Something like putting one's elbows on the table.

'Well, do you remember how they told you that Dad had called Sebastian from the hospital after he was hit?'

'Yes.'

'Well, that wasn't exactly true. When Sebastian arrived at the hospital they were still taking x-rays of Dad's leg. At that point he still hadn't had a chance to call anyone. It was Ibarra who phoned Sebastian to tell him what had happened.'

I waited a moment to gauge her reaction, to see if she got the drift.

'The rude man?'

'The very one.'

'And how did he know what had happened?'

'Well, that's exactly what Dad is all worried about.'

'I don't get it. If that man is so worked up about your

father, why on earth would he have bothered to tell Juan Sebastian that he got into an accident?'

My Mother has always been even denser than I am when it comes to following movie plots. Sometimes I think that the shortcoming is hereditary. On the other hand, both of us are pretty good at inventing stories, all you have to do is listen to the excuses she dreams up to justify her Visa bills to my father. They're worthy of a soap opera.

'He wasn't making a courtesy call, Mom. He called to make it very clear that the accident was no accident. That he was behind the whole thing.'

'Good lord! Do you mean to say that he was driving the car?'

'Nooo . . . what I mean to say is that he hired a couple of goons to scare Dad.'

I could hear the rush of air as she sucked in her breath. She was clearly frightened now, and with good reason. Of course, it would have been far worse to have told her the truth . . . *All right, Mom, listen: not only did they ram into Dad but someone has kidnapped Sebastian and his lover, but we can't call the police because they'll just make a bigger mess out of all this, and that's why I, your wayward son, have to take charge of the situation, with the assistance of your daughter-in-law who, by the way, is sexually frigid, probably a drunk, and finds girlfriends for your irreproachable older son.* No. Lying was definitely the better option. And that was what I needed, to have her sufficiently scared so that she would stay home for a couple of days. Of course I couldn't just leave her hanging – all the Valiums in the world wouldn't calm her down for long in that case.

When she finally digested the information she spoke again, this time in a pained voice.

'Why didn't you tell me any of this? Don't you think I have a right to know about this sort of thing?'

'I talked it over with Dad, and he didn't want you to get frightened. So he asked me not to say anything. He'd rather you think it was some maniacal fantasy of his.'

'And how did you find out?'

Ooh. How *did* I find out?

'Uh . . . I was in Sebastian's office when the call came in about the accident.'

'But you just told me on the phone that you found out because Juan Sebastian had called you at home.'

Beeep. Mistake.

'I said that?'

'Yes.'

'Well, I figured it was better to pretend I didn't know anything until I got to talk to Dad.'

Luckily my Mother was far too perplexed to look for inconsistencies in my line of defence.

'Have you called the police?'

'Don't worry, Sebastian is taking care of that. For the moment he's trying to trace Ibarra's phone call in order to have something substantial to give to the police. Obviously he can't prove anything against them, but we warned Ibarra that the police have been following his activities, and that should be enough to stop him from trying anything else against Dad. In fact, they're most likely perfectly satisfied with having broken his leg. I doubt they'll try to do anything else, but we just want to be sure. The whole thing should be resolved in a couple of days.'

MH no longer seemed very interested in my explanations.

'Sebastian. I have to speak with Juan Sebastian so that he can explain what the devil is really going on here.'

Danger.

'You won't find him, Mom. He's in Bilbao.'

'Bilbao? And what in Heaven's name, pray tell, is Juan Sebastian doing in Bilbao? For God's sake, this sounds like some secret plot . . .'

'He went to Bilbao specifically to look into the phone call from Ibarra. He wanted to do it himself. According to the computer connected to his office's phone box, the call was made from Bilbao.'

MH, just like the telemarketing girl, is one of those people who believes that computers can actually do that sort of thing.

'Well, it's all the same. I'll call him on his mobile.'

Shit. The mobile. In all likelihood, he still had it. In reality, I assumed that Lady First had already thought of calling him on the mobile, although I didn't remember her mentioning it.

'I don't think he'll answer it. I think he disconnected it, to avoid getting interrupted by the office.'

My mother, at that point, held the phone away from her ear for a moment to call out to Beba.

'Eusebia, what on Earth is going on with that Valium? I'm going to have a fit if you've turned against me too . . .'

In the background I could hear Beba answer her.

'I am not giving you one more Palium because you took the last one only two hours ago. If I give you one more you're going to keel over. If you want I'll make you a tea and that's it.'

'Eusebia! Don't tell me you're getting smart, too. Or is it just that everyone in this house has lost all respect for me?'

I decided to get back in the fray.

'Mom. Listen. You have to promise me that you won't breathe a word about any of this to Dad, all right?'

'Of course I won't say a word. If he hasn't deigned to

tell me anything, I'm not going to let on that I know anything either . . . And I am still plenty ticked off that he sent me to the kitchen, for God's sake.'

'Fine. And one more thing: promise me that you'll stay put in the house with Eusebia for a couple of days.'

'Well, this afternoon I have a canasta game, but I suppose we can move it here if we have to. Good god, this is like a spy novel . . . It won't be dangerous for my friends to come here, will it? Mrs Mitjans will be beside herself when she finds out.'

'No, no, there's nothing to worry about. But better not mention any of this to anyone, okay? And remember, above all, not a word to Dad. And forget about Sebastian until he gets back from Bilbao. I imagine you can survive a few days without your favourite son?'

'Do me a favour and drop the sarcasm, Pablo José. I am not in the mood for your issues with Juan Sebastian . . . My God. I think I need a massage. Right now. I'm going to call the gym so that they can send someone up. Gonzalito, I need Gonzalito . . .'

'That's right. Have a sauna at home and then get a massage. And don't worry about anything. I'll make sure to keep you informed. *D'accord*?'

'What?'

'I said da-kord. All right?'

'Pablo José: do you know that I find that you are behaving extremely oddly?'

I hung up as she was about to sip her tea and call her Gonzalito, a bodybuilder with about a hundred kilos on his frame – distributed far differently from my own – and gayer than a pink satin hat. That's the latest fad: at this rate we're all going to end up queers. As I hung up I realised how tense I had gotten from the conversation. So I prepared another joint, flopped down on a chair and smoked it with relish before I took my second important step of the day. I looked at my reflection in the television set once again. Superficially nothing was very different. Once again it was me, in my robe, and with the same living room chaos surrounding me on all sides. Yet, nothing was the same. Everything was much worse. Or maybe much better. I'm never quite sure how those things work. The point is, everything was different now, and my inner peace had most definitely been perturbed.

I got moving, so as not to enter a vortex of self-reflection.

Out on the line, my clothes were as damp as they had been half an hour earlier. I unhooked the brown pants and a white shirt that seemed to match pretty well and brought them into the living room. In the storage room, I rummaged about for a hair dryer. Found it. It was part of the domestic equipment my mother had sent me after I had moved in to one of my father's buildings after having gotten thrown out of my last apartment for lagging on the rent. It must have arrived along with the Corte Inglés delivery, with all those blenders, choppers, juice squeezers, electronic scales, robot dehumidifiers, gadgets for regulating the temperature of my shower gel, videotape rewinders, and all those things that my mother thought were of utmost importance to electrically domesticate her son the savage. The hairdryer, like everything else, was still unused, still in its corrugated carton box: an imposing machine, the shape of an elongated snail. It came with an attachment that allowed it to stand on its own, and I hooked the thing up: that way, as the dryer oscillated left and right, I could spread the clothes out on a chair in front of the blower and forget about the issue. Breakfast time. Steak and fried eggs, which took me half an hour to prepare and eat. After finishing, I checked in on the clothes: still wet despite the nautilus airblower. I tried with an iron. My efforts were rewarded: the shirt was rendered almost dry but the pants proved to be a bit trickier. I stopped trying, and ended up, as always, hunting through my closet for some forgotten item with which I might cover my nether regions. I opted for the bottom half of a dark-blue Dacron suit with a zipper that almost made it up to the button. With the help of a belt and a shirt with the tails sticking out, I could hide my little bang-up job and head out to the street. It was after one when I checked myself out in the vestibule. Not exactly Cary Grant, but I'd seen worse.

It took me almost fifteen minutes to reach The First's family home, given that I was focused on taking very tiny steps so as to prevent my zipper from opening mid-trip. But I was a man on a mission; there was no stopping me. I entered the building, beneath the suspicious gaze of the blue-bathrobed doorman, and took the lift up to the top floor. Veronica opened the door. This time her t-shirt read 'Department of Biology' which confirmed my hypothesis regarding her political inclinations. In her arms she carried the toothless creature whom I wasted little time in greeting. Veronica then pointed toward the kitchen and there I found Lady First coating various hake fillets in an egg-and-flour batter. She looked me up and down, rather brusquely. My fashion decision had inspired a stupefied horror that she could scarcely hide.

'You cook?' I asked, by way of a greeting.

'Of course. What did you think?'

'I thought that elegant people didn't touch food with their hands.'

'Whoever told you I was elegant?'

'You look the type.'

'Well, now you know. Can I get you something to drink?'

'I could do with a beer.'

'Take a look in the refrigerator – I can't, my hands are all sticky.'

I opened the door and hunted for the beer and glass according to her instructions and then leaned against the doorjamb observing her as she handled the fish. She seemed a little subdued. Of course, that was to be expected if the story she told me the day before was true.

'All right. So tell me about these ideas that you've come up with.'

I lit a cigarette to stall for time.

'I think we should hire a private detective,' I said, finally.

She stopped what she was doing for a minute and just stared at me, her eyebrows raised.

'A detective?'

'Well, this is what they're for, wouldn't you say?'

'I don't think that's a very good idea. This is not your typical infidelity case. I don't think a detective would be useful at all.'

I had expected some resistance to the idea, and I had already prepared a convincing argument.

'Look, Gloria. I'm going to be straight with you. I don't want anything bad to happen to my brother, but I'm not particularly interested in getting mixed up in his problems, know what I mean? So he disappeared. All right then, we have to find him, and to a certain point it's logical that you would come to me for help. But I think the best thing we can do is turn the case over to a professional. I can't come up with anything better than that. I already told my mother some cockamamie story to explain away his absence for a few days, so that she wouldn't get too alarmed. And I'll tell my father some other story if I have to – basically

I'll try to steer the trouble toward the office. But aside from that I don't think there's anything else that I can really do.'

'What did you tell your mother?'

'That Sebastian had to go to Bilbao to wrap up some business.'

She stood there thinking for a moment.

'And it didn't strike her as strange that he didn't stop by to see her? Sebastian goes over there every two or three days, and always before he goes away on a trip.'

'Don't worry, I already figured something out to keep her calm and quiet. I told her that you went with him, so don't call her because as far as she's concerned you're in Bilbao. I thought that would make things easier for you: if she doesn't try talking to you, you won't have to lie to her.' That last part was bullshit, but I thought it convenient, given the circumstances.

'She didn't ask you about the children?'

'No . . . she must've assumed your parents were looking after them. Don't they take care of them when you two go away?'

'Yes, sometimes. But it's odd that she wouldn't ask after them.'

'Well, she's a bit frazzled, what with my father's accident and all.'

'How is he?'

'Fine. I saw him yesterday. He got distracted on the street, checking out some girl's cleavage, and a car that was turning a corner hit him. He's being completely impossible, but it's nothing. He's just grumpy because of the plaster cast.'

'I would have liked to see him . . .'

But I wasn't interested in continuing the discussion about my Father's Highness.

'So, well, what do you say about the detective?'

'What do you mean, what do I say? I don't like it at all. I'd rather you look into the situation yourself. Firstly because we can't just let any stranger go poking through Sebastian's papers, and secondly because I don't care to reveal the details of my marriage to anyone.'

'Well, we don't have to tell him the whole truth. And if you want, I'll deal with going through his papers.'

She abandoned one of her hake fillets, leaving it on the tray mid-batter, and turned to me.

'I don't get it: what use is a detective that doesn't know what's going on?'

'There are plenty of possibilities that aren't occurring to us. Those people know where to look, I don't know, airports, hotels . . . They have contacts – with the police, for example. In two days they can cover way more than we can in a month. Plus, we can get him to tail your friend the secretary, what was her name?'

'Lali.'

'Lali. We can hire the detective on her account, you know, say we're friends or family or something. That we're worried about her. He can start sniffing down that trail, see what he comes up with. That way we can get ahead on things until the envelope you mailed arrives. Then we'll take it from there.'

She turned back to the flour, utterly unconvinced by my proposal.

'I think it's mad. And I don't know . . . awfully contrived.'

'Okay, but in any case we can't lose anything by trying. At the worst, all we lose is the money for his fee. That was why I asked you if you had money in the house. Plus, I need some for myself. Yesterday Sebastian was supposed to have paid me for some work I did for him. How are you doing money-wise?'

'I have about five hundred euros in the house. But I also have credit cards. If you want I can give you Sebastian's cash card. I have a copy of it here, with the PIN number, too.'

'Would there be enough to pay for a detective for a couple of days plus some money for me?'

'Well, it's his pocket money, but yes, I suppose so. He usually has some extra money in the account for unexpected expenses. Take what you need and you can settle accounts with him afterwards . . . when he comes back.'

'Perfect. Listen, one other thing. I was thinking, it wouldn't be a bad idea for me to have a car, more than anything just in case I need to move around to do some investigating. Do you have Sebastian's car keys?'

'Which car?'

'I thought you only had one car.'

'No, we just bought another one, one of those SUVs, with adaptable seats, for the kids, you know . . .'

'I'd be better off with the BMW.'

'We don't have it anymore. Sebastian treated himself to a sports car.'

'Do you mind if I use that?'

She shook her head. It seemed there was something else she was concerned about.

'Listen, I'm not altogether convinced about your detective idea. What are you planning on telling him?'

I made like I was thinking aloud.

'Well, um, I don't know . . . Maybe you could pretend to be Lali's sister and I'd be her brother-in-law. You wouldn't really have to act, just lie about a couple of minor details.'

'Oh, sure. If you think lying about the two of us being married is just a minor detail . . .'

'Well, do you have a better idea?'

Silence. Half-turn, back to the hake filet and the batter. This was the moment to make it easy for her, convince her once and for all.

'Listen, I'll deal with calling a detective agency and making an appointment for us to meet here, all right? Trust me, I'd feel much better if we do it. How about at eight tonight?'

Finally she relented.

'All right, all right. Whatever you say.'

'I'll call you to confirm. And uh, if you don't mind, could I get the car keys and the cash card? I have to go now, I'm a little pressed for time.'

She rinsed her hands off and went out into the hallway toward what I imagine was the executive suite. I downed my beer as I waited for her in the kitchen, not because I was so polite but rather because I wanted to avoid the frightening prospect of running into one of her Adorable Children again. I would have loved to have seen the bedroom of Lord and Lady First – generally speaking, the conjugal bedroom offers a wealth of privileged information – but I held back. After a few minutes she returned with a La Caixa cash card and one of those remote control car keys, both of which seemed to promise great things.

'This also opens the gate to the parking garage, but you shouldn't have to use it. There's a guard there, and it's always open. Our spots are fifty-six and fifty-seven.'

I took both items, and couldn't help but glance down at the insignia on the keychain: 'Barcelona Tennis Club' it said, framed by two little racquets and a golden ball.

'The PIN number is 3-3-4-4. Easy.'

'Thanks. Listen, have you tried calling Sebastian on his mobile?'

'No. He left it here.'

'I thought he always had it on him.'

'Not always. Only when he knows he'll be difficult to locate.'

'So he thought he'd be locatable for a while.'

'Yes, of course.'

'Do you mind if I take it with me?'

'The phone? No . . . I'll go fetch it for you.'

She turned and went back toward the bedroom at the end of the hallway and came back with the phone. I scooped up everything in one hand and got ready to leave. Lady First walked me to the door.

'Oh, I forgot to ask. Have you spoken with anyone from the office today?' I asked her.

'Yes, I called in sick for Sebastian again.'

'And did you give them any kind of diagnosis?'

'No. Just that he still had a fever and that we were going to call the doctor this morning. I didn't want to invent anything specific. I'm a terrible liar, it scares me to death.'

'Oh. One more thing. I think you'd be better off if you didn't leave the house for a couple of days.'

'Yes, I already thought of that. That was why I didn't send Merche to school today.'

Once I was inside the lift, I noticed that the last button was different from the rest, a white 'P' for Car Park, against a blue background. I hit it.

The garage occupied an entire floor of the building. I saw the guard's post from a distance, at the foot of a ramp illuminated by a glow filtering in from the sunny outdoors. I looked for spots fifty-six and fifty-seven. In the first spot I found a humungous blue-green all-purpose vehicle and in fifty-seven, the sports car. I had underestimated my Magnificent Brother. I had assumed he had gone for one of those Japanese jobs that you can get for twenty-five or thirty thousand euros, but instead I found a first-class two-seater: metallic grey, thirty-centimetre wheels, and a crouching-tiger shape, a real little *bête noire*. I moved closer to the snub nose and admired the brand-name tucked in between the retractable headlights: Lotus. The top of the car reached just past my belly button, and I wondered if I was going to be able to fit myself into that microscopic cubicle which flashed an ominous red light, indicating that some kind of security device was being employed. I decided to give it a go. I pressed the little button on the keychain and heard a muted 'stuuuk' which opened, in unison, the locks on the two doors. You don't enter this type of car, though: you slip it on, not unlike the manner in which you slip on a condom. The toughest bit was getting my right thigh under the steering wheel, but once I managed it, I had the full and total sensation of making the most intimate contact imagineable with a machine capable of digesting a full 300 kilometres an hour, the maximum velocity promised by the speedometer. It smelt faintly of leather and the dry, aromatic notes of some kind of ambient fragrance. I turned the key in the ignition. First the dashboard lit up and then frzzzz, a light buzz from the open door indicated that the engine was indeed running.

I turned it off immediately. This wasn't the moment to play racecars. Exiting the contraption proved more difficult than entering, but I did it, zipped up my zipper, which had not resisted my various bodily contortions, and walked toward the exit ramp and the street outside. That way the guard would see me, most especially considering that the Black Beast could not have escaped his notice. I waved goodbye, but he was reading something and barely even glanced in my direction.

As soon as I left the building, I headed toward the La

Caixa branch on Travessera-Aviación. Now that I had given the car a once-over, it was time to check out the potency of the cash card I had been given. The inside teller windows were still open to the public, which meant that it wasn't two in the afternoon yet. I decided to go with the cash machine. Secret code, balance enquiry, short wait for the little slip of paper to come shooting out. At first I was nearly indignant to read that the available balance was only 12 euros, 65 cents, but upon closer inspection I noticed that only two of the three zeros following the 1265 were to the right of the decimal point. That's right – when do you ever see three zeros after a decimal point? And so the revised amount was, in fact, twelve thousand, six hundred and fifty euros, no doubt about it: one, two, six, five, zero, zero, zero. The decimal point after the first zero. I knew that The First could never leave the leave the house with his pockets empty, but more than twelve thousand for petrol and restaurant expenses surpassed all my expectations. I quickly withdrew two hundred and fifty euros out of that hot little oven before anyone could regret having put them at my disposition and, once I felt their warmth penetrating my pocket, I tried to take out two hundred and fifty more. *No problemo*. They came out as docile as little baby lambs.

After that, it seemed almost sinful to return home and eat fried eggs and chips and so I flipped through my mental file of neighbourhood restaurants in which one could ask for something more than just the daily bureaucrat special. I didn't have to think for long, because right before my eyes, one such restaurant beckoned: La Yayá María. I had never been inside, but it looked like it fit the bill: superb quality but in smallish portions, one of those coy little joints where what you really want is to order three appetisers, three main courses and three desserts, a kind of excess that requires at least a hundred euros. I made my entry. For a first course, I had cream of carrot soup, a shrimp omelette and fava beans, *a la catalana,* of course. And then for the next course, stuffed red pimientos, grilled swordfish and a fricassee. Then for dessert, dried fruit compote and lemon sorbet, plus wine, a café cortado, a shot of icy vodka and a Rosli. One hundred and twenty-five fifty. They were so thrilled with my appetite that the chef came out to say hello.

I walked home, en route to my siesta, feeling like the king of mambo, but I made the mistake of smoking a joint before bed, and had quite a tough time falling asleep even though my body desperately craved it.

THE MONK FROM ROBIN HOOD

I woke up from one of those free-fall dreams that have you thrashing about your bed in an attempt to cling to something stable. I looked at the alarm clock: four in the afternoon. I could stay in bed for maybe another hour, but it was so goddamn hot there was no way I would be able to fall back asleep.

I ducked into the shower to shake off the suffocating heat between the sheets, and then I made some coffee. Radio. Joint. Ten minutes of relaxation in the living room. *Ah se ela soubesse que quando ela passa/ O mundo inteirinho se enche de graça/E fica mais lindo por causa do amor.* When I felt sufficiently awake I lowered the volume, booted up my computer and connected to the internet. I entered 'private detectives AND Barcelona.'

I scanned the first ten results and clicked onto 'ACBDD, Regional Detective Association', which offered a listing of affiliated agencies by province. I looked specifically for Barcelona, postcode 08029, and hit the link for the 'Total Research Agency.' It sounded like something out of a Schwarzenegger movie, but I had to start somewhere. Of course, the second I connected to the site, a MIDI launched with the Pink Panther soundtrack, which seemed so unpromising that I didn't even bother to wait for the rest of the page to load. I went back to the ACBDD page and picked out another site that corresponded to the 08029 postcode. There were no bells and whistles involved in this one, just text, which read:

> PRIVATE DETECTIVE
> LICENCE NUMBER 3543
>
> *Enric Robellades i Vilaplana* is a Private Detective authorised to operate by the Institute of Criminology at the University of Barcelona and by Governmental Licence number 123, issued to him by the Police Department of Barcelona.
>
> Mr Robellades is an investigator who has gained considerable knowledge and experience with professionals in the fields of Investigation and Security Consulting, and applies his skills toward the gathering of information and necessary evidence to find solutions to your problems in an **EFFECTIVE** and **EFFICIENT** manner.

His very conscious distinction between efficient and effective, in boldface capital letters, convinced me. It was as if he wanted to highlight the fact that he was *extremely* effective but didn't want to be too superlative about it. And anyway, in general, I never trust people who write perfectly. I have observed that when it comes to practical matters, the best professionals are always the worst writers, the kind that try to use rhetorical conventions but don't quite finish them off the way they should. I once met an internationally-renowned cardiologist – a friend of my Magnificent Family – whose Christmas cards always read 'To our Friends Valentín and Mercedes: Wishing you a Merry Christmas and Happy New Year, and extending each wish to your children', which to me always came off sounding like some kind of gypsy curse that never fully explained exactly which wish my parents were to extend to me, and which was meant for Sebastian so that we could have a halfway decent holiday. This Enric Robellades, private detective, did not make quite so obvious a gaffe in his statement, but he was promising enough and so I continued reading the section on Fields of Investigation, which had four sub-links that provided more detail on each of the various fields: Investigation of Businesses, Investigation of Accidents, Investigation of Personal Matters, and Urban Rental Investigation (whatever that meant). I clicked onto 'Investigation of Personal Matters', which seemed the most appropriate for my case, and was led to another page, which read as follows:

Investigation of Personal Matters

- Marital Infidelity. For filing papers of separation or divorce.
- Child Custody. This category includes asserting the above, as well as proving the spouse's insufficient dedication and capacity to fulfil such obligations, if in fact this is the case.
- Pre-Nuptial Report. For the purpose of gathering the necessary information regarding the past and present of the potential spouse, with the goal of helping the client make such an important decision.
- Child Behaviour, Prevention of Drug Use and Involvement in Cults. For an accurate assessment of the child's situation, and for the preparation of a plan of action.
- Missing Persons' Search. For locating family members, in and out of the country.
- Anonymous Threats

– Incapacitation, Excessive Spending, and Inheritance Matters
– Pre-Contractual Reports on Domestic Employees

I was completely convinced by this guy, and went straight back to the home page to look for a contact number. I found the address, telephone, fax and email and then printed out the page, disconnected and rolled another joint before making the call. When I had the thing lit, I dialled the number.

'Robellades, good afternoon.'

It was a woman's voice, not too young. I don't know why I imagined Mrs Robellades herself working as her husband's receptionist/secretary.

'May I please speak with Mr Robellades?'

'Which one?'

'Enric, Enric Robellades.'

'Father or son?'

Families that toil together are loyal together. I decided to go with the father.

'Who may I say is on the line?'

'A client.'

'Your name, please?'

I almost identified myself as Pablo Miralles, but luckily, just in the nick of time, I realised that this was not in my best interests.

'Molucas. Pablo Molucas.'

I could have just as easily said Pablo Marbles, but the important thing in these situations is to say whatever you have to say as naturally as possible – and anyway, I happen to use Molucas often. Besides, it's never a good idea to go around changing your assumed identity too much. The woman asked me to wait a moment. Shortly thereafter the family elder came on the line.

'Yes?'

'Mr Robellades?'

'Speaking. What can I do for you?'

'I've found a reference stating that you are a private detective and I am interested in soliciting your services. If you might be able to meet with me today, I would be much obliged. It's a rather urgent case.'

'What is it about?'

'A disappearance.'

'Who has disappeared?'

'My sister-in-law.'

'How long has she been missing?'

'Two days.'

'That isn't very much time, Mr . . .'

'Molucas. Pablo Molucas. No, it isn't much time, but I have reason to believe that something quite serious may have happened.'

'Very well, if you could fill me in on the details . . .'

'Of course. But I'd rather not do it by phone. Would it be possible to meet later?'

'Yes, we could do . . . what time is good for you?'

'Around eight. Would you mind coming by my home? I live close to your office, on Calle Numancia. You see, I'd like my wife to be present, and she has to stay home with the children.'

'No problem at all. If you'll just give me the address and telephone . . .'

By this time I had detected a strong Catalán accent, possibly from somewhere near the Tarragona region, where everyone turns their zeds into melodious 's' sounds, and add a 't' to the end of certain infinitives. I consulted my address book for The First's building and telephone number, located it and gave it to him.

'At eight, then?'

'On the dot.'

I made it through another joint while doing a quick mental recap to ensure that I hadn't left any detail hanging. I hadn't thought much about giving the detective a fake name, and I was slightly worried that it might create some inconsistencies. One would assume that a detective pays attention to details, after all, and who knows, maybe he would actually take the time to look at the letter box in the entrance hall of The First's building, or something like that. I ruminated on this as I got dressed and continued to think as I walked up the street toward the Illa shopping centre. I wasn't sure of what kind of mess I had gotten myself into but I did have one thing clear: before The First reappeared I had to take full advantage of his cash card, even if only to fuck with him a little. And anyway, it was in my interest to work up some kind of disguise: given the way I dressed, the claim that I was married to Lady First would be a tad unbelievable.

Once inside the shopping centre, I entered the first boutique that seemed to have appropriately informal attire to outfit a thirtysomething married man who possessed two children, a 150 square-metre penthouse on Calle Numancia and a Black Beast in the garage. The only free salesgirl watched me enter the shop like a matador about to be pounced upon by a 600-kilo Miura bull, and the gum she was chewing was suddenly rendered immobile between her teeth. Impassive, I surreptitiously ascertained that my zipper hadn't come undone, and then I approached her, unfazed by her childish attempt to act as though she hadn't seen me by pretending to hunt for something behind the counter.

'Hello. I need shirts, pants, shoes.'

'Shirts, pants . . . ?'

'And shoes.'

Once she realised there was no way out, she stopped playing hide-and-seek.

'What sort of shirts are you interested in?'

'Big ones.'

'Big . . . Hmm. Do you see anything you like here?' She indicated a wall-to-wall shelf lined with all sorts of shirts. A little group of solid, quite flashy colours caught my eye: red, emerald green, violet, and grey and black as well. Those were okay. They were the sort of shirts that you would expect the gangsters in *Guys and Dolls* to wear.

'Those are all right. Do they come big?'

'Uh . . . yes, I believe we have some larger sizes, yes. What colour do you prefer?'

'I'll take one of each.'

She stood perfectly still for a moment, halfway between me and the shelf, but didn't dare challenge me. Instead she simply picked out one in each colour, and piled them onto her right arm.

'There are nine different . . .'

'That's fine, nine then. You're sure they're large enough?'

'XXL. That's as large as they come . . .'

'Right. Now I need two pairs of pants.'

She pointed toward the opposite wall: another shelf with a pile of jeans in various colours, and below them, more serious-looking pants on hangers. I can't stand jeans, there's never anywhere to stuff your gut. Plus I tend to favour trousers with quick priapic access – if you don't have your prick perfectly situated, erections can become torture in a pair of jeans. So I went for the hangers and entertained myself for a while looking at the roomier models, cotton and acrylic blends. I picked out a slate-grey pair and another, more pearly grey pair that would look all right with any of the shirts.

'Like these but in my size, please.'

'Do you know what size you would take . . . ?'

No idea.

'I've no idea.'

She examined my abdominal contours, practically out of the corner of her eye, as if it was too obscene to actually gaze directly upon that part of my anatomy. I raised my arms and spun about, to give her the full picture. The girl was going to have to initiate herself sooner or later, and she might as well be de-flowered by me instead of some other cruel customer.

'Aren't you going to take my measurements?'

She stood there staring at me, her sky-blue eyes reflecting back at me the full terror of a little girl trapped in an ogre's den. But she nodded yes, made a neat half-turn and ran for cover in the dressing rooms where another salesgirl was assisting a very politically-correct looking man who had come shopping with his matching girlfriend. She returned with a measuring tape wrapped around her hands. I checked my fly again and waited there with my arms up.

'I'm all yours.'

She approached me and tried to wrap her arms around my waistline. To cover my full perimeter, however, she would have had to hug me, and her arms were far too short for the distance involved. I tried to make it a little easier on her; she'd already had quite enough for one day, I imagined.

'Wait, wait. I'll hold the tape here and you measure.'

I held one end of the measuring tape below my navel and guided her, as she held the other end, around my waist until the circle was complete. We exhausted the full length of the tape, though, and so we had to palm it from where she held her index finger, just above my love handles.

'One hundred . . . one hundred seventeen centimetres.'

'See how easy that was?'

'I'll go check to see what size that makes you.'

She consulted a small framed chart hanging on the wall, and then quickly entered the storeroom. I killed time looking at the shoe display in the middle of the store; each different model was perched atop its own little wooden cube. A black, solid number caught my eye – weren't clunky military-style shoes in vogue at the moment? Anyway. Two minutes later the girl re-emerged bearing two pairs of pants, though they weren't the ones I had picked out.

'In that size we only have this model.'

The trousers in question were made of a very fine wool, very formal, dark grey. I took them off the hanger and held them against my body to see if they were long enough. When I confirmed that they were, I asked her if she also had them in light grey and subsequently added the two pairs of pants and one pair of shoes, size forty-five, to my shopping list. Over three hundred euros, all told. I was already paid up and on my way out the door with my bags when I suddenly spotted a silky Hawaiian shirt in the window: red, blue, green, papagayos, philodendrons and a South Seas landscape behind them. Eighty euros for that one alone, but it was worth it. I went back in. My girl, having realised I was so docile, had finally overcome her fear and now came bounding toward me, delighted that I was back.

'Sorry, I wanted another shirt, like the one in the window.'

'Large, right?'

As I left the building I looked up at the clock in the snack bar at the supermarket entrance. I was all right on time. I went through my mental map of the neighbourhood and remembered that there was a hair salon on the following corner, just before Travessera.

The hairdresser turned out to be a guy around my age, sporting a short goatee. He seemed thrilled by my visit. He had the air of a man who truly enjoys his profession, and so I decided to add some extra spice to the afternoon.

'Listen, I'm putting together an outfit for a masquerade party. Let's imagine that I'm a man from a very well-to-do family, I work hard at my own business, and I drive a James Bond-type sports car. How do you think I should wear my hair?

'Age?'

'Mmm . . . thirty-eight, give or take.'

'Education?'

'Tons. Masters degree in Important Stuff from Harvard and all the extras you can dream up.'

'Married?'

'Extremely. Two kids. I play tennis and go to the gym every day.'

'That's some disguise . . . Pardon the sincerity, but you'd be better off going as that monk from Robin Hood. With a brown habit and a beer stein you'd be perfect.'

'Well, to tell you the truth, I need to impress a woman. She likes the solvent type. I've already got the car and the clothes, I just need a haircut to match.'

'Oh. That's another story. Sit down and we'll see what we can do.'

The guy knew what he was dealing with. He looked me over – up, down, back, forth – and when he seemed to have a pretty good idea of my head's possibilities he got to work.

'Listen, if I were you I'd go with a long, thin moustache, like Errol Flynn. A slightly fascist look would make the most ideal contrast, because in reality you look much more like a . . . well, something else entirely. If you start working on it at home, in a few days you'll have it just the right shape and length. Don't let it grow too much: it has to look just like a little French garden, very well manicured, you know what I mean?'

'Exactly. Yes, I'll go with the little moustache. Listen, do you have any expensive cologne?'

'Extremely expensive.'

'Well, give me a good splash. And note down the name for me.'

By the end of half an hour, I looked like a family-sized Bart Simpson.

On the way home, I ducked into a perfume emporium to purchase a minuscule bottle of Godknowswhat by Christian Dior – eighty euros – and then stopped at a dry cleaner's half a block from the entrance to my building. I asked how long it would take them to wash and iron nine shirts. They said they could have everything ready in an hour. I left the goods there and went upstairs.

The first thing I did was call Lady First.

'I made a date for us with a private detective. Eight o'clock, your house.'

'Are you sure you know what you're doing?'

'Don't worry. I'll come by at around seven-thirty to go over the details.'

When I hung up I looked up at the clock in the kitchen: just after six-thirty. I had one long hour to kill. I then remembered my emails from the Metaphysical Club and decided that a quick look at John's Primary Sentences might be just what I needed to get my mind off the mess I was in, at least for a little while. When I get into them, especially if I accompany the reading with a thick three-paper joint, I experience what feels like an odd kind of jump in hyper-time that suddenly brings me an hour and a half ahead in real time. I opened the Word document and began with the first sentence. It was completely unintelligible: '1. Every route is an opening of the paths.' John must really have thought this phrase especially brilliant. Whatever. Two and three were these extremely long, dark paragraphs, and I spent a while trying to crack them. Four was also long, but looked like it might actually be comprehensible, at least at first glance. Once I read a bit more though, I could tell he was going to start in with the Rationalists – he was already salivating to the effect for the past three sentences. Bingo: number five was fully devoted to the scientificists, their arch-enemies. John is always trying to come up with an axiomatic definition for Invented Reality, but he always ends up shoving all his assertions down everyone's throat. If we left everything up to him, we would end up a bunch of anti-rationalists mainly known for being a pain in the arse. I swear. The other danger was that of being identified as irrationalists, also a minority and an opposing faction, but very different from us (without taking into account that from time to time we do ally ourselves with the mainstream). And then we have also been confused, occasionally, with the solipsists, which is really abominable because as far as those guys are concerned the whole world ends up making a big void out of them (what else can you *do* with a solipsist?). The truth is, this philosophy thing is very reminiscent of politics and John always ends up arguing with absolutely everyone. And if I call him on his expository disorder he tells me that under no circumstances will he submit to some kind of syllogistic girdle because he is a John-Pablian Inventivist and that way he side-steps the Aristotelian logic bit entirely. And if I then tell him that in this case the best thing to do is write a discursive essay and not a simple list of laws, he says sure, fine, but first he wants to get his ideas straight and for that the brief assertions are useful. Anyway. After skimming number six, which I almost thought was a joke ('6. The sceptic is not certain of being a sceptic.'), I ended the session.

At seven sharp I went down to the dry cleaner's. It was exquisite – not only had they washed and ironed the nine shirts by the agreed-upon hour, but they had taken them all out of their packaging and handed them over to me, carefully hung on hangers, free of all pins and tags. Spain sure is starting to get like Europe, no doubt about it. I went back upstairs and showered for the third time that day, to fully free myself of all those extra little hairs that had been left behind on my neck from the haircut, and then I tried on the pants, the shoes, and one of the shirts. The aubergine one. Now, I don't mean to exaggerate about my fine appearance, but let's just say that beneath the Bart Simpson hairdo, the Errol Flynn moustache and the Bud Spencer silhouette, I began to see a certain resemblance with the venerable master, Baloo. Peeking out of the flat top, even, were some jaunty little bangs that harmonised so nicely with the prominent nose and bear-like features.

When I arrived at Lady First's building, I stopped to look at the letter box for a moment. Despite my impeccable appearance, the blue-jacketed doorman refused to take his eyes off me and I didn't dare try and fuck with the thing. 'Gloria Garriga and Sebastian Miralles, penthouse 1a' it read. I could always come down with Lady First and change the name, or at least cover it up. As I waited for the lift, I saw the doorman remove his robe and rummage about in a little room behind the counter. It looked like he was finishing up for the day and getting ready to go home. In all likelihood he would be gone by the time Robellades arrived, which was a very good thing, because prepping him for the possibility that Robellades might ask for us under a false name would have been a touch tricky.

I rang the bell at Penthouse #1. Lady First herself answered the door. It took her a good five seconds to recognise me.

'I decided to go under cover. How do you like the disguise?'

'You're very . . . handsome.'

'I don't think handsome is quite the word. To be exact, you might have said "cool." Didn't they teach you to use adjectives carefully, Miss Authoress?'

'I don't know, darling, but you got it right.'

'That's better. The important thing is to look like I might have somehow, sometime, inspired you to marry me. Let's see: if you had met me looking like this, would you have married me?'

'Instantly.'

'Perfect. Listen, what do you say if we go into the living room and make ourselves comfortable, chat a bit?'

'Sorry, of course. It's just that you've left me rather stunned. Come in . . .'

Suddenly it was as if we had been best friends forever. It's pretty incredible what a change of image can do for a person. Once we sat down in the living room, I went straight to the sofa and flopped down. She repaired to the bar and offered me a beverage.

'Give me one of those things you always drink. But we should control ourselves, we want to have our wits about us for this guy.' She served herself a whisky on the rocks and handed me one of the same. There wasn't much time to lose so I went straight to the point.

'We're meeting a Mr Enric Robellades, private detective. Now, I told him my name was Pablo Molucas, so don't be surprised if he addresses you as Mrs Molucas. The idea is that your sister – that is, my sister-in-law – has been missing for two days and we are very worried. I will try to do most of the talking, you can kind of just follow along. Now, one would assume that you know your sister better than I do, so he will probably try to get an idea of what kind of person she is by asking you for some specifics about her. Now, don't get all worried, you told me yourself the two of you have been friends since childhood, right? So whatever he asks you just tell him the truth. Be completely straight about everything, with only one exception, and it's an important one: you know where she works but you have no idea that she's shagging her boss.'

She nodded in assent and took a brief sip of whisky.

'Another thing: presumably you and I are married, so our conversation and mannerisms should suggest this somehow. Don't overdo the role-playing, just be careful not to stick your foot in your mouth. For example, don't drop any reference to my house when you refer to me, or anything. I think we'll be all right on that, but we'd probably be better off if the kids don't come out to the living room while this guy is with us, okay? They could ruin the whole thing.'

She nodded her head again.

'Your first name is Gloria, and your surname is . . . oh, and what's your friend's surname?'

'Robles.'

'Robles. Now, you don't want to tell your parents about this because you don't want to worry them, and you also don't want the police involved because then your parents would find out. We've decided to hire a detective because you can't find her anywhere – not at home, not at the office. At work all they know is that she's been out since yesterday morning. She's not with your parents, either, you've already checked that one out.'

She looked me straight in the eye, still taking tiny sips of whisky, as if trying to digest and retain everything I had just said.

'Do you have a recent photo of her?'

'Yes.'

'Well, he'll definitely ask you for it. What else . . . ? Oh, yeah. What time does the doorman get off?'

'Half-seven.'

'Perfect. All right, I don't think I missed anything. Repeat what I just said to you.'

'My sister Lali disappeared two days ago. She's not at home, she hasn't gone to work, and I can't find her anywhere. You, my husband, see that I am visibly worried and have decided to hire a private detective to investigate. We don't want my parents to know, so we have to ask him for a bit of discretion on that end. Did I leave anything out?'

'Only one thing: we want him to be discreet not only with your parents but in general. Get it? We don't want anyone at the office or any of her friends to know that we're looking for her.'

'What do I do if he asks me about the kind of people she runs around with, or about the kind of men she dates?'

'Do you know her friends, or of any other boyfriends apart from Sebastian?'

'Hmm . . . I don't know. Years ago we had some friends in common, but now . . .'

'Okay. If he asks you, then that's what you should tell him. Like I said, it's better if you're completely straight about everything except her affair with Sebastian. And if at any time you don't know how to react, pretend to be disoriented or something, or turn around as if you don't want him to see you crying and I'll take over.'

'Can I have another whisky before he gets here?'

I thought about it; maybe it was better for her to drink up a bit. The less nervous she was, the better.

'Go for it.'

'Do you want another one?'

'I don't usually drink before dark. Listen, do you mind if I go downstairs for a second and flip over the name plate on the letter box? Just in case he decides to check it or something . . . Meanwhile, you can go and tell Veronica not to bring the kids into the living room.'

She stood there with her back to me as she poured herself another whisky and nodded her head yes. It seemed so odd that this was the same Lady First who hardly ever even looked at me during all those Christmas Eve dinners at my parents' house. Now she surrendered to me like an obedient little girl doing whatever Daddy told her, even asking permission to have another whisky. This was what went through my head as I waited for the lift, but once the doors opened and I saw myself in the mirror I couldn't help laughing out loud, a cackle that reverberated through the hallway. There I was, dressed up like some kind of City Planning Consultant, about to impersonate my Magnificent Brother. Some joke.

The name plate on the letter box turned out to be slightly more complicated than I had anticipated. It was screwed in, and so I had to use the Black Beast key to loosen it up. Maybe instead of turning it around I should just take it off entirely, I said to myself. No name plate at all might seem more natural than one that had been fucked with, so I took it off and placed it on top of the bank of letter boxes.

According to the living room clock it was already five minutes to eight by the time I went back upstairs. I think Lady First had snuck another whisky while I was downstairs; her glass was far too full to still be that standard first drink she had poured for herself. I didn't say anything, though, and focused on the objects in the living room, thinking that Robellades would be sure to check them out. Way up high on one of the bookshelves I spied a framed photo of Lord and Lady First, ten years younger and in their wedding clothes. I suppose The First and I bear some kind of resemblance, but not so much that I could actually pass for him.

I placed it face down.

'He shouldn't see this,' I said.

'I'm scared,' she blurted out unexpectedly.

'Scared of what?'

'Of saying something I shouldn't. Are you sure we haven't forgotten anything?'

'When lying, it's always helpful to leave a bit of room for improvisation. Remember, you can have doubts about things even when you're telling the truth, hasn't that ever happened to you? You make a mistake and then you correct it. Well, you can do the same thing when you're lying. Believe me, I have experience with this.'

I sat down on the sofa to toss back my whisky. Lady First sat down in front of me, just as she had before.

'You know something? You're a strange guy . . . I sure would like to know who you are, for real.'

Good god: already exchanging confidences in the twilight. I shrugged my shoulders.

'What you see is what you get.'

'But you seem different today. And I don't know, I've always had the feeling that you have, I don't know, another side to you.'

'Well, don't worry about it too much. Everyone lives in the world that they themselves create. In your world, yes, I suppose I have another side. That's all.'

She sat there for a moment, thinking, looking at me.

'What do you mean by that?'

'I mean that reality is always an invention.'

She raised an eyebrow as if to disagree, but I was then saved, literally, by the bell – specifically the tuneless buzz of the intercom from downstairs. I gestured for her to get up and answer it and then walked over to the door with her.

'Mr Molucas, please? I'm Enric Robellades,' the voice said to Lady First. She pressed the button. I noticed she was still a bit tense and so I offered one final confidence booster.

'Relax. Just follow my lead and don't be surprised by how I act. It'll all come off just fine.'

I half-opened the door and waited for the lift to arrive, like a perfect host. After a few moments, two men emerged, unsure as to which way to turn in the hallway. The one who came out first had Robellades Senior written all over him: short, chubby, sixtysomething. The little hair he had beyond his receding hairline was combed back. Directly behind him was a younger, thirtyish man, taller, thinner and with the same receding hairline only in a slightly earlier phase of balding. Both wore dark suits and ties, the older one in brown and the younger in blue.

'Mr Molucas?'

'Yes.'

'Enric Robellades. This is my son Francesc. He works with me.'

All right. He had at least two sons. There was probably an older one named Enric.

'My wife Gloria,' I offered.

Lady First extended her hand in a limp display of courtesy. I tried to avoid lapsing into silence and ushered them into the living room.

'Please, have a seat. Can I offer you something to drink? A cocktail, a coffee, some fruit juice? Gloria, do we have some fruit juice for these gentlemen?'

'Yes, I think so.'

'Thanks, but we just had a coffee at the bar downstairs.'

The father wore the pants in this team, clearly. I guessed that while he, the expert, gathered more direct information and entertained us with his conversation, the younger one was in charge of focusing on the more environmental details, a task he began immediately, checking out the living room, looking left and right. Both of them remained standing, undecided as to where would be an appropriate place to sit. I sat down on one of the sofas to help their decision and they, in turn, settled into a pair of leather easy chairs. I looked at Lady First and indicated the spot next to me, patting it repeatedly with my open palm. She stopped for a moment at the bar.

'I hope you don't mind if I have a cocktail.'

'Please, of course not,' said Robellades Senior. For a moment I feared that Lady First was going to ruin the entire operation and so I tried to help her out.

'You need it, love. A cognac would do you a world of good. Or maybe a whisky would be better. Do we have any whisky? Excuse us,' I said, turning to our guests. 'We're both a little nervous – all of this has been a bit overwhelming for us.'

'That's perfectly understandable, of course it is.'

'Thank you, you see – my wife and her sister were very close . . . that is, they *are* very close. She lives alone and we're concerned that something has happened to her. We didn't want to call the police so as not to worry her parents.

They don't know anything about this, and we'd rather not alarm them unnecessarily.'

'Unnecessarily?'

Give a liar a free rein and he'll hang himself with it. So they say. This guy was sharp, you could tell just from looking at him. Now that I could study him at close range, my eyes travelled up and down his face: a dense beard cast a long dark shadow across his greasy, drooping cheeks and his small nose came to a point at the tip, which was reddened by a web of tiny capillaries. I went back up his face and gazed into his blue eyes, somewhat porcine and extraordinarily bright, as if swimming in a pool of water. For a moment I felt like a secondary character in some police story. Someone, somewhere, had to be writing the story of Enric Robellades, private detective, who had been hired by a young, well-to-do couple that looked as though they were lying through their teeth half the time they opened their mouths.

Still, I refused to be intimidated.

'What I mean is . . . well, my sister-in-law is a young woman and . . . well, perhaps this is nothing more than some romantic adventure that we have unintentionally overestimated . . . do you see what I mean?'

Lady First arrived with her glass and sat down next to me. She did a pretty good job of it – meaning that she didn't sit down next to me as if I were her worthless brother-in-law. She sat very close to me, like we were a team.

'Of course, it's perfectly understandable. Yet you've nevertheless called upon us . . .'

'Well, there are a few details that strike us as strange. It's odd that she simply disappeared without calling anyone, not even the office where she works. In addition, she's very close to her sister, close enough to tell her about her romantic interludes . . . and so her disappearance does strike us as strange enough to call in a private detective but not quite worthy of alarming the entire family.'

'I think I understand. Now, has she ever gone away without telling you before?'

'Not that I know of . . .'

Lady First, quite properly, entered into the game.

'No. Well, for a period of time we did fall out of touch for a while, but for the past two years we've been seeing each other quite regularly, so no, never . . . We speak on the phone almost every day. Sometimes we go shopping together . . .'

'Right. Now, normally I would ask if you have any idea as to why, or with whom, she might have . . . gone away, if you will. But now if you knew that you would have already told me, wouldn't you? So instead I'll begin by asking you for some personal information so that we may start the preliminary phase of the investigation. This usually takes a couple of days. If by the end of this first phase we haven't come up with any clear lead, we will have to enter into a more . . . intense phase of the investigation, if you will. Our fees are two hundred euros per day, plus any expenses that may come up: trips, that sort of thing. But we would naturally advise you before incurring any significant outside expenses.'

Now that he had launched into his speech, a few things had become more evident: his very pronounced accent, his preferred expression and the funny way he smiled every time he said it or finished a sentence in that complicit, confidential tone of voice. Each time he made this gesture a golden tooth on his upper-right jaw would peek out of his mouth, and I asked myself how the hell a private detective could allow himself to reveal such obvious tics.

'I think that's reasonable. If we don't discover anything in the next two days, it would be appropriate to notify the police. In the meantime, please, we'd prefer it if nobody knows that you are investigating our case. This is extremely important to us.'

'You don't have to worry about that. We tend to make very little noise, if you will. And as for whatever you decide to do after the first phase, that is entirely up to you. We can continue the investigation or end it then and nobody has to know . . . That is, of course, unless we discover something that obliges us to alert the authorities about you or the case. Naturally, we have to comply with certain . . . legal requirements, if you will. *Aviam: Francesc, ves prenent nota, si us plau*,' he finished off in Catalán, and then turned back to us. 'Let's see, now: the missing person's full name?'

Robellades Junior extracted a pen and pad from his jacket pocket, and I prayed with all my might that Lady First would remember her friend's second surname. She came through: Miranda. Eulalia Robles Miranda, and Lady First also remembered her address, age, job location and title – that last one was easy, of course. As the father ticked off his questions, the son took notes and then Dad finished off with a request for a photograph. Lady First put her whisky down for a moment and walked over to a door in the hallway to get it. Robellades Senior then began the attempt to rise from the big leather easy chair, not an entirely easy feat for him.

'Very well then, Mr Molucas, I think we're off to a good start . . .'

The son got up, and I followed suit.

'Let's see, today is Friday, Saturday, Sunday . . . on Monday morning we will be prepared to hand in our first report. Shall I call you on Monday to arrange a time?'

'That's fine. We'll wait for your call.'

'And don't worry, er, in our field this is a very common type of case. They almost always end up being nothing more than a bit of a fright, if you will. Nothing to worry about, not usually.'

He waved his hands round, as if trying to downplay the gravity of the case. At this point, he'd loosened up somewhat and seemed more open, more relaxed than he had been at the beginning of the meeting. He was even a bit condescending now. The son, on the other hand, was still one hundred per cent business, perhaps because of his inferior position in the duo.

Lady First returned with the photograph. She approached Robellades and asked him if it was good enough to go on. I managed to catch a glimpse of it from behind. The first thing I noticed was a shock of copper-coloured hair that was so perfect it had to be a dye job.

'Good photo, yes, indeed . . . you can see her face perfectly. Very attractive lady. Very attractive, indeed . . . In that she certainly resembles you . . . if your husband doesn't mind my saying so, of course.'

He allowed himself a light titter and turned back to me, flashing his gold tooth. I conceded, nodding my head slightly as if grateful to accept the compliment on behalf of Lady First. We all shook hands. Then I walked them to the door and waited there with the door open until they entered the lift and the door had closed.

By the time I returned to the living room, Lady First had already served herself another whisky and was trying to reach up to the bookcase shelf where I had concealed her wedding photograph. As I poured a long shot of whisky into my own glass I weighed the potential significance of such a rapid attempt to put the portrait back in its original position. After that we fell silent for a short while, with her on the sofa and me standing by the bar.

'So, fine. See how easy it was?'

'Do you think we did a good job of it?'

'Of course. You couldn't tell?'

'I don't know, I'm so nervous.'

'Well, you didn't show it, not one bit. Listen, I'm sorry but I have to run. As soon as I can be sure the Robelladeses won't see me leave. I'll call you tomorrow and we can talk then, I don't have time right now.'

I downed the rest of the whisky and went over to the front door. Lady First, resigned to being left alone with her whisky, walked me to the outer hallway and pushed the button for the lift. Then, an absolute shocker: suddenly she slid her hand behind my neck and planted a kiss on my cheek – a real kiss, not one of those meaningless cheek-brushers. She smelled good under – or was it over? – her boozy breath. I hid my surprise by winking at her, Sam Spade style, and stepped into the lift.

I went down to the parking garage with the intention of taking the Black Beast out, but at the last moment I decided that I might be able to coax my whisky-induced drowsiness into some real sleep. I ended up leaving via the car park and as I walked up the ramp I was able to demonstrate my presence to another of the guards, probably the night guard this time. Once I got home I called the Telefónica wake-up call service to wake me up at midnight, and got ready to snooze for the next three hours. If I was going to stay up all night to start the real investigation, I was going to have to be well-rested.

THAT SUPERFINE POWDER

A medieval orgy in all its splendour: long wooden tables and benches, huge platters piled high with succulent meats, fowl stuffed with all sorts of delicacies, suckling pigs, ribs, carafes of wine. In the centre of the hall, the drunkest of the lot dance in their peasant jigs atop a round table amid cheers and general party mayhem that drown out the melody of the troubadours. The guests are having a tremendous time of it – everyone except me, that is, because I can't stand eating with my hands – those bourgeois weaknesses of mine again. Sitting directly in front of me, at the table of honour, is Prince Charles, with those ears, those red cheeks and his family crest prominently displayed on the breast of his garnet-coloured velvet jacket. He is mesmerised by the meal on his wooden plate, and he plunges his fingers into the mounds of food, coming up with a hunk of meat which he devours with glee. To his right, elbows on the table, Queen Elizabeth imbibes the juice of a snail with the gusto of a bear trampling a honeycomb. Further over to the right, the Queen Mother licks her plate clean of every last bit of sauce that a servant-boy has ladled out for her. I am just about to call the Prince's attention to his porcine table manners when I suddenly hear the sound of the telephone ring joining into the troubadours' musical arrangement. The wake-up call. I emerge from my dream and lunge toward the telephone.

I picked up the phone waiting to hear the message from Telefónica, but instead I was greeted by a strange, pregnant silence.

'Pablo?'

'Yes?'

'How *are* you . . .'

Good lord.

'Shit, Fina . . . What time is it?'

'Just after ten . . . What are you doing?'

'I was sleeping.'

'Did I wake you up?'

'It's okay, I can't stand eating with my fingers.'

'Huh?'

'Forget it, just one of those things.'

'So? What are you up to?'

'For God's sake, Fina, I just told you. I was sleeping.'

'All right, all right, don't get mad at me. I only wanted to see how you were . . . and to see if you felt like going out.'

'I've got things to do tonight. I haven't even eaten yet.'

'Me neither. If you want I'll take you out for a pizza somewhere.'

I meditated on this for a moment until my brain recovered some semblance of lucidity. Now, without the aid of more alcohol there was no way I'd fall back asleep, and dinner with Fina might have a nicely relaxing effect, a calming return to the world of the familiar. But this was no day to be eating pizzas in some dive joint.

'I'm treating tonight. Get yourself dolled up and I'll come pick you up in the Black Beast in a little while. I'll buzz you when I get there.'

'In the what?'

'You'll see.'

We agreed to meet at eleven. After hanging up I went

to check the clock in the kitchen: ten twenty-five. I put some coffee on, splashed my face with copious amounts of water, brushed my teeth and rolled a joint which I smoked as I drank my coffee and tried to wake up. I then took my fourth shower of the day and got dressed. I don't know what had gotten into me – all of a sudden I'd become completely obsessed with personal hygiene. I thought about putting the aubergine-coloured shirt back on – it still retained that recently-ironed crispness – but at the last minute decided to debut the black one. I patted myself here and there with some cologne and then left the house in the direction of The First's car park. I entered via the exit ramp, jangling the car keys so the guard would notice me, and I arrived at space number fifty-seven whistling a little tune to myself. The Beast was waiting there obediently, absolutely still in its electronic dormancy.

'Stuuk,' it beeped.

I got in, fired up the ignition and looked about for the button that controlled the retractable headlights. I found it, turned on the lights, lowered the window and positioned myself as best I could behind the wheel. As I gently raised the clutch, the Beast purred and moved forward smoothly, like a panther preparing for attack. I waved hello to the guard and stopped after the curve in front of the barrier at the foot of the exit ramp. I tapped the accelerator and zooooom, the car literally fell up the ramp as if the force of gravity had suddenly inverted. Luckily the wheels were pointed in the direction of the ascent, but I did have to slam on the brakes when I reached the end so as not to smash into whoever might be standing on the sidewalk. That moment marked the beginning of what would be a continuous battle to shift into second gear, mainly in the stretches between streetlights: too little time for shifting.

But I made it out all right, and drove until I reached the driveway in front of Fina's building. Only when I stopped did I notice the incredible tension that had gripped all the muscles of my body. I felt as though I had just taken a trip up and down a roller-coaster in one of those tiny little bucket cars.

I buzzed up ('Fina, it's me, downstairs.'), went back to the Beast, and sat on the hood to wait for her. There we were, just the two of us: Baloo and Bagheera reflected in the glass door of Fina's building. Tonight, the wait was brief: I had smoked my way through no more than three Ducados before she appeared, rounding the corner from the lift and out the building. Who would have guessed it, but she was also dressed in black, a vaguely iridescent black, flat slipper shoes, tight skirt down to her knees and a slick jacket with shoulder pads beneath which I could make out some kind of white, silky thing – maybe a bustier or a spaghetti-strap number that highlighted the presence of a pair of first-class knockers. Despite her eco-alternative hairdo, it was a sophisticated, alluring look. I let her pass by me and walk toward the corner – she hadn't even noticed me – so that I could admire her more freely. I whistled. She turned around. I waved my arm up high. She looked at me, looked at the Beast and, without showing any sign of being interested in either of us, turned back around and strutted to the corner. I tried again, calling out her name this time.

'Yo, Fina! It's me.'

'Pablo? Holy shit. I was thinking, who's the arsehole trying to pick me up? God, what did you do to your hair?'

'A little remodelling. You like it?'

'I don't know . . . strange . . . are you letting your moustache grow in?'

'The Errol Flynn look.'

'I'm not a fan.'

'You, on the other hand, look quite tasty, you practically can't even see all that weight you lost.'

She was standing in front of me now. I wrapped my arms around her waist as I kissed her on the cheek and pointed toward the Beast.

'What do you think?'

'What's that . . .?'

'An automotive vehicle. No reins, it's guided by a small steering device that makes the wheels go in the proper direction. See? That round thing is a steering wheel.'

'Right. And you brought it here yourself?'

'*It* brought *me* here is more like it.'

'Are you dealing hallucinogenic narcotics or something?'

'It's my brother's. Come on, get in and I'll explain on the way.'

I opened the passenger-side door and gallantly helped her in as she rather sceptically inspected the interior before deigning to enter, first placing her arse on the low seat and then tucking her legs in. I spun over the hood and got in on the other side. I discovered that by imitating her movements it was far easier to wedge my thighs in under the steering wheel.

'Are you sure you know how to drive this thing?'

'I'm learning.'

I decided to put the car's abilities to the test by heading towards the Diagonal, which would eventually get us out of Barcelona and onto the A7 motorway in the direction of Martorell. From the days when I used to actually leave the neighbourhood, I remembered a restaurant outside of the city that wasn't half bad: one of those refurbished country homes, with a massive stone fireplace in the main dining room and a healthy selection of sausage products.

I figured I had about two hundred euros on me, but after midnight I would be able to replenish the cash supply at any cash machine, so we could easily spend the dough free of worry. Definitely enough for some good wine and choice ham.

'Does this car have air conditioning? It's so hot . . .'

'I'm sure it does, it has everything. Take a look on the dashboard.'

As Fina inspected the equipment I focused on trying to shift into second gear. On the last stretch after taking Travessera toward Collblanc, I hit it.

'It has a CD player,' mused Fina as I narrowly missed sodomising a hapless little Renault Twingo that had darted out in front of us. She had located the sound system and underneath, in some kind of storage unit, she found CDs.

'Shit, man: Schubert, *Musical Moments*; Bach *Suites 2 and 3*; Schumann, *Renana Symphony* . . . Your brother's a real wild guy, huh?'

'He's very high-culture. Put the radio on, something's bound to come out.'

Fina worked the tuner until hitting 'Der Komissar', a song that always brings back good memories. It must have held the same charm for Fina, too, because she started dancing in the front seat as she resumed her search for the climate control. Once on the Diagonal I took advantage of three straight green lights and managed to shift my way up to fourth, and Fina abandoned the A/C bit and began frantically patting about, looking for the seatbelt. After our last stop on the Diagonal, all that lay before us was a beautiful, multi-lane motorway. Traffic was light, just a few odd cars that, along with the music, made it feel like we were on the opening screen of a video game. Green. I slammed down on the gas to fire up the engine; the heart of the

Beast howled behind our necks and just as the revolutions began to slow down, I loosened up on the clutch and went full blast. We lost a bit of the propulsion as the wheels slid over the asphalt, but as soon as it restabilised we tore out of there like a hundred bats out of hell. Five seconds later the engine purred to the beat of 'Der Komissar' and soon began to sound like a Moulinex on pureé; the speedometer crept up to 100; I pumped down on the gas again in second until we hit 140; third, 170; I didn't have the balls to go into fourth: 180, 190, 200, and we were glued to the back engine, which zoomed from behind like an automaton as we began to pass cars, leaving them in the dust like hats falling out of the window of a train. 220, 230, 240 . . . the motorway seemed to contract, until it felt like a country lane full of sneaky little twists and turns.

'Pablooooo!'

I was getting scared, too. I lifted my foot off the gas and stopped pushing, so that we might slide a bit with the clutch down, and I shifted into fifth so that we could level off at 200kph, and pass the few cars on our right, staying far enough away from them so as not to jostle them too much.

I lowered the volume on the radio.

'Not bad, huh?'

Fina's hand had fluttered up to her heart.

'For a second there I thought I started to get my period, and I'm not due for another week. What the fuck is this, anyway?'

'Some kind of Lotus. I should slow down.'

By now we were on the final stretch in Molins de Rey, turning off the exit ramp – a 270-degree turn, as good an occasion as any to test the car's suspension. I cranked into second and the centrifugal force sent me slamming against the door. Fina started screaming 'Pablooo!' and clung to her seatbelt for dear life, as tense as a cat, but the machine hung tough, barely losing its horizontality at all, and the tires gripped the asphalt like Velcro. It would take much more than the Molins de Rey exit ramp to throw off the Beast: good for Bagheera. Fina actually seemed to be having a splendid time – afterward she claimed not to have experienced anything like it since she went up the Dragon Khan roller-coaster at Port Aventura. When we reached the driveway of the country-house restaurant we were dripping with sweat. I parked the nose of the car headfirst into the kerb, and as we got out we straightened our clothes and hair and went through the front door of the restaurant arm-in-arm, like a couple of newlyweds on their honeymoon with that exhilarating recently-fucked feeling you get from a damn good car ride. The hostess who greeted us was a fortyish lady with blond hair pulled back into a bun and a gold-lamé blouse that would have made Elizabeth Taylor proud. Her outfit went rather dismally with the rustic decorating scheme, but that's women for you. Fina asked where the toilet was and I busied myself picking out a table.

The main dining room was empty. Of the twenty or thirty tables scattered about, only one table was occupied, by two old couples that looked like vacationing foreigners. Despite the time of year and the air conditioner, the stone fireplace was nevertheless crackling away. I picked a table close by: in addition to the ham and the wine, this was the main attraction of the place. When Fina returned from the toilet I followed suit and went to the gents to wash my hands, and after a while we were both sitting there studying the menu. I focused on the Rioja wines. They had my beloved Faustino I, but I feared that might be a bit heavy, both for Fina's palette as well as the fine sausage delicacies we were going to eat. I also dismissed the 1973 Conde de los Andes due to the high price, and wavered between the Martínez Lacuesta Special Reserve and the 1985 Remelluri. The Lacuesta is perfect for ham, but Fina liked the Remelluri because, according to her, it was so smooth. Plus it was cheaper and it was still unclear how much fun those two hundred euros would buy us, especially if we ordered desserts.

'This place sure is nice . . . listen, do you have money? All I've got is a twenty.'

'I've got two hundred. What are you going to order?'

'Your call, Fittipaldi.'

I scanned the menu.

'Let's see, what do you think of: an *escalivada* to nibble at while we wait . . . , smoked trout . . . , a platter of cured pork loin and a couple of platters of cured ham. And ciabatta with tomato; they roast it on a woodburning fire. Then we'll see. If my memory serves me right, they have a stellar manchego.'

'I put my taste buds in your hands.'

I turned around to look for a waiter. The only one in the dining room quickly repaired to our table. Evidently he was slightly bored at the lack of clientele. I ordered. In the end I went for the Remelluri, and asked him not to serve it to us too warm. What with the usual routine of serving red wine at room temperature, they usually end up serving you a lifeless Rioja at twenty-five degrees.

As soon as the waiter retreated, Fina began her interrogation.

'All right. What's this business with you in your brother's car?'

I don't like lying to Fina. I don't like it at all.

'How about if you explain to me, first, exactly what

you are doing here with me. Wasn't your husband supposed to come home today?'

She lowered her head, eyes down. When she opened them again her pupils travelled up to a faraway point somewhere in the corner in the ceiling.

'Meetings . . . They have to report back to their boss about the Hewlett Packard scene in Toledo . . . the usual. I got angry and told him that I would just go out with some friend – a male friend – and not to wait up for me.'

I lit a Ducados to allow her to continue on in that vein or change the topic of conversation.

'I don't know what to do, Pablo . . . Look at me, I spent all day waiting around for him like an idiot . . . I was excited to see him, really, to go out to dinner somewhere, I don't know, have some quality couple-time together . . . But no, "oh, we hung about the office for a while to talk," he said. I could have killed him, I swear. Sometimes I think he stays with me just so that it looks like he's a normal person, you know? Like, it's natural and normal to be married, so he gets married and that's it . . . I don't know how many weeks it's been since we last had sex. I'm going to look for a lover, I'm serious. Damn right I'm serious, I'm sick of this . . .'

'Did you try talking to him?'

'I tried. And you know what he does? He tells me I'm neurotic! As if all this was just some crazy hysteria of mine. "But baby! We never fuck!" See what I mean? But no, nothing. He puts the telly on for a bit and then as soon as the clock strikes eleven he goes to bed. Because he has to wake up so early, you know . . . And then Saturday comes along and the least little thing comes up and we don't do it, and the day goes by and I get nothing for another week. Last week it was because he was going to

Toledo, the week before it was because we had to go to Girona to see his parents and ended up coming back late, the week before that I don't know what the fuck happened but we didn't do it then either . . . And now I'm the one who doesn't want it anymore. So that's that.'

The conversation was interrupted by the arrival of the wine and a few slices of cold cuts that the waiter served as a pre-appetiser before launching into his wine-presentation number. I told him he could just pour it and then he left us alone.

'All right. So tell me about the car. I don't feel like talking about my husband.'

'Nothing to tell. My brother gave me a surveillance assignment and I needed a car to use as an observation post.'

'What's it about?'

'I don't know, some deal he's cooking up. He's got his eye on some property in the neighbourhood and wants me to find the owner. Five hundred euros are mine if I get the name for him by Monday.'

'So what are you going to do, just wait at the front door until someone comes out?'

'Something like that, yeah.'

'Well, that little machine is not exactly going to go unnoticed. You'd be better off in an Opel Corsa.'

'Maybe. But my brother doesn't have a Corsa. He has a Lotus.'

'And are you planning to do the stakeout tonight?'

'That's the idea. We have dinner, then a drink at Luigi's and then I head over there.'

'I went by Luigi's last night, I was sick of tossing and turning in bed. I tried you on the phone but since you didn't pick up I figured you'd be there. Roberto said you'd pulled some disappearing act.'

'I went for something to eat on the Parallel.'

'And after that, a hooker, right?'

I shrugged, with a gesture somewhere between innocence and resignation. Still she was intrigued enough to keep at me:

'And so? How was it? Real special, yeah?'

'Oh, nothing you and I haven't done. You know me, when it comes to screwing and snuggling I'm pretty unimaginative.'

'I think I'm going to go and do the same thing one of these days, go out and find myself a gigolo.'

The food arrived. The *escalivada* was a touch warm for my taste; the pork loin a bit gamey, as if they had it in the icebox for too long; the cured ham was superlative, oily and aromatic; and the trout was fine. The ride in the Beast had whet our appetites, but Fina still found the time to continue with her little inquiry.

'Okay. So this image change of yours?'

'I had to do it. For this job he gave me . . .'

She sat there looking at me, rather suspiciously, even though she didn't know quite what to be suspicious of.

'Well, you know what? I think you're acting kind of strange. The haircut, the clothes, the car . . . , all that extra cash, expensive cologne . . . Plus you're so serious tonight, you haven't even cracked a joke yet.'

I couldn't think of a single joke right then.

'My brother left me his cash card to cover my expenses . . . I don't know, maybe it's just that having good clothes and money to spare gives a person character. And anyway, I'm not used to driving a millionaire's sports car.'

'Yeah, so? Do you like it?'

'Hmm . . . it *is* fun. It's a change, anyway.'

'Well, if you like it, why don't you do something about

it? Your parents are loaded, your brother, too, and you're a partner in the business, aren't you? You could have all the money you want . . .'

'Don't bother, I've heard that speech before. I know it cold.'

'I just don't understand why you don't try and make more of yourself. I don't know, if only just to be able to go out for a drink whenever you want instead of racking up bar tabs all over the place. You're a guy with a brain, you know that. Use it.'

'Actually, I think if I had a little less brains I'd be a lot more intelligent.'

'There you go again. You say the weirdest things sometimes.'

'See? That's the way my mind works, I'm like a modern day Bugs Bunny.'

I put a Bugs Bunny expression on my face, Bugs Bunny with his carrot, digging a hole, outsmarting everyone. Fina had to cover her mouth with her hand so as not to toss her *escalivada*. But she blasted back at me as soon as she had the giggles under control.

'I don't get it, really I don't. Why can't you just do what's expected of you? And don't give me another one of your analogies . . .'

In general I despise it when people demand explanations about what I do or do not do – I've got enough on my hands with FH's sermons and my Magnificent Brother's sarcastic comments. But this time it came in handy because it allowed me to direct her attention away from my wardrobe transformation and onto something else, to steer the chit-chat elsewhere.

'Fine. I am going to answer you with a true story that will serve as a parable.'

'Only if you promise to do the Bugs Bunny face after.'

'We'll see about that. First, listen to what I have to say.'

'I'm all ears.'

'Now, then. This is the story of a young man who set off for the Yukon during the height of the gold rush. His father, a prosperous merchant, had just died of old age in his hardware store in Omaha, Nebraska, and left his son a certain amount of money. With that, plus what he made from selling the old man's business, the young hardware-store heir figured he would have enough money to travel north and try his luck there. So this young man journeyed all the way to Seattle, crossing half the American continent, and from there, took his first steamship to Skagway, close to the western Canadian border. Shall I continue?'

'Well, now that you've started . . .'

'Fine. Now, the thing is, I don't want you to picture the usual opportunist fortune-hunter type. This person was more of an . . . adventurer, all right? More than gold, he was searching for the privilege of perspective – he wanted to see the world from the Absolute North, he wanted to climb the cusp of the planet Earth. That sort of thing.'

'A dreamer.'

'Exactly. You've got it. All right. The guy leaves Skagway on the back of a mule that's part of a great horse-and-livestock caravan heading further and further north toward Dawson. Six hundred kilometres of a most infernal route: avalanches, barely enough grass for the animals to survive, and an arse-whipping chill despite the spring season. In those days, Dawson was the last outpost of civilisation, a place where one could stock up on goods and supplies before going deeper into the great unknown. It was kind of a last stop from where adventurers departed for the Polar Circle.'

'Sounds like a Jack London story.'

'More like Jack Lunkhead. You read too much, it'll ruin your eyesight.'

'I don't get enough action, what do you want?'

'So the deal is, once he gets to Dawson, he's suddenly not into the idea of sticking his feet in freezing water and breaking his back to look for signs of gold dust that most of the time only appears in the most ridiculously microscopic quantities. So he decided to spend a few days in the city. Dawson had still not reached its heights of splendour. It had only just begun to be regarded as the Paris of the North, but you could drink champagne, eat caviar or hire young French maidens to dance a can-can for you in lacy undergarments – all of this at nouveau riche prices, of course. And mixed in with the men who spent all their gold dust in these dancing saloons were hundreds of poor slobs who slunk around, utterly unable to pay the fortune these places charged for a plate of green beans and a hunk of bread. It wasn't long before this scenario became a powder keg far beyond the control of the Canadian police force. Can you picture it? Now, turning back to our man from Nebraska: he had money in his pocket and after two days he couldn't care less about the north and its privileged perspective. A week went by, then two, three, and in between glasses of champagne and gold-dusted fucks that didn't require him to get his feet wet in the least, he ended up pissing away the money he'd inherited from his father.'

'I don't know why, but somehow I knew that was coming.'

'Wait – I'm just getting to the good part. So when he was finally down to his last few bucks he realised he had no other choice but to leave. He bought a sack of provisions, tossed a coin in the air to decide which way to go, and toted his satchel, mule, and sieve in the very same direction as the other fortune-hunters: Klondike upriver. But the Klondike was already more trashed than those madcmoiselles' lace undergarments – there wasn't a foot of river that hadn't been claimed, and the same was true in all the principal tributaries, and so our dreamer friend busted his arse to climb up some microscopic creek where nobody had ever found the tiniest speck of gold dust. And so, after a month of stretching his supplies and climbing up the Mackenzie Mountains, he finished off the last of his provisions. The future was looking very grim indeed. Other men might have been able to survive the harsh winter by hunting and fishing, but this Omaha hardware-store heir could hardly tell the difference between a salmon and a rabbit, and he certainly hadn't the foggiest notion of how to catch either. And so: one day, doubled over near a little creek, so hungry he could have taken a bite out of his mule, he found himself face to face with a Siwash, fishing in the water.'

'A what?'

'Siwash. An Indian from the North country. Anyway, the Indian could tell that the hardware-store boy was in desperate straits, and so he carried him off to his family. In the summertime, the Indian's clan generally set up camp near a well just a little bit upriver, and that was where he brought our man. The Indian's people gave him food to eat and before long our boy from Omaha fell into a deep sleep beneath the watchful gaze of the Indian's entire family, none of whom were at all accustomed to having such blond, hairy men in their midst. The hardware scion slept the whole day through and when he awoke, he felt much better. It was nearing nightfall when he got up and walked over to the well, hoping just to clear his eyes in the cold water. That was when he saw it.'

'Gold!'

'Exactly. Gold. In the bottom of the well: a golden sheen that sparkled in the oblique, late-afternoon sun, like a bottle of Freixenet held against the light. He practically choked. At first the Siwash didn't understand what the fuss was about, but the grandfather of the clan finally came up with a plausible explanation: that dust had to be some kind of cosmetic substance – the golden pigment that gave colour to the hair atop the Pale Face's head and the brilliant locks that covered his chest and clustered about his mouth.'

'You're making this up . . .'

'No, really. Those people were not used to seeing blond people. They had only seen white men from very far distances, looking for some invisible something in the bottom of the rivers. Think about it: next to a Siwash, a Dutch-descendant knickerbocker shines in the sun like a Marian apparition, just like the bottom of that well. What with all this fuss, our young friend realised why nobody had gone up this particular creek. Generally the gold nuggets travelled downriver, dragged by the current. The gold diggers normally tried their luck in areas shallow enough to sift in themselves; if they found something they would continue sifting further upriver, and if not they would abandon the creek entirely and try somewhere else. But as it turned out, in that tiny well, ten or twelve metres deep, the current was very slow – so slow that the gold would just settle there, like a fine shower of glitter, and the superficial water would continue to flow downriver, entirely clean of gold. In other words: the well was a kind of natural decanter that allowed gold to simply accumulate at its bottom. The only thing left to do was find out exactly how thick that golden layer actually was. More wine?'

I poured for both of us, did a quick recon of the ham plate and revisited the warm *escalivada*, which still didn't win me over, though a healthy splash of thick, greenish olive oil and a dash of salt improved it somewhat. Fina took advantage of the moment to pick at the trout and sink a couple of bites into the ciabatta toast. I waited until she covered her mouth with a napkin and asked, 'Well? What happened?'

'Well, as it turned out, a perfectly Bugs Bunny idea suddenly occurred to our hero. Out of sheer curiosity he went into the well, about three metres down, and filled his hat with the dust at the bottom. Once he returned to the surface, he knew that there was tremendous wealth in that sand, almost equal parts quartz and gold, and as soon as he realised that he was now immensely rich, he suddenly became extremely disaffected by the prospect of having to dive down like a duck for days on end to extract his treasure. And so, the only thing he could think of to do was to take a crash course in hunting and fishing with the Siwash. After all, the gold would remain there, for however long he had to wait. On the other hand, the Indians never remained at the same campsite for more than a week and it was highly improbable that he would ever find them again. And so he stored his hat away in the mule's saddle-bags, and decided to forget about the whole thing until the moment arrived when it was time to really get to work, something that could easily wait for a few days.'

'And he stayed with the Indians . . .'

'He didn't just stay. He went with them. And not only did he learn how to tell the difference between a salmon and a rabbit, he learned to tailor-make traps for each one, depending on the situation. And since he was a dreamer with a good head on his shoulders, he used all the skills he had honed in the back room of his father's hardware store and invented an ingenious system for retrieving felled animals that left the Siwash utterly speechless. A week went by, then two, then three, and before long it dawned on him that he actually liked the nomadic life, and he followed the Indians from camp to camp for the rest of the summer, and for part of the autumn, too.'

I paused again, for another sip of wine and slice of ham.

'And the well?'

'With the first few frosts, the Indians began to descend the mountains toward the south, and our hardware-store heir decided that the moment had arrived to retrace his steps and get to work on extracting that gold. He knew that he must have travelled some two hundred kilometres with the Indians in the general direction of the Yukon, but he nevertheless employed his recently acquired skills as a predatory trap-setter on the long road to the North. The first snowfalls came and our friend was still only about halfway there, busy tanning rabbit hides to protect himself against the growing chill. He then tried to speed things up a bit, but the winds and snow began to make the road more and more difficult to travel on, and it took him an entire week to cover the last twenty kilometres before reaching the well.'

'And when he arrived, it was full of people digging about.'

'Not exactly. We can safely say that no man could have gotten into that hole even if he had tripped right over it. And there was no water there anymore, just a huge block of solid ice, covered by hard snow.'

'Bummer.'

'Very much so.'

'So then . . . ?'

'Well, he had no other choice but to return to Dawson with the original bit of gold he had put in his hat which was now in his mule's saddlebag. The gold would be completely inaccessible until springtime, and even then it would require several men and various days, or perhaps even weeks, of work. Why, they would have to put together a veritable mining camp. But it didn't end there, either, because our friend was struck by another Bugs Bunny idea: what would a normal person do in this circumstance? A normal person would get busy hiring other normal people, a small group of experienced miners who had been successful in their own individual efforts, and who wanted to round out their fortunes by working for someone else for a week or two. But what did our blockhead of a hardware scion do? Well, he decided to play Mother Teresa of Calcutta and went around Dawson looking for poor souls.'

'What for?'

'Well, he was alive and rich thanks to the generosity of a few Indians whom the rest of the world shunned, and so he figured the moment had arrived when he should return the favour by sharing his secret with a score of needy souls. Working as a group, they could extract the treasure from under the ice and then they could all go home with their pockets bulging, to set up comfortable lives for themselves.'

'That doesn't sound like such a bad idea to me.'

'Sometimes, Fina, I think you're a bit of a dreamer as well: all that NGO nonsense has ruined your common sense. Can you imagine what happened when that man, dressed in rabbit skins, began to tell his story to the bunch of poor, ragged folks staggering about half-drunk through the town of Dawson? They laughed in his face. Who was about to believe a playboy who everyone remembered for throwing away his riches in the local saloons and who now bumbled down the local skid row telling drunkards stories of riches beyond their wildest dreams? And they were even less inclined to believe him when, in an effort to back up his story, he started talking details and began to tell about his days with the Siwash. You see, George Carmack, the local hero to whom the Bonanza discovery is attributed, was a white man who was such an Indian sympathiser that he actually married a Tagish woman, and in fact, he made his great discovery through one of his wife's brothers, an Indian known as Skookum Jim. So when our Omaha dreamer began to get specific about his Indian adventure everyone pretty much agreed that not only was this poor man a liar but a dreadfully unimaginative one at that. He turned into a kind of local dunce who wandered in and out of the local saloons ranting on about golden wells of great wealth and riches. Everyone lost respect for him, and the more he insisted the more insane they took him to be.'

'But he still had the gold that he put in his hat, didn't he? That would prove that his story was true.'

'Ah, yes. That also occurred to him, too. One day he took out a handful of gold dust, walked into a saloon with his palm open wide and shouted 'Look! I have a whole pound of this stuffed in a hat, so whoever wants to come and see for themselves . . .'

I stopped for a moment and took a sip of wine, looking Fina straight in the eye all the while.

'Well?'

'Well, the people most interested in the gold dust were a couple of mounted policemen. If that bravado about the hat was true, it had to be because the guy had stolen it from some honourable citizen. They detained him. Interrogated him. After two hours he found himself obliged to make up an excuse and so he said that he had invented that pound of gold just to impress the people in the bar. Even so, he had a pretty tough time explaining away the handful of that superfine powder he'd shown the barfolk. Luckily, that evening a dancer from one of the saloons on the main street accidentally tossed a lamp out the window during her show and half the street caught on fire. At the time, the city did not have a fire house and the police had so much on their hands that everyone more or less forgot about our poor luckless friend.'

'What a bad scene . . .'

'Very bad. And that is where the story ends. It was already the beginning of December, and the idea of having to wait seven months to go back to the well, in that place where everyone took him to be a suspicious drunk, was more than the poor fellow could bear. And so he set out on the long trip back to Omaha, disillusioned and full of anger.'

'And the gold in the well?'

'A mystery. The hardware scion never went back. It might still be there, but I doubt it. Nowadays, that area is part of a tourist route for saloon aficionados. Someone must have found it at some point, maybe the Canadian government. Or maybe not. Gold fever didn't last very long, only a couple more years. Go figure.'

We didn't say anything for a few moments. Fina, very serious, seemed to be meditating on what she had just heard, as if trying to hit upon some kind of allegorical meaning that was presently escaping her. I took advantage of the moment to ask the waiter for a dry slice of manchego cheese. She didn't want anything more to eat, not even dessert.

'Hey. You're not pulling my leg or anything, are you?' she asked.

'Why would I do that?'

'Because you like to do that sort of thing. It's like you.'

'You know who told me the story? Greg Farnsworth, Junior, the only son borne to our hardware store heir, many years later, of course. I spent a few weeks working at his petrol station outside of Aurora, about 150 kilometres from Omaha.'

'Oh, really? I didn't know that you'd worked at a petrol station.'

'Just that once, in the summer of '86. I needed a few bucks to get to Denver and he needed a pair of hands to organise his warehouse. I usually went over to see him and old Annie to drink iced lemonade on their porch as the sun went down. They didn't have any children to tell war stories to, and so they told them all to me, a foreigner passing through town.'

'But how do you know if the story is true? I wouldn't be so sure . . . it still sounds a lot like a Jack London story to me.'

'Fina, come on . . . do you think a couple of old farts with one foot in the grave would make up a story like that just to fool me? That man treasured the memory of his father, he told me about his adventures as a way of keeping him alive somehow, to keep him from getting lost in the dust. And apparently, he felt that I was worthy of hearing the story – I was worthy, in fact, precisely because I was a traveller passing through town. He gave me all sorts of details – names, dates, places . . . Maybe I reminded him of that dreamer who went up North in search of a privileged perspective on the world, I don't know . . . Plus, he showed me the gold in the hat. He had it stored away, along with the rabbit skins and the mule's saddlebags, like religious relics.'

'Reaaally?'

'A wide-brim hat, brown, completely deformed but hard as a rock, moulded by the gold dust to the inside of the saddlebag. And the dust was really gold, brilliant gold . . . If you touched it, it left a little sparkle on the inside of your hand, just like a fine shower of light. It's one of my most treasured memories: that superfine gold dust.'

Silence. The fire crackled. Suddenly the mood had gotten intense; I felt the need to crack some kind of joke. As an emergency measure I made like some thick-lipped black guy and began to tap my feet to some Georgie Dan dance steps:

'*When people criticise me, saying that*
I spend my life thinking about nothin'
It's because they don't know I'm the man
who's got the greatest coffee plantation in the land.'

'And now,' I declared, 'we are going to have a couple of glasses of champagne and a little spot of coffee, how about it?'

Fina finally broke into a smile again.

'Oh, no . . . first you have to do the Bugs Bunny face again. You gave me your word.'

I did a brief Bugs Bunny impression to make her happy and then called the waiter over. The end of the dinner was inevitably slow and lazy; we drank the champagne and tried to talk, about anything, but it was clear that a change of scenery was in order. I asked for the check – ninety and change – and we got up and tried to get out of there. I say tried, because while we had been eating dinner another couple had entered the dining room and sat down at another table. I had seen them but Fina had been facing the other way and didn't notice them until we got up to leave.

'Oh my God! Toni and Gisela! Good God, I haven't seen you since forever!'

Shit. When Fina bumps into someone in a restaurant, you know you're fucked. It's always been centuries since she last saw them and she always insists on getting the full update on their life and times right then and there. The couple – thirtysomethings that looked like the typical childless couple that can still indulge in the luxury of going out to dinner mid-week – duly recognised Fina and waited for her to approach them, displaying a full repertoire of enthusiastic gestures. I could see that this was going to set us back at least an hour if I was willing to enter the game, and so I improvised a distraction manoeuvre.

'Oh, God, Fina, I'm going to piss my pants. I'm going to go to the toilet while you say hello to your friends and then I'll just wait for you in the car. Don't be too long, all right?'

She agreed without paying too much attention and went straight over to the table, full of glee.

I didn't bother stopping at the toilet because I wasn't, in fact, pissing my pants, and went outside instead. It was hot. Late spring evening. We were far enough away from Barcelona to be able to see the stars. That and the scent of the log fire have a way of making a person feel bucolic and pensive. I reached the Black Beast, did the 'stuuk' bit and got in, opened the window and let myself get lulled into the cric-cric of the crickets and that sleepy, post-dinnertime glow.

BROTHER BERMEJO

The interior craftsmanship of the Black Beast may very well have been perfectly calibrated for speeding down a motorway, but it is rather difficult to fall into a deep sleep in a seat that locks you into a position more suitable for a race-car driver. Even so, I managed to fall into a sweaty dream state, obsessed with the idea of setting a bunch of crickets' chirps in four-four time, but I kept getting distracted; every time I heard a few steps upon the gravel road, or the sound of a car driving past me, I was brought back into surveillance mode. After a while, though, aided by large gulps of the evening breeze, I soon felt the indescribable pleasure that one feels when falling deep inside oneself. I began to dream that I was driving full speed down a bunch of lonely mountain roads, amid clouds of buzzing insects reflected in the haze of the streetlights, always toward a remote valley awaiting me in the distance, with its tiny village, houses and soft single beds that would finally allow me to sleep with my legs fully stretched out.

An unbearably suffocating feeling jerked me out of my trance, however, and my arms flailed about in the air as I tried to escape something that felt as if it were sealing my nostrils shut with a pair of tweezers. Once I fully came to, I found Fina laughing at me from the other side of the window.

'Where did you go? I thought you were going to the toilet.'

'Fina. Shit, don't do that again, all right?'

'What?'

'Hold my nose while I'm sleeping. I can't stand it.'

'All right, all right. You don't have to go and get mad at me.'

'Right. Just don't do it again. I fell into a perfectly fine sleep and you had to go ahead and cut off my breathing. You know what that feels like?'

She walked around the car and got into the passenger seat, glowering. Now she was playing the I'm-offended routine in an effort to get out of the little joke she'd played on me.

'So what now? We're leaving?'

'What time is it?'

'Just after one.'

'One? How long were you bullshitting with those two?'

'I don't know, honey, I thought you'd gone to the toilet and were coming back.'

'I told you I was going to wait for you in the car. The problem is, when it doesn't suit you, you decide not to listen to me.'

She fell silent. Still glowering. I tried to adopt a more conciliatory tone.

'All right, now. Why don't you put on the air conditioner?'

'You put it on, Mr Perfect. How am I supposed to know where to find it?'

'Shit, Fina. It's only right in front of your face. See the little picture? Red for hot air, blue for cold.'

'Fine, then. If it's so obvious then put it on yourself. I'd love to see you hunt for it as you fire down the motorway.'

'The one all fired up is you, baby. Come on, put on some music. Think you can find the button yourself, my little *fleur de lis*, or shall I help you out with that, too?'

She turned away and gave me a little slap on the shoulder as if teaching me a little lesson. I took that as a good sign.

I gunned up the Beast, and we slowly made our way back to town via the National motorway. Fina reviewed the CD case and found a Dinah Washington greatest hits album. By the time 'Mad About the Boy' came around to smooth things over, we were back on speaking terms.

'Who were those two, anyway?'

'Toni and Gisela? We went to university together. You don't know them.'

We stayed like that for a while, Fina telling me all about her friendship with Gisela, me driving under 120 and listening without much interest, and Dinah Washington doing her best to create a smooth atmosphere. Once we were back in the neighbourhood, I turned at Nicaragua and took a moment to double-park in front of the La Caixa cash machine at Travessera. Technically speaking, another working day had begun; I didn't know what the limit was on my brother's Magnificent cash card, but given that the machine had spat out five hundred big ones only a few hours earlier, there was no reason it wouldn't do it again.

Smooth sailing. Fina's eyes grew as big as saucers when she got a load of the dough.

'Why are you taking so much money out at once?'

'Didn't you learn anything from the story of the hardware scion of Omaha, my little *fleur de lis*?'

'Call me *fleur de lis* one more time and I'll slug you with my purse.'

We got back into the Black Beast and I had to drive circles around the block in order to end up not 500 metres from where we were before – that is, directly in front of Luigi's bar. Car issues. We triple-parked in a tiny spot sandwiched between the thousands of taxis and the City Guard van parked in front of the bar (sometimes Coyote and Roadrunner bring the van with them). From his spot behind the bar, Roberto saw us pull in and as he recognised us let out a 'sonofabitch!' which was, in fact, audible from where we were. Still in his apron, he immediately ran outside, heading straight for the Beast and staring at us with wild eyes as we passed him on the sidewalk. Fina and I followed him inside the bar, but Roberto's sudden stampede had caught the attention of the bar clientele. Five or six taxi drivers, Coyote and Roadrunner, the usual drunks plus a second-rate artist formed a human wall at the entrance to Luigi's bar, watching Roberto as he walked round and round the car. Fina and I managed to penetrate the wall of rubberneckers, though only to be greeted by Luigi's suspicious gaze, which focused, for once, on me rather than Fina. It seemed that he had decided to refrain from commenting on my appearance until a later point, so as to find out what the hell everyone was staring at. Roberto wasted little time: he was soon back in position at the bar, with a perplexed expression on his face.

'Holy Mary, Mother of God: a Lotus Esprit. 007's car!'

That was enough to let the crowd know exactly what kind of machine we were talking about, and the group pounced on us, demanding an explanation. The first time I had seen Bagheera, I knew it was worthy of someone with a licence to kill, but I had no idea that it was the very same car that James Bond drove.

I sat down, feeling the need to minimise the impact of the situation.

'I thought James Bond drove an Aston-Martin . . .'

Roberto was beside himself.

'No, no, that was only with Sean Connery. Roger Moore drove the Lotus Esprit. You saw *The Spy Who Loved Me*, didn't you? Remember the scene when he dives into the ocean in a white sports car that turns into a submarine? This is the same car. Well, this is the newest model, V8 GT. And did you see *Basic Instinct*?'

'No, but I saw *Meatballs Two*.'

Roberto had the entire bar hanging on tenterhooks with his deluge of informative details. Everyone seemed rather shocked at his display of automotive knowledge, although in reality it didn't amount to much more than a bit of old movie trivia. This kind of expertise did not exactly fit with Roberto's personality.

'It also shows up in *Pretty Woman* . . . a classic, exceptional automobile, a gem . . . 550 horsepower, 32-valve biturbo engine, acceleration from one to 100 in 4.9 seconds, maximum speed of 272 kilometres per hour, limited only by the electronic system's control unit . . .'

The taxi drivers began to gaze upon me with the resentful sneers of men who own diesel-fuelled Renault 21s painted like Maya the Bee. I decided that Roberto had to be cut off as fast as possible, and so I whipped out the keys and plunked them down in front of him.

'Want to take her for a ride?'

He stood there, staring at the keys like a man hypnotised. At first I thought it was the shock, but little by little a sheepish, puppy-dog smile came over his face and his eyebrows rose up high as he murmured, with the infinite sadness of a man without means.

'Well . . . you see, I don't have a licence for driving cars.'

For a few seconds everyone was frozen. Then, as soon as Luigi overcame his asthmatic breathing and let out his first 'hah!' the congregation followed suit. And then some. One of the taxi drivers, unable to hold in his laughter, grabbed Roberto by the head and planted a loud kiss on him, smack in the middle of his forehead, which only exacerbated the hysteria surrounding the poor buffoon who hung his head as he rubbed his hands against his apron, once again at his post behind the counter. Taking advantage of the general fracas, we quickly headed to the back of the bar and grabbed a table. Before sitting down I asked Fina what she wanted to drink.

'Whisky on the rocks. I feel like getting drunk tonight. But make it a good one – I don't want to end up with a headache.'

I asked Luigi for a Vichoff for me and a Cardhu for Fina. I don't know if Vázquez Montalban is aware of this, but the world has him to thank for the fact that even the worst deadbeat losers now order single malt whiskys instead of regular whisky – they think it makes them connoisseurs or something. Anyway. Luigi returned with my Vichoff, his own Cuba Libre and the Olympic nectar that Fina had requested. Then he took it upon himself to sit down with us and subject me to my second round of questioning that evening.

'Right, then. Think you can do us the favour of explaining what the fuck is the meaning of that car out there and that snappy look you're walking around with tonight?'

I nudged Fina under the table so that she would shut up and let me talk. She flashed me a stern, let's-see-what-you-come-up-with-this-time look. But she kept her trap shut.

'We happen to be celebrating our anniversary,' I replied.

'Anniversary? What anniversary?'

'Fina and I met twenty years ago today,' I said, which was almost true. Fina and I met on the night of San Juan, the summer solstice, if not twenty, then twentysomething years earlier. 'And we have decided to celebrate the occasion by availing ourselves of a radio programme that offers a very special evening, all expenses paid, to the listener who promises to go on the air the following day to spill all the details of the date. They hired the car we asked for, they paid for our dinner, and all the drinks we want. And we even have a suite reserved at the Hotel Juan Carlos I.'

'You're fucking kidding . . .'

'Tomorrow night, just tune in to Radio Amor and you'll hear us talking about your very own bar. The show starts at midnight, it's called "A Hard Day's Night." I'm definitely going to tell them all about the scene with the Lotus: the audience will love that one. Do you want me to say something specific about the bar, mention the excellent tapas, or something like that? Take advantage of me – it's free publicity, you know.'

'Go to hell. I don't believe you for a second.'

'Oh, really? Well, right outside you have proof positive of the machine that'll get Sharon Stone going at 100 kilometres per hour in 4.9 seconds. Where else do you think we got it? Do you know what it costs to get a car like that for a night?'

'I couldn't care less. I still don't believe you for a second.'

'Well, we could have gone to Oliver Hardy's for a bottle of Dom Perignon. Instead, however, we chose to come here, to share our festivities with you. And you go and treat me like some common liar.'

'I know what you're up to. Now you're going to ask me for a receipt and you're going to tell me that they pay for the drinks tomorrow, when the radio people give you the money for your expenses.'

I rummaged through my pockets slowly and pulled out

the wad of bills which I counted in his face. Then I left a twin set of blue euros on the table.

'Keep the change, waiter.'

'Forget it. God only knows where you got that cash. All right, now, Fina,' he said, turning to her. 'If you tell me the bit about the radio show, maybe then I'll buy it.'

Fina glanced over at me, let out a little titter, turned back to Luigi and nodded her head in a mini-gesture that wouldn't have convinced even the most gullible of men. He got up from the table triumphantly, placing his index finger beneath his eye in a little I-get-it gesture. I shrugged my shoulders, looking at Fina, who looked at me imploringly, like an actor in some kind of Italian musical comedy.

'Now. What I would like to know is how on earth you expect me to believe your gold-rush stories if you go around telling lies to everyone who crosses your path?'

'And what I would like to know is why everyone is so obsessed with telling the difference between truth and lies. What is the big deal?'

That last comment launched us into a half-hour discussion not at all worth repeating. Suffice it to say that it gave us enough time for another round of whisky and Vichoff. What with the wine at dinner, the glass of champagne, the two hefty tumblers of Cardhu, Fina was starting to get sassy. After a while, the clock behind the bar counter struck two and I decided it was time to get to work before the proverbial well froze over.

'Listen, Fina. I gotta go. You know the deal.'

'Al-ready? Noooo, don't gooooo, I don't want to go home now . . . I'll go with you. Every detective needs an assistant, right?'

'But it's going to be really boring . . . I'll probably spend all night in the car.'

'Well, at least you won't fall asleep if I'm there. We'll bring something to drink, we'll put on the radio and we'll have a little party in the Lotus. How does that sound?'

I thought about this, briefly. It was completely stupid, but knowing Fina, it was likely to take me a good couple of hours to get her home anyway. When she sets her mind to something, she can be the queen of sabotage – she would have come up with a thousand different tricks to put off the farewell. Anyway, what the hell, I didn't have much desire to hole up in a car for the night, even if it was James Bond's car. So I put on an all-right-you've-convinced-me look, good and resigned, and I went over to the bar counter to find Luigi.

'Listen. I need to buy a couple of bottles of Cardhu off of you, plus the vodka you keep in the freezer for me, and a bag of ice. I'll pay for it up front.'

'Whaaat? Are you mental? And how much do you expect me to charge you for all that?'

'I don't know. Whatever you'd charge me if you were serving it to me glass by glass.'

'Right. About a hundred seventy-five.'

'Fine. I've got that. Take it while you can.'

He turned around and went into the back room, muttering under his breath, and came back out, vodka bottle in hand. Then he pulled the whisky bottles from the display and plunked them down on the bar, trying to hold back a snort that somehow snarfed itself out of his nose.

'Bring me two of these tomorrow. At least as full as these are.'

'Done. I also need a bag of ice and two glasses, if you don't mind.'

'And where do you think I'm going to come up with a

bag of ice around here? What does this look like, a petrol station?'

'For Christ's sake, Luigi, just stick a handful of ice cubes in any old bag, do I have to spell everything out for you? And add up the fifty from last night plus whatever I owe you for tonight.'

'From today and from yesterday morning too, remember? You ran me up for a coffee and a pack of Ducados.'

Luigi has such a sterling memory.

After we put the bottles in a bag, Fina and I made our exit and walked over to the Beast. Suddenly she started getting all sentimental on me, insisting on hugging me and the like. Danger. This called for abrupt behaviour.

'Shit, Fina. You're all over me today.' She gave me another little slap and jerked back, in a dramatic gesture of feigned offence. We got into the car and coasted down Jaume Guillamet in silence until we reached number fifteen. I made a left on Travessera and double-parked a few metres from the corner.

'Wait here a second. I'll be back in two minutes.'

'Where are you going?'

'To take a piss.'

I got out of the car and walked over to the intersection, back to the corner and then down toward the house, my hands in my pockets, as if I had planned to meet someone there and was killing time, pacing about. The lights were out in the house, or at least the shutters were closed, so that you couldn't see anything from the street. I stopped for a moment by the gate in front of the garden, pretended to tie my shoelaces, and looked up at the lamppost where, as before, the red rag fluttered in the night air. Then I got up, untied the rag very calmly, stuck it in my pocket and returned to the car.

As soon as I turned the corner and saw the back of the Beast with the lights on, I heard the muffled sounds of The Police singing 'doo-doo-doo-dah-dah-dah', which must have been on full-blast inside the car. The silhouette of something that looked suspiciously like a Muppet, bobbing up and down inside the car confirmed the fact that Fina was most definitely feeling the effects of the whisky.

'Are you mental? Do you know what time it is?'

'De-doo-doo-doo, de-dah-dah-dah, de-na-na-na-na-na-na, bu-boom, de-doo-doo-doo . . .'

'Fina! For Christ's sake! The windows are wide open!'

I lowered the volume as soon as I got in. Fina had decided to get cute on me, and started chiding me in the voice of a drunken rich girl.

'Oh, come on, ever since you got a little cash on you you've started getting so fussy . . . de-doo-doo-doo, de-dah-dah-dah . . .'

Now she was singing in a kind of whispery parody, continuing to move about like the Cookie Monster. I turned on the ignition, planning to move down the block.

'Fina, if you don't behave yourself, you're going to screw up the entire plan, and I'm talking about five hundred big ones.'

'Oh, excuse me, sir. It won't happen again, I promise.'

Abruptly her attitude changed: suddenly she got very serious and fiddled with the radio until locating a classical music station that was playing some kind of baroque music, solemn as all hell, and she began to wave an imaginary baton for the imaginary quartet she was directing, her face brimming with an almost religious ecstasy. I started to laugh which, of course, was what she was trying to get me to do in the first place, and she stopped pretending to be the master of ceremonies, pinched one of my chubby cheeks and exclaimed, 'Oh, my big little boy!'

'Fina, please. Drop it.' It was hopeless. As soon as she hits on something that she knows pisses me off, she won't stop until I'm about ready to kill her. I decided to focus on the issue at hand and wait for her to get tired of caressing and pinching me. There were no parking spots to be had as we drove up Jaume Guillamet, but about fifty metres from the house, across the street, I spotted a couple of driveways that led to an auto-repair garage. 'Body work and painting' said the sign. I decided to park the Beast there; it was highly unlikely that anyone would need a paint job at two in the morning. From that vantage point I could keep my eye on the entrance to the house, and both the distance and the shadows from the street lights guaranteed us a modicum of discretion – that is, as long as Fina didn't start singing again, something she is wont to do during phase C of her drinking jags. For the moment, however, she had settled on a pop station that was playing some kind of modern reggae.

'Are we there yet? I thought we were going to take a spin in the Black Beast. Full speed, wheeeee . . . But wait, wait: where is this place that we have to check out?'

I pointed to the house.

'The house with that little garden? What a pit!'

'Exactly. Do you know how much money you can make putting up a residential building on that lot? Just do the numbers: six floors with two flats on every floor, at five hundred thousand euros a piece. Times twelve. Six million big ones.'

'Well, I like it just the way it is, with its little garden and those little trees.'

'Didn't you just say it was a pit?'

'Well . . . yes, but all it needs is a bit of fixing up, really.

Anyway, what? Aren't we going to have a drink? What do you fancy?'

'Pass me the vodka bottle, please.'

'Straight from the bottle? Well, I am going to have a whisky in this tall glass right here, with ice and everything . . .'

She dropped three ice cubes into the glass and poured just enough whisky to coat the ice cubes completely. A double, by anyone's standards. I tried to drink straight from the bottle, but between the measuring gadget at the tip, which complicated the flow of liquid, and the Beast's extremely low ceiling, which did not allow a full elbow angle, I gave up and served myself a glass with a couple of ice cubes. The strains of a Mike Hammer-style version of 'Can You See Her?' began wafting through the speakers, which was dangerous with Fina around, because this particular song always gets me a tad sentimental. To fortify myself, I downed the vodka in one go. Vodka softens the heart, they say, but it also softens the prick, which I wanted to keep flaccid for the moment. And so I served myself another healthy dose of my anti-aphrodisiac tonic and continued sucking it down in short gulps.

'Listen, Pablo: you and I get along pretty well, don't we?'

Good God: an aerial attack.

'What do you mean, exactly, by "get along pretty well"?'

'Well . . . we laugh a lot . . . we have a good time together . . . I don't know. For example, I can't sit in a car drinking whisky at two in the morning with my husband.'

'That's because your husband is a normal man.'

'Normal? Do you think it's normal that he leaves me at home so that I have to call you to relieve my loneliness?'

'Well, there you have it: you're here with me now not because you have a better time with me but because he's left you alone for a night.'

'Don't confuse me now. That's not what I meant to say. Ooh, listen: the song from *Grease*.'

True enough. The radio DJs had gone seamlessly from Mike Hammer to Olivia Newton-John and John Travolta's 'Summer Nights'. That, however, was not enough to get her off the subject.

'You know what? I think that if you and I had gotten married we would be a normal couple by now, with a little flat and a couple of kids . . . I'm sure of it, we would really be happy.'

'Don't be ridiculous, Fina. That's the whisky talking. Must I remind you of the scenes you and I have lived through together?'

'What scenes?'

'What do you mean "what scenes"? I don't know if you recall but we shared a flat for fifteen days and we fought the whole bloody time. If we had gotten married you and I would hate each other by now. Deep down inside you have the soul of an old-fashioned housewife, no matter how much you buzz-cut your hair and dress like a goth queen. And I drink like a fish, I like sleeping with hookers, I spend most of the day sleeping and I get acne from the mere thought of working eight hours a day. We wouldn't have lasted a year together.'

'I disagree. To start with, if we had gotten married, you would be leading a totally different life by now.'

'See? The person you think I am has no relation whatsoever to the person that I happen to think I am. You project on me the image of the person you wish I were. That person exists only in your mind.'

'There you go again, saying strange things and making everything so complicated. Why do you always have to go around saying strange things and complicating everything?'

'Complicating everything? What, because I don't want to assume responsibilities for third parties? That is what I call simplifying things.'

'It may seem that way to you, but running away from responsibilities is merely a sophisticated way of complicating things.'

'Oh, really? Well, now I think you're the one saying strange things.'

'It's only because of you, you get me all mixed up. If you didn't make such a mountain out of the simplest little mole hills . . .'

'Look who's talking. Anyway, you didn't marry me. You married José María, and nothing is going to change that. And if you have issues with him, it's not because he isn't like me. He's the kind of man you need: serious, focused, hard-working. The problem is that José María is so serious and so hard-working that he doesn't have any time to kill with you, but you can't fix that by shacking up with the first mental case that makes you laugh. And anyway, I haven't got the time, either. Not for you or anyone else.'

'I wouldn't exactly call you "the first mental case that made me laugh." Anyway, what do you mean you don't have time? We spend a ton of time together.'

'But those are bonus hours.'

'What's that supposed to mean?'

'It means that a few hours here and there are all fine and good, but I couldn't face seeing you tomorrow morning when I wake up with a pounding hangover and all I want to do is smoke a joint in silence. To begin with, you wouldn't even let me puke on my bedroom floor tonight. And then you'd make me put all my dirty clothes in the hamper, and then you'd nag me for wasting away my brain-cells and all my family connections, and then you'd make me shave off my Errol Flynn moustache and remember your birthdays and worry about your orgasms. That is what living together is all about. Maybe you love the idea, but I don't: I happen to believe that people should suck it up and deal with their own birthdays and orgasms without driving their fellow man mad.'

'That's because you don't love anyone, not for real.'

'Maybe. But it took me long enough to learn to love myself. I don't know if I can go through all that business again on someone else's behalf.'

'Well, that's your problem right there.'

'Listen, Fina: if you want to play psychoanalyst I better warn you I know the game. And moreover, if you absolutely must play your little girlfriend-disciplinarian role then you ought to give me a hand job first, and good – or at least let me touch your tits. It's only fair. If you're going to force me to endure the disadvantages of cohabitation, I ought to be able enjoy at least some of the advantages.'

'You are a filthy pig.'

Big mistake. That is, to have allowed myself to engage in a serious discussion with her. There I was, concerned about the welfare of my Magnificent Brother, the health of my father and the mental stability of my mother, sitting in a ridiculous car straight out of an action movie so that I could stake out the entrance to a house that looked straight out of an Edgar Allan Poe story. And there was Fina, bathing herself in whisky and trying to convince me that I was an immature egomaniac just because I didn't seem altogether enthused by the hypothetical idea of marrying her.

I rearranged my facial mask. Then I leaned in closer to her and placed my hand on her shoulder.

'Come on, Fina, come on. Won't you give me a hand job, just a little one?'

'You leave me alone. I'm angry.'

I slid my hand between her thighs.

'Well, fine, then I'll do it myself, but just lemme touch your cunt a teeny bit, to get in the mood, you know? You wearing panties?'

'Stop that, Pablo, stop that right now! I'll start to scream . . .', she threatened.

She slapped me again and tried to act serious, but I could tell she was on the verge of surrendering. I began whispering like some Argentinian latin lover.

'Picture it, picture it . . . you're already doing it, yeah, *chup-chup*, sucking me off. Can't you see that lovely little cunt of yours has a heart of its own, beating away for me . . .'

'Pab-lo!'

'Come here, come here, skinnybone, let me take your blood pressure, let me stick my finger in and I'll tell you what the reading is.'

She couldn't take much more. She leaned forward, pressing hard with her thigh muscles so as to stave off my manual advances, but then collapsed in a wave of those compulsive yelps that she emits as a form of laughter. Triumphant, I took the glass out of her hand and poured her another healthy serving of whisky. I also replenished my vodka and then reassumed the pilot's position. This seduction-and-laughing fit seemed to be an extended version: all I had to do was give her a seductive tango-singer leer, and she would surrender to another spasmodic yelping fit.

'You look like one of the shrimps on the Pescanova can!'

Now Stevie Wonder was putting sunshine in our lives from deep within the radio, and so I exchanged my canned-shrimp face for that of a blind dude with dreadlocks, exalting in the sounds emanating from his keyboard. Fina was already in permanent laughter mode – anything I said or did was apt to send her howling at this point. Better. Then came U2, 'With or Without You', which gave me the chance to assume the persona of a brooding heartthrob who makes profound statements, and that was followed by the Lambada – proving that the DJ was clearly as drunk as Fina. I pumped up the volume and opened the door so that I could at least move one leg comfortably. Fina followed suit and started in on me. The curve on Molins, luckily, had not been enough to dislodge the Beast's suspension, but the Lotus engineers had not built their machines to fight the two elements I was dealing with now, however, and the Lambada duet threatened to destabilise the emergency brake. Fina ended up completely outside the little cubicle-sized space, and began jiggling her legs around in full public view, as if trying to shake off her pelvic bones in a most colourful display of centrifugal motion, fuelled by her frenetic, furious crescendo of pleasure. I think more liquor ended up on the leather upholstery than in our respective bodies, and by the time our dance number was over, we were desperately thirsty and had to immediately replenish ourselves straight from the two bottles. 'Bad Moon Rising', by Creedence, served to slow the rhythm down a bit, and 'Knocking on Heaven's Door' completed the deceleration process. According to my calculations, Fina must have ingested the equivalent of six or seven normal whiskies: slumber would only be a few minutes away now. I can put away a bottle of vodka in two or three hours without losing my marbles, and so I would be able to remain alert until the early-morning hours. I put on the air conditioner and turned off the radio. Fina protested, so I decided to try my luck with the New World Symphony CD

I found in The First's mobile music collection. The long intro to the main piece, along with the air conditioner's comforting artificial breeze encouraged Fina's slumber. I told her to take off her shoes so that she would be more comfortable, and she obeyed. I took mine off, too.

As soon as my newly minted detective's assistant fell asleep, I repositioned myself with my glass of vodka, which I drank with utmost caution so as not to make the ice cubes clink against each other. I lowered the music some more and sat there, looking outside. It was rather odd: now that it was night-time the street didn't seem quite so gloomy, maybe because that stillness, coupled with that slightly desolate atmosphere, is normal at night, and doesn't seem out of place at all. Even so, the sight of that ridiculous island in the middle of the city did remind me of the mess I had gotten myself involved in. It was Friday (or Saturday, if you went by the calendar), and it had only been two or three days since The First had called me to offer me that mini-job, and yet it somehow felt like weeks ago. Too many developments in too few days – I'm used to a slightly slower pace of life. I began to mentally reconstruct those past three days, to refresh my memory, now dulled by the alcohol, the low-quality sleep and the intensity of the recent turn of events. And I guess I did it also to occupy myself for the next couple of hours before sunrise. I tried hard to remember everything, allowing for no more than half-hour lapses in between events. What I came up with was a dense, minute-by-minute narrative, exactly as I have recounted it up until now.

An hour later, I still hadn't made it to Thursday: I was immersed in the memory of my walk through the Boquería market and the sight of that beautiful Queen of the Seas, when I suddenly realised that the door to the house at number fifteen had opened. Opened!

I rubbed my eyes and hunched up closer to the dashboard to get a better look. A man emerged, leaving the door ajar behind him. He was tiny, bald, hunchbacked, and I could even make out his aquiline nose and gnarled hands. He wore something very baggy, maybe brownish overalls, that went down about mid-calf. He went straight to the point: first he separated the mat of ivy that partially hid the lamppost; the absence of the red rag seemed to disturb him. He unceremoniously tugged at the ivy, looked left and right, his hands on his hips, and went back into the garden out front without closing the door behind him. This, I thought, might be just the moment to start the car, coast past the house and check out the inside of the garden, but that would entail driving down to the stop light and circling the block, which might mean I would miss the man's next movements. I turned off the music and sat there, waiting. Not thirty seconds later the man reappeared with a red rag in his hand. He stood up on tiptoe in order to tie it to the lamppost, and then stepped back a few paces as if to check that it was in position. After glancing left and right once more, and then toward the balconies across the street, he finally went back into the garden and closed the door behind him.

I turned Fina's wrist toward me so I could see the time on her watch. Five on the dot. 'Matins,' I thought, though I don't quite know why. Maybe because that little baldy looked sort of like a monk. He reminded me of a math teacher I had at the Marist Brothers' school: Brother Bermejo. Kind of out of it, but not an altogether bad guy. Fina, uncomfortable, opened her eyes and stretched her arms down about her knees.

'We're going, *fleur de lis*.'

'Huh.'

'We're going to bed. We're done working for the day.'

'Mmmm. Did you find anything out?'

'Yeah. I've got a lousy assistant.'

I bid my Sleeping Beauty farewell at the door to her building, and waited for her to disappear through the glass doors and up the lift. She looked as if she had just returned from an initiation session in the Eleusian mysteries and I thought about how it sure would be better if good old José María were still sleeping. After leaving her, I couldn't bear the thought of having to drop the Beast off at the parking garage, and so I tried my luck parking in the street, as close as possible to my building. The First had to have some kind of deluxe all-risk insurance policy for the car, down to bird shit. I found a space about twenty metres from my doorway, recently vacated by one of those eccentric types that gets up at five in the morning. I gathered up the bottles and glasses and went upstairs. I wasn't tired; I hadn't gotten sufficiently drunk for that, and I felt as though I had left a job half-finished. I undressed down to my socks and boxers, lit a joint, and finished off the remains of the vodka bottle. Then I resumed my reconstruction of the chain of events that had ensued from Thursday night until the present time.

Only when I had finished the total recap and the sun had begun to glint off the empty vodka bottle did I finally feel the urge to embark on the thrilling adventure of falling asleep.

DENTOMAXILLARY DYSFUNCTION

Fina insists upon showing me something absolutely fascinating, something that involves some friend of hers. She won't say anything more than that, she just takes my hand and drags me through a series of anonymous streets, although I can tell we're in Barcelona – the smell and the traffic noise are unmistakable. We arrive at the main gate of a public garden enclosed by a fence. We go in, and walk down a wide footpath until reaching an elegant Victorian mansion that rises up in the middle of the park. We knock at the door, which is then opened by an old servant woman with a little cap on her head. She seems to know Fina, and she ushers us in. We enter without saying a word, with Fina always in front of me, walking as if she knows exactly where she's going and wants to arrive as soon as possible. Next we pass through an elegant parlour with a log fire burning in the fireplace. We see an old woman sitting in an easy chair, doing her knitting, impervious to our interruption. I also notice the sofas, the rugs, the patterned fabrics, porcelain knick-knacks, but I can't explore at great length because Fina keeps on opening new doors, walking through them like a madwoman, and I'm having trouble keeping up with her in the labyrinth. From the parlour we go into a corridor, from there to an entranceway and then to another parlour, where another old woman sits there, doing her knitting in front of a log fire. The parlours are always different, as are the chimneys and the old women with their knitting, but the situation and the characters are always the same as we move from room to room. Puzzled about this, I ask Fina to explain.

'Shhh,' she says in a low voice. 'They're the guardians.' I then become aware of the fact that we have been walking further and further inside the mansion for quite some time now, and not once have we seen a single window, which makes me realise that we must be in deep inside what must be an uncommonly massive building.

'Heart of Darkness,' I say to myself. 'We're looking for Mr Kurtz.' That's it. We then arrive at an immense room with vaulted ceiling, a special chamber somewhere within this monumental edifice. The crackling of the fire, an open book face down on a table and a half-empty glass of wine betray the presence of someone who, for the moment, we cannot see. Fina finally seems to have found the thing she was so desperate to show me: an electric bass guitar, made of natural wood, though damaged by a tremendous wallop that has unhinged the D peg. Only three strings remain, but it is nonetheless connected to an amp and the slight brush against it resounds deeply through the entire room – *boo-oo-ong*. Fina hands it to me – cautiously, tenderly, as if handling a newborn baby. I slip the guitar strap over my head and try to play a simple melody, but it is impossible: the neck has been warped and the strings are all out of tune. The noise has nevertheless caught the attention of Mr Kurtz, who suddenly appears in the doorway, drying his hands with a towel. He is a young man, wearing camouflage pants, military boots, and a tank top that exposes his muscular arms. As he looks over at the bass, a melancholy smile comes over his face, a sad smile that seems to suggest he is caught in the memory of something lovely that he has lost forever. Introductions are unnecessary, he knows us and we know him. He looks at me.

'How is Mom?' he asks.

'All right. She thinks you're in Bilbao.' Fina then gets soft and sentimental, and kisses the both of us, sandwiching her head between our two heads in a hug.

'They're on their way,' Mr Kurtz says. I look about me: the silence of the defunct bass guitar has awakened the guardians from their knitful dreams. Imperceptibly, from behind the several doors that open onto this room, the guardians enter the room. They still look like harmless old ladies, but their determination transforms them into something absolutely terrifying. Inexorably they continue moving forward, invading each and every inch of the parlour until they crush our bones, and when they are finished, they self-destruct as they fulfil the implacable instinct for destruction that governs their souls.

A horrifying scenario. I woke up, paralysed with fear by the image of the soft, roly-poly face of my maternal granny. Goddamn dreams. I tried to go back to sleep, but I couldn't get her image out of my mind, and I opened my eyes so that the light filtering in through the blinds might reassure me that I was, in fact, safe and sound in my everyday, normal world. The worst part of it all, though, was the realisation that my everyday, normal world had changed so much that it was, in and of itself, a nightmare, a nightmare inhabited by little bald men that emerged from their lairs under cover of night to tie little red rags on the gates of some madhouse.

My hangover was just what I expected it would be: headache, dry mouth, and various extremities which felt as though someone had beaten them to a pulp. According to the kitchen clock it was past five in the afternoon. At least I had caught up on all that lost sleep, but the yellowish light from the street indicated the imminent sunset, and I hardly felt like plunging into another long night. I drank water, lots of water, and for the first time in years, as I clung to the tap, I felt an intense desire to be in the countryside, enjoying a brisk spring morning. This sudden change of heart had to be remedied, on the double. I located the bottle of Cardhu which I had left on the table, and filled half a water glass with its contents and gulped down the alcohol as if it were medicine. After that, I put some coffee on, rolled a joint and sat down to smoke it, though somewhat impatiently. I knew that smoking a joint and drinking coffee would kill my appetite, but I figured that I had eaten enough the day before to endure a few more hours before refuelling. I would have loved a line of coke right then. Maybe now that I was flush I could score a gram off Nico . . . I thought about what I might have in the house that could serve as an acceptable substitute, and rummaged through my medicine chest until I came up with a box of aspirin that I remembered having bought a while back. They had expired more than a year earlier, but I took two anyway and chased them down with a slug of the Cardhu, and then smoked another joint as I took a few sips of coffee.

After twenty minutes, I was Pablo Miralles again, and I was even able to brush my teeth and shave – carefully, of course, being careful to respect the boundaries of my stylish new moustache.

Next up: I started to worry about what I was afraid I would have to worry about. My first plan of action had been executed to completion the previous night; all I could do now was think some more. I did this and came up with at least two potential avenues of investigation. I decided to opt for the first, simple and easy. On the dining room table I looked for The First's mobile phone, which was one of those tiny jobs with a fold-out mouthpiece, and I focused on unravelling its various mysteries. I was sure it had to have some kind of telephone directory, and maybe I could even investigate the source of the last phone calls he had received, or at least the last phone calls he had made from the thing. In no time at all, I figured out how to use the directory function, and discovered a total of sixteen memorised numbers, all of which I jotted down on a piece of paper. Given the names and also by comparing them to the numbers listed in my own address book, I confirmed that four of the numbers stored on his mobile were known quantities: that of my Parents' Highness (*PaMa*), that of The First's residence (*house*), that of the office (*Miralles*) and mine (*P.José*). Other numbers like *Taxi, Insurance*, and *Pumares* were relatively easy to identify and the list was whittled down to seven unknowns. The telephone number of The First's secretary was probably one of them, but I couldn't remember her first name. Probably it was the one that went with that very familiar *Lali*, but to save time I decided to put in a call to Milady.

'Gloria, it's me, Pablo. Any news?'

'Nothing. And you, have you got anything?'

'Nothing concrete. Listen, I'm calling you because I need your help with something. Do you know how Sebastian's phone works?'

'Well, it's like any other mobile, I suppose.'

Some help.

'One other thing: have you got paper and a pen handy?'

She did not. I was put on hold as she went to locate them.

'I want you to copy down some names I'm going to read off to you, and tell me if any of them rings a bell. I found them in the phone directory in Sebastian's mobile. And I want to know whose numbers he has stored. Ready?'

'Ready.'

'Okay, so here goes the first. *Llava*. L-L-A-V-A. Sound familiar?'

'No.'

'Okay, second one: *Vell Or*. V-E-L-L space O-R.'

'Vell Or, no, nothing.'

'Number three: *Mateu*. M-A-T-E-U.'

'Well, that one, yes. That must be Lluis Mateu, our lawyer. We had dinner together once, with his wife. He looks after Sebastian's legal matters, has done for years.'

'Very good. Next one. *Lali*. L-A-L-I.'

'Yes, that must be Lali's . . . 410 7690, is that right?'

'Right. Our friend the secretary?'

'Yes.'

'That's what I figured. Okay, next: *Villas*. V-I-L-L-A-S.'

'No idea.'

'Next one: *JG*, looks like a pair of initials. Are you writing this down?'

'Yes. But I don't recognise that one either.'

'Next one: *Maria*. The usual, only no accent.'

'I don't know, I suppose I know a lot of Marias . . . maybe your father's old secretary, the one at the reception desk now?'

'Good idea. I'll check that out. Here's the next one. *Tort*. T-O-R-T.'

'Nothing.'

'All right, here's the last one: *Fosca*. F-O-S-C-A.'

'That must be the house number at Fosca.'

'What?'

'Fosca. It's a beach, near Palamós. We have a little house rented there. Does it have a Girona dialling code?'

'972. Yeah, I guess so. That must be it. Listen. I want you to take another good look at that list, see if anything pops out at you, all right? And if it does, call me. I'll be at home for a while, but if I'm not here just leave a message. Do you know how to activate the phone company's answering service?'

Star ten, double hash. I tried as soon as we hung up. Nobody deigned even to say go rot in hell, no pre-recorded chit-chat or anything. I hung up and then picked up again to see if it had activated. 'The Telefónica answering service informs you that you do not have any messages waiting for you.' Bingo.

The next order of business was to call the office. It was about five to seven, there would still be some employees in action there. As always, Maria picked up.

'Maria, it's me, Pablo. Listen, is your telephone number 323 4312, 93 dialling code?'

'How did you know . . . ?'

'I'm taking a class in telepathy. How about this one: does the name Tort mean anything to you?'

'Yes, he's the branch manager at the Banco Santander office downstairs. He comes around here a lot.'

Two down. I asked her to put me through to Pumares, and recalibrated my voice to a tone that would be convincing enough for him to take seriously the instructions he was about to be given by the good-for-nothing brother of his boss.

'Yes, Pablito, tell me . . . how is your brother doing?'

'Convalescing. But better, thanks. In fact, he just told me something he wanted you to do for him. He needs a list of all the phone calls that have been made from the office in the last month. He's sick of lying in bed and wants to use the time to figure out how to reduce phone costs.'

'He wants a whaaaaat?'

'A list. A compilation of information organised in lines, called "entries", and columns that are commonly known as "fields." Since the advent of the computer they are a very common sight in offices.'

'Don't give me that, Pablo, I know what a list is. What I mean is, where the hell am I supposed to get that information?'

'I suggest you call Telefónica.'

'Shit, Pablo, that costs money . . .'

If the order had come straight from The First, Pumares would have busted his arse to get it done on the double, but when someone like me came along, all he did was whine and moan as if I had woken him up at three in the morning with an order to bring me a strawberry parfait. I could have reminded him that his hiring contract also had my signature on it, as an equal partner in the company, but this wasn't the moment for arguing. And anyway, pulling rank is almost always useless when pitted against twenty years of conditioned reflexes.

'Listen, Pumares: I told you this is my brother's request, he's completely lost his voice and the doctor told him not to talk under any circumstances. Of course, if you don't believe me and prefer that he tell my father to call you . . . you do trust my father, don't you?'

The mere mention of the patriarch always has an astonishing effect. A long pause ensued, during which he let out a deep sigh before finally conceding,

'Very well. Tell your brother I'll see what I can do.'

The list of unknown phone numbers was now down to four, and so I made a second list with the remaining names to get a clearer picture of things and to see if anything jumped out at me. *Villas, Llava, Vell Or, JG* . . . It would have been perfect if *JG* stood for Jaume Guillamet, but things don't usually work out quite so neatly in real life. I decided to try a kind of reverse-deduction method: what telephone numbers would The First logically have saved on his mobile directory? His office, my house, his own house, my parents' houses in Barcelona and Llavaneras . . . *Llava*! I cross-checked in my own address book, and there it was, the phone number of my parents' house in Llavaneras. Bingo. I was all ready to kiss my reflection in the mirror when the phone rang. It was Lady First.

'Pablo. It just occurred to me that Sebastian, Lali and I often go to a restaurant on Marqués de Sentmenat . . . its called "El Vellocino de Oro." He often calls in advance to make the reservation for us. I thought maybe that was the "Vell Or" on the list. Does that make any sense?'

'All the sense in the world. I'll look into it right now. I'll ring you right back.'

I dialled the number. A male voice answered.

'Vellocino, good afternoon.'

I claimed a wrong number and crossed one more suspect off the list. The only ones left were *Villas* and *JG*, and so I mulled over them for a while, trying to identify the street locations by the three numbers following the Barcelona 93. *Villas* was a 430, a classic Les Corts exchange, specifically covering the vicinity of my own house, as well as The First's penthouse and office. JG was a 487, which meant nothing to me, although I thought I might try my luck by calling information. I dialled the number.

'"*Welcome to the Telefónica directory information service*" . . . Good afternoon, this is María Ángeles speaking.'

'Hello, María Angeles, how are you? I need to confirm a bit of information. The first three digits of a telephone number identify a specific geographic zone in the city, is that right?'

'Umm, yesss . . .'

What the hell did that mean, "ummm, yesss . . ."?

'Well, can you tell me what neighbourhood corresponds to 487?'

'Do you have the full number?'

I read off the number.

'Sarrià-Sant Gervasi.'

'You can't give me the exact address?'

María Ángeles was very sorry but she was not authorised to do so.

Sarrià-Sant Gervasi. That had to mean from Plaza Calvo Sotelo all the way the hell out to nowhere up the mountain toward Tibidabo. Who knew, that could even include Pedralbes, or even Vallvidrera . . . I never did get the hang of all the weird municipal zones within the city and I certainly didn't feel like getting up to speed right then. Anyway, wherever that *JG* lived or worked, he could just as well be The First's shrink, his antiques dealer or the crusty old tailor who makes those custom-made pretty boy suits of his (Jesús Gatera, Jacinto Garrafones, Juanito Gazuza, who knew?).

Enough hypothesising, I told myself, and decided to ring *JG* right then. I punched in the number, and had to wait before anyone picked up.

'Jenny G, good afternoon.'

Good God: kitty-cat voice, perfect enunciation. She sounded thrilled to have made my acquaintance. Whorehouse. Unquestionably. It threw me for such a loop that I had to stall a couple of seconds, to think of what to say. I solved the dilemma by faking the voice of a fortysomething gentleman looking for some exotic-type action.

'Yes . . . uh, Jenny, please.'

'Are you . . . ah, a friend of the house?'

'No, no, not exactly. I'm calling on behalf of a friend of mine.'

'I'm terribly sorry, sir, I think you may have made a mistake.'

Good, good, good. Not only was my Magnificent Brother shacking up with his secretary, but he also got his rocks off at a whorehouse with a receptionist who was probably a Literature student in her spare time and said things like 'I'm terribly sorry.' At that rate, the prostitutes were probably descendants of the Romanovs. I began to envision The First in a whole different light now – suddenly he had morphed into a Magnificent Gangster with a camel-hair coat and monogrammed cigar.

I didn't want to leave anything hanging, and so I tried the Villas number next. After a couple of rring-rrings, it picked up but there was no answer on the other end.

'Good afternoon?' I said. 'Hello? Hello?' Nothing. I hung up, redialled to see if I had made a mistake the first time round, but once again, nothing. No sign of life. I even tried a third time, to no avail. Anyway. For the moment, I considered my telephone investigation concluded and turned on my computer. I logged on to the Internet and typed in 'Jaume Guillamet' on the Alta Vista dialogue box.

A vortex.

I started out by reading a report by the Spanish Association of Dentists and Odontologists which stated that sixty per cent of the adolescents in Granada currently suffer from dentomaxillary dysfunction due to maxillary overcrowding. To make matters even more interesting, a scientific study had revealed that only thirteen per cent of medieval skulls show evidence of this disorder. This tremendous discrepancy had led experts in the field to believe that a very serious pattern has emerged, though it was not clear whether they meant in Granada, in the Judeo-Christian Western world, or in the entire galaxy. Next up, I tried my luck with an article on the historical-pathological aspects of periodontal reconstruction, and then another item on the appropriate dental bridges for handling such reconstructions. At this point, I began to suspect that someone named Jaume Guillamet was a dentist and, in fact, found a number of documents bearing his signature, along with the title 'President of the Promotional Delegation of the Executive Committee of the Society of Spanish Ortho-Maxillary Surgeons and Gastroenterologists', a position which definitely smelled of dentist – and the expensive kind, at that. But this was only the beginning: after a bit of surfing I learned that there were various Guillamets involved in the Steering Committee of the Figueres Sporting Club; one Guillamet who had photographed the gravestone of Kiki de Montparnasse and who was currently the curator of the artistic patrimony of Andorra; a Miss Eva María Guillamet who, on her personal website, declared that her interests included Agatha Christie novels, camping, and meeting interesting people (not like her). I even found a taxi driver in Manhattan named Sylvester Guillamet, who had something to do with the New York Taxi and Limousine Commission. In mentioning the Taxicab Rider's Bill of Rights he did make special note of the passenger's right to oblige the driver to provide 'a radio-free (silent) trip.'

After half an hour of learning things that I had no need to learn about, I clicked on to the 'advanced search' option and entered 'TEXT: (('jaume guillamet *15 OR '15* jaume guillamet') AND 'barcelona') NEAR ('dir*' OR 'address' OR 'mail')' and waited to see if luck was on my side. It was. Only a few links came up, maybe half a dozen, and that is always an encouraging sign.

I clicked on to the first one. It was an enquiry regarding traffic fines that had been sent to a consultancy service. The enquirer had parked his Citroen BX, number plate B-blah, blah, blah next to a construction site located at Jaume Guillamet number fifteen. Apparently the city towing service had been obnoxious enough to tow the car and leave a triangular-shaped sticker stuck to the kerb in its place. The letter was dated January of 1998, which must have been when the work began on the apartment building across the way from the little house with the garden.

Alta Vista's search engine seemed to be in top form, though it wasn't doing me much good.

I clicked on to the second link and was greeted with an untitled page. The first line of text read '22th Juny' and underneath it, a massive list of schedules, names, and addresses. I scanned the first few paragraphs: the addresses were in cities all over Europe: Milan, Bordeaux, Hamburg, organised in what appeared to be a rather arbitrary fashion. The word 'worm' was repeated across the bottom of the page, sort of like a mosaic, with a dark grey, fake bas-relief background. The first thing that came to my mind was the conventional English meaning of the word: worm. I tried searching the site for the word *Jaume* and came up with, in English:

00:00 a.m.
G.S.W. Amanci Viladrau
Password: 25th Montanyà St.; 08029 Barcelona (Spain)
Address: 15th, Jaume Guillamet St.; 08029 Barcelona (Spain)

Interesting. I tried the third link, which turned out to be a mirror of the same page, only in French. The next link was in German, and the last one in Spanish. That was it for the search engine's responses. I couldn't imagine what the hell it could possibly mean, but it was weird, definitely weird enough to continue down the trail.

The domain of the mirror site was worm.com, and so I went there. The first thing that popped on the screen was an undulating message which promised vengeance in the form of a virus to anyone who dared enter the site, and it immediately executed a MIDI with a depressing musical jingle. The idea was for it to look like some kind of system message, but it looked a lot more like the Mummy's curse. They were clearly trying to scare away the casual, easily impressionable surfer who had happened to chance upon the site. Precisely for that reason I decided to forge ahead.

For the intrepid web surfer who chose to load the page despite the ominous warning, the site had another initiation test prepared. Once the adagio was through, a chorus of voices came on singing 'worm, worm, worm', like a voodoo club about to sacrifice someone amid the echoes of their otherworldy howls. The screen had morphed into a black background with red and gold cabalistic symbols, and the visitor who wished to continue was asked to fill out a personal information form. Once finished, 'Worm' would send a password to the email address provided on the form. This tactic is pretty standard practice for dissuading the majority of visitors – people don't usually like giving out their email addresses just like that. I, however, have a collection of mail accounts at a variety of different servers, and it's about equal to the number of fake names I use on the street, so *no problemo*, as they say. I filled in the blanks – Pablo Molucas, thirtysomething years old, a fictitious Barcelona address, a random telephone number, *pmolucas@hotmail.com* – and hit enter. Instantly a dialogue box popped up saying 'OK.' In a few minutes, it said, I would receive a message with a password. I opened up another Navigator window and went to Hotmail, entered pmolucas and my password, and checked my In Box. Nothing had arrived yet.

I poured myself another coffee and lit a joint to kill time. It was almost hot. For the first time since the previous autumn I opened the living room window, and a mixture of air, carbon monoxide, and heavy industrialised metal fumes wafted into the room. After a few seconds the entire room smelled like bus exhaust fumes – but they were fresh, comforting fumes, and the atmosphere that had hung in the room for the past winter in comparison seemed downright stale. I love the smell of Barcelona – I don't know how people can survive in the country, with all that raw air drilling away at your lungs. I felt so content that I stood there and leaned out the window for the duration of the joint. Twilight in late June. Above the death rattle of the traffic, I could already hear the sound of a few firecrackers that some kids, unable to wait for the San Juan holiday, had fired off. Actually, I'm not a big fan of firecrackers, or fireworks, or any of those pyrotechnical displays that supposedly bring us back to the ancestral rites of traditional sun-worship, or some such bullshit. They always seem so progressive and modern to me, all that pseudo-populist paraphernalia.

I returned to the Hotmail window and refreshed. I had one email waiting in my In Box. 're: Worm Key' it said. I opened it and read the following message: 'Tell the WORM you are pmolucas_worm.'

All that mystery, and this was it? Anyway. I went back to the page with the chorus of ghouls and entered 'pmolucas_worm' in the little box, though it only led me to the third step in the initiation process. This was all starting to feel like an Indiana Jones movie, and so I decided to give them exactly fifteen more minutes of my time – any more and they could all to go to hell. This time, a message appeared telling me that if I wanted to continue on the site I had to read a text passage and answer a series of questions about what I had read. First I looked at the questions, to see if they could be answered without reading the thing, and despite the fact that the possible answers were limited by a drop-down menu with multiple-choice answers, they all made references to very common first names and asked for specific facts relating to a story I had never heard of before. For example, what Lord Henry was carrying in his hand when he met the Queen. That sort of thing, twenty questions in all. I tried first by picking answers at random from the drop-down menus, but when I hit enter, all I got was an unequivocal 'Read *The Stronghold* and try again', and was then returned to the questionnaire page. *The Stronghold* was the text they wanted you to read in the earlier frame. I wasn't very sure what 'stronghold' was supposed to mean, and so I clicked on the right-hand button on my mouse to enlist some help from the Babylon translator. 'Fortress,' it said, or 'strong fort.' Very interesting. For the moment, I chose to click on the link that said 'Download The Stronghold, 1kb', and saved it on my hard drive. Once the transfer was complete, I disconnected and opened it in Word: seventy pages of text, divided into stanzas. Too many. I thought about skimming over a few verses onscreen, figuring I could avoid reading the entire thing. I had my reasons: I was hungry, I had a Magnificent Brother to rescue, and this wasn't exactly the time to dive into a discourse of esoteric gibberish, most especially if it was written in that convoluted English pock-marked with unintelligible monster words. But there was no way around it: even before I got through half a page, I got the sense that I had hit the bullseye with this one.

It went something like this: rainy night, someone arrives at the door to a citadel. The entrance has an awning that protects the visitor from the rain, an iron doorknocker in the shape of a hand curled around a ball, blah, blah, blah, four or five other atmospheric details and then – attention, please – a red rag tied to the lantern that illuminates the threshold.

Very coincidental. Too coincidental. So I had no other choice but to fill up the paper tray and print the entire document. It would easily be half an hour before it was ready, but I decided to be patient and wait to have it all down on paper so as not to waste away my eyes on that medievalesque madness.

In the meantime, I sat down in the living room to think about how in the hell I was going to spend the following few hours. I had to eat something. I *always* have to eat something. Sometimes this is a marvellous thing because I actually feel like it, but other times it is nothing more than the bother of an empty stomach, or else the signs of physical weakness forcing me to interrupt my drinking or smoking or some other enjoyable activity. One thing is for sure, though: when I have money in my pocket it's always easier to resolve the matter. And at that particular moment I had money. All I had to do was get myself over to a restaurant and order. The Vellocino de Oro, for example – why not? I might even be able to find something else out about my Magnificent Brother, who seemed to have been abducted by a cult of fanatics – *worm, worm, worm*, etc. Clearly it would be better to show up with a date. Preferably a woman. When attempting to get information out of a waiter, it's always far less suspicious when you do it as a couple, and in any event it's always more entertaining than eating alone. Fina, though, was not a possibility – eating two days in a row with her could very well prove slightly indigestible, and if my memory served me right, it was Saturday, a likely reconciliation day with good old José María.

The more plausible alternative, then, was Lady First. With her, it would be even easier to get in good with the restaurant staff. They knew her: her, her husband, and her husband's lover. The Lalala trio.

I went back over to the phone and rang her.

'You were right: *Vell Or* is a restaurant.'

'I figured as much.'

'Listen, I was thinking maybe we could go there for dinner. That way you can get out of the house and at the same time try and find out if Sebastian and Lali were there after I last spoke to him. What do you say?'

'Well, the children . . . Veronica leaves here soon, at seven.'

'Why not just ask her to stay until midnight? Afterwards, if you want, I can drive her home.'

'On a Friday? She must have some kind of plans for tonight.'

'Ask her.'

She moved away from the phone for a moment and I waited. From the sound of her voice, she seemed kind of amused by the invitation. After all, she had been holed up in that apartment for three days already.

'Pablo. Veronica says all right.'

We agreed that I would pick her up at ten. That gave me four hours to kill. I hung up and sat there, staring at The First's mobile. Would I be able to get all the information I needed out of that thing, all alone, no instruction manual? Where the hell had I seen another model like it? I tried to visualise the scene. Suddenly a hairy hand came into view, rubbing it with a delicate touch, a thick silver ring on the thumb, short beard around a pair of lips just like Edward G. Robinson's. I even thought I could make out a strange accent, a voice kind of like Cantinflas . . . ah, that was it. Roberto. That resolved the telephone issue, but it was a task I knew I should leave for later. Right now, my time would be better spent by taking a look at the text that my printer was currently spitting out.

And so that was what I did.

I should point out – now that we are getting to know each other, you probably expect as much – that ever since I decided to repress my bourgeois interests in literature, reading has become a terrific bore. In fact, advertising is about the only thing capable of providing me with some degree of aesthetic satisfaction, as well as a profound sense of moral well-being, a kind of spiritual peace. I say this to give an idea of how unexcited I was about reading that damn document all in one go, and to warn you that I have no intention of summarising the insane story that I so copiously read that day for the first time. Moreover, in the last few months I have had to bust my arse reading the thing so closely that I could practically repeat it word for word if I had to, and if I manage to record the conclusion of this story, perhaps it will be clear why. And anyway, at this point I am completely saturated by the thing. I will only say that it recounts the trials and tribulations of Lord Henry, a young gentleman who, one rainy evening, arrives at the door of the Fortress, grabs the red rag hanging from a post and knocks on the door. From there, he enters this edification, a kind of castle of infinite dimensions, and embarks on a Kafka-esque plot which includes only six characters, strongly archetypal ones at that: the King, the Queen, the Wizard, the Troubadour, Lord Henry (who turns out to be a kind of crown prince) and a Lady Sheila (who functions as the betrothed princess). Of course, the infinite fortress immediately reminded me of Mr Kurtz and the knitting brigade, which only served to confirm, once again, the oracular quality of my dream life, but it also reminded me of something else, something even more important. It was extremely obvious that this entire, absurd tale only had meaning when seen as an allegory, and in that case the various episodes could be interpreted as the exposition of a series of historical-philosophical systems, specifically in their more metaphysical variants. The odd thing, though, was that the writing did seem genuinely medieval, and as I read it I half-expected the author to start in with the Ionic philosophers and end up around Francis Bacon (or Kant, in the event the author was a guy with a vision for the future). But no: he continued on for centuries and centuries, all the way down to Russell, Wittgenstein, and even further on. But – attention, please – how much further can you get than Wittgenstein?, the pre-university student may ask. Well, for example, John Gallagher and Pablo Miralles (as opposed to Baloo, who is more a moralist than a strict metaphysic). I don't mean to get heavy but, to give an example, toward the end of the poem I found something very evocative of a certain Theory of Communication whose defence had forced an extremely renowned Semiotics guru (who can't bear people who disagree with him) to leave the Metaphysics Club, indignant. Pure avant-garde. And in verse, no less. Signed by some guy named Geoffrey de Brun.

Seriously flabbergasted, I tried to make some sense out of my thoughts – I had been reading for three hours straight, smoking one joint after the other, not to mention the Cardhu-and-aspirin breakfast. I reread, at random, some verses in an attempt to find the trap, but my English is exclusively contemporary and as soon as something sounds vaguely like Laurence Olivier doing Hamlet, it's instantly medieval to me. The next step, then, was clear: I would have to send the thing to John and ask him to read it and, if he found something strange about the narrative form, ask him to send it on to someone able to perform some serious linguistic stomach-pumping on the document.

At that, I got up from the sofa, approached the computer, rapidly wrote out a message for John and attached *The Stronghold* to the email. I logged on, sent it to him, and then returned to the sofa to light my umpteenth joint. It was eight in the evening. I had over an hour to kill. I was thirsty, so I got up with the intention of going into the kitchen for something to drink, but after a second my arse was back down on the sofa, victim of a sudden drop in blood pressure. And since fainting, to me, is an unacceptable manifestation of weakness, I took advantage of the moment instead to take a little twilight nap in the living room and save my image just in case anyone had installed secret cameras in my living room.

Appearances have to be kept up. In the end, they're all we've got.

THE INCORRUPT ARM OF ST CECILIA

There is something magnificent about falling asleep, but there is also something equally grand about waking up, feeling that the world is, in some way, a new place. To be awake all the time must be utter madness: I heard somewhere that a cat subjected to sleep-deprivation torture will eventually develop suicidal tendencies. I don't know if that has been proven, but I believe it. And if it hasn't been proven, it wouldn't be due to a flawed hypothesis, but rather a flawed cat that simply didn't fulfil it. *I know that, so it is*, as John would say.

I was starving, but my brief siesta had at least restored some of my strength. Eight-thirty. Definitely enough time to take a shit. Then I felt like showering again. Clearly, I had gotten caught in some kind of compulsive hygiene cycle. Well, whatever: it wasn't anything serious, so I gave in to it. Anyway, dinner with Lady First at a twenty-five-star restaurant definitely called for a bit of personal grooming and outfitting and I actually dedicated a whole minute to selecting the shirt I would wear. I had already used the black and the aubergine, which left seven immaculate specimens from which to choose – plus the Hawaiian number, but that didn't seem appropriate for the occasion. I tried the orange one, and the man I saw reflected in the mirror was none too shabby-looking: I looked like I could be the Flintstones' gas-meter guy. Or no, better yet – Bill Gates's gas-meter guy. I even rehearsed a few rapper moves, as if I were some dude arguing with a traffic cop in the middle of the Bronx. Then I recited the Our Father in English, as an improvised underground rap lyric. I knew my histrionic side would come out sooner or later – I have to eat, crap, sleep and act like an idiot at least once a day. If not, I start feeling under the weather. I can go without drinking, on the other hand, for up to forty-eight hours, and without fucking, much more.

I gave myself a splash of the expensive cologne and went out to the street, remembering to bring with me The First's mobile and the keys to the Beast.

I made my way to Luigi's bar at a leisurely pace.

Roberto had already begun the night shift.

'Roberto, you wouldn't happen to have one of these walkie-talkie things, would you?'

He craned his neck a bit to see what I was talking about and nodded yes.

'Uh-huh,' he said.

'And does it have a memory that saves the calls it receives, like with the number and everything?'

This marked the beginning of a lengthy discourse on the topic. I can't reproduce it exactly because I didn't understand most of what he said, but I do recall him discussing the differences between receiving a call from a regular phone, from a mobile (pre-pay or monthly calling plan), from a Spanish transmission station, from a European satellite, and on. A frighteningly complicated mess.

'Okay, Roberto. Focus. Now, if I want to find out the number of the last call this thing received, what the fuck am I supposed to do?'

He snatched the mobile from my hands, hit the little button that lights up the display and after a few moments pronounced: 'It's blocked. You need a password.'

This did not seem like a good sign.

'And so . . .'

'Well, if you don't have the password you can't access that part of the telephone book. Unless you buy another phone card.'

Immediately he launched into another technical lecture, on mobile phone cards and satellites, and this time I let him ramble on as my mind wandered onto something else. It was a long shot, but maybe Lady First knew the goddamn security code. In any event I didn't have time to think about it much more because, all of a sudden, the phone began to ring, peep-peep, some queer sound that nevertheless jolted me. Roberto stopped cold and gave the mobile back, his face looking shocked at my own shock. I thought fast: I have to answer it – it could be a lead, I told myself – I can't let it ring and not know who called. So I hit the little button that had the little picture of an unhooked telephone receiver.

'Yes?'

'Pablo José! Would you mind explaining what you are doing with your brother's telephone?'

My Mother's Highness: categorical tone of voice, somewhere between shocked and reproachful, like when I was little and she would catch me snooping in The First's bedroom for something meaningful to steal from him. For a second I was afraid that she was going to order me out of there im-med-i-ate-ly and threaten to tell my Father's Highness.

'Well, you see . . . Sebastian lent it to me.'

'He lent it to you . . . ? Where are you two?'

'I'm alone . . . here, near the flat.'

'Now, don't tell me that you went all the way to Bilbao and back just to get your brother's mobile phone.'

'No, no. He left it at the office. He must have forgotten it.'

'Didn't you just say he lent it to you?'

'Yes, well, over the phone he gave me permission to use it.'

I still felt as if I was trying to get out of some childish prank I had played.

'Pablo José, don't you dare lie to me. I despise it when you lie. Maybe you can fool your father, but not me. You know that. I have been calling this number for two days straight and nobody has picked up, not once. And now suddenly you appear at the other end of the line . . . What do you mean Sebastian called you and not me? Will you please explain ex-actly what kind of a game you are playing, or would you like me to have a fit this instant?'

When my Mother's Highness threatens to succumb to a fit, measures must be taken im-med-i-ate-ly or else she follows through on her word – she's got the kind of mind-body control that would make the Dalai Lama look like an epileptic.

'Well, there's been a bit of activity . . . But I don't want Dad to know, and I'm afraid you'll let it out . . .'

'Pablo José! Tell me right now what is going on!'

Right. Nothing occurred to me at the moment. The best thing, when this happens, is to say the first thing that comes to mind.

'It's Torres. He's been hit by a car. He's at the hospital, in intensive care.'

'Who?'

Anyone who saw me at that moment, in the bar, in front of the counter with the cognac bottles, would have had no doubt as to where I found the inspiration to improvise that last name. And I had to thank Providence, once again, for not having placed a bottle of Licor 43 in front of my eyes. I got even more out of the bottle, too.

'Torres, Ricard Torres. Don't you remember him?'

'No. Not at all.'

'He was one of Dad's business partners. Right around the time of the Ibarra mess. Remember what I told you about Ibarra?'

'Yes: that rude man who had your father hit by a car. What I don't see is what one thing has to do with the other . . .'

I feigned impatience.

'Mom, you're not paying attention. The fact that in the space of two days they hit Dad and then his business partner, doesn't that tell you something?'

Silence. Deep, shocked breathing on the other end of the line.

'Good lord! Do you mean to say that that . . . obstinate man is continuing to . . . ?'

Only my Mother's Highness would think of calling such a person 'obstinate.' She inherited the tendency from my Magnificent Grandfather, who initiated her in the art of adjective collection at a very early age.

'Extremely obstinate. The situation is more serious than we thought, and Sebastian had to extend his trip. He called to warn me that he's filed a formal complaint against him in the Court of First Instance in Bilbao.'

I have no idea whether the Court of First Instance is the proper place to file this kind of complaint, but my mother was not terrifically interested in the institution's exact title. My mother does not collect names, only adjectives, and if I had told her he had filed a complaint at Benito Villamarín it would have made no more of an impression upon her.

To recap: the rest of the conversation was an endless

litany of all the domestic tribulations she was enduring. I did manage to ascertain that my Father's Highness was as foul-humoured as he had been before, that they had not exchanged a single word for the entire day, except when Beba was around to mediate, and that they hadn't left the house for the past two days. They had, on the other hand, received a visit from Gonzalito the masseuse as well as the regular members of MH's canasta club. Apparently, FH had been particularly disagreeable with them, and had refused to go to the library to smoke his smelly Montecristo – hence, the reason behind the silent treatment he was now receiving from her. Beba, on the other hand, had refused to serve the visitors their muscatel and tea cookies, stating that she was not a bartender and that if those gasbags wanted to play cards they could go and do it at a saloon. Beba does have her moments occasionally, and I know she does not like my mother's friends, but this time I did have to side with my mother: I mean, she really shouldn't have called her guests gasbags. And I also agreed that it was unpleasant on the part of my father to begin inhaling noxious fumes without first asking the ladies' permission, even if he was in his own living room. Anyway, everything was still under control, or rather under the systematic, habitual lack of control. The real down side of the conversation, though, was the fact that just as I was about to say goodbye I completely walked into the trap that she laid for me.

'I suppose you'll come over for dinner tomorrow night . . .', she suddenly said, as if it was so obvious it almost wasn't worth mentioning. As it happened, the next day was her birthday. I don't remember anyone's birthday except for my own and Albert Einstein's – two great men, born on the very same day – and even those two occasionally slip my mind, and so I rarely celebrate them. But considering the recent state of affairs, I thought it would be cruel to say no and confirmed that I would indeed be present. After all, my mother was turning sixty, a round-enough figure to justify the exception. As always, however, this bit of stupid sentimentalism only opened the door to a new set of problems. I didn't see the trap until after I'd already said yes.

'Marvellous. We'll be exactly five couples, then: a family dinner.'

'Five couples?'

'Five, in addition to your father and me: Aunt Salomé and Uncle Felipe, Aunt Asunción and Uncle Frederic, the Blascos, their daughter Carmela, and you . . . You know, Carmela – the girl I told you about . . . the bohemian.'

And a brave bohemian she was, to have accepted an invitation to dine with her parents at the home of my parents, in the additional company of two older couples whose masculine halves were, respectively, a bigwig in the conservative Convergència i Unió party and an ex-General of the Spanish Army. Of course, knowing my MH, it was highly probable that the unsuspecting Carmela had also gotten herself caught up in my mother's matchmaking shenanigans. My Mother's Highness is capable of getting the president of the Gay and Lesbian Alliance to put on a mantilla and attend a mass for the head of the Opus Dei. It's one of her specialities. Anyway, after I agreed to turn up at their house at nine on the dot she let me go without any more hassles.

Roberto, seeing me all wrapped up in such a complicated discussion, had disengaged himself and was now fiddling with the remote control for the television. He appeared to be looking for a station with the most aesthetically offensive content, and ended up settling on BTV,

Barcelona Television. It was ten to ten according to the clock behind the bar, just enough time for a vodka shot before picking up Lady First. But as I contemplated the TV people conducting an interview with a young painter in the heart of the Barrio Gótico, I started to get depressed and decided I had to get out of there, my taste buds dry and unsatisfied. I don't know what it is about those progressive trendsetter types, they always end up depressing me.

Once I was back out on the street, I looked for the spot where I had parked Bagheera. There she was, laying low as usual. Someone had left a bunch flyers on the windshield: pizzas, a car-wash, a parking garage, a parking ticket . . . I leaned over to remove the sheaf of papers, blew Bagheera a little kiss and left her there, where she was clean and happy. I arrived at the home of Lady First just before ten o'clock and buzzed her from downstairs. She answered it herself. She was ready.

'Be down in thirty seconds,' she said, which gave me time to take three or four drags off a Ducados before she came bounding out of the lift. At least she didn't make me wait forty-five minutes like Fina had.

'I didn't think you would be so punctual. You're not exactly known for that,' she said as she walked out the front door of the building.

'I'm sorry, I didn't mean to disappoint you.'

I actually meant that, but I think she took it as a joke. She was wearing a pair of eggshell-coloured pants, turtleneck sweater, navy blue jacket, and navy blue shoes. The outfit revealed a slim, well-shaped silhouette – not exactly my type, but she did make you kind of want to check her out from the corner of your eye. She wore her hair in that Greta Garbo style that was so very becoming. When completely tranquil, she had a rather mysterious, and not entirely disagreeable air about her: a woman with a past, Oscar Wilde would have said about her. We didn't speak at all as we walked over to the restaurant, which gave me time to think about what kind of attitude I ought to adopt for this encounter, but I came up with three different points of view that spawned so many alternative solutions and options that were so incompatible and contradictory that I decided to blow them all off and improvise as the evening unfolded. We only walked for a couple of blocks, but the silence was as thick as that of a championship chess match.

We reached the vestibule of the restaurant: a potted plant with hibiscus flowers, a stand with the menu and a golden sign proclaiming 'El Vellocino de Oro', traditional country cuisine. It was one of those places I had passed a thousand times without ever going in. Until then, I hadn't even noticed that it was a restaurant.

Once inside, we were greeted by a girl in a black vest and white lace cap, who was in charge of the reception zone and the coat-check. She seemed to know Lady First.

'A table for two, please, Susana. The usual one, if possible,' said Lady First.

'Of course. I'll go tell Don Ignacio you're here.'

Don Ignacio, no less. For a moment I envisioned Paco Martínez Soria, dressed up as a rural priest, but I was only half-right on that one, as I would soon find out. The Susana chick wasted little time in nodding her welcome. We walked through one of two passageways framed by velvet curtains and entered the main dining room. On either side of the entrance were two huge goons dressed up in dark suits, with their arms crossed over their chests. If there's one thing I don't like, it's guys who are bigger than me, much less two at a time, much less on either side of an exit door. The decor of the restaurant was dark, very dark: a dozen tables at the most, lit with little candles. From the back of the room, a kind of Minister of Foreign Affairs approached us with unbridled enthusiasm.

'Mrs Miralles: we thought you'd abandoned us.'

He even dared to take the hand of Lady First in his and plant a light kiss on it. As far as I'm concerned, there is nothing dodgier than a guy who kisses ladies' hands (unless the lady in question has just smeared Ponds on her face, in which case kissing her hand is the only viable option), but experience proves that the sweeping majority of women eat that stuff up. And if that's what they like, then the fools deserve to be treated like sexual objects.

Lady First seemed to be expecting this treatment, and had even raised her arm up to facilitate the manoeuvre.

'Don't be silly, I was here having dinner with Lali and Sebastian not two weeks ago.'

'Precisely: two weeks without so much as an appearance is absolute cruelty on your part.'

I began to get an idea of just how much dough the Lalala trio dropped in this joint. The guy smiled from ear to ear and maintained that perfectly obsequious mien, leaning forward ever so slightly. Fiftysomething, good height, silver hair, skin well-burnished by exotic sunlamps and wearing an impeccable dark suit, with a little hankie in the breast pocket to boot. No a trace of Paco Martínez Soria – he looked more like Mario Vargas Llosa, only with less teeth. He didn't even look at me until Lady First did the honours.

'I'd like to introduce you to my brother-in-law Pablo Miralles, Sebastian's brother.'

The guy offered me his outstretched hand as if he was about to award me a medal for belonging to my Magnificent Family.

'Mr Miralles . . . a pleasure to meet you. Please know

that the brother of our most favourite client is also our favourite client.'

I smiled.

'I wouldn't be so sure, Don Ignacio. You should know that the transitive property is not necessarily applicable in just any case.'

'Very true, but I am sure yours is not just "any case."'

Clever guy. He turned back to Lady First.

'Your usual table?'

'Please, if that's possible.'

He ushered us over to a little corner with a round table set for four, protected by two screens that were, at the moment, folded up. Then he went through the little routine of pulling out Lady First's chair and pushing it back in, practically up her arsehole, as she sat down.

'May I offer you a drink while you look at the menu?'

'Yes, for me the same as always.'

'And for you, sir . . .'

I could have gotten conventional so that the game could continue in peace, but I went a little overboard.

'Do you know how to make a Vichoff?'

'No, I'm afraid not, but if you tell me how . . . our bartender will do what he can, I'm sure.'

'It's easy: ice-cold vodka mixed in a blender with a few drops of lemon juice. Served in a tall glass with plenty of ice. Add equal parts of very cold Vichy water, and a sprig of mint if you wish. If you are out of Vichy water, any kind of soda water will do. And if you are out of bartenders, any kind of waiter will do, as well.'

The guy remained implacable.

'Nothing to fear, in this restaurant we never run out of anything, not even patience. So . . . Campari with an orange twist and a . . . Vichoff?'

My companion nodded her head. The guy took a step backwards, made a half-turn, and left us alone in a silence that was interrupted only by the light clink-clink of cutlery against plates. Two-nothing. Good for Don Ignacio.

Lady First seemed to have enjoyed the little banter.

'I should warn you that he is quite accustomed to dealing with the devil himself. And I mean that literally.'

'Yeah, he does kind of look like one of Satan's helpers . . .'

'No, I don't mean it like that . . . he studied theology in Rome. He took his vows as a priest and went to Rome to be one of Paul VI's advisors. Among other things, he was in charge of documenting the exorcism solicitations that the Vatican received. You could spin your neck 180 degrees and speak to him backwards in Latin and he would still come up with an answer for you.'

'Right. And the devil tempted him with avarice and so he ended up opening a posh restaurant in Barcelona.'

'He hung up his habit when the Pope died. Well, in reality, he fell in love with one of the nunzio's nieces. Ever since then, he's travelled a great deal and has a daughter who is the living image of her mother, who died during childbirth. Very novelesque, the whole story.'

'I'd say you've grown rather fond of the Exorcist. Are you planning to write some 500-page Tolstoy-type thing?'

'I don't write anymore. I drink, which is more satisfying.'

Just then a bow-tied waiter arrived with the drinks. Then the Exorcist reappeared and waited for my verdict on the Vichoff. I pulled out the mint sprig, tried it, and nodded my assent. With a reverential flourish he withdrew, and I turned my attentions back to Lady First. What with all the chitchat we hadn't even looked at the menu. I opened one and gave it a quick once-over: sea bass a la *ciboulette*, sole with blackberries and other such exaggerations. I asked Milady to order me something elegant. She asked me about my preferred dishes. I told her general edibles and left it at that. When the bow-tied waiter reappeared to properly set the table, Lady First ordered a vegetable consommé, *txangurro*, Solán de Cabras water and an unspecified white wine to start. Once again we were alone. I thought it wiser to wait for the appetisers to arrive before launching into the Looking-for-The-First issue; by then we could be sure that we wouldn't be interrupted again. Personally, I would have been perfectly content to just sit there quietly sipping my Vichoff, but Lady First seemed determined to get me to talk.

'So. Now it's your turn to tell me about something interesting.'

Shit.

'Did you know that dentomaxillary dysfunction due to jaw overcrowding affects sixty per cent of adolescents living in Granada?'

Silence. A baffled batting of the eyes. I quickly offered more details, to see if that would get her eyebrows to return to their normal position.

'As it turns out, the medieval crania that have been analysed only show thirteen per cent of this disorder, which makes for a rather striking difference. One would be inclined to look for a reason for the incremental shift, especially if one is a dentist.'

'But we are not dentists.'

Fina would have cared less about not being a dentist. With her, I would have made a face – that of a dentomaxillarially overcrowded child – and she would have laughed her arse off, with those noises that make her sound as though she's running out of petrol. But Lady First wasn't familiar with that kind of game.

'And what makes you think the explanation is a dental one?' I replied, as if trying to embarrass a lazy student. But it didn't have much of an effect.

'Well . . . I don't know . . . I don't understand what you're trying to say.'

'Pff, forget it.'

I tried to focus my concentration, once again, on my Vichoff. But the respite was brief.

'All right. He's back again now,' said Milady. For a moment I thought she meant the Exorcist and I even turned around to take a look, but she quickly clarified her statement.

'You're back to being the Pablo I've always known.'

'That you knew when?'

'Before this week: at my wedding, at the Christmas Eve dinners, at your parents' birthdays . . . scornful and pedantic.'

I overlooked the 'scornful' comment, because I almost agreed with her, but the 'pedantic' bit was really untenable. Me, pedantic? Me? After having resigned myself to maintaining a relationship with the members of my family, which is, in and of itself, an unprecedented show of humility?

'Excuse me, but I am not pedantic. You see, when a person is truly great, no amount of modesty can conceal his true stature.'

I said it so seriously that she sat there for a moment, staring at me with an equally serious look on her face. Then, very slowly, her mouth began to curl into a grimace of utter condescension.

'You know what I think?'

'Something very impertinent, I'm sure. If not you would have just come straight out with it.'

'I think that such tremendous self-confidence only serves to hide some kind of inner weakness.'

'Maybe. And maybe that weakness just happens to be my greatest strength, Miss Enigma.'

She was silent for another moment. Then her face changed completely, and her features reassembled into a complex expression of utter yet complicit resignation, if in fact such a face can be transformed as such.

'And you know what else I think?'

'Now it better be something flattering, to compensate for previous impertinence.'

'I think that outside of Sebastian, you are the most intelligent man I've ever met.'

She must have thought that was some kind of compliment.

'Oh, really? What about the Exorcist, then?'

She didn't have a chance to answer, because the aforementioned Exorcist suddenly appeared, asking if we were ready for our appetisers. Lady First nodded yes. Then the guy turned to me.

'I thought that sir and madam might like a Txomin Etxaniz *txacoli* to accompany the *txangurro*. A simple but appropriate wine for your selection. Fresh and very slightly acidic. I thought I would serve it at eight degrees centigrade.'

I thought about asking him if the appropriateness was due to the *txacoli* itself or to purely phonetic reasons. But I decided to keep my trap shut because arguing about the wine with this dude was not part of the plan for the evening. In any event, the way he insisted on talking to me in the third person was incredibly annoying, because it was such obvious derision on his part – derision toward the supposed vulgarity of my orange shirt, my flat-top hairdo, and the very notion of Magilla Gorilla dining at the Vellocino de Oro. But I chose to hold off on the full-frontal attack until a more opportune moment. Instead, I continued to address him as if he were a parish priest.

'I leave the wine in your hands, Don Ignacio,' I said, making sure not to forget the folkloric form of address. He nodded, turned and walked away with a glint of irritation in his eyes. No: avarice was most definitely not what the Devil had tempted him with, nor was it lust: it was pride, and that perfect maitre'd submissiveness he so masterfully imitated was just his particular form of penitence for all the copious sins he had surely committed. I thought about this as I watched the bow-tied waiter approach us with a little cart bearing our appetisers and wine. That was when the total feeling of major negativity washed over me. It happens to me very rarely, but when it does it is extremely unpleasant. I didn't like the place, I didn't like Lady First, I didn't like the Exorcist . . . I had to do something, immediately, something ridiculous, some kind of stupid practical joke, something truly worthy of Magilla Gorilla: jump out of my seat and start a rain-dance, anything to demonstrate the utter lack of order in the universe, to show that it is we who impose the order and that by just changing the vibe a little the entire universe will change and adapt around us. In other circumstances I would have done something, but this time I held back and sought solace in the thought that later on I could go to Luigi's bar and get good and drunk, drunk enough to fall asleep so that I could wake up again, hit the universe's reset button and start another goddam chapter all over again, in some other, better way. But now – now that I have the time to think at leisure about all that went on that night – I can safely say that my perturbed state that night was due to fear. I recognise this because I can now understand that it was a kind of premonition of another, sharper and more specific fear I would begin to feel in the days that followed. At that moment, it was nothing more than the undefinable, blind fright I hadn't felt since I was a child – background fear, light but constant, like the fear of darkness, the fear of that place that is calm for the moment but where anything could suddenly come popping out.

I got hold of myself. I finished the Vichoff and attacked the *txacoli*. It was time to cut out the game-playing and get some useful information out of Lady First.

'Are you familiar with a place called Jenny G?' I asked her, before filling my mouth with a small spoonful of *txangurro*. I pronounced it American-style, and fast enough so that anyone who didn't know what I was talking about would have to ask me to repeat the question. Her facial expression indicated that yes, she was quite familiar with the place known as Jenny G, but that she wasn't very interested in admitting it just like that.

'Jenny G? No. Why, should I be familiar with it?'

That was proof positive. She had repeated the name in perfect Spanish-ised English – *cheni chi* – as if she had seen it written down somewhere before. I didn't think much before answering, to tell the truth.

'Well, because from what I gather it's a whorehouse that counts your husband among its clientele.'

As soon as I said it and saw the uneasy expression come over her face I realised how unintentionally clever I had been. In the event that she had not known, the information was important enough to oblige her to adopt an attitude that would be very difficult to fake: incredulity, shock, indifference . . . in any case, it would have been extremely difficult to improvise.

She chose to surrender.

'You certainly haven't been wasting your time, I see.'

'I should remind you that it was you who asked me to investigate the situation.'

'I didn't think this would come up.'

'Is this another one of the secrets between you two?'

'I told you, your brother and I understand one another.'

'And Lali, too: you understand each other with respect to her, too?'

'Don't start in with that, it's not worth it. If Sebastian's disappearance had something to do with Jenny G, I would know about it. And that is all I care to share with you regarding this topic.'

'Well, now . . . you are back to being you again, my dear sister-in-law. The cold and disdainful woman I know from those Christmas Eve dinners.'

'Is that how I seem to you? Cold and disdainful?'

'Only when you drink Solán de Cabras water. Under the influence of whisky you seem much more compassionate. But I'd rather not waste time discussing our common relationships. I have a brother to save.'

'Don't forget, he's also my husband. And the father of my children. And you are investigating this issue because I asked you to.'

'Right. So we will be much better off if we can work together.'

'Just as I told you: this Jenny G business has nothing to do with Sebastian's disappearance.'

'How can you be so sure?'

'Please, just take my word for it.'

At this point, Lady First's word did not inspire much, but for the moment I had to accept it. And anyway, just then the Exorcist came back to aggravate us with more of his cloying courtesy.

'Was the consommé to your liking, Mrs Miralles?'

'Superb.'

'And the gentleman's *txangurro*?'

It was delicious, to tell the truth, but it pissed me off to admit it.

'Fine,' I said. Lady First then ordered our main dishes. Sea bass for her, and thighs of quail in onion sauce for me. When the dude finally left us in peace I reassumed the attack.

'What do you know about WORM?' I asked.

'What's that?'

'W, O, R, M: WORM.'

'As in, insect larva?'

'Exactly.'

'Does it have something to do with Sebastian?'

'I don't know.'

The main dishes arrived on the same cart, pushed by the same waiter, and followed by the same Exorcist who now came bearing a bottle of wine as if it was the incorrupt arm of St Cecilia.

'To accompany the quail, allow me to suggest a bottle of 1981 Anniversary Julián Chivité Gran Reserva vintage: tempranillo wine, aged in oak barrels. I brought it out from the cellar at eighteen degrees. Shall I serve it immediately?'

'That's fine. Just make sure those aren't Fahrenheit degrees, I can't stand my wine rock solid. And would you be kind enough to bring us a calendar that lists the saints' feast days, please?'

Luckily I had had the foresight to end the little show

with a question that would preclude him from striking back, leaving the game at two-to-one. He glared back at me with sparks flying out from his pupils.

'A calendar with . . . the saints' feast days?'

'Yes, one of those wall-hanging ones would be fine.'

'Very well . . . I'll see if I can find one in the kitchen.'

He hesitated a moment, as if trying to remember, and then retreated. Lady First waited for the waiter to finish serving us before asking me anything.

'What do you want a calendar for now?'

'You just follow my lead.'

I focused on my food, in search of a bit of personal privacy. The quail thighs were exquisite – I had to admit that, in addition to his ecclesiastical talents, the Exorcist had a very respectable kitchen. And now that we were halfway through the bottle of wine (mainly due to my indulgence), the world had started to seem like an amenable place again. Good grub and good booze. My fly even got a little loose, an effect I often observe after eating well. I suppose it's the idea-association thing: food-sleep, sleep-bed, bed-sex. The pressure of my boxer shorts was encouraging the process along, and I had to reposition my chair so that I could loosen my trousers a bit and leave room for the expansion. Luckily my cock has more volume than length, which made the manoeuvre less complicated than it otherwise might have been. It occurred to me that it might not be a bad idea to swing by Jenny G's later on, in the interest of the investigation. Maybe there I could find a professional sufficiently vulgar for my tastes – hints of cellulite, or an imperfect nose, for example. I didn't get too carried away with that line of thinking, though: from what I can tell, I must be the only guy of my generation who likes typical females. All the rest dream of Julia Roberts and grudgingly fuck the derivative specimen they resign themselves to marrying. It's sad for the women, but they deserve what they get, the foolish twits.

These profound sociological reflections lasted for the duration of the main course. Then the Exorcist returned. He appeared distraught.

'I'm so sorry, the kitchen calendar doesn't have the saints' days. I sent someone out to enquire at some of the neighbourhood establishments, but they're all closed at this hour.'

'Don't you have a date book, or a diary of some sort? Gloria, have you got one on you?'

Lady First did, indeed. She removed it from her purse and handed it to me. I began talking as I flipped through the pages.

'There's this client of my brother's . . . I can't seem to remember his name, but I have an idea. You see, Sebastian once mentioned that he had come here for lunch – or maybe it was dinner – on this client's saint's day, just before going off to a little party for the client. It was this week, I'm almost positive. Now if I knew the exact day, I would find his name listed among the saints of that day . . .'

The Exorcist came to my aid:

'Mr Miralles did come here on Monday, in the company of Lali and another gentleman.'

'Perfect. Let's see: Monday the 15th . . . St Modesto. That's it – Modesto Hernandez. Thank you so much, that was all I needed to know.'

'A pleasure to be able to help you. Would you like to see the dessert menu?'

We ordered coffees and then he trotted off.

'I didn't get lucky this time,' I said to Milady.

'Just to find out when Sebastian was last here you had to go and invent that ludicrous story about his client's saint's day? It was so complicated and farfetched, my God. I could have just asked him myself.'

Colombo clearly would have done a better job of it, but after all I am only an amateur.

'Did you know that Sebastian was here on Monday night?'

'Yes. With Lluis Mateu. The man who takes care of his accounts, the one I told you about over the phone.'

'Right. So we don't know anything new.'

Lady First did seem a bit amused, though.

'Good lord, what a name: Modesto Hernandez.'

'Well, it could have been worse: Filemón, Agapito . . .'

'Just like your "Molucas" alias. How did it ever occur to you to invent such an unbelieveable name as Pablo Molucas? I don't know how on earth that man believed you.'

'Who, Robellades?'

'Yes . . . speaking of which, where did you dig him up?'

'I found him on the internet. His website was so bogus I figured he had to be pretty legit.'

'Well, he looked like an encyclopedia salesman. I had trouble not laughing out loud just at the thought of having to pretend I was a "Mrs Molucas."'

'I don't know what's so unbelievable about it. I'm sure there's someone out there named Pablo Molucas.'

'Right. But that's his real name. Nobody would ever think of using it as a fake name.'

'That's exactly why it makes a good fake name. Listen, I once met a man whose name was Juan López García. He was once stopped by customs agents at the airport in Medellín, Colombia. They asked him his name, and he told it to them: Juan López García, from Spain. And can you guess what happened?'

'What?'

'They threw him in a cell behind bars and stuck their fingers up his behind to see if he had something hidden there.'

'And did he?'

'No. But after that, whenever a policeman would ask him his name he would say it was Herminio Calambazuli. When he said it he would pronounce every syllable, very clearly. Ca-lam-ba-zu-li, as if he was dead tired of the phone company sending him bills with his name misspelled. After that, nobody ever bothered to ask him for his passport. Of course, he actually ended up a whole lot worse off, but that's another story.'

'Why worse?'

'Because one day he decided to take advantage of the newfound impunity afforded him by his new name, and he smuggled in a hundred grams of coke. He forgot about the fact that those police dogs aren't exactly housepets. Six years. It could have been even worse, though,' I said.

The very thought of all this seemed to horrify Lady First, but she did seem intrigued. Writer stuff.

'And how on earth did you ever meet that kind of person?'

'I met Calambazuli 150 kilometres off the Norwegian coast. He had just gotten hold of a bottle of ninety-six-proof alcohol and he came knocking on my door one night, looking for some sugar.'

'Sugar?'

The waiter arrived with our coffee. I took the sugar packet and shook it in front of Lady First's eyes.

'You can't drink ninety-six- proof alcohol just like that. You need to dilute it in water and add sugar until it tastes like cognac. It's not Remy Martin, but it does get you good and wasted.'

'And may I ask what made him think that you would be able to supply him with sugar, 150 kilometres off the coast of Norway?'

'I was a kitchen prep.'

'On a ship?'

'On an oil tanker. Alcoholic beverages were prohibited, but it was a pretty boring place to be, so the boys did what they had to to get by.'

'No library on board, hmm?'

'Yeah, though I do think I once saw a couple of Simenon novels in Norwegian, somewhere on the ship. There were movies, too, though the programming wasn't exactly top-notch. If you like Kurosawa I wouldn't recommend you look for work on an oil tanker.'

'Right. And you like Kurosawa . . .'

'I get by on a bit of 96 proof with a dash of sugar.'

Lady First looked at me with very strange eyes, as if she was trying to turn me into a three-hundred-page Hemingway novel. They say that two tits have a hell of a lot more pull than two trailer trucks, but I know the real weapon, the secret weapon that women use for trapping men: the weapon of overt and obvious signs of admiration. Fortunately I am aware of this particular trick and I try to focus on the tits when I can.

'I didn't know that you had worked on an oil tanker.'

'Just that once. Three months.'

'And after that?'

'I went to Dublin to spend the seven thousand five hundred dollars I'd earned.'

'Why Dublin?'

'Because I met a guy, John, on the tanker. He invited me to visit his country so I took off with him.'

'You don't seem like the type that makes friends so fast.'

'I'm not.'

'So?'

'John had started work in the kitchen a few days after the rest of the preps. Some joker thought it would be a real gas to piss in his coffee cup and he thought I had done it. He called me a goddamn sonofabitch in Gaelic, I told him he was a shit-eating cocksucker in Spanish. In order to bring our words to life we gesticulated a bunch until we were finally *mano a mano*. He was pretty scrawny, but had that proverbial Irish spirit, and so he gave me a black eye as fast as he could. Which meant I had to use my sure-fire weapon against him.'

'You have a sure-fire weapon?'

'Of course.'

'And may I ask what it is, or is that top secret?'

'The Obelix Method. You'll find the reference in any respectable library. It basically consists of butting against your enemy at high speed.'

'And it works?'

'As long as the buttee is not much bigger than you. The one drawback is that you never know exactly what you're going to butt against, nor how you're going to land, so you run the risk of ending up as knocked-out as your opponent. That time we both ended up in the infirmary, in traction. And for two weeks we had no other choice but to talk. We started off insulting each other and we ended up revising the pillars of analytic thought.'

'Do you still see each other?'

'Not much. He's a professor of Ontological Thought at the University of Dublin now, but we founded the Metaphysical Club together and we stay in touch over the net.'

'The Metaphysical . . .'

'Club.'

'Philosophy?'

'Top-level philosophy. Cutting edge.'

Once again she looked at me as though I was a 300-page Hemingway novel.

'You are a very odd person, you know that?'

'I think you've expressed that idea at some other moment.'

'Obviously, but the more I get to know you, the odder you seem to me. There's something very radical in you and at the same time something extraordinarily conventional. A bit like Ignacio but another style entirely.'

'Right. I'm an unrepentant drunk and he is a respectable exorcist.'

'No, it's something else . . . For example: you don't seem very religious.'

'Well, I am. Quite devout at that.'

'I don't believe you. I can't quite picture you receiving communion.'

'It's just that I'm not a Catholic. I am an orthodox ego-deist. Hey, do you think the Exorcist will serve us another drink? All this talking has dried out my mouth.'

'Shall we take it in the salon?'

I had gotten everything possible out of this interview, and wasn't terrifically interested in prolonging the evening, but I felt it would be unkind to rush my companion home directly after dinner. Why not stay a while – I could start getting drunk right there and turn up at Luigi's later. We got up from the table and walked through more velvet curtains into another room, this time with easy chairs, low tables and a real bar with a real bartender, distinguishable from the waiters by his cherry-coloured jacket. There was also a little stage, or dance floor, presided over by a black grand piano. The First seemed to have a need for the presence of a piano at all times.

At the bar we ordered a whisky sour and a Vichoff, and sat down somewhere nearby to drink them. Lady First turned out to be one of those people who has never travelled at all, but who still believes it to be one of life's most enriching experiences, and so she peppered me with questions about peeling potatos, pumping petrol, and painting staircases to earn a living in various godforsaken corners of the earth. By the time we ordered the second round of drinks she had resumed her Miss Gloria persona, that of the lady who had discovered her unsuspecting, wayward brother-in-law to be both intelligent (not, as she had pointed out, as intelligent as his Magnificent Brother) and chock-full of real-life adventure tales. I tried to convince her that the one useful lesson I had gleaned from wandering around the world was that there wasn't much point in leaving the ten square kilometres surrounding my bed. She kept at it, though, choosing to interpret that comment as an exaggeration borne from my essentially cosmopolitan character, and paid no attention to me on that account. Anyway. To make matters even worse, at exactly twelve midnight, the woman who appeared to justify the presence of the piano came out onto the floor. And I say 'worse' because she was the kind of chick that drives me mad: two breasts like a two giant melons and a full, round bum that came together to create a silhouette reminiscent of a cello. On top of it, as she sat down on the piano bench, her dress rose up above her knees, and to reach the piano pedals she had to open her legs in a delicious allusion to that centre of gravity all women have, the kind my little man likes so very much.

I began to feel pressure in my diaphragm and realised

that I would not be able to focus on anything else, and so when that little mental-distraction machine started to warm up with 'Dream a Little Dream', I decided it was time to retire.

'Listen: what do you say if we go somewhere else for the last drink?' I asked Lady First.

'Right now?'

'I feel like stretching my legs a bit.'

'Well, if you want we can dance . . .'

Good God: dance.

'Impossible. I suffer from intercoastal hypochondria.'

'What?'

'A strange, fictitious malady that prevents me from dancing in any and all circumstances.'

She didn't hear me because I was already getting up (I had to reposition my little man before doing so), and she didn't seem very interested in arguing the point, so she got up as well. I was already headed for the entrance, trying not to look at the source of my discomfort, but Lady First stopped dead in front of the piano and actually exchanged kisses with the pianist, who continued arpeggioing D-majors to stall the tune she was about to play. Evidently they were friends. And when Lady First made a certain gesture, the lady actually turned to take a look at me. She smiled. I smiled. Then she let her eyes fall in such a way so that she could check me out unobserved. Then she turned back to Lady First. For a few seconds I had a flash: the room is empty, it's just her and me. I walk toward the piano, take a little nibble out of that bare neck of hers, unobstructed by her upswept hairdo. She is aroused down to the tips of her shoes. I kneel down before the piano bench, I expose her breasts, bury my nose in them . . . then I get to work between her legs, on the delicate skin on the insides of her thighs. She goes mad with desire, throws her head back, and frantically tries to wiggle her way out of her dress, thighs stretched up heavenward . . .

Lady First returned to my side and gave me a let's-keep-it-moving yank just as I was about to drop my pants. The bill was two hundred some-odd euros, including the drinks. I left a fifty so that Don Ignacio would see that I, too, could be generous with my Magnificent Brother's money. And finally we got out of there.

Street. Night. Moon. Etcetera.

'Where do you feel like going?'

'I don't know. I told Veronica that I'd be back by around one and it's almost half-twelve. Do you want to come upstairs and we can have something at the house?'

Well, that might abbreviate the procedure. I asked her if she wanted me to take the babysitter home, but it turned out that she lived in the same building. We arrived to find her watching a National Geographic documentary on the telly. That younger generation sure is something – as soon as they're alone they sit around eating bowls of Twixies with milk, mesmerised by entomological pollinisation in Bora-Bora. I left the two of them sorting out the domestic tasks for the following day, and went out to the terrace with the rest of the Havana bottle that I hadn't finished off on my previous visit there. Lovely view. I was still perturbed by the effect of the piano player, and all I wanted to do was jerk off right then and there, but I had so much alcohol in my body that I was liable to take off at any moment. Barcelona exhaled the first inklings of summer, *súbete a Colón, su-be-te a Colón.* Once again, I felt the urge to sing out loud. But this time I did it: *súbete a Colón, su-be-te a Colón,* without a thought to Lady First and Veronica. 'Human etiology, lesson number one: given the fact of a drunken man filled with desire on the eighth floor of a flat on Numancia, the man will sing.' *Súbete a Colón, su-be-te a Colón.*

I remember very little of the rest of that night with exactitude. I know that I hastily said goodnight to Milady, and I also know that I stopped at the Grupeto for a Vichoff refresher before continuing on to Luigi's. I also know that I drank everything I could get my hands on and tried singing everything from Jorge Negrete to more contemporary tunes. I remember Roberto doing backup ranchera music vocals, and Coyote and Roadrunner waving their silver-tipped hats and Luigi threatening to call the City Guard if we didn't stop making such a scene. I was delivered to my house in Coyote and Roadrunner's patrol car singing "*de piedra ha de ser la cama/de piedra la cabecera-a*" . . . I was unable to hit the elevator button, so I went up to the first floor on all-fours. I do remember having laughed at myself for that one – Magilla Gorilla crawling up to his animal cage.

What I can't quite figure out is exactly how I managed to get the key in the lock. But I must have done.

MICROSCOPIC EYELASH SPECKS

I wish I could say the Holy Virgin herself appeared before me that night, but what I saw was not terrifically Marian, at least not in the Biblical sense. Let's just say that a Feminine Deity did appear before me, but in a 3.0 version with an individual-use diving helmet and pressurised suit. For all intents and purposes, however, she was the Virgin Mary – one can recognise the archetype even if she isn't wearing a gossamer gown. She poised her begloved hand on my temples and smiled through the helmet visor. Very young: so young and she was already the Virgin Mary, I thought. Not even twenty years old. I perceived a balsamic, fresh aroma. My breath fell into rhythm with the sound of her breathing apparatus – though it wasn't Darth Vader-esque at all; it was more like an exquisitely perfumed breeze. The bed stopped moving, the room stopped its senseless oscillation, and everything was suddenly comfortable and calm. It must have been around dawn. After that, I was able to fall into a deep sleep. It was an intense experience, but I don't want to be too annoying about it because it isn't very polite to have privileged relationships with divinity.

At seven p.m. I opened my eyes. Plock: that was what the clock hands told me. My first move was to take a quick survey, evaluate the damage. With time and experience I have come to classify my hangovers in various categories:

there's the hammer-hangover, the heavy-duty hangover, the weird-hangover, and then there's the non-existent-hangover. I cite them all individually, though they generally present themselves in combination form such as the dry-hammer or the strange-existent-heavy-duty hangover. Well, this one was a new strain, a rare and marvellous variant: clearly, the twelve or fourteen hours of sleep seemed to have diffused all the unpleasant aspects of my condition. I could even entertain the thought of digging up a mop and cleaning up the little puddle of alcohol with bits of *txangurro*, croutons and minced onions on the floor. My Magnificent New Shoes had received some extremely imperious mouthfuls and the sheets were also somewhat affected, so I decided this was a good moment to change the bed linens – something about their jaundiced appearance suggested the need for drastic measures. I actually did all this before wrapping my lips around the mouth of the tap. I prepared a pot of coffee, smoked a pair of joints and, resigned to my newfound obsession with hygiene, I showered and shaved, and when I was finally finished the kitchen clock read nine in the evening. Hunger, serious hunger. The idea that I was using up my reserves, burning the fat that is part of my innermost being, alarmed me slightly and I went running to the refrigerator in search of something that might stop the weight-loss process. I de-plastified a package of vacuum-packed Vienna sausages and ate half of them as fast as I could. As far as everything else was concerned I was clean and freshly shaven and in possession of an abundant closet of clothes. This time I chose to debut the Hawaiian number and it wasn't long before I was ready to leave the house.

I arrived at the entrance to my parents' house in the company of Bagheera. I hesitated for a moment, undecided as to whether I should park right there or head into the car park. FH owns only one car, which he never uses – invariably a navy-blue Jaguar Sovereign that changes as Jaguar updates the models – but he keeps four or five parking spaces in the building for visitors. The way he sees it, more than one car would be ostentatious, but fewer than five parking spaces would be rude. So I decided to go into the car park.

The guard must have recognised my Magnificent Brother's Lotus because he didn't utter a peep as I entered. To tell the truth, though, I was none too amused at the ease with which I entered the building: what good was a guard in the hall if anyone at all could get into the place? I consoled myself thinking that an unfamiliar car wouldn't have had it so easy, and searched for the Jaguar that would indicate the location of the Miralles domain. Next to the Jag was a silver Mercedes, a huge Audi, and a Golf – cars that I assumed belonged to my Illustrious Aunt and Uncle and the other guests. I left Bagheera next to the Golf, went up the private lift to the penthouse and arrived at the main entrance to the family duplex. I never like ringing the main door of my parents' house because I never know who will answer, but it was too late to rectify the situation. This time the kitchen maid opened the door. She had seen me the last time I had come around, but I guess she hadn't really noticed me – plus, since then I'd acquired a new look, so I found I myself obliged to introduce myself.

'Hello, I'm Pablo. Pablo Miralles. Mr and Mrs Miralles' son.'

She seemed a bit awkward, as if not quite sure how to address me.

'Would you mind waiting a moment while I announce you?'

So I stood there, admiring a most opportune Romanesque Annunciation scene that clashed horribly against a Ming vase. Absorbed in this contemplation, I assumed that the maid would return with permission to advance toward the domestic nucleus, but as it turned out my mother decided to do this in person. It was quite a sign, for my MH does not appear in the vestibule for anything but the *creme de la creme* of Barcelona society.

'Good lord, Pablo José – you look like a gangster!'

My mother always has a way of finding me somewhat vulgar. If it isn't a truck driver, it's a gangster or a construction worker or Al Capone's urologist.

'I'm sorry, Mom. Happy Birthday.'

Just then it dawned on me that I hadn't brought her a gift. I was about to apologise but she didn't even let me get a word in edgewise.

'Where on earth did you get that?'

She was referring to my Hawaiian-print shirt.

'Well . . . they were selling it in one of the shops.'

'Couldn't you have worn something more appropriate for the occasion? Carmela has arrived in a stunning evening gown. You are going to look perfectly awful next to her. And that thing there . . . ? Pablo José, will you im-me-di-ate-ly explain to me what that thing is on your face?'

She was referring to my Errol Flynn moustache.

'My razor messed up while I was shaving.'

'Well, you look like you're about to have a meeting with the Medellín drug cartel. Go, go in there into your father's dressing room and find something to put on.'

I obliged. What alternative did I have? Apparently, this Carmela chick was wearing a cobalt-blue number, and my Mother's Highness elected a silk shirt to go with it, along with a strawberry-coloured tie and a blazer in a bizarre wild-fruit-yogurt colour that, fortunately, did not fit me – my Father's Highness may be shorter than me but he is considerably wider in the gut area, and so she substituted this with a sky-blue suede jacket. I didn't find it particularly attractive, but at least the colour was slightly easier to describe. I decided not to look at myself in the mirror, and since my mother had gone back out to attend to her guests I went to the kitchen to see what Beba had to say before I turned up in the living room.

'You look like that actor with that nice voice, but with more hair . . . and you're more manly, too. Gorgeous, really, she said.'

Given the vagueness of her comment she could have been referring to anyone from Oliver Hardy to Woody Allen. Anyway, we weren't the only ones in the kitchen – a couple of bow-tied waiters (presumably the helpers lent by the catering outfit) were hovering about, and Beba always gets suspicious when there are strangers messing about in her kitchen, so she was probably more focused on taking care of her cutlery and glassware than on answering my questions.

The time had come to make my appearance in front of the guests. I took a deep breath, crossed myself and stepped forward into the threshold of the living room, for all the world to see. There were my illustrious parents, Aunt Asunción and Uncle Frederic, Aunt Salomé and Uncle Felipe, a sixtyish couple that looked to be the Blascos, and Carmela had to be lurking about there somewhere, probably hidden behind some Ming vase. I assumed this because at the moment she was nowhere in sight. As far as my aunts and uncles, I can say that my Magnificent Maternal Grandfather – collector of adjectives – had done quite a job of pairing off each of his daughters to a different interest group. Aunt Asunción had married into the pro-Catalonia bourgeoisie; back then it had been easy to see that their stock would go way up once the dictatorship ended. Aunt Salomé had gotten stuck with the armed forces and the fundamental pillars of the regime, and my Mother's Highness had been married off for cold, hard cash, which always comes in handy when any of the other apparatuses require greasing. It should be noted that my Father's Highness, though by far the most well-endowed of the family in financial terms, does not come from old money at all. He is, rather, a convert – the son of a carpenter, just like Jesus of Nazareth, though from what I have gathered my paternal grandfather was a bit more of a bruiser than St Joseph. My father, as such, retains a vivid notion of the common people, an understanding of what it means to make your first million, etcetera. The other two consorts, on the other hand, have surnames that go back for generations, and the most common people they have ever laid eyes on are their full-time drivers. Uncle Frederic – I believe I mentioned this earlier – belongs to the inner circle of the conservative Convergència i Unió political party and is up to his eyeballs in what he always calls '*el govern*' in Catalán. He says it like that even when he speaks in Spanish – a blasphemy he only succumbs to under extreme duress. Uncle Felipe is a military officer who retired with the rank of Major General. He wears eyeglasses with tinted lenses and a moustache very similar to my own, although I sincerely doubt his is a homage to Errol Flynn. As far as my aunts, I should prefer not to even attempt to characterise them at all – it would be pointless, really. All I can say is that the two of them should have switched boyfriends before getting married: some odd calculation error on the part of my Magnificent Grandfather produced two oddly star-crossed couples. And the third party of this exemplary group was the Blasco couple, who seemed to be a pretty well-off pair: I put them down for no less than five hundred thousand euros' worth of Banco Argentaria stock. In short: the scene was more than enough to populate a Tod Browning movie. And me? A vision of tranquillity.

The first one to attack was Aunt Salomé.

'Pablo José, darling, come and give your Auntie Salomé a big kiss.'

I began to distribute smooches at the rate of two per lady (aunts and non-aunts alike) and handshakes to the tune of one per beard, except in the case of my Father's Highness which required two extra kisses. When the round was over I was so wiped out that I almost forgot that there was still the missing bohemian to kiss. I looked around like someone scrutinising a Where's Wally picture, convinced that I would see at least her head, peeping out from behind some giant antique or something. But no: in addition to bohemian, the girl was apparently a midget or else I was as blind as a bat. My Mother's Highness resolved my doubts, taking me by the hand and pulling me out to the terrace.

'Pablo José, I would like you to meet Carmela.'

Fear.

I didn't like the first thing I saw as I stepped into the terrace garden. About ten metres from where we were, clinging to the one stretch of railing unconsumed by the abundant foliage, a tremendous cobalt blue bum suddenly appeared before me, round as a plum, a gluteus maximus that abruptly bloomed out beneath her waistline and with her little diamond mine very well-insinuated indeed under those evening clothes. I cursed my luck and wished with every bit of strength that she would have a case of rampant acne or – I don't know – chronic halitosis, or something extremely unpleasant.

When she turned around, I discovered to my dismay that she was also quite delectable from the front. But there was something even worse.

'Pablo, I'd like to introduce you to Carmela. Carmela, Pablo.'

'I think we've met before,' said the Bohemian Girl.

'Hmm. I'm not sure I remember,' I replied, trying to sound sincere.

'Oh, you already know each other?' said my mother.

'Yes, yes, I'm sure of it,' said the Bohemian Girl.

'Well, what a timely coincidence, wouldn't you say? I'll just leave you alone then, darlings,' said my mother, who rapidly disappeared from the scene after inventing an excuse.

There was only one way out of this: to be as grotesque as possible.

'Am I that bad a piano player? You didn't even stay for the first song.'

'Oh, yeah, right, right . . . The Vellocino de Oro. Sorry, I didn't remember you. Listen, do you mind if we go inside? It's a little cold out here.'

I said it in a slightly impatient but polite tone of voice, as if I was trying not to sound obnoxious, which of course is the best way to sound obnoxious. The chick reacted on the double:

'What's the rush? I'm sure your mother can find something to wrap you up in.'

With that, she turned her back on me to gaze down at the Diagonal, leaving me to face her sublime bum once again. I don't understand why these things always happen to me. I was tempted to rebutt the comment, but at the last moment I decided to behave sensibly and turned to go back inside to the living room. The last thing I needed was to start worrying about what this fraudulent bohemian thought of me, no matter how succulent she was. But my diaphragm had already wrenched itself into a little ball. Shit, shit, shit. It wasn't even going to be easy to get drunk tonight.

Inside, the conversation was split into two camps: the women were discussing cleaning supplies and maids, and the men, politics and business – in my family, you see, stereotypical upper-class social mores are strictly and faithfully observed. So I tried to distract myself from the knot in my stomach by floating about the room as if it were a museum exhibit. The truth is, my parents' living room is actually the perfect place for that sort of activity, I'm surprised they don't get school groups in there. I paused in the Contemporary Art section, next to the piano, and discovered a new acquisition – a Miquel Barceló, placed between the Juan Gris and the Pons that had always hung there. It was a bullring illuminated by the late-afternoon sun, painted from an aerial perspective, giving the spectator the feeling of being suspended in a helicopter high above the bullring. The effect was a bit strange, I don't know why, maybe because the idea of a bull together with a helicopter isn't a particularly harmonious image. It was a pretty repugnant painting, almost scatological. The spectators were represented by little blobs of brownish-greyish oil, like a mushroom colony languishing under the sun. It was a bullring, but it could have just as easily been a depiction of the scene inside a toilet bowl of a bar on the Parallel.

My plastic ecstasy was interrupted, however, by the sound of my father's crutches.

'I think I recognise that jacket,' he said.

'It's yours. The shirt and tie, too. Mom asked me to put them on because she didn't like what I was wearing.'

'Listen, do me a favour. Keep the jacket, at least. She makes me put it on for Sunday Mass, I end up leaving the house looking like the Virgin Mary. Take the tie, too, but don't let your mother know. You can stick it in the pocket, nobody will notice.'

So. The jacket was still a Maurice Lacroix, of the finest suede chamois, and with a t-shirt underneath it would have a completely different look. FH, however, quickly lost interest in my borrowed wardrobe, and was now facing the Barceló, his eyebrows furrowed.

'You like it?'

'What . . . ?'

'The painting.'

My Father's Highness is even more reactionary than I am when it comes to artistic manifestations, especially if they are contemporary ones, and so I knew that our conversation was in for a turn; it was just a question of leading him in the proper direction.

'Eighty thousand. You know him, this Barceló?'

'He's in the top ten, Dad.'

'Well, tell me, do you see a bullring anywhere in there?'

I made a face that said yes, kind of.

'Why are the spectators green, then?'

'Dad. Expensive paintings haven't been getting the colour right for over a century now. And anyway, if you think this one is weird, the Pons on the right is even worse.'

'My boy, I really don't know . . . At least the Pons is happier . . . it's got nice colours, at least. This one looks like some kind of lumpy cow. And the worst of it is that Barceló isn't going to die for ages . . . don't get me wrong: I don't wish harm on anyone, but as a rule I don't ever buy paintings by artists who are younger than me. Your brother picked this one out for your mother's birthday. He promised me that in ten years' time it would double in value. Speaking of which: do you know where your brother *is* these days?'

'Didn't Mom tell you?'

'I asked her, but she told me some cockamamie story. She's a terrible liar, gets worse and worse all the time.'

'What story?'

'That he had to go to Bilbao on business.'

'Well, that doesn't sound so weird to me.'

'Oh, really? And why is it, then, that you're driving his car?'

'How do you know I'm driving his car?'

'The guard at the car park downstairs told me that he saw Sebastian's car come in, but without Sebastian.'

'And how did you know it was me?'

'Because a big, fat man who drives Sebastian's car, screeches the tires, parks in one of my spots and goes straight to the private lift to the penthouse could only be you.'

'I didn't screech the tires.'

'You have done nothing but that ever since you got your driver's licence. What happens is, you don't even hear it anymore . . . And I am also aware that for the past several days you have been driving around in your brother's car and using his cash card. And that the day before yesterday you hired a private detective: Enric Robellades, ex-policeman and formerly the head inspector at the station at Laietana, number 83.'

I suppose I had some kind of dumbfounded look on my face.

'Don't underestimate your father, Pablo. Don't forget, when I came to this city forty-five years ago, I had nothing but a bag over my shoulder, a change of clothes and five hundred pesetas in my pocket. And can you guess the sum total of the recent estate appraisal I requested, to update my last will and testament? Come on: take a guess.'

I wasn't in the mood for guessing.

'I don't know, Dad . . . five million? Ten million?'

He held both crutches in one hand, grabbed my neck with his free hand and pushed my head towards his with a satisfied smile.

'The most conservative estimate put it somewhere close to twenty-five million. In more favourable circumstances that number could very well double – that's ten times what it was when I retired. Do you know what twenty-five million euros are?'

'A rather good measure of what you're worth.'

'Exactly: the measure of what I'm worth. And the measure of what you and Sebastian are worth, too. Either one of you is worth that amount. Did you ever think about that? Or did you think that you could just cease being who you are by living like a pig?'

'Dad, please do me a favour, stop beating around the bush already. Just tell me what the hell is going on.'

His smarty-pants expression changed into an impotent grimace.

'I don't know what is going on. I know that Sebastian disappeared with his secretary on Wednesday afternoon and I also know that you are looking for him. I know every single move you've made since you left here on Thursday afternoon. What I don't know is what's become of Sebastian.'

'You have people following me?'

'Of course I have people following you! If your brother's disappearance has anything to do with him being my son, then you're in as much danger as he is. Are you listening to me?'

I was listening, of course, but for a brief moment I felt a sense of relief that made me feel strangely absent.

I am not the kind of person who can endure the burden of secrecy for very long – the responsibility of behaving like a silent machine that pretends everything is all right it's too much for me. Years ago my life was so plain and simple: I fed myself with the cheapest items I could find in the supermarket, slept until I was sick of lying in bed, got drunk, got myself the occasional fuck, and maintained nonsensical email relationships with four other nuts scattered around the world. The truth is, I had managed to turn my life into a Baloo paradise, a peaceful existence in the jungle of life where everything I needed was within arm's reach. But then all of a sudden the world has a way of coming down on you, like a huge garbage truck lumbering down the middle of the road in which you are nothing more than a tiny car that gets bashed into. And for what I think was the first time in my life, at least in my adult life, I was glad to share something with my father, to not do things behind his back, to dump at least some of this bogus burden onto his shoulders.

'Do you think they've kidnapped him? That they're going to demand some kind of ransom?'

The look on my father's face said yes. Or at least it didn't say no.

'Well, I don't think so,' I said to him. 'To begin with, a kidnapper isn't going to go and slam into his ransom-payer before carrying off his kidnapping stunt. And they hit you, didn't they? I also don't think it's such a terrific idea to go and kidnap someone with their secretary included, someone nobody is going to pay to rescue, but who could very well cause problems. And that's not even considering the fact that nobody has gotten in touch with you to demand anything, or have they?'

'No, but that's not so strange. They always wait a few days to establish contact, to give you time to get nervous.'

'Whatever, but I doubt this thing has anything to do with you or your twenty-five million.' I almost felt bad disappointing him with that. 'Look. On Wednesday at noon, Sebastian rang his wife and told her to stick some documents in an envelope and then mail it to himself . . . I think all this has something to do with some dodgy scheme of his. Who knows what kind of mess he's gotten himself into, trying to cut one of those sweet deals you two love so much.'

FH shook his head left and right.

'But if all that were true, it wouldn't explain why a couple of goons went and crashed into me.'

'Maybe. Maybe it's exactly the opposite of what we're thinking: they decided to hurt you as a way of pressuring him.'

He seemed to be warming up, at least somewhat, to my own doubts.

'I don't know . . . I've been going mad the past two days.'

'It didn't occur to you to phone the police?'

'The police don't move a finger until the disappearance really turns into something odd, and in the meantime I'd rather not let Gloria and your mother in on the details.'

'You mean about Sebastian shagging his secretary?'

There. It was on the table.

'I didn't know you knew.'

'And I didn't know you knew. Gloria was the one who told me.'

'She knows?'

'Plenty.'

Now he was the one with the dumb look on his face.

'A modern marriage,' I said, careful not to mention Jenny G, just in case he hadn't gotten up to speed on that part. I also didn't mention anything about Jaume Guillamet 15. It was good to share a bit of the pressure with him, and I even liked that rather unfamiliar paterno-filial camaraderie that had sprung up between us – no reproaches or attacks – but I also knew from experience that it was better not to tell FH everything. Anyway, as far as the Jaume Guillamet issue was concerned, my suspicions still did not amount to much more than a pretty unreliable intuition on my part. Then, as if to confirm for myself that discretion was most definitely the order of the evening, I saw MH approaching, looking ready to scold us for huddling in a corner together.

'Would you mind telling me exactly what you two are plotting over here?'

'Nothing: I was showing Pablo the painting Sebastian gave you.'

'Incredible, isn't it? It has light, it has texture, it's so . . . so . . . ethnic,' said MH.

'Well, I still think it's a lumpy cow,' replied FH.

'Valentín: you simply do not know how to admire a good painting. You're better off not looking at it at all. You'll ruin it, I tell you.'

'Right. I may be no good for looking at paintings, but I'm good for buying them, aren't I?'

'Don't be so vain, my darling: anyone can do that.'

'Anyone who has eighty thousand euros to spare . . .'

'You and that obsession with the eighty thousand! Can't you think about anything other than money, even for a second?'

'Yes, I can. Why don't you ask those pretty boys you brought in here to serve us dinner already? It's after nine-thirty.'

'That was exactly what I came to tell you. Dinner is served.'

FH pretended say something to me, his eyes still firmly fixed on the painting.

'Let's hope that this time she ordered something to actually fill our stomachs. Last week we invited the Calvets over and we ended up eating some kind of coloured vomit. I can take the modern paintings, but don't mess around with my food.'

'Valentín: it is my birthday today and you will eat exactly what you are served. End of discussion.'

'Well, I'm warning you, if I'm still hungry I will go straight to Eusebia for a couple of fried eggs. And I will eat them right in front of your pretty-boy waiters.'

When we arrived in the dining room, the table was already set with a first course of whole baby lobster, completely peeled – claws included – and a dressing that consisted of two clumps of herb-type things that turned out to be seaweed, one bluish and the other sort of orange-coloured, which matched the smooth skin of the dead crustacean they accompanied. I had been placed between Aunt Asunción and the aforementioned Carmela. From what I could tell, the girl was still pissed off about the scene on the terrace and did not even grace me with a glance. Fine with me – that way I could concentrate on the lobster and avoid looking at her tits, which were currently teetering above her plate. Otherwise I wouldn't have been able to eat a bite. I tried the seaweed and found it to be completely indigestible: extremely bland and with a light fishy taste that did not jibe with their vegetable origins. But I was so hungry that I was the first to finish the thing, which left me with no other choice than to listen to the table conversation until the arrival of the second course. Uncle Felipe

– with his "For God and for country" moustache – was about halfway through a story about the evil conspiracies of the Masons, a topic he always brings up when he wants to piss off my father. As it turns out, my Father's Highness has always had a tendency to expiate his opulent lifestyle through philanthropy and, as such, he worked his way up to being the Grand Master of one of Barcelona's main lodges of the Ancient and Accepted Scottish rite. My Magnificent Brother is a Fellowcraft of the Temple (though his is a clear case of nepotism) and I suppose I would be at least an Official Security Guard if, when my father brought me to a First-Degree white-apron initiation meeting when I turned eighteen, I hadn't laughed out loud in the middle of the opening rites. I know that it was rather rude of me, but as soon as I heard my Father's Highness, gavel in hand, declare that thing of 'Let wisdom preside over the construction of our temple!' I couldn't help it and yelled out 'May the Force be with you!' Naturally, everyone heard me. I wasn't all that far off, however, because once the plebs stopped laughing the Entered Apprentice on duty answered with 'May the Force sustain you!' and by the time the second round of laughter finally subsided, I was fully convinced that George Lucas had to be a Mason, or at least a sympathiser. Ever since then, FH has barred me from coming within one hundred metres of the lodge, and so that was the beginning and end of my initiation process. Big deal: they don't even give you a light sabre – after thirty years of selfless dedication, the only thing my FH has ever gotten out of that bunch was a gold-coloured carpenter's square and it isn't even real gold.

'Well, I think you should accept women into the lodge,' exclaimed my Aunt Salomé, who is kind of a feminist.

'There have been cases. But I don't think it works. At

least not at our lodge,' replied my father, who is not at all a feminist.

'Oh, really? Well, I don't see why it shouldn't work,' said my mother who, while not a feminist, does like to disagree with the Grand Master whenever she can.

'Because we can't spend our meetings worrying about what dresses the women are wearing.'

Though I was very careful about expressing my agreement, in this case I was completely on FH's side. I'd love to see the smart little fellow who's able to concentrate on some harebrained ritual when he's got a pair of beautiful tits bouncing around the noonday pillar. I, for one, wouldn't have been able to touch the lobster.

'Well, you know what I think? I think the idea of men getting together exclusively with other men is pretty suspicious stuff.'

That was Aunt Salomé again. She likes to read the psychology columns in the home decorating magazines, and occasionally gets analytical on everyone.

'Suspicious of what?' My father was getting really pissed off now.

'Well . . . after all, cases of latent homosexuality are very typical among men who join exclusively masculine, strictly hierarchical organisations. The army, the clergy . . .'

This is where Uncle Felipe almost choked on his seaweed.

'What do you mean by that?'

'Meee? Nothing!'

'What do you mean, nothing? Am I supposed to listen to my own wife calling me a homo? I would think that you, of all people, would have proof of exactly the opposite.'

'Oh, Felipe, for God's sake, forget it, a person can't have a normal conversation with you . . . I am simply making a very general statement.'

'Oh, really? Well keep in mind that in fifty years I've never seen a single queer at the base. Now, things would be different in Spain today if the military service was still mandatory, I can assure you that you wouldn't see so much homosexuality all over the place. Television is disgusting nowadays, every time you turn it on you get assaulted by some built-up muscle hunk dressed up like a lounge singer . . .'

'Those aren't homosexuals, Felipe, those are drag-queens,' my mother piped in.

'Well, I think Felipe has a point,' interjected Aunt Asunción, slightly more subdued but also with well-formed opinions. 'To a certain degree, I think everyone should live the way they want to, but when it comes to airing one's dirty laundry on the television, what do you want me to say? Really, I just don't see why people need to go to such extremes.'

'I don't see anything wrong with the idea that people should be able to openly express their sexual preferences,' was the unexpected intervention from Carmela the Bohemian Girl, who seemed to be gunning for everyone to come out of the closet as soon as possible.

Sparks now flew out of her mother's eyes, which were firmly focused on her daughter. Was it possible that this respectable matron was a co-conspirator in my mother's matchmaking pretensions? The fact is, every time our eyes met her face quickly morphed into expression that had Magnificent Mother-in-Law written all over it, a Magnificent Mother-in-Law who would be overjoyed to see her aging Bohemian Girl daughter married off to the hapless millionaire. The father, on the other hand, seemed more interested in separating the seaweed from the lobster, an attitude that made me predisposed to liking him.

Soon after that, a rosemary sorbet (repugnant, period)

arrived, and immediately following that, roast beef, swamped in some kind of papaya sauce in which tiny little pasta bow-ties floated. No doubt MH had tasted such a thing at the banquet of some Very Important Spaniard and had decided to let us all in on her big discovery. Luckily, with a bit of knife-scraping I was able to offload much of the sweet mush and discovered that the meat beneath it was reasonably edible. By the time we got to dessert I was still trying my best not to utter a peep or make direct eye contact with anyone, while everyone else was busy expressing their firmest convictions. Everyone except Aunt Asunción, who tends to be a bit more discreet, and the father of the Bohemian Girl, who also knew how to keep his mouth shut in between mouthfuls.

Now, the part of these dinners that strikes the greatest terror in my heart is the after-dinner conversation. Just around the time coffee is served, when my Magnificent Parents have exhausted all possible topics relating to Culture and Society, they begin to ask me personal questions – almost invariably related to my marital status, my professional prospects, or my medium- and long-range life expectancy. There was a time when I enjoyed shocking them by improvising all sorts of aspirations that would be completely unacceptable for a young, upper-class brat like myself – getting my taxi driver's licence, or working on an assembly line, things like that. But at this stage of my existence – and, more specifically, given the circumstances at that time – I didn't feel much like scandalising my aunts and uncles. After all, the poor old farts hadn't committed any sin other than that of being conservatives (or right-wing, to be more exact) and that is an eminently easy sin to forgive for someone who has had the opportunity to mingle with left-wing intellectuals and ecological types – two groups that are way more difficult to deal with, as far as I'm concerned. And so, I somehow managed to apologise to my fellow diners and arise from the table as soon as we were through with the sweets. FH looked at me disparagingly (for the Grand Master, meals are not over until he lights a cigar), but I got up anyway. If I could hide out for a while, wait around for about as long as a good shit would take, I had a better chance of returning to a fresh conversation topic, one that was unrelated to me. And so I wandered around the apartment until I got to the back stairs, intending to go up to my old bathroom. Maybe I *would* actually end up taking a crap. After all, stinking up the main bathroom in the house's public space wasn't exactly part of my evening plan. But as soon as I opened my old bedroom door, I suddenly felt as if a time-machine had transported me back to the past.

I suppose, if I had been born into a normal family, the clan would have turned my bedroom into an ironing room, but in a duplex apartment of 700-plus square metres, with five suites, a library, servants' quarters, sauna, and an upstairs–downstairs terrace that wraps around the perimeter of the building, there is no pressing need to reconstitute the bedroooms of emancipated offspring. As such, my expensive, rich-adolescent trinkets were all there, exactly as I had left them fifteen years earlier. Even the huge bookcase overflowing with books hadn't changed. I confess: I have read books – I was young, naive. When I caught on to the plot I thought of burning that mountain of paper, but I eventually came to understand that burning books is as excessive an act as reading them: the best thing one can do, simply, is ignore them, like those microscopic specks that live on our eyelashes. Things got even worse after my book bout – that was when I got bit by the travel bug, which is an even bigger rip-off. Anyway, a little light-bulb went off in my head as I gazed at the spine of the first volume of Antonio Escohotado's *History of Drugs*. I approached the headboard of my old bed and opened the vertical cabinet where Beba used to store my pillow and my pyjamas. I stuck my arm in, all the way to my armpit, and patted about in the dark corner. Bingo: the hash box, a silver case, now tarnished with age. I opened it and found an old half-empty sheaf of Esmoquín rolling papers and a considerable amount of hash. All I had on me was a pack of Ducados, but it wouldn't be the first joint I ever lit with unfiltered cigarettes. I warmed up the rock: 1983 vintage, purchased at the Plaza de la Virreina. It still smelled exactly as it was supposed to smell. I sat on the sofa to roll the joint and went outside to smoke it, as I did in the old days, to avoid contaminating the room with the tell-tale aroma.

The upper level of my parents' terrace looks kind of like a ship's deck, with its teak railing, *Love Boat* style beach chairs and four ancient pieces of gym equipment that my Magnificent Brother was quite addicted to in his day. I approached the railing on the side that faced the water, just above the university's Department of Pharmacology. Fifteen years since I had last smoked a joint in that part of the world, right at the spot on the railing where I used to stub out my joints just in case The First, tattler that he was, caught me in the act. Fifteen years and the only things of mine that remained were my twin predilections for weed and alcohol (I discovered whores a bit later). The affinity for weed, alcohol and a millionaire father. Twenty-five million. Twenty-five. Which included properties, entire buildings in the centre of Barcelona and Madrid, various summer homes in the Costa Brava, rental apartments in Castelldefels and Salou. And then there were the stocks, the bonds, the shares in various companies, the industrial outfits, the works of art, the jewellery, the gold, the safe-deposit boxes spread over various banks, the contents of which only FH knew about. Surely it would be a piece of cake to slap together a hundred thousand in cash. And what is a hundred thousand in exchange for a Magnificent Son, an Architect of the Temple and Master in Dodgy Financial Deals? It hadn't occurred to me before. Kidnapping for ransom . . . This possible resolution to the issue brought with it a tremendous sense of relief, but something inside of me told me it couldn't be so simple. Maybe I was loath to give up my little investigation, the Jaume Guillamet mystery, the trials and tribulations of Lord Henry in that big old citadel, Jenny G and her high-class hookers, Lady First and her romantic intrigue. Without meaning to, I had begun to envision myself as a double-oh-something secret agent, going head-to-head with a cult of evil philosophers, and the movie I had begun to film inside my head had made me use all my wits, all my might, all my mettle. And now, suddenly, all Indiana Jones had to do was get Daddy to pay the ransom and the bad guys would free the hostage, his hair a bit mussed but no worse for the wear. I struggled with this, trying to identify the place inside of me where this stupid urge had come from – what dark corner of my past was making me feel this idiotic need to be useful, to dazzle my Father's Highness and my Magnificent Brother? I decided to attribute it all to the sinister influence of the setting – my room, my books, the scorched hole on the terrace railing that belied so many forgotten joints. I didn't have time to finish the thought, though, because Carmela the Bohemian Girl suddenly appeared on the grass-covered surface of the terrace just below and slightly in front of me. She approached the railing, rested her forearms on the edge and stretched her thigh backwards a bit, resting the tips of her toes on the terrace floor. She looked just about ready to kick back and have a smoke while looking out onto the post-twilight sky. Immediately I thought of running for cover just in case she looked up toward me but, helpless in the presence of that body, I tried to etch the image of her hind quarters in my mind so that I would be able jerk off in their memory at some later date – as soon as I had the chance, in fact. Just then, I hit a fat knot of hash in the joint and the aggressive drag I took caused me to cough, loud and violent. As soon as I start to cough, my twenty-five years of abstinence from all sports other than the living room variety come back to haunt me.

'It's cold. You should have put on a warmer jacket,' the little smartass said as she turned up to get a look at me. Someone should have told her that evening gown necklines are not designed to be viewed from an upstairs terrace. In any event, I swore that I would not allow myself to be ridiculed once more.

'I was lying when I said that bit about the cold,' I called down to her.

'Oh, really? And do you lie to everyone or just to piano players?'

'I lie whenever I can get some kind of advantage out of it.'

'And what kind of advantage did you gain from lying to me before, if you don't mind the question?'

'I'm glad you asked that. It just so happens that you are so fucking hot that if I spend five minutes in your presence I will have to go straight to the bathroom to jerk off and I don't want to go blind. You know.'

'In that case, I have another question: are you this crass with everyone or just with piano players?'

'I thought you believed that everyone should freely express their sexual inclinations.'

'I'm afraid that yours are not sexual inclinations; they are plain and simple insolence.'

'Shall I assume, then, that only gays have acceptable sexual inclinations, or do you just find it inappropriate that someone might be turned on by your body?'

'I find you, in general, to be inappropriate.'

'That's why instead of fucking you I'll have to settle for jerking off. Obviously that's the only thing about you that interests me.'

'Oh, really? Why is that the only thing?'

I couldn't believe it, but the chick was eating this up. It was a serious calculation error on my part: I forgot that every so often you end up with a mental case.

'All right, all right, skip it already.'

'No. Why should I?' she asked.

'Why? Why?'

'Right. Why don't you want to jerk off with me?'

All I could think of right then was to be completely straight with her. When the first lie malfunctions, you don't have too many options left.

'Because the only thing about you that interests me is your body. I don't know anything about the rest of you, but I'm not really interested, either.'

'So what? . . . I don't care much about you beyond your body, either. I like you. Guys like you turn me on. I get the feeling you'd be a good fuck.'

Good God. There is nothing worse than not living up to this type of expectation – and there are, after all, certain girls that fantasise about giant cocks so I decided to take extra precautions.

'I wouldn't be so sure of that if I were you.'

'Well, anyway, it's all the same to me – if you've got a little prick or something it's not like I'm going to laugh at you. So what's it going to be? A fuck? Can I get up to that terrace from here?'

'Hey, hey, hang on a second . . .'

She had already walked over to where the upper terrace jutted out over the lower one. She looked left and right to make sure the coast was clear, shrugged off the spaghetti straps of her evening gown and removed her breasts from her bra cups.

'Look. Take a look at my tits. I want you to touch them.'

My little bird went flying up to attention. I couldn't help it.

'Come on, tell me how to get up there, I'm all hot and bothered now.'

I was completely unable to maintain a normal train of thought. I should have said no, straightaway, but those tits were like two bundles of heaven. Instead, I began to babble.

'Swear it, swear it or promise me on your honour that never again after this night will you ever take a single step to try and see me again.'

'Whaat?'

Oh, fuck it. From up above, I pointed the way toward the other side of the terrace, where there is a little staircase one can climb up without running the risk of being seen from the living room. She tucked her two little treasures back into her dress, hopped up the steps without making too much noise and I received her with open arms. At the first open attack my fly took on the proportions of the Mikerinos pyramid; she pushed her cunt against me and as soon as she felt the bulge she extricated herself from my arms and dragged me over to the bit of wall that led into the bathrooms. She shoved me up against the wall with a sharp thrust, and told me to shut up as she began to take off my belt. Suddenly, she seemed unable to hold back and planted her hand on the zipper as if assessing the contents underneath. Then she lowered the zipper, stuck her hand in and tried to massage the bulge in my boxers. A difficult task. She changed her tactic, and crouched down before me, pushing her way through until she had my boxers down around my ankles and my shirt-tails fluttering in mid-air. Her panting calmed down a bit when she parted the shirt-tails and my genital apparatus appeared before her eyes, in full attack mode. She contemplated it for a moment and then rubbed it with all her might.

'Well, it's no cause for fireworks, but there's enough there,' she said, which assuaged my nerves a bit – I mean, at least it got an 'enough.'

And so then, suddenly, I felt a smooth, unmistakable warm feeling, and as I lowered my gaze I found her clinging to the recently approved item. It's unbelievable: the minute you drop your guard these bohemian babes pounce on you to suck you off.

'No, no, wait . . .' I said. She turned her head up, puzzled, looking at me with my prick in her hand.

'You don't like it?'

'Not so much. Come on, get up on your feet.'

The blow job had set me back a bit, and so I stalled for time by raising her skirt to pat around a bit, here and there.

'What is it that you like, then?' she asked.

'This little thing, right here,' I answered, having covered just enough terrain to be able to identify what I meant with full precision. She raised a thigh, resting her knee against the wall behind me, giving me room to lift up her panties and sink my middle finger in the little crevice that was exposed. Pure spring water. She started kissing me, all over my face, thanking me for that little trickle as if the accomplishment were mine. Full-fledged flow. Siphon-like. Niagara.

'Give it to me,' she said, a proposal that I found most opportune. I raised her dress even more, lowered her panties with my hand so that she could step out with at least one foot, and I invited her with my body language to climb up and rest her thighs around my hips. She did so. She was heavy, and I couldn't quite raise her up enough and so my prick ended up squashed against her cunt, hairy and wet as a feverish racoon. We had to turn about 180 degrees and rest her back against the wall – if not, there was no way we would be able to finish off the event. I managed to pull it off by taking three little leaps with my feet together, and once we had positioned ourselves against the wall in a flurry of sighs and frantic movements, I did not make even the most minimal attempt to restrain myself: after a scant few deep thrusts she was already pronouncing the letter O and then, very soon after, my legs had begun to shake under the weight of her body, clinging to mine like a creeping fig bush. I tried to hold the position so that she could continue coming in short spurts, with those delicious spasms, but I was only able to let her rub up and down with relish for a few seconds. I wasn't straight-on anymore: my cock and I had been reduced to one massive, inconsistent blob, a sad giant with feet of clay.

'Listen, I'm sorry but I'm going to have to lower you because my legs are going to buckle any second and that'll kind of kill the mood.'

I must have sounded very serious because my comment made her howl with laughter. Just what we needed. What little bit of strength I had left was not enough to raise her up on my own. I needed some cooperation from her –

otherwise her entire dress would scrape against the rough surface of the wall. She continued laughing hysterically, which made me laugh, too, and so we continued slipping and sliding until we were halfway down in a rather difficult position: me with my boxers at half-mast and her with her skirt up around her ears and her panties hanging from the heel of one of her shoes.

Not a Kodak moment, exactly.

'Listen, I didn't put a condom on,' I said, once we had assumed a certain degree of verticality, and she had recovered the dignity required to say something coherent.

'That's all right. I won't get pregnant, for sure.'

'And AIDS, and all that?'

'Don't worry, I usually use a condom. Tonight was an exception.'

'I'm not saying it for your sake: I'm kind of promiscuous, that's why.'

'And when you are being pretty promiscuous do you use a condom?'

'Yes. Always.'

'Well, then . . .'

Right.

'Hey, I have a favour to ask,' I said.

'What?'

'I'd like to take a look at your tits. After all that, I never did get to see them up close.'

She was into it, and so she showed them to me. With pride, I would even venture to say. I took the right one in my hand and kissed it, and then took the left one and kissed that, too. Then I helped her back into her bra, and that was when she planted a transversal kiss on my Errol Flynn moustache. It's a shame that I'm so very fundamentally a bachelor, because there certainly are some very lovely things about life when you are part of a couple – like that bit about chimpanzees taking out one another's lice. That sort of thing.

'You know something? I actually find you to be tender,' she said, as she finished rearranging her clothes.

'I'd be better off if you didn't let that one out.'

'I don't plan on telling anyone.'

'People would probably have a tough time believing it, anyway.'

My legs continued quivering, as if they were made of gelatin. Then she said that a bathroom would do her a world of good, and I told her to follow me along the upper terrace until we reached the entrance to my room. I pointed the way to the toilet.

'There must be towels in some closet around here. Under the sink, maybe.'

I closed the door behind her and looked for someplace to sit down and calmly have a smoke. Only when I lit up, sitting on my old bed, did I realise the gravity of my transgression. And I realised it precisely because I suddenly found myself wanting to kiss her tits again, the tits of that presumptuous Bohemian Girl who was currently taking care of her personal business in my bathroom. Yes: my bathroom, in the end. It's one thing to go chatting up hookers – as soon as you feel like kissing the girl-of-the-moment again, the taxi has already transported you far away from the scene of the crime, and so you run no risk of succumbing to temptation. But this individual, this beautiful individual whom I was dying to hold again in that delicious, quiescent abandon that had flowed down my balls (I could still feel, in fact, the tickle of a tiny droplet behind my scrotum, and I had to shimmy my package a bit so that the cotton of my boxers might soak it up), was going to emerge from the bathroom at any given moment, and I . . . I could not risk exposing myself in her presence.

So I went to hide in my Magnificent Brother's old bedroom.

It was empty. Wherever The First goes, he takes his entire past with him, piano included. The bed was still there, though. And so I lay down for a moment, confident that the quivers would subside in no time.

WELCOME, MR CONSUL

Fast asleep on The First's bed, I started to notice how much my shoes were annoying me – they were comfortable but they were also brand-new, which is the worst thing a shoe can be, and so for the brief duration of my extemporaneous siesta, I dreamt that I was floating along with the burbling current of a turbulent river, sitting astride a tree trunk, my legs danging in the buoyant rapids beneath me. That was when the piranhas started to appear: little piranhas, with little borzog teeth. To make matters worse, as I woke up I realised that had made a mess of the mattress, which was now all wrinkled and dirty from some massive scuffing by my new shoes.

I looked out at the night sky, filtering in through the terrace window. I entered the bathroom. As soon as I lowered my zipper to take a piss, a brief reminiscence wafted up toward my nose, bringing me back to the recent scene out on the terrace: it was her smell, mixed in with the scent of the perfume she wore, and, I suppose, my own smell as well, which was slightly more difficult to identify given that it was so familiar to me. Boom: an adolescent-sized erection. The scent of a woman is so goddamn good, there's nothing comparable to it, except maybe the aroma of a good pipe, delicious and ever-so-slightly acidic. 'The Nectar of the Gods,' I called it, in a momentary bout of lyricism. Of course, this line of thinking was not going to help calm my erection and despite my best efforts to get a decent angle, I ended up pissing on the toilet bowl lid. Naturally, I denied myself the pleasure of jerking off in memory of Carmela: to err is human, but to err twice, in rapid sequence, is dubious at best. And so instead I doused my prick with extremely cold water as a form of penitence. As a result, it subsided somewhat, though the technique hadn't liberated the juices, now slightly dried-up, that Carmela had left behind on the little hairs on my balls. Now, I don't particularly like bidets, but I found myself with no other choice than to sit on the thing and wash myself a bit more carefully. As I completed the manoeuvre, shamed by the serious violation of one of my most basic survival codes, I began to whistle something, anything, to cover it up. I frequently do this: hide things from myself – by whistling, humming, anything to distract myself. The worst part, however, was yet to come, the acid test of my inevitable re-encounter with Carmela. I couldn't remember how one was supposed to treat a woman one has just recently fucked – was I supposed to act especially friendly, attentive, silent? Would we exchange conspiratorial looks? Would our elbows brush up against each other at the table? Would I have to take her to the movies on Sundays? I was suddenly overcome with stage fright – I would just get out of there without saying goodbye. But I didn't.

'Fuck it. Chin up,' I said to myself as I left my Magnificent Brother's quarters and went downstairs.

In my parents' house it is customary practice to savour the second round of after-dinner drinks in the living room, but everyone was still seated at the table, which meant that I couldn't have been sleeping for very long. Well, everyone was at the table minus Her.

'Pablo José, darling, where on earth have you been?'

'In my bedroom. I went inside for a second and got

distracted looking through all my old things. It's been years since I last . . . looked at . . . my things.'

Way too much explaining. Very rarely do I trip up when telling lies, but when it happens it is dreadful – there's nothing more painfully obvious than an expert tripping all over himself. But as long as money isn't involved, people are pretty easily foolable.

'Well, Carmela just left. She had a show at ten, and it was getting late. She asked us to say goodbye to you.'

'Oh . . . great.'

'She was out on the terrace alone for quite a little while . . . you didn't even have a coffee with her,' MH stated.

My mother's comment was aimed directly at me, but she said it in a such way that included the rest of her co-conversationalists, which effectively aborted the group's previous conversation – that is, if there had been one at all. Her tone wavered somewhere between reproachful and saucy, an attitude that was reflected in the faces of the other seven souls sitting around the table. Clearly, I was not to be let off quite so easily.

'*I què, Pau, com va la feina*?' That was my Convergent uncle Frederic, inquiring after my well-being in Catalán. Uncle Frederic, who can't stand to be addressed in Spanish as Federico, and who always addresses me as Pau, my name in Catalán. The usual routine: he starts in with an innocent question like that, and ends up trying to tempt me with various executive vacancies in some or other official institution of indecipherable nomenclature and always with some previous affiliation to our own little *cosa nostra*. It took me years to figure out how to interpret this absurd insistence of his, but after a while I finally realised that those ridiculous job offers were just his way of making an oblique joke at my expense.

I answered the question as laconically as I could, to see if I could nip this one in the bud. Nothing doing: I only blew wind in his sails and Uncle Felipe, coming in from the rear with heavy artillery, didn't give me second to turn the bow around.

'What you need to do is find yourself a girlfriend and get married. It isn't very healthy to be a bachelor at your age,' proclaimed his Excellency the General. At least he refrained from emphasising this admonition with the customary 'At ease!' His military airs have gotten weak with age, I guess. But the crossfire continued for a while, and my lower decks began to accumulate water. For the moment I held tight, but as soon as FH entered the fray, I had no other choice but to let air into the sails, and when my Mother's Highness joined in, I had already said something scandalously inappropriate and was fully prepared to weather the rest of the storm by letting loose every last rope I could. Even the Magnificent Mother-in-Law candidate entered the skirmish. Only Aunt Asunción and the Father of the Bride remained neutral, which means they didn't try to help me, either. Aunt Salomé, as usual, was the most difficult of the group. With the intellectual airs she had acquired as an avid reader of so many pseudo-scientific magazine articles, she insisted on questioning me at length about my 'romantic disappointments.' According to my well-informed Aunt Salomé, it was obvious that my patent misogyny could only be attributed to a clearly neurotic reaction to the premature frustrations of my romantic experiences. She was so insistent on this point that I had to sabotage her notions by letting out my blunt lines with an equally convoluted analysis which I couldn't possibly reproduce here. In short, I stated that perhaps my problem was not a question in misogyny but rather one of garden-variety misanthropy. No dice, though. The more people get caught up in these scientific theories, the less common sense they seem to have. It was quite the topic. In any case, the coffee hour finally ended, concluding the regulation courtesies required by the family dinner event. I managed to say my goodbyes with the regulation kisses and handshakes, after which my Father's Highness, in a wholly unprecedented move, insisted on walking me to the door. I knew I was in for something, though I didn't know what – maybe he wanted to finish off the conversation that had been interrupted in the Contemporary Art wing. At that moment, however, I was still pretty pissed off and kept my distance from him. Just after we had opened up to each other in front of that painting, he had to go and start in with me at the dinner table – conspiring, no less, with two of our most despised common enemies. This was not very nice of him, I thought. My father can be a real pain in the arse, but even I have to admit that he has a kind of noble character that puts him in a league of his own. And so I attributed his fair-play routine to the whims of old age. Nevertheless, a twinge of resentment still gnawed away inside of me.

'Wait. I have to change my clothes. I left my shirt in your dressing room.'

'Don't forget to take that jacket with you, though.'

'I'm sorry, if you want to liberate yourself from that thing, you'll have to include it in your last will and testament, along with the 12.5 million I've got coming to me.'

The old fart seemed to have forgotten he'd done wrong by me and was confused by my cool attitude. His face did break into a half-smile, though, as if politely acknowledging a joke he didn't quite get. I can be a bit hard on him sometimes – though that is definitely the sentimental softie inside me coming out. A sentimental softie: that's what I am. Anyway, I went into the kitchen to say goodnight to Beba and as I came back out to the vestibule, I almost felt sad as I saw him waiting there for me, clinging pathetically to his crutches. I even gave him a conciliatory pat on the shoulder, not very hard, so as not to tip him over.

'Take care of yourself, okay?' I said.

'You take care. I'm not going to ask you to come over again, but at least ring us on the phone. And don't even think of mentioning a word of all this to your mother.'

I got into the lift feeling horribly guilty for something, and I thought about what I might do to remedy this bad head scene. I didn't feel like getting drunk – I can only get truly drunk when I am completely happy – but I couldn't think of anything else to do with my mortal body. Only when I was sitting behind the wheel of the Beast did I decide that the next two hours should be spent breaking speed records with the aforementioned car. I tooled down the Diagonal, heading for the A7 motorway, keeping my eye firmly fixed on the rearview mirror. I stopped at the Molins de Rey petrol station so that Bagheera could fill up to her heart's content before getting the hell out of there. Right behind me, a white Opel Kadett, an old GSI model, followed me off the road. I asked the attendant to fill the tank and went into the shop for cigarettes. One of the two guys in the Opel entered the shop as well and bought a bottle of water. Around thirtyish, slightly tough-looking though definitely not the law-breaking type, he carefully avoided looking me in the eye. I went to the toilet and when I emerged the Opel was still there, with the tough guy pretending to check his tyre pressure. Shortly after I returned to the motorway they followed suit – I could still see them in the rearview mirror – and I cruised for a while at about one hundred kph but they didn't pass me. There was no doubt now that these were the guys my FH had hired to follow me. Now they were going to get theirs.

An hour and a half later, fully mesmerised by the joys of making tracks on the motorway, I suddenly found myself approaching the cupolas of the Basílica del Pilar in Zaragoza, and decided it was time to start heading back to Barcelona.

I was concerned about the precise extent to which my father had had me followed. In addition to the simple decorum/propriety issue, had they seen me the night that I had stood guard on Guillamet, in the Beast with Fina? And if so, what had they made of it? Had they discovered my interest in number fifteen? Thousands of little circumstances for which I had no answer.

In retrospect I know that I had been smart to think these things through, but at the moment I couldn't help but feel a bit ridiculous. Obviously these people had kidnapped The First with the intention of demanding a ransom – it was just a matter of hours before someone made contact with FH. Even so, as I approached Barcelona, taking the long way around so that I could enter the city via the Meridiana, I decided to swing by Jenny G's. Clearly, this had everything to do with my reluctance to give up my newfound adventure, but I fooled myself into thinking that I only wanted to solve the mystery and say my farewells to Bagheera and the cash card with a bit of a bang. Before long I would once again be Pablo Baloo Miralles, cash-free pedestrian. And that was when I made the painful realisation that, if I had to choose between eternal life on the Internet and the ephemeral pleasures of driving a Lotus Esprit, I most definitely and infinitely preferred the Esprit. But it was too late to change my life for another one.

I drove down Villarroel and found a car park whose yellow billboard said it was open all night. I went inside the car park and took out The First's mobile. Right there I dialled the number in question in The First's directory. According to the clock on the digital display it was 3:04 in the morning.

'Jenny G, good evening.'

Strong English accent, just like the time before.

'Hello. Listen, I'm a friend of the house and I was thinking of coming by for a drink, but I wasn't sure if it would be a bit late for that.'

'Not at all.'

'Marvellous. Now, I don't think I remember the exact address . . .'

Some number of some street in the far reaches of the neighbourhood of Sarriá, where the city fades off into the mountains. I hailed a taxi as I exited the car park. Crowded House ballad on the radio, the remains of some woman's perfume on the upholstery, well-mannered driver. On the way over I checked my pockets and located six hundred ninety-three wrinkled euros among my keys and smoking paraphernalia. A bit close, I thought, and so I asked the driver to stop at a cash machine in the Sarriá plaza and withdrew three hundred more as backup. I got back in but we still had a little ways to go. Once we arrived at the probable location of the number I had memorised, I got out.

I had to walk a bit, but I quickly identified the building. It was a massive neoclassical mansion about five or six stories high, encircled by gardens. Despite its imposing bulk, the resulting volume was harmonious, balanced, and well-turned-out. The white-and-yellow facade was enhanced by the green ivy and the lilac colour of the sprawling bougainvillea. The place could have easily passed for an old-age home or one of those private universities where they teach people how to earn large quantities of money, and for the second time that evening I regretted having donned the Hawaiian number back at my apartment. I walked past a hut with a couple of guards who were there to check in whoever came by car – 'Yep, right, hello' – and went through the front part of the garden. As I stepped up the small marble staircase I felt my thigh muscles call out in protest, tired of so much extra work. At the top I found myself facing a glassed-in wrought-iron gate, behind which was a breezeway which must have been used in the olden days for letting horse-drawn carriages through. Beyond the glass wall, two sets of steps lay before me, one of them leading upstairs and the other downstairs, both profusely decorated. I pressed the bell that was ensconced in a hard golden casing. It said 'Jenny G' beneath an etched-in adornment that looked like a rod of tuberoses, although maybe they were magnolias or something – I am a bit uneducated in the area of flowers. I was tempted to search the outer premises for a red rag, but I exercised restraint when I saw someone come forward to open the breezeway door, a girl in a jacket and suit, sort of a not-too-aggressive executive look. I couldn't get rid of the déjà-vu feeling until much later, but in any event it was a false déjà-vu, because I was actually eminently aware of its origins.

The girl worked the same accent I had heard over the phone. I told her I had just spoken with her and she acknowledged remembering me.

'Are you a member, sir?'

'No.'

'Your first visit?'

'Yes.'

'Your identity card, please.'

'I have to give you my identity card?'

'It's a formality we require.'

Well, whatever – mine had expired a few years earlier, but I always carry it with me, along with my expired passport: a habit from my travel days. The girl didn't notice the dates; all she did was enter the numbers into a keyboard. A few seconds later an already-laminated card came spitting out of the printer.

'Let me explain a few things. You will need this, it's a magnetic card. The staff will record all the services you solicit during your stay. The entrance fee is three hundred euros. If you'd like to consult prices, there are various price lists throughout the establishment.'

It seemed to me that the old-fashioned fake-name routine was, in fact, a whole lot easier, but I nevertheless accepted the card with the tuberose logo along with my identification number and a bar code on the flip side. Something gave me the feeling that I was entering a theme park, but that thought was quickly dispelled when I spied a young gorilla with a black turtleneck and a Prince-of-Wales plaid jacket. He had partially emerged from a room beneath the staircase that led upstairs. From that same area I could hear the gentle murmur of conversation in English, which evoked, in my mind, a corps of guards in a military barracks. The man who had stepped out was at least six feet three, all shoulders and pecs – I almost wanted to stick a yogurt in his hand and snap a photo or two. He hesitated for a moment, as if waiting for the girl's thumbs-up regarding my arrival and, seeing that all was well, returned to his cubicle with a movement that displayed a dark bulk underneath his blazer, around the level of his armpit, which meant that it wasn't exactly a turtle dove. I wasn't terrifically pleased at that little discovery, but now that I was here I decided, as per the receptionist's suggestion, to go up the stairs and walk through the threshold of the upper floor that seemed to lead the way into the definitive entrance to Jenny G's.

No old ladies sitting before a fireplace in this joint: a slight bend in the corridor led me straight into a grand salon which looked like the main bar – even bigger than the vestibule at the entrance downstairs. That was when I thought of an old beer ad in which a young diplomat is sent to a remote country and, once there, finds himself in a most exotic setting that promises the most glamourous of worldly adventures. 'Welcome, Mr Consul,' was the ad's catchphrase. I had been more or less expecting the glamorous bit, but the exotic aspect of the place came off as rather strange: perhaps it would seem exotic from the perspective of a foreigner in Barcelona, I don't know. It was this very quintessentially British type of club even though it was physically located in the far reaches of Sarriá, and every corner of the place oozed that very subtle geographical difference, down to the very architectural style of the building, the sepia prints of the Paseo de Gracia at the turn of the century, the modernist chairs, the massive ceiling fans, the luminous blue of the wall-coverings and the immense, tropical and very un-Mediterranean *kentia* plants that finished off the colonial-style ambience. I liked it, though. Enough that I even felt like getting drunk again or, in the event I found an adequate companion, who knew – maybe I would land my second fuck of the night, what the hell. Sounds of jazz, playing very low, emerged from somewhere. I'll never understand why jazz is always the background music in places that are supposedly elegant – I'd love to know what Charlie Parker would have to say about that. But anyway. In front of a massive picture window with tinted panes that looked out over the garden and the city I spotted a bar, and for the moment that was more than enough to keep me happy.

I wasn't too interested in complicating my life at that point, so I just ordered a simple Havana with a lemon twist from the waiter – a guy of mediumish age, in a black vest and the inevitable bow-tie, though this one didn't speak in an English accent, at least. I passed him my card and once he had served me the drink I stood there observing him as he slid the card through the slot of a rather odd keyboard that was visible from where I was. Then I spun around on my bar stool to inspect the crowd.

About fifteen or twenty people scattered about the immense room: two guys negotiating something at a table that was slightly separated from the rest of the action; a couple that you could somehow tell wasn't a real couple; four people sitting on a bank of sofas in the middle of the room . . . It seemed like a perfectly fine, relaxing place to get wrecked, even though you could sense, in the middle of all that glamour and Barcelona a-la-Britannia, an enigmatic *je ne sais quoi*. The staff, either alone or in little groups, contributed to this atmosphere of intrigue by wafting in and out of the many entrances to the salon, which were actually corridors with conveniently placed corners that neatly hid from view whatever happened to be going on beyond the main room. The back room was definitely an intense little spot, I thought to myself, and figured it wouldn't be long before I found a companion. I was not mistaken: no sooner had I polished off the Havana when I was approached by one of the sweet young things that had come in from the mysterious inner rooms. Elegant carriage, black dress that looked more like a negligée, thirtysomething, medium-length reddish Head & Shoulders hair. When she turned to greet me, I saw that she was unusually attractive – pretty face and big green dragon-lady eyes. She wasn't exactly my type, but she did kind of make you want to try her out, even if just for a change of scenery. She placed her evening bag on the bar, a couple of seats away from where I was, and very politely said hello. I reciprocated, with the best diction I could muster, so as to give the impression that the Hawaiian number was merely an eccentricity, and I continued taking mini-sips of my rum. She turned to the bartender and ordered a Campari with an orange twist (odd coincidence, that one), and I took advantage of the opportunity to order another Havana with a lemon twist. Then I started planning my move.

'May I take care of that for you?' I offered.

Meaningful look, smile, good vibes all around.

'Thank you, much obliged.'

Brief pause so as not to seem impatient. Back to business: 'Lovely evening.'

'Marvellous, yes.'

'Summer solstice: a perfect moment for an evening drink. Sleeping, on the other hand, always proves a bit difficult on a night like this.'

'Yes . . . sometimes I think sleeping should be done exclusively in wintertime.'

'Well, the secret is to shift your sleeping hours toward the daytime.'

I got up from my bar stool and found another one for her, at exactly the perfect distance from both me and the bar.

'Excuse me, would you like a seat?'

There was something about this girl – she couldn't have been more than a few years older than me, but she made me want to talk to her in the formal. It was some kind of turn-on, don't ask.

'I don't recall ever seeing you here before.'

'This is my first time. I heard about the place from a friend who comes here quite often.'

'Perhaps I know your friend, then.'

'His name is Eusebio. I'm Pablo. Pablo Cabanillas. Pleased to make your acquaintance.'

I extended my hand, and she accepted it as women often do, offering up only her fingers, bent at the knuckles.

'Beatrice.'

'Lovely name. May we speak informally, Beatrice?'

'I think so.'

'And you? Do you come here often?'

'Two or three times a week, always on Saturday. What is your friend's surname?'

'Lozano. Eusebio Lozano.'

'It doesn't ring a bell. Of course, there are some people that don't like to use their real names here. Some people like a bit of fantasy.'

'Oh, really? For example?'

'I don't know . . . invent a new name, pretend they're someone else . . .'

'Innocent entertainment.'

'That depends on who it is, and who they're pretending to be. Of course, it is possible I simply don't know your friend. Lots of people come through here.'

'I thought this was an exclusive sort of club.'

'It is. Very possibly only one in ten thousand people can indulge in coming here. But even so, that's over three hundred thousand candidates, if I'm not mistaken.'

'Including Chinese men?'

'I've met one or two here, yes.'

I fully drained my Havana in one or two long gulps, so I ordered another one, plus a Campari with an orange twist for my lady friend. She demurred, however, saying that she had barely touched her first one. Clearly, Jenny G's hookers didn't score a commission off the bar.

'Hey. You know what I'd like?'

'What?'

'For you to show me around. My friend has told me some incredible things, but I'm sure I'll miss the boat if we stay here at the bar.'

'Would you like a Cicero? Very well, bring your drink with you.' She glanced over at the bartender. 'Gerardo, we're taking our drinks with us.'

She seemed amused by the idea of showing me around the joint. She even took me by the hand and tugged me a little.

'Well, now: what would you like to sample first, heaven or hell?'

'There's a choice?'

'Of course. Didn't you study your catechism?'

'My head must be somewhere else . . . let's go to hell first. I'd rather save the best for last.'

'What makes you think Heaven will be better than Hell?'

'Well, one supposes that the words carry with them certain connotations that give them a more complex meaning.'

'Chomsky is such a cretin.'

'I knew it.'

'The Chomsky reference?'

'No. That you're a philologist.'

'Wrong. I read History.'

We were out of the main salon now, walking down a wide, well-lit (or better put, skilfully lit) corridor that was very similar to the corridor of an upstairs theatre balcony:

all the salon exits converged here. Armoires, tapestries, paintings, rugs, doors, hallways, a variety of staircases, even a few lifts. There was also a small crowd milling about: a pair of cute-looking, impeccably-dressed young ladies, a couple whispering to one another, a fat man in shirtsleeves. The entire building had to be some kind of insane whorehouse, but we were still in the zone where everybody still behaved themselves.

'Would you like something before we go downstairs?'

At first I thought she meant something to drink and I raised my glass to show her it was almost full. She then pointed to her little purse. Ohhh. Well, yeah, a little whatever would be just fine, I thought. We turned around and went through an unremarkable door, behind which was a row of sinks and massive mirrors surrounded by naked light bulbs, like in a dressing room.

'Have you got a bill?'

I gave her a fifty and she rolled it up. She rolled it up even before taking the mirror and the little package out of her bag. Coke, probably, I thought. She prepared two very generous lines and offered me the mirror. I did half a line through each nostril – coke, indeed – and passed the paraphernalia back to her. She sniffed her ration and then stored everything back in her purse, including the fifty I'd just given her.

'How do you know I'm not a cop?' I asked, trying to dig at her conscience a bit. No luck.

'What would you prefer, to take the stairs and go floor by floor, or the lift?'

'Floor by floor.'

'I warn you, there are quite a few. Does the Divine Comedy ring a bell?'

'Very much. But you can't get satellite TV from where

I live. Listen, I hope this isn't going to be some big allegorical thing, because I'm in the mood for something else.'

'Everything in this world is allegorical, darling, but if you'd prefer we can get straight to the point. Let's see: do you like to eat, drink, watch, be watched, boys, girls, groups, suffer, make someone else suffer, lingerie, fetishes, some kind of picturesque philia – copro, zoo, geronto, necro – or do you prefer something a little more commonplace? The only limit is that it can't be illegal. Everyone here is a legal adult, of sound mind, and has come here on their own initiative.'

'I put myself in your hands. You're the expert.'

'Very well: third basement. I call it the department store window. It's a good place to get acclimatised.'

It was kind of more Corte Inglés than Dante's Inferno: 'Semi-basement level: lingerie and ménage à trois; look for our sodomy specials.' I must admit, though, that it was all pretty impressive – I would never have imagined such a place existed a mere four or five steps away from the centre of Sarriá. Now, as we descended a second set of stairs that led us below ground, the windows disappeared and, with them, all outside references: first, to the city – a distant, but calming reference – and second, to the little hut with the guards that controlled the various domains of the mansion, and thirdly the tops of the trees in the garden, which were visible from the main salon. I wouldn't say that I was scared – I was in the company of a very nice girl who walked with utmost confidence through the labyrinthine passageways, and the security of the clientele was ostensibly guaranteed by the elegant gorillas that one bumped into here and there in the hallways. And anyway, I was used to pretty heavy scenes, heavier than this at least – I was reminded, for example, of a kind of floating slum

I once visited in the outskirts of Saigon, and after that you've pretty much seen it all. No, no, it wasn't fear exactly, but I did feel an odd presence in the pit of my stomach, one that precluded me from being fully able to enjoy the Havana with the lemon twist. It's funny how both fear and excessive sexual stimulation can have the very same effect. Anyway, coke always has a stimulating effect, and this particular batch definitely made its own statement.

We soon arrived at the floor in question – the Department Store Window, as she called it, three stories below the salon bar where we had begun. In the access room, one of the gorillas swiped my card through another one of those keyboards with a slot on the side, and we entered a most complex daedalus. At first, as we went deeper and deeper, from one room to another – I somehow realised that we were going deeper inside even though my sense of orientation had been completely fucked by the twists and turns of that complex labyrinth – I still didn't see anything that grabbed my attention. The decorating scheme was about the only thing that was at all entertaining. The orangey rug, the erotic drawings hanging on the walls, the chaise longues and the upholstered easy chairs were definitely an improvement over the *kentias* and the ceiling fans from before. Then, all of a sudden, when it seemed that we were approaching a kind of interior gallery, an old man came walking toward us – old, white as a sheet, bald, super-skinny, dressed in nothing but a white shirt that hung down mid-thigh, like a kind of tunic. When he saw us appear at the other end of the corridor, he stopped cold in front of us and raised the tails of his shirt up high, to show us his sexual organs – a very long, skinny penis that hung listlessly from a peach-fuzz mound of surprisingly dark pubic hair. His eyes implored Beatrice to look at it – he seemed to want her to look at him first, maybe because she was in front of me. I could tell she obliged, and as she lowered her head to look down at the old man's genitals, I could see the glint of appreciation in his eyes. Then, once she was through checking him out, it was my turn to fulfil his request. Our eyes met, though only for a moment, because I found it much harder to stand there and stare into those beseeching eyes than to look down toward the spectacle he was so intent on showing off. I concentrated on that wrinkled little snake, whose length was accentuated by a bit of protruding foreskin, and I quickly looked back up at his face, to conclude the encounter right then and there. I don't think I had ever seen such an old man naked before, and I was taken aback by the smooth, transparent skin and the slack genitals that had endured such an excess of gravity. It was jarring to observe the effects of ageing on body parts that are normally hidden from view – the same effects that are nevertheless so familiar on a face, or a pair of hands. After we had passed him, I spun around and saw that he now had his back to us, though he had turned his neck about so that he could continue looking at us. Now it was his arse that was on display, a yellowish, wasted bum that he tried to frame with his hands, so that it would be eminently obvious what our new focal point should be.

That was only the beginning. We arrived next at a giant, square-shaped atrium that cut through the entire building; each floor was flanked by a balcony, and from this vantage point we could look down and up onto the other floors. That was where we began to see even stranger things. To start off, the building itself was rather breathtaking: there was a full ten-story void between the mosaic-green pool that swished and bubbled down at the bottom floor of the basement, and the glass roof that let the night sky take over as the building's ceiling. We began our journey around that open space in the centre, like a married couple at an automotive fair – the only difference being that the objects on display at this unique fairground were piles of people focused on fornicating in any and every which way they could. The first thing I saw, on a long bench just to our left, was a couple trying to achieve, without much success, an *ad mode ferarum* fuck. Our presence seemed to arouse them and they panted a bit harder, though I think it was more an attention-grabbing ploy than a real demonstration of self-stimulation. A bit further on we saw two very similar-looking men – both physically and fashion-wise – necking furiously, like a pair of incestuous twins. In another area where a long modular sofa snaked around the wall, I spied a long lineup of people piled against each other, forming one giant mass of human livestock, stroking each other with gusto. Other people simply walked around, ostentatiously revelling in their own nudity and their complicated and occasionally frantic solitary caresses. One man, less interested in his own exhibitionism and more interested in the people around him, walked about masturbating himself disinterestedly, as if testing out the arousal capacities of the other performers. Here and there you could also spot people like us, just taking a stroll through the premises, stopping before a particularly impressive scene, or sitting down for a smoke. As we walked, occasionally we had to scoot out of the way of people with their bums high up in the air, doing things like sticking magic markers up their anuses. Finally we completed the first side of the immense square atrium. It seemed quite clear that my companion's intention was to guide me around the perimeter of the room until we arrived back where we started, so I just followed her lead. A bit further on, we reached a more intimate corner that was a kind of continuation of the nook where we had started our tour. Here, Beatrice stopped before a small group of ten or fifteen people. To tell the truth, so much action had whetted my curiosity that I followed her willingly. The centre of this little gathering, partially hidden by the observers, was an odd trio comprised of what looked like an older, perhaps married couple – both of them equally chubby, dressed like a well-heeled lawyer and his wife – and a delicate young girl with the most innocent blue eyes; she couldn't have been more than eighteen years old. These three characters, unlike the others we had passed by, were focused exclusively on their complicated intertwined manoeuvrings and seemed utterly indifferent to the interest they had aroused among their observers. The wife, sitting on the rug and resting her shoulders on the bottom part of a sofa, had opened her varicose-veined legs as far as her constitution would allow, using her hands to create an open space in the soft triangle between her thighs. In the middle, you could see her wide-open vulva, like a fleshy flower with a bulbous white clitoris quivering from the stimulation provided by the ring-finger of her right hand, an instrument she also used for penetrating her vagina. The man was completely clothed, though the head of his cock peeked out from his unzipped trousers, purplish and smooth like an overfed slug jutting out from his spare-tyre belly. This is where the young girl got into the act. Seated on the sofa next to the man, she very gently clasped the tip of his prick between two fingers, and judging by the restrained vehemence of his instructions, she was attempting to strike just the right balance necessary to keep the cock's proprietor teetering on the edge of ejaculation. The woman, revelling in a discreet bout of prolonged ecstasy from her own manipulation, stared straight at the man's zipper; he, in turn, stared back at her nether regions in the exact same manner. The girl alternated between her manual responsibilities and the facial expressions of this respectable couple, while the spectators, whose complete and total silence was punctuated only by the man's instructions – "faster", "stop", "that's it" – and the wife's light moans, observed this precision exercise as if it was a three-way pool game. Looking directly at the main action made me feel kind of funny, so I decided instead to observe the observers, some of whom had sat down on the two sofas, in the free spaces unoccupied by the lusty trio.

The scene had a truly pictorial quality, like one of those Renaissance paintings where everyone seems as if they've been frozen around the centre of the composition. At the most, someone would dare to move an arm to take a drag off a cigarette, or change their focus from one to another of the revellers. The most unbearable thing, though, was the awful tension that hung in the air – it was as if everyone was waiting for the spectacle to end so that they could finally applaud. This gave me an especially nasty vibe and so I turned to my Havana for solace, but the momentary clinking of the ice cubes broke the blue-eyed babe's concentration and almost provoked a major cataclysm, a fatal imbalance in this sublime show. Various disapproving looks were shot in my direction, and I began to feel ridiculous – yes, me – with my loud shirt and my neophyte interruptions. I looked over at Beatrice, hoping for some sign of complicity in her eyes and fortunately I was not rebuffed: me and my reaction were as important to her as the scene we were witnessing. I made an I've-had-about-enough-of-this-one face and we continued our tour round to the other side of the square.

'Ugh. This rug is giving me a headache,' I said.

'Let's go.'

She seemed amused by my discomfort. We lightened up the little stroll, but she did make a point to stop in front of a series of three tiny rooms separated from us by a glass wall; each room was almost entirely occupied by a massive bed in the centre. The first two rooms featured empty beds, but in the third we saw a young couple, completely nude – I think they were the only people I saw completely nude, everyone else was always in some half-undressed state – and copulating with the kind of gymnastic effervescence you see in those porno flicks with techno-pound soundtrack – *chump, chunga-bum, chump, chunga-bum.*

'This is what I call the Department Store Window,' said Beatrice, pointing to that aquarium-like room.

'Those two look like professionals.'

'They may be. I once saw Rocco Sifredi mixed up in one of these numbers. He was in Barcelona for the Erotic Film Festival.'

'Right. So you're familiar with all of the Inferno?'

'Well . . . there are areas that I can't really take, areas that offend my sensibilities. I despise unpleasant smells, for example, and I can't bear the sight of blood. Would you like to go down one more level? The next floor is still tolerable.'

'I'd rather get some air.'

'All right. Let's go upstairs, then.'

We were far away from the central gallery by now and as we walked way back toward the elevators we made a pit-stop for another line of coke. Naturally the previous banknote I had provided wouldn't do this time around, and she asked me for another.

'What's on the upper floors?'

'Heaven.'

'Right, but what's there?'

'If Hell is the earth, matter, flesh, you can just imagine it . . . Heaven is air, the mind, the spirit. Downstairs is for satisfying the body, upstairs is for comforting the soul. There is physical contact up to the second floor, but after that people don't touch at all. They just speak.'

'And on the seventh floor there's group therapy and a confessional.'

'Well, not exactly.'

'So what floor are we going to, then?'

'The top floor.'

'Cool.'

'Well, don't get too excited, everything comes full circle. Both the highest and lowest floors offer direct communication with the city – the view up top and the car park down below. Reality is comprised of both Heaven and Hell. Pure allegory, as you can see.'

The top floor, in fact, was occupied by a kind of central snack bar surrounded by a solarium from which you could see the city once again. It was still dark, probably somewhere between five and six in the morning. The air felt pure and clean, and Beatrice and I both took deep breaths as we sat down at a table on the rather desolate terrace and waited for a waiter to come by. Beatrice ordered another Campari and I opted for a bottle of ice-cold vodka and a glass with ice. I poured myself a glass and in a single breath I just about drained it, down to the tips of the ice cubes. As my body shivered from the effect, I continued taking little sips. Beatrice, meanwhile, began theorising. Bosch, Goya, Golem, Guy de Maupassant, Pío Baroja's witches, Nietszche, the songs of Maldoror . . . a hodgepodge of references with a common denominator that attempted to theorize, in a rather convoluted fashion, on the basis of ideas that invariably led to another universe of thought: Faust, Freddy Kreuger, Dorian Gray and then back again.

'So – are you a hooker?' I asked her when I started getting sick of all the deep thought.

'Excuse me?'

'Are you a hooker . . . a prostitute . . . ?'

'Why do you ask?'

Suddenly a slightly mad idea entered my head.

'Nothing. Just curious. I thought this was a whorehouse.'

'Umm, not exactly.'

I couldn't tell if the "not exactly" referred to the whorehouse bit or the prostitute bit, but it didn't much matter.

'Listen, I'm going to be honest with you . . . I'm a private detective. I've been hired by a family to look for someone and it's possible that you might be able to give me some information. You'd be compensated, of course.'

'I knew it.'

'What?'

'That you were a detective. As soon as I spotted you that's what I thought.'

Was that a touch of irony I noted in her voice?

'Well, I didn't think it was so apparent.'

'You fit the bill. Plus, I'm a good psychologist.'

'Excellent, yeah, I can see that . . . Listen, you said something before about knowing the regulars here . . .'

'Almost all of the people who show up at the bar. But I don't want trouble.'

'No, I'm not trying to get you mixed up in anything. Does the name Sebastian Miralles mean anything to you?'

Her face didn't move.

'Has something happened to Sebastian?'

'You know him?'

'Yes. Has something happened?'

'We don't know. He disappeared a few days ago and his family has hired me to do a bit of investigating.'

'Did Gloria hire you?'

Shit: the family that plays together, stays together.

'You know Gloria, too?'

'Yes.'

'And Lali, Eulalia Robles?'

'As well.'

What was it that I found strange about the way she said 'as well'?

'Have you seen them here recently?'

'No, not for a couple of weeks.'

'Do they come together?'

'Sometimes . . .'

'I've been thinking that his disappearance may have something to do with the fact that they are clients here. Does this make any sense to you?'

She looked at me with a poker face.

'Listen, I think I've told you too much already.'

'But you haven't told me anything I didn't already know.'

'Discretion is extremely important in a place like this.'

'Look, I don't give out the details of my investigations to anyone. I look for the guy, and if I find him, great. If not, I present a general report and charge the minimum fee. That's all.'

'And who did you say hired you?'

Why did I get the feeling she was making fun of me and didn't believe for a second that I was a detective?

'Gloria. She gave me this address,' I said, and then repeated my initial question, which was still unanswered. 'Do you think his disappearance has something to do with this place?'

'This place has the reputation of being one of the safest in the city.'

At that point the roles changed, and suddenly she was the one asking all sorts of questions about the case: how, when, why, what for, etc. That was about when I realised I had exhausted her as a possible source of information, and that from here on in she would be the one running the inquiry. To think that after all I had learned, nothing was new except for the fact that the Lalala trio frequented this building as a group, which didn't seem so strange at this stage in the game.

By then the last day of spring had dawned, although the brisk air of the previous evening still prevailed, as well as a bit of darkness which was punctuated by the street lights outside. About a quarter of the ice-cold vodka bottle still remained untouched, and I started to feel like going home. I told my guide that I hadn't slept for three nights, and that was enough to convince her to let me go without hassling me with more questions. She even offered to walk me down to the entrance hall.

Once we were alone in the lift I rummaged a bit in my pockets and took out two more fifty-euro bills.

'This is for you. In case you want to do a couple more lines.'

She took them with ease, said thank you and offered me her hand as a farewell gesture.

The whole joke, totalled by the executive babe at the reception desk, came out to more than seven hundred euros – including cover charge, drinks and extras – which explained the reason for my Magnificent Brother's high-octane credit card. Of course, they did call me a taxi, which appeared on the double just outside the entrance gate, and they didn't charge me for the call.

It was a relief to get into the taxi and head down to Les Corts. The radio announced the World Cup football games on tap for the afternoon and I was overjoyed to see that the human race still watched football games, that television, radio announcers, and tabloid magazines continued to exist. Once the newsagent at Carlos III came into view and I saw that he was already open for business, I actually felt like buying a newspaper, to grab hold of something familiar, anything.

I asked the taxi driver to stop for a moment and quickly returned with three newspapers: *La Vanguardia, El País*, and *El Periódico*. Of course, it didn't even occur to me to actually open the papers and read what was inside, not in the taxi and not when I got home, either. That was a good thing, though, because otherwise I might not have ever gotten into bed and slept a little.

STRESSED THE FUCK OUT

Since I don't have anywhere to sleep, Miquel Barceló (the painter) comes around and lets me crash at his studio. It's a ground-floor affair, very pleasant, with a whitewashed patio teeming with potted planters overflowing with flowering geraniums that fill the room with their pungent aroma. It is a warm spring morning, and the sun bathes the studio in light, illuminating unfinished canvases, paint cans, pieces of old, paint-stained furniture. It would all be perfect, and I would be able to sleep like a baby if it weren't for the animals. They're everywhere: fowl, dogs, cats, as well as other more exotic types – mandrills, parrots, etcetera . . . most specifically, it is a family of gorillas and a pride of hyenas that are causing the greatest nuisance. They prefer to squabble amongst themselves out on the patio, but I still find them annoying: the hyenas laugh like a bunch of idiots and the gorillas explode in loud roars to free themselves from the harassment to which they are being subjected. The gorillas are much stronger, but there are only three adults among them; the rest are kids. There are about a dozen hyenas, on the other hand, and they're an excitable bunch. The altercation grows louder, so much so that I stick my head out to see what's going on. Various hyenas have pounced on the gorillas, who have been forced to take serious action to repel the attack. Some of the hyenas are already out of commission, rendered helpless and useless by a giant gorilla wallop that has slammed them against the wall, while other hyenas are turned into mincemeat by the ever-powerful gorilla embrace. The offensive team, however, has managed to destabilise the family-based gorilla defence and the full pack starts chasing the two little baby gorillas that are now on the run. One of them narrowly escapes getting chewed to bits by ducking into a hallway, and in one big sigh of relief, moves toward the inside of the studio. Given that I naturally side with the gorillas, I run after the little gorilla baby to see if I can help him by shutting a door behind him or something like that. But by then a group of hyenas has broken into the studio, hot on the trail of the baby gorilla. They growl as if possessed by the devil himself – they're enraged, so enraged that they even lunge toward me, flashing their bloody fangs, and I freak out and jump up to safety via a ladder that I find leaning against a huge bookcase. From that vantage point I can observe the hyenas in their chaotic, hot pursuit of the gorilla, who howls for help like an innocent, vulnerable child. I scream out to him to come back to me and climb the ladder, but by the time he reaches my outstretched hand, it's too late, he doesn't have time to climb up. They pounce on him. They've got him. Several sets of jaws nibble away at him, though rather indecisively because they know that this piece of flesh is the property of another hyena – the most frightening one – and that they'd better beat it and go look for another victim. At this point the only ones left in the room are the little baby gorilla, now paralysed with fear, the massive hyena sniffing about him, and me, fascinated by the imminence of something I sense will be shocking and terrible. I see the baby gorilla, tummy up, at the mercy of his executioner. I see the hyena rising up like a satanic serpent to the point of actually achieving a certain level of anthropomorphism. I see how he brandishes the handle of an axe in his front claws. He raises it up high and releases it downward in a clean slice that amputates the little gorilla's hand, just above his wrist. The hyena, indifferent to the spurt of blood that wets the hair of his back paws, raises the axe and cuts off the gorilla's other hand. The little gorilla is completely out of it, caught in a series of tremors that have his little baby stumps shaking, and I want to think that at this point he is unable to even suffer, given the enormity of his wounds. Finally satisfied, the hyena retreats, bearing his two trophies, with which they will create a series of macabre ashtrays. And now that I look around, I realise that these ashtrays are everywhere, filled to the brim with stubbed-out cigarettes. I am horrified, but suddenly the phone rings and I have to climb down. It must be Miquel Barceló; I have to tell him what happened so that he can get those motherfucking hyenas to behave themselves. I pick up the phone, yet it continues to ring: some goddamn phone is ringing somewhere, though I have no idea where.

Ah. In my living room. Ring-ring. Ring-ring. I jump up to answer it, still not fully emerged from my dream state.

'Pablo.'

'Gloria. What's going on?'

'Have you seen the newspaper?'

'What newspaper?'

'They've killed Robellades' son.'

'Who?'

'Robellades, the detective.'

'Whaat?'

'Are you asleep?'

'Give me a second, will you? And start at the beginning.'

By the time Lady First had calmed down enough to

slowly explain what she was talking about, I had already figured out the basic gist of things but I let her talk anyway.

'I just read it in the *Periódico de Cataluña*, on page twenty-two, it's got a photo and everything. He and his car careened off into the pit of some construction site, last night, right here, in this neighbourhood. And it's not clear whether it was an accident. They've started an investigation because there was another car involved.'

'Hang out, wait a second, I've got the newspaper here with me. Let me read it and I'll call you back.'

Page twenty-two, Society section, News Briefs subsection. 'Spectacular fatal accident in Les Corts.' Two columns. Photo: just beyond a piece of crushed metal railing, the camera breaks out onto a massive excavation site. At the bottom, right next to a giant crane, you could make out the image of an upside-down car. Caption: 'The vehicle crashed into the security railing and fell into the pit.' Article: '*El Periódico*, Barcelona. Francesc Robellades Marí, 28 years old, was taken to the Clinical Hospital in Barcelona early this morning and pronounced dead on arrival. The death has been attributed to the severe wounds he sustained when the vehicle he was driving fell into the pit of a construction site where a car park is currently being built, located at the intersection of Travessera de Les Corts and Jaume Guillamet. Also involved in the accident was a second automobile which, according to a material witness who offered testimony to the City Guard, left the scene shortly after the accident occurred, close to midnight last night. A search team has already begun an investigation to track down the second vehicle, a Red Renault 600, to clarify the facts of the occurrence and to assess the possible responsibility of the driver who left the scene of the accident. A source representing the construction company responsible for the site declared that "the area in question was appropriately lit" and that "all security measures required by the law currently in force for this type of excavation were taken." According to these same sources the fatal outcome of this accident could only be explained by an unusually violent crash, caused in part by the fact that the vehicle in question was driving at a velocity far beyond the legal speed limit. Several neighbourhood residents who heard the thunderous crash from their homes confirmed this hypothesis when they described the sound of the engines and the screeching of the tyres that preceded the spectacular fall from 12 metres high. Unfortunately, the unusual circumstances of the accident complicated the rescue attempt and despite the efforts of the emergency medical workers and the firemen who arrived on the scene, it was impossible to save the life of the young driver of the vehicle, who died en route to the hospital.'

Holy shit.

I went over to the phone and dialled Lady First and she immediately picked up.

'Don't worry, it could have been an accident. Things like this happen every day . . .' I said, to see if I could calm her down a little.

'An accident? What do you think? That they're going to put a Post-It on the corpse to say that they murdered him? No, there is no question about it: the police are already looking for a second car . . . and it happened 200 metres from this house and Sebastian's office, so don't tell me you think it's a coincidence.'

Right. Not to mention the bit about Jaume Guillamet and the small red second car, neither of which she even knew about.

'Well . . . it's probably related, but we can't be sure. In any event, we ought to try and prove it first.'

'Prove it? How?'

'I could call the editorial office of the newspaper, or the hospital, I don't know . . . I'll take care of it. For now, just stay calm and don't leave the house.'

'Don't leave the house? Of course I'm not going to leave the house. I'm still terrified. I have two small children here with me . . .'

'I'll take care of that, too. I'll get my father to send someone over as soon as possible.'

Somehow I convinced her. I guess she was so nervous that she was glad to have someone who could fend for her.

'Have you looked in the letter box? To see if that envelope you sent yourself arrived yet?'

'Yes, I checked this morning . . . but the letter box was empty. Plus our name plate was missing. And then I remembered how you'd gone down the day the Robelladeses came over and took it off for God only knows what. You didn't put it back?'

Shit. No. I hadn't put it back. When I'd left the house that afternoon I'd forgotten all about it. The envelope should have arrived days ago and because of my stupidity we might have lost it for good. Although if the package had no return address on it, it most likely would have been returned to the district post office and would be waiting there for someone to claim it.

'I'm going to need your identity card to get it from the post office. Or wait . . . did you send it to my brother?'

'I sent it without a name. Just the address.'

'The same address on your identity card?'

'Yes.'

'What time is it?'

'Nine.'

'All right. Listen, at some point this morning I'm going to stop by your house to pick up the ID card. If the guys my father's sending over come by first, give them a description of me so they'll let me upstairs.'

'What kind of a description?'

'I don't know, toots: tell them I'm attractive, elegant . . . and just in case, add about twenty kilos, a Lotus Esprit and a blood-red shirt, that's what I'll be wearing.'

Nothing like breakfast with a dead man to help you wake up and face the day. I felt badly for the kid, he seemed like a nice guy, and I felt almost worse for the father, probably because I remembered his face a little better, and it's easier to feel badly for someone whose facial features you can recall. They had irrevocably embittered his old age, and his golden tooth would shine a bit less brightly from now on. And then, I was hit by something that has happened to me less than five times in my entire life: I got really, truly, negative, thinking about Robellades Junior, Robellades Senior, my father and his getting hit by a car and even for The First, so mysteriously disappeared. The whole thing was entering a totally different phase. Now we were going to have to seriously roll up our sleeves and get to work. For the moment, however, my next move was to put together a good Sicilian defence for us.

I rang my parents' house. Beba picked up and I had to do a little dog-and-pony show so that she wouldn't suspect anything. She sounded so sad – she didn't have the foggiest idea of what the hell was going on, but she had a hunch it was something major. She told me that FH had been up all night in his office, and in the morning fired the kitchen maid. I asked her to send the call into his library.

'Dad?'

'What?'

'We need a couple of tough guys to go over to Sebastian's house.'

'Now you tell me.'

'Have you seen today's *El Periódico*?'

'Yes, and *La Vanguardia, El País, ABC, El Mundo* . . .'

'So you know?'

'If you're referring to Robellades Junior, I have been aware of it since two this morning.'

'Why didn't you call me?'

'I tried calling you from four-thirty to six in the morning, at least twenty times. And listen, the next time you try to throw off the people I hire to follow you, please at least do me the favour of listening to your phone messages. I have half of Spain's Civil Guard waiting for a Lotus to drive by at 250 kilometres per hour.'

'I'm sorry. I had no idea what was going to happen.'

'Well, don't rush. You're not going to escape quite so easily this time.'

Had they hired a McLaren with driver included? He was perfectly capable of something like that. The fact is, he'd had Lady First's residence under surveillance since early that morning, but hadn't told her anything because he didn't want to alarm her. The guys he had watching Robellades Senior had alerted him about the accident. He had already gotten in touch with someone from the Ministry of the Interior (FH never gives out names) which meant we could safely assume that the big guys were on the case now – discreetly, Miralles style, as one might say. No forms to fill out in the local police station.

'Eusebia told me about the maid.'

'Yes. I told her about the situation without getting into

too much detail, and told her she could take a few days off until things got back to normal. But she decided to leave for good. This isn't her war. And to tell you the truth, I'm much calmer now. I signed a check and that was that.'

'And Mom?'

'Still refuses to speak to me. Incidentally, it wouldn't be a terrible idea to come over and see her, if you don't mind. Every conversation between her and Eusebia ends in a fight.'

'Right. I'll stop by at some point later on today. Can I bring you anything?'

'No. They bring us everything we need.'

'OK. Listen, tell the goons over at Gloria's house to make themselves known to her. She's already read about Robellades in the paper, and she'll be much calmer when she knows she's got protection.'

For the first time in his life, I think, my father accepted my instructions on something.

All right. Given that my father was now shouldering the majority of the defence in his own way, it was time for me to pull my own strings. In my telephone book I looked up John's number in Dublin and rang him. Monday mornings he doesn't have class, and so Sunday night is technically still the weekend for him. His voice, as was to be expected, sounded something akin to the hangover-hammer: 'Come on, leave me alone, could you please? I'm hangovering, and I'm not your arsehole of a . . .'

I didn't give him time to finish. What I tried to do was get him to understand that something big was going down, and he finally let me talk.

'John. Listen. You're gonna just be quiet now for a second and listen to a bunch of questions I have to ask you, one by one. All right? Now let's go. One: have you received my email?'

'What email?'

'Good, we're on the right track. As soon as you hang up I'd like you to do me the favour of connecting to the Internet and looking at your email. Read what I send you and then send the document to someone who knows something about English literature, I want them to date it for me. Don't you have some respectable philologist on campus somewhere, or are they all like you?'

'I could send it to Woung. He went home to Hong Kong for the summer, but I've got his email. Listen, can I ask you . . .'

'Just read the document and when you finish, you'll be the first to know where it came from. Another thing. I need a hacker. The best one you can find.'

'A hacker?'

'What was the name of that German group that infiltrated the main Interpol system?'

'Stinkend Soft?'

'That's it. You're friends with one of them, aren't you?'

'With Günter. We met at one of those country meeting things that they organise with other groups . . .'

'Right. That'll do fine. I need them to find out everything they can about the domain worm.com. That's where I downloaded the document you're going to read for me. I want to know where their server is, what they do, and if possible I would like to get access to their main system hard drive. And write this down, will you?' I waited as he went to fetch pen and paper. 'Jaume Guillamet 15. It's a Barcelona address. I'm very interested in knowing what, if any, relationship exists between this address and the domain name I just gave you. Think you can get all that out of the Germans?'

'If I nudge them enough, they'll move, but they aren't like Woung. These guys only move when they want to, and if it doesn't sound interesting enough they won't go for it.'

'Don't worry about that, they'll have plenty of fun with this. The first thing I need you to do when you hang up, though, is get in touch with them. And then second, read the document. Something like seventy pages. I'm giving you three hours. I have to leave the house in a little while, though. When can you confirm for me that you've made contact with your friend Günter?'

'I don't know, I can try set up a meeting in the Metaphysical chat room. And I can get Woung in on it, too. Say about five o'clock?'

'You can't do it sooner?'

'Sooner? You sonofabitch: the only way to locate Günter is by phone, in Berlin, and he may not even be at home . . . and anyway this is all your goddamn . . .'

'John!'

'What?'

'Thanks.'

'Go to hell.'

That last bit was in Gaelic, and was immediately followed by the cluck-clong of the telephone hanging up. Right away, in a brief bout of hyperactivity, I looked at the masthead of *El Periódico* and dialled one of the numbers I found there.

'Front page, good morning.'

'Good morning. I was interested in finding out some additional information related to a news piece that appeared today in *El Periódico de Cataluña* . . .'

'Just a moment, please, I'll connect you to the news desk.'

At the news desk, another young lady connected me to

Society and in Society they patched me in to News Briefs. Finally I got to speak to someone who actually seemed to know something, but he turned out to be the sassy type.

'What company are you calling from?'

'Well, I'm calling on my own behalf.'

'And what is your name, if that isn't too much to ask?'

'Pablo Cabanillas.'

'Any relation to the politician?'

'No. No relation at all.'

'Any relation to anyone worth mentioning?'

Motherfucking son of a bitch and servile peon, I was going to say. But I refrained.

'I'm a private investigator, I don't mind giving you my licence number if that's necessary. The issue is that this accident may have something to do with one of my clients.'

'I'm sorry, Mr Detective, but we can't give out any information other than what we publish in the paper.'

'Yes, I assumed that, but I don't expect anyone to tell me anything that I couldn't find out by going over to the scene of the accident myself. I simply thought that the reporter who was there might be able to save me a bit of work, that's all.'

'We can't make any exceptions to the rule. Anyway, the reporter who covered the story isn't here right now.'

Ah, fuck it. Only about one out of every ten thousand guys is like that, but when you get stuck with one of them there's nothing you can do about it. I assumed that the police would be even less explicit, so I decided to pursue another avenue of investigation. I looked for the number of Robellades's office among the papers still sitting in my printer tray and called him. A voice answered, different from the other time I had rang. Twentysomethingish.

'Good morning,' I said. 'Mr Robellades, Senior, please?'

'Who may I say is calling?'

'Pablo Molucas, a client of his.'

'Oh, yes. Mr Robellades left a report for you last night. He'll be out of the office for a few days due to a death in the family. There's nobody else here, but if you can't come by to pick it up I can send a messenger out. Unless you'd rather wait a few days and speak to Mr Robellades yourself about it . . .'

I told her that I'd read about Robellades Junior's death in the papers and asked after him. She told me they would be burying him the following day. This very morning they would be transferring the body to the Sancho de Avila funeral chapel. I asked her to give me the office address again, and said that I would most definitely stop by that morning to pick up the report.

Apparently, the anatomical-forensic people had finished examining the corpse. What conclusion could I draw from that? No goddamn idea. I took advantage of this moment of doubt to prepare my first cup of coffee of the day, smoke a six-euro joint, shower and dress. I figured maybe the activity would help banish the major wave of negativity that had come over me.

Out on the street I was greeted by the sun and the spring entering into its finale: sidewalks all lit up like fashion show catwalks, housewives running breathlessly through the markets, clusters of office workers going back to their cubilces after breakfast, old men soaking up the UV rays and scraggly pigeons nibbling away at trash on the street. Fortunately, the Play Station generation was safely in school, which meant there was no one around to drive you batty with bicycles and balls. I arrived at the intersection of Travessera and Guillamet, not paying much attention to the path I had taken, turning here and there, more focused on sticking to the shady side of the street.

When I arrived at the corner where the accident had occurred, there was nothing at all that even suggested an accident had taken place that morning. The yellow barriers that had been put up to provide a walkway for pedestrians were back up, and the other one, a metal barrier that went all the way around the excavation site, had also been repaired. I had to look closely to identify the exact spot of the crash, but once I spotted the first tell-tale sign, the other evidence stood out more clearly: bits of broken-glass dust glittering against the asphalt, a few gnarled metal crossbeams, but most especially, a massive, curved tyre mark, a bit darker than the rest of the road, indicating a serious slamming of the brakes. When I tried to envision the logical continuation of the car's path based on the skid marks, it looked as though the car had come out from Guillamet and had taken too wide a turn round the Travessera curve. There were signs of another brake-slammer, too: the marks were shorter and shallower, and stopped short just before cutting off the longer tyre tracks from the side. This seemed to indicate that two cars had been cruising at top speed and had tried to stop short in the middle of a curve. One car had taken the barriers head-on and had jumped the metal railing, whereas the other car had managed to hit the brakes a bit earlier, or maybe had crashed into the first car, judging by the tiny chips of yellow plastic, possibly the smashed-in headlights, gleaming on the asphalt.

To clear up any lingering doubts I tried to discern whether the fallen vehicle had any kind of lateral dent, and so I stuck my head into the excavation site, just above the railing. It was a sheer drop: three or four stories' worth.

It couldn't be very easy to haul a car up from all the way down there, but it was nowhere in sight. Given the situation, the only possible line of investigation was to go back and follow the tyre marks of the brake-slammer and try to establish the precise spot where the chase had begun, if in fact there had been a chase at all. Traffic was light on that stretch, and so I walked down Jaume Guillamet in the street, intently focused on the road surface. Less than fifty metres beneath number 15 (right next to the auto-repair shop) I found another set of tyre marks: someone had torn out of there like lightning, no doubt about it. That was exactly what I had been looking for, but I didn't want to hang around the scene for too long and so I kept walking down the street. That was when I thought of passing as a journalist to try to get some information out of one of the neighbours mentioned in *El Periódico*. It wasn't going to be easy to identify them, I realised as I looked up at the block of flats on that stretch of road. And I also realised that it was slightly absurd to start investigating the death of a detective whom I had hired specifically to investigate a case of my own. Absurd and possibly very dangerous.

I had smoked an entire Ducados before I spotted a free taxi. I hailed it and asked the driver to take me to the main entrance of the Clinical Hospital, thinking I might sniff around there a bit before going to pick up Bagheera – it was only a few blocks away from the car park on Villarroel where I had left it the night before.

'I'd like to know if the body of Francesc Robellades is still here at the hospital, or if it has been sent to some outside morgue. He died last night in an accident,' I said to the lady at the information desk, very solicitous. She looked into the mystery by consulting a computer screen that, from my position, I wasn't able to get a look at.

'The body has already been transferred to the Forensic Institute. They must be preparing to take it over to Sancho de Avila by now.'

'Would it be possible to speak with a doctor who knows about the case?'

The lady started to say something about medical information hours, but warned me that as a rule the hospital generally spoke with family members only. I am aware that Sam Spade would have gone straight to the wing in question, marched down the hallway disguised as a neurosurgeon, and examined the cadaver with his own two eyes. To say nothing of what Mrs Fletcher would have managed. But the thought of inspecting the corpses of accident victims until I hit the right dead man made me a little woozy. I had no choice but to withdraw on this count.

I had already said thank you to the information lady when another idea suddenly popped into my head.

'Would you happen to know if someone by the name of Gerardo Berrocal is registered as a patient here?'

Stairway eleven, second floor, orthopedics, room forty-three. Right upstairs. Berri.

'Would you be able to tell me the nature of his medical problems?'

The lady looked at the electronic file on him: contusions, a broken tibia with open wounds and a pretty smashed-up wrist. Not very pleasant, but he'd make it back onto a motorcycle eventually.

I left the hospital and walked down to the car park on Villarroel, took Bagheera out and drove back to the neighbourhood, cruising at slow speed. On the way, I remembered I had two Guardian Angels on my tail and peered into the rearview mirror looking for the white Opel Kadett.

There they were, but they weren't alone: they seemed to be flanked by a giant Honda motorbike that was hovering near me as well. In point of fact, it amounted to no less than 750 cubic centimetres under the command of a little tough guy decked out in head-to-toe leather and topped off by a heavy-duty helmet. Sufficient for keeping tabs on a Lotus Esprit tooling down the motorway.

I pulled up in front of The First's building, left Bagheera double-parked with the lights on and went inside, hoping that the goons stationed there would let me go upstairs to pick up Lady First's identification card.

In the front hall, I found the doorman – different from the one I'd seen on other occasions – accompanied by a serious gorilla. God only knew how my father had managed to convince the neighbours to let that kind of guy stand guard in the entrance hall of an otherwise respectable building, but he'd done it. Thanks to Lady First's description he recognised me with no problem – I could tell because he immediately looked away, turned around, and raised his hand to his ear and spoke into a tiny microphone hidden somewhere in his blazer. I said hello. They responded. I went straight over to the bank of letter boxes, patted around on the top surface until I located the overturned name plate and affixed it to the corresponding box. They let me be until I started walking over toward the lift. Then the doorman popped out in front of me.

'Pablo Miralles?'

'Yes. I'm going up to see my sister-in-law.'

'She's trying to get some sleep. She left this for you.'

It was her ID card: Gloria Garriga Miranda. Fine: she saved me a trip up to the penthouse. I went back to Bagheera. I was starting to get stressed the fuck out.

At the post office there was a reasonably short line. Its

brief length, however, was more than compensated by the eternity each customer took, which made the wait sufficiently irritating. A "no smoking" sign was posted on the wall. A school-free and leash-free child trotted around the office beneath the indulgent stewardship of his poor excuse for a mother, while a dog was forced to wait at the door as his/her master licked large quantities of postage stamps. The dog was reasonably quiet and was not even wearing fluorescent socks, which only seemed to prove how very wicked the human race can be. Just as I was on the verge of immobilising the child via a direct hit in the solar plexus, it was suddenly my turn at the window. Saved by the bell, as they say, though this bell came in the form of a post office bureaucrat with eyeglasses, who looked at me with a face that seemed to say "and what the fuck do you want?"

'I'm here to pick up an envelope.'

'Do you have the notification slip?'

'No, but . . .'

No matter what I could have said, it was utterly irrelevant to him. After my long, involved explanation, the guy repeated the same question over again, although this time around he framed it in a tone that expressed the infinite patience he had for the collection of morons who came into this office every day to bother him. I tried to explain it from the beginning all over again, but he didn't even look at me this time; he seemed far more interested in one of his fingernails.

'I cannot give out any packages without the notification slip.'

As far as I was concerned, the issue had entered Phase B.

'Right. I'd like to speak with the supervisor of this office, then. Im-mediately.'

'I'm sorry, that isn't going to be possible.'

'Really? Well, if he doesn't come out right away, see that chair over there? I'm going to put it in the middle of this room, get up on it, pull down my pants, and if the supervisor still hasn't come out, then I'll just start wanking off right there in front of everybody: women, children, dogs too. And I'll make sure to ejaculate as far as possible – and let me warn you, I have damn good aim. So do whatever you think is best.'

'Excuse me: I already told you the supervisor cannot come out. And if you continue to insist upon it, I will have to call the police.'

'Do what you have to do, but warn them to bring a couple of sponges because they'll be able to open a sperm bank with all the come I'm going to leave on that wall. I've been saving up for a couple of weeks now.'

'What do I care?' he said. 'All right. Next in line, please.'

He fancied himself quite the tough guy, but he didn't know who he was messing with. I turned halfway around, picked up the chair that I had been referring to and, making all the noise I possibly could, placed it in the middle of the office and climbed up on it, not without a slight bit of difficulty given that my body was somewhat unfit for any type of climb. Then, from that high vantage point which only emphasised my triumphant mass, I struck up a bit of a sorcerer's pose to ensure I had sufficiently stolen the audience's attention. Then I began the spectacle, slowly unbuttoning my shirt.

'The itsy bitsy spider went up the water spout . . .'

I sang the tune with my right arm raised, with the appropriate manual choreography as accompaniment. When my left hand had undone all but the last two buttons of my shirt, I saw the postal clerk scurry toward a door that led to some unidentifiable back office. I quickly got down from the chair, put it back in its place and buttoned up by the time the lackey had returned with his superior, so that I would seem like any other, vaguely normal person waiting at the counter. The superior in question was a fortysomething woman in a grey jacket and a little postal office name tag on her lapel: a model of efficiency. I told her that due to construction work that was being carried out in my sister-in-law's building, the identification on her letter box had been removed, etcetera, etcetera. After a bit of hesitating, she finally handed over the envelope and made me sign some paper and asked for my own ID card in addition to that of Lady First. Luckily she didn't seem to care that it had expired.

I returned to the Beast and parked on the sidewalk to examine the envelope at my leisure.

I opened it up and extracted a manilla folder filled with papers. Many papers. The first one was a multi-page report that had been drawn up by an American company specialising in commercial assessments. I scanned it quickly. The second thing was a brochure for some gym equipment, which I immediately disregarded. Had Lady First placed these papers in the envelope exactly as they had been placed in that desk drawer?, I asked myself. A detective's job is never as easy as it looks: you have to ask the right questions, naturally, but you also have to know how to interpret the answers, and my syllogistic intelligence tends to be stymied by an excess of imagination, such that as soon as I arrive at the only possible answer to an enigma, I immediately think up another twenty-five possibilities that get in the way. So I sat there for a while, flipping through the papers over and over again to see what jumped out at me. It was a real mishmosh of things: copies of letters to clients, a business card (Bernardo Almáciga, Coiffeur), more commercial assessments, a bill from a posh mechanic for a tune-up and an oil change (five hundred euros plus VAT), a Gucci tie catalogue, a few Microsoft Access printouts, a note written in my Magnificent Brother's magnificent penmanship ('Half is less than what one may think,' it read) and . . . toward the end of the little pile, various computer-printed pages, stapled together, with a long list of addresses. June 22 was the date on the document header, followed by a list of addresses, in various European cities: Bordeaux, Manchester . . . Very quickly, on page three, I found this:

G.S.W. Amanci Viladrau
Password: 25th Montanyà St;
08029-Barcelona (Spain)
Address: 15th, Jaume Guillamet St, 08029-Barcelona (Spain)

I found it so quickly partially because I was looking out for it but also because it was highlighted with an irregular circle that made it stand out on the page. Just outside of the circle, in the same pencil and in the same superlative penmanship, one single word had been written.

Pablo.

A shiver ran up my spine, and I almost tossed the paper aside from the shock. Seeing my name there seemed like some kind of jinx, I dont know, it was like the graphic representation of me, standing in front of that little walled-in garden on Jaume Guillamet, like a sinister premonition that was only just beginning to be fulfilled.

I had started up the engine when something suddenly hit me: my Magnificent Brother always calls me Pablo José, just like my Mother's Highness. And he does it precisely because he knows I dislike it when people address me as such. Even on the Post-Its he uses for himself, he always writes "P. José", just as he had my number recorded on his mobile. So you can imagine the vertigo I felt when it occurred to me that my Magnificent Sister-in-Law just might have forged the note, imitating her husband's handwriting expressly so that I would see it and take special note of the address.

Once again, the more I knew, the less I knew. But instead of allowing myself to drown in the abyss, I chose to drive over to Robellades' office.

The traffic was a major drag. The Barcelona board of education must have opened its cages right about then, because a couple of human mutts toting school bags (or those modern substitutes, with wheels and other accessory attachments) trotted over and tried to get close to the window so they could check out Bagheera's interior. I growled at them and they went running for cover behind a postbox, where they proffered me a fuck-you gesture with their arms. Ignatius J. Reilly was right: there is no such thing as geometry or theology anymore. There isn't jack shit.

Half an hour later I arrived at the Robellades consultancy, which occupied the second floor of an old building. The girl who greeted me at the reception desk was the same one I had spoken to on the phone. Now that she saw me in person, I think she kind of dug me, maybe because for women I seem to represent all the things they've been taught to despise. And that is often quite a little turn-on for them. Given the severity called for by the rather grim occasion, however, she limited herself to being polite and properly cordial. I collected the envelope, paid the three hundred euros requested by the invoice she then handed me, and after another few seconds I was downstairs again, face to face with a traffic cop who was taking note of Bagheera's number plate.

'Ticket?'

'Yes, sir. You've parked in a zone for loading and unloading, commercial vehicles only.'

'Would it be worth anything if I said I came to load this envelope?'

'And are you also going to tell me that this is a commercial vehicle?'

'It's a Kuwaiti taxicab, sir. You know what those sheikhs are like . . .'

'Right: they put Barcelona number plates on all their sport-model taxicabs.'

'The B is for Burqan, south-west corner of the country. Funny coincidence, wouldn't you say?'

'Nice try. But you're going to have to tell your sheikh that if he really wants, he can to try to appeal it.'

Forty euros. I thought about paying it on the spot, but I decided it would be better to have them just send it on to my Magnificent Brother, to piss him off when he returned. I rounded the corner and pulled over on another wide sidewalk, the Carretera de Sarriá, to read the report. Another decent-sized envelope, but thinner than the one I'd picked up at the post office. This one contained only three typewritten sheets of paper.

Barcelona, blah, blah. Mr and Mrs Molucas, preliminary report on the blah, blah, blah, disappearance of Eulalia Robles Miranda (why did that last name sound so familiar?), etcetera, etcetera, etcetera, and another page and a half of etceteras that I more or less disregarded and then at the end, a bold-face conclusion.

'With all due caution, we believe that her disappearance is most likely related to that of Sebastian Miralles, who seems to have a certain conflict of interest with a certain real-estate company, that is most probably based in or around the city of Bilbao. His disappearance is very likely due to the pending resolution of this real-estate issue.

'Finally, given the aforementioned information, we cannot discard the possibility that the two aforementioned people may be travelling together of their own free will, and may be located at the present time somewhere in the north of Spain.'

Too much. The Robelladeses had done a good job – I realised this as I reread the report from start to finish in the interest of following all the steps of the investigation that had led them to their conclusions. I also realised that the last source with whom they had been in touch had no doubt been my Mother's Highness, the queen of misinformation. If the KGB had hired her, Texas would be part of the USSR today: only she could have suggested that bit about the Bilbao property-management company, which could only be the Ibarra that graced the jar of mayonnaise in my kitchen. For a moment, though, I did feel liberated from that invisible weight on my shoulders when I double-checked that no mention had been made of the house on Jaume Guillamet. There was nothing at all to suggest that there was any connection between the guy's death and my case. Of course, right then I remembered the tyre tracks and the little bits of yellow headlight glass scattered not fifty metres from the little garden on Guillamet. If it was a coincidence, it was quite an unusual one. It seemed far more likely that Robellades Junior had hit upon some new lead after his father had already drafted the report, and had decided to follow it up himself – all the way down to the bottom of an excavation pit for a new neighbourhood car park, four stories below street level.

I still had a wad of bills that I had stuck in my pocket when I'd left the house, but I stopped at a cash machine anyway for six hundred more. Then, as I went down Travessera again, I thought of going to look for Nico. Maybe I could buy some coke off of him, and in any event it wouldn't kill me to stock up on hash – with all the activity, my stash had diminished considerably. I double-parked for a second and went into the plaza.

No sign of Nico.

On my way back to the Beast I bumped into the same Guardian Angel I'd seen before at the gas station. He had gotten out of the Kadett and followed me through the plaza.

'Sorry to have made you break into a run. I just stopped for a second to look for a friend,' I said.

'No problem, do whatever you want. Occupational hazards, you know.'

'Have you got the time?'

'Two.'

Time to start thinking about the old tummy.

'Hey: how would you like some lunch? It's on me.'

'Hmm . . . I'd have to ask Lopez about that.'

Lopez, it turned out, was the other Guardian Angel, who had stayed behind in the car. We approached him. He was a pot-bellied fiftyish type, dressed in an outmoded blazer. I repeated the invitation through the window.

'Thanks, but we can't do it.'

'Come on, man. I'm hungry, and when I go into a restaurant I take a long time before coming out. What are you two going to do until then, park outside the door and order a pizza?'

'It wouldn't do for us to be seen together.'

'Well, we could agree to meet at some out-of-the-way joint and then leave here separately. I doubt anyone could follow both of us.'

The guy was still hesitant. I kept at it.

'Come on, I'm having a bad day. They've kidnapped my brother, smashed into my father, and killed the detective I hired to investigate the situation. I'm not in the mood to eat alone.'

He softened up a bit. He asked me if I liked paella. I said yes.

'Do you know those outdoor cafeterias at Las Planas, in front of the train station? Take the Vallvidrera road there. The motorcycle will follow you. We'll lag behind, tailing you.'

He removed a hand-held radio from a unit in the centre of the dashboard and said something to someone who was listening in from somewhere. The pot-bellied dude was sharp: the continuous zigzag of the Vallvidrera road gave the motorcycle an advantage over almost any other car. Anyway. There was paella and lamb chops for everyone, plus some cheap red wine – refrigerator-cold, though that was remedied by some sweet fizzy *gaseosa*. Followed by shots and a round of cheap cigars. And then there was the conversation, which was straight out of central casting: Lopez, a former cop, had plenty of lurid stories under his belt, and Antonio had his share of low-rent shenanigans as well, having been a common carjacker in his day. The motorcycle dude and I mostly listened to the other two. Good guys. By the time we made our way back to Barcelona – slowly – we were all a little tipsy. I'm sure all they wanted to do was park in front of my building and take a little nap in the car.

When I arrived home, in fact, that was exactly what I felt like doing, but I had to connect to the internet first.

I went straight to worm.com, entered the site, introduced the password "molucas_worm" in the space and found myself back again on the page with the questions related to *The Stronghold. What was Harry holding in his hand when he met the Queen? A red kerchief* was the answer. *What did the King do on the castle ground? Training* was the answer to that one, and it went on and on until I finished the twenty questions, which were not always quite so trivial as those first few. Two or three times, in fact, I had to consult the printout before being able to select an answer from the drop-down menus. I hit *submit* and crossed my fingers.

Bingo. Now, beneath the sign that read 'Welcome to the Worm Gate,' were three sentences written in modern English:

The road is long and difficult. One life is
not always enough.

Ask your conscience. Impoverished is he who
approaches with impure intentions.
He will never reach the heart of the worm,
but he will nonetheless be pursued.

Ask your conscience. Welcome is he who
approaches with a pure soul.
He will not reach the heart of the worm but he
will nonetheless be well-loved.

In short: three rings for the eleven kings under the sky and the fat lady sings. That was it, along with a link that led to the email address mail@worm.com and a button that said "First Contact." It was all so childish, but I don't know . . . Anyway, I did have good reason to think that all these threats were not empty ones. Oh, God. I summoned up all my cojones and hit the button. Luckily I had given them a fake snail-mail address the day before when I had filled out the first form to get the access code – close to my real address, which was handy because when the page finished loading, a name and a telephone number appeared, and it seemed to have been assigned based on geographic proximity to the information I had given them. Specifically, this name and telephone number were *Villas, 93 430 1321*

Of course, I instantly bolted from the chair and went looking for the slip of paper where I had taken notes on the numbers in The First's mobile phone directory. There it was: *Villas, 93 430 1321.*

I returned to the screen. 'Call this number and tell the Worm you are Molucas_worm,' it said below the telephone number.

Too fast. Too goddamn fast. Calm. Serenity. Let's think for a second. I had already rang that number. I had rung it, they had answered and then immediately hung up. I remember it perfectly, I had tried it one or two times, in fact. Was it because I hadn't given them some kind of password? Now I had it, but was it in my best interests to use it?

After a bit I decided I was better off waiting until I had a better idea as to the authenticity of *The Stronghold*. This led me to the realisation that in less than an hour I would have to be prepared to face another trio, one that was aeons away from my Guardian Angels. An Irish metaphysic suffering from a severe hangover, a German techie, and a

Chinese philologist specialising in Medieval English Literature.

Keeping things calm and copacetic in life sure is one hell of a job.

OBERON IN THE WOOD

I tried to sleep, but I couldn't. Too many ideas running through my head.

I got out of bed, but there was still a bit of time to kill before the chat, and since patience is not my strongest suit, I decided to get a jump-start on things and rang John anyway. He answered in a fine display of foul humour.

'I hope you don't mind my asking what the fuck is wrong with you. I just spoke to Günter not five minutes ago. Says he can't do anything from home. He's punished.'

'He's what?'

'Punished. His father says he can't hook up to the Internet for a week. What's the matter? Don't they punish you in Spain when you misbehave? Or don't they – and that's why you turn out to be such immature adults?'

'How old is he?'

'Günter? Thirteen. Why?'

This was the last straw. For God's sake, there must be a hundred thousand hackers in the world who also happen to be legal adults, and I had to end up with an adolescent punished with modem confiscation. Luckily, John assured me that all was not lost. The kid could go to Stinkend Soft's clubhouse and connect to the chat and at the same time look into the problem for us. By the end of the afternoon, he would be able to give us some kind of answer.

'Have you started *The Stronghold*?'

'Are you gonna get off my arse? Yes, I've been reading it this morning.'

'Right. So listen, do you mind connecting now and we can talk in the chat room? Calling Dublin costs a fortune from here.'

He grudgingly agreed. I gave him five minutes to connect and went over to my own computer to boot up. Our home page on Metaclub.net featured a few new design tweaks that I would have liked to examine a bit more closely, but I didn't have time for that. I went straight to the chat section and entered the general room. There was John's nickname, "Jhn", in the attendance box. The conversation went as follows:

Pbl> Right. I'm here.

Jhn> I hope you're happy, you've ruined my entire day. Would you mind telling me what this madness is all about?

Pbl> You said you read *The Stronghold*, right?

Jhn> Yes, what about it?

Pbl> You didn't notice anything strange?

Jhn> Was I supposed to?

Pbl> Shit, Jhn, how old is it? How old would you say the text is?

Jhn> Middle English, 14th century more or less. Maybe earlier. Woung could tell us for sure.

Pbl> Don't get sulky on me, I can't handle it right now.

Jhn> What?

Pbl> Have you read the full text of the poem?

Jhn> Yesssssssss.

Pbl> And you don't find it strange to see Freudian references popping up in a 14th century text?

Jhn> Come on, Pablo: Freud is anything but original, he's all over the entire canon of world literature.

Pbl> Well, what about Russell, then? There is a complete

explication of the language-portrait theory, and that's strictly 20th century.

Jhn> Thanks for the clarification. I have a real tough time remembering what century Russell wrote in.

Pbl> I'm serious. The theory is there, almost word for word, in about a dozen verses down toward the end of the poem.

Jhn> If I'm not mistaken, the language-portrait theory literally proposes the isomorphism between language and reality. Is there some verse in there that mentions that, in such a literal way?

Pbl> You know as well as I do that it can be explained in other words . . . Remember the part where Henry tries to draw a sketch of the fortress structure? There's a couple of stanzas where he makes exactly the same assumptions as Russell: the idea of studying language to understand the structure of reality, the same combination of blindness and clarity. And in the *Tractatus*, Wittgenstein discusses the propositions of language as 'paintings of that which is real', and that is exactly the same expression used in the poem, the reference is obvious, all you have to do is read it.

– Woung from Hong Kong is joining the chat at 17:01 (GTM +1)

That was the little message generated by the system to alert us that the Chinese guy had clicked on.

Woung> Hello, Jhn and company.

Jhn> Woung, I'd like to introduce you to Pablo, my associate in Barcelona.

Woung> Pleasure to meet you, Pablo. I've heard quite a bit about you.

Pbl> Hi, Woung, thank you for coming.

– 121 from Berlin is joining the chat at 17:02 (GTM + 1)

Another newcomer to the chat room. The nickname didn't ring any bells.

Jhn> What can you tell us about the text, Woung? Pbl is ranting on about some anachronistic content-form hypotheses.

121> Hi, jhn. are you john?

Woung> Well, I haven't had time to read the entire poem, just a few stanzas here and there. Interesting.

– Puck from Norway is joining the chat at 17:04 (GTM + 1)

Things got difficult from this point on. A chat with four guys and an elf is not the easiest thing to follow.

Jhn> Yes, 121, I'm Jhn. Are you Günter?

121> yes, günter. hello for all. my english not so good.

Jhn> I'd like to introduce you all to Günter: the best hacker this side of the Mississippi.

Pbl> Hi, 121.

Pbl> Woung: can you give us a preliminary estimate of a date for that document?

Puck> 121: are you really a hacker? Did you hit the NASA computers with a virus?

Woung> Middle English: most definitely later than the 12th century.

Pbl> Woung: can you be a bit more specific? What's the

very latest date you would put it at? That's what I'm mainly after.

Woung> Not so easy to place an upper limit on the date. I would say 14th century, but it could also be 13th or 15th. Strictly basing my judgment on the language used, I can't get more specific than that.

121> puck: i not cracker who plants virus.

Jhn> puck: never ask a hacker if he is a hacker.

Woung> A precise dating requires a content analysis plus a fair amount of historical research and documentation. This is usually done in teams with specialists in different areas. I haven't even read the whole poem.

Puck> Why can't I ask?

121> puck: i not cracking. i like hacking. much admire.

Pbl> Woung: It's a shame, because there isn't a single explicit historical reference in the entire text – like battles, wars, recognisable characters. Is that what you meant?

Jhn> Puck: because a real hacker would never introduce himself as such. It is an honour that others confer upon him.

Pbl> 121: has John told you about what I need?

Puck> What's cracking?

Pbl> 121: the text I am discussing with Woung has to do with the domain worm.com.

Woung> Not just specific historical references, but the whole environment – clothing, furniture, customs . . . They help a great deal with dating.

121: yes, pbl. jhn told me a little.

Puck> Is someone going to tell me what cracking is?

121> Cracking is bad cyberpunk. Hacking no never zerströrend. Hacking good construction for liberty.

Jhn> Puck: the idea is that the crackers are bad and stupid and the hackers are good and intelligent.

Pbl> Woung: do me a favour, write down everything that came into your head when you read those stanzas. I'm interested in anything that might have occurred to you. I'll read whatever.

Pbl> 121: can you get the information I need?

121> hacking is information for all in harmony.

Jhn> There are some cracker movements that denounce the hacker hypocrisy, and propose a kind of purification by fire, revolutionary style.

Puck> 121: but have you broken into NASA?

Pbl> Jhn, do you mind, if you can't help at all at least don't be a nuisance. Don't get 121 going, come on.

Woung> At first glance, we find a poem of 500 some-odd dodecasyllabic verses, with a consonant ABABA rhyme, very typical of the 12th century.

121> pbl: yes i can give you information. but better with help.

Jhn> Listen, you shithead, you dragged me out of bed at nine in the morning and now I can't talk about what I want to talk about in my own club? If you don't want to read me just hit ignore and stop being such a bloody pain in the ass.

121> yes i have done hacking in nasa.

Woung> The lexicon most likely corresponds to the late 13th century, which makes the versification even older.

Pbl> What kind of help, 121?

Pbl> Keep going, Woung. I'm still listening.

Puck> LOL.

Woung> The spelling could also be dated to the 13th century, although it seems to be more representative of the 14th. In any event, it isn't later than 15th.

Jhn> What are you laughing at, Puck?

121> Pbl: help from friends.

Woung> I'm not stopping, Pbl, I just can't type that fast.

Puck> Your 'shithead' comment was very funny. I thought this was a philosophy chat room.

Pbl> I'm sorry, Woung. I really appreciate your help. Keep going however fast you can.

>>121: help from friends? Can you get it? Have you been able to find anything out?

Jhn> Puck: it is, it's very philosophical.

>>Pbl: Speaking of which, shithead, have you read those Primary Sentences I sent you?

Woung> From what little I've read I can tell you that the document includes some characters that are typical of the quest: the knight, the king, the enchanter, the queen . . . all of which recalls the old talktales; it's possible that the story has something to do with a Breton legend that evolved into a series of different written versions.

Puck> Pbl: you worried about something?

121> i tested with satan. good security there. must try with password generator. a few hours if lucky. maybe a trojan. very important to enter?

Jhn> SHITHEAD: I WANT TO KNOW IF YOU HAVE READ MY PRIMARY SENTENCES.

Pbl> I'm sorry Puck, I'm not in the mood for chit-chat. Another day.

Woung> In short: I would bet that it is from the 14th century, but I can't be completely sure. It's always difficult to know for sure. There are Robin Hood tales that people have studied for years and they still can't figure out if they're from the 12th or 14th century.

Pbl> 121: what is 'satan' and 'trojan'?

>>Jhn: STICK IT UP YOUR ARSE FOR A WHILE, WILL YOU? YOU AND YOUR PRIMATE SENTENCES.

Woung> It would also not be uncommon for the text

to be a compilation of fragments that were expanded upon or reinterpreted in successive versions from various different time periods.

Pbl> Woung: could this be an apocryphal text? false? i mean, it is possible that it is a contemporary imitation of an archaic style?

Puck> 121: does NASA have information on extraterrestrials?

121> satan: security analyser, basic hacker tool. trojan is a program that enters system like trojan horse. spy program.

Jhn> Listen shithead, the only "primate" here is you. And I should remind you that we have work to do. I may be the one appointed to draft these things, but if you don't even make the effort to read what i send you its going to be years before we have a minimally presentable theoretical corpus. Up to you.

Woung> I don't believe the text is false. The possibility always exists, but I think it's small in this case. For this to have been written by a contemporary writer the author would have to be not only a very erudite philologist but also an excellent poet. If we were only talking about a few stanzas, maybe, but over a thousand excellent verses . . .

121> too much information in NASA, fun to enter but too much info to look and look.

Pbl> [*private to Jhn*] I haven't been able to read them all, John. Don't get angry, I'm sorry. I'm in a real fucking mess right now. We'll talk later. I'll send you an email or we can talk on the phone.

Puck> 121: can't you show me how to get into NASA? That's a fun site to wreak havoc on.

Woung> John tells me that you found the document on the web. What surprises me is that I've never heard of it before. There aren't all that many extant Middle English documents, period, and I'm pretty familiar with the principal sources. Maybe if by looking into the website you found it on you'll come up with more information.

121> what 'havoc' mean?

Jhn> [*Private to Pbl*] I hope so. I'd like to hear how you plan to justify what you've put me through today.

Pbl> 121: "havoc" means *schelmenstreich*; don't pay attention to Puck: Puck is another name for poltergeist. So you can't tell me anything, absolutely anything about the domain that I'm interested in?

>>Woung: I'm on it, 121 is investigating the origin system.

Puck> I'm no poltergeist, I'm a sprite.

Jhn> Puck: How the hell did you end up in this chat room?

Woung> If you come across any more info send it to me at woungw@usa.net. I'd appreciate it. Meanwhile I'll read through the poem. Can you give me an email?

Jhn> [*Private to Pbl*] I already told you that you have to nudge Günter a little. He's just being lazy. Present the job to him like some kind of fascinating mystery that he may be able to crack, if not he'll forget about you the minute he leaves the chat and turn his attentions to something other than your paranoia.

121> I'm sorry Pbl, I haven't found anything out yet.

Jhn> Puck: Poltergeist means 'sprite' in German. See how this is a serious chat, we even speak German.

Puck> Jhn: us sprites like to butt in where we don't belong! Like in NASA for example.

Pbl> Woung: miralles@metaclub.net. That's my metaphysical club email.

Puck> This is getting boring.

>>Jhn: why don't you tell all those funny things you told me in private about Pbl.

Woung> Incidentally, Pbl and Jhn, I heard about a student in Richmond who is interested in writing a thesis about the ideas that you exchange on the site. Right now he's trying to get the Philosophy Department to accept the idea, and it looks like they will. I've heard some very attractive versions of that Invented Reality theory of yours. You're very much the rage in the humanities departments on the East Coast. I was there this winter.

Jhn> I don't know what you're talking about, Puck. I haven't sent you any private message.

Pbl> Puck: I think we can safely say you've gotten caught with your pants down.

Jhn> If Pbl drank a little less and worked a little more we'd be able to publish something coherent, but as of now we don't even have a formal definition for the theory, it's just a pile of email messages scattered across the net. I wouldn't mind if you put me in touch with this student, though. Maybe he can help us assemble it all. We could use an intern.

Puck> Ah, who cares, anyway? . . . you're really boring you guys. I'm going. Maybe I'll find Oberon in the wood . . .

– Puck left the chat at 17:26 (GTM + 1)

Jhn> What a pain in the arse, that sprite.

Pbl> [*Private, to 121, Jhn*] Günter, I have to clarify something for you. Your help and the help of your friends is extremely important. I know it sounds insane, but this is the short version of the story: we are trying to determine the origins of a 14th century poem that (pay attention) contains information as to things that have happened in the six centuries that followed. Woung is working with us: he is a specialist in Medieval English Literature, and in fact has just confirmed the age of the text. We know that the domain worm.com has something to do with the poem and we think that if we can get to the system where it originated we can gain access to more information. Do you understand how important your work is to us? Experts all over the world are involved but we need a crack tech team. In a way, we're trying to obtain information about the future. So please, send me an email when you have some information. I'll be waiting for your message. And be discreet, please, this can't get out to too many people, just inform your closest colleagues.

In the end, I guess I did get a little carried away, but I figured my words had done the trick. For a thirteen-year-old kid, adventure is still a possibility, no matter how mental it may seem. At the very least, he did promise to do something that afternoon, and to send me an email as soon as he had any information. As far as everyone else, the message mania went on like that for a few more minutes, but I'd already gotten all the information I could for the moment, and so I disconnected as soon as my minimal sense of courtesy permitted it. As always, my investigative efforts had proven fruitless: on one hand, *The Stronghold* did seem genuinely ancient, but on the other hand I wasn't so sure that that was such a weird thing. And it is true that the entire history of philosophy is a continuous process of formulation and reformulation – behind every supposedly contemporary idea you can always find some precursor.

The fact is, the mental stew I had cooked up had gotten

pretty potent by then. I had to cool off, detox somehow, and given that there was nothing left for me to do from home, I figured that I would pay the visit I had promised my family. At the same time I could check in and see if my father had found out anything interesting vis-à-vis the Robellades Junior accident.

I was just walking out the door when the phone rang.

'Heeeeey, how are you?'

Just what I needed.

'Well, you know. Here, answering the telephone.'

'So? What do you have to say for yourself?'

'I have nothing to say, Fina. Absolutely nothing. I'm simply waiting to hear why the hell you're calling me.'

Before she would tell me, I had to apologise for being so unkind and then I found out that José María was going to be coming home late from the office, and so she had decided to make a date to see me. That is, of course, as long as I behaved as if she were the one doing me the favour. But I had other plans that evening.

'I can't, Fina. Let's hang out tomorrow, if you're free.'

'Oh . . . and may I ask why you can't today?'

Shit. More improvising.

'Well . . . I have a date.'

'A date? You? Not with some tramp?'

Totally on the fly, I followed her lead:

'She's not a tramp.'

'I knew it . . . One day you suddenly turn up in a posh sports car, dressed up like some flashy thirtysomething, running around dropping loads of cash . . . but that's not even the worst part. The worst part is that you don't even crack jokes like you used to anymore. You're . . . fogged out.'

'I know. I thought, shit, at my age this sort of thing couldn't possibly happen to me.'

I said it in a little lamb voice, as if I was chagrined by it all.

'That little slut . . . so who is she, if I may ask?'

'I met her at my mother's birthday dinner. Our parents are friends. I'm meeting her for dinner . . . and then a few drinks, maybe . . .'

'Really. Well, after I hang up, you will never hear from me again. So you dump me for the first amateur whore that crosses your path, is that it?'

'Fina, come on, it's just part of life . . .'

'That's a low blow. You made me a promise, or don't you remember? You promised me that if you fell in love with anyone one day it would be me.'

'Don't be ridiculous, Fina. What kind of promise is that?'

'Your kind of promise, obviously. And now you're giving me that "I've-fallen-for-the-bitch-daughter-of-my-parents'-best-friends bit" . . .'

'I have said nothing of the sort. And don't call her a bitch.'

'Why not? After all, she did seduce you like she would a . . . a teenager. You get all dressed up, put on expensive cologne, and start acting all . . . absent. And what? Have you fucked her already, or is that what you have planned for tonight?'

'Fina, please . . .'

'"Fina, please . . ." You know what I say? I'm going to go out on the town tonight. By myself. I have admirers, too, in case you weren't aware.'

Anyway.

Once I got downstairs, I advised my Guardian Angels of my plans. They were still in the Kadett, playing cards to pass the time. The motorcycle dude was nowhere to be found. I supposed that, now that I had stopped trying to dodge the surveillance, my FH had relieved him of his duties. I didn't feel like walking over there, though, and briefly considered taking Bagheera out, but a taxi was scooting past the Kadett just at that moment and so I stopped it, almost as a reflex. I'll never know if that taxi saved my arse or put me in even more serious danger that day, but I guess I did live to tell about it.

I found neither Mariano the doorman nor the uniformed security guard in the vestibule of my parents' building. The battalion of gorillas had escalated to another level entirely: two of them were pacing up and down the street, two more were parked in front of the building, and two more were stationed up above, at the door to their apartment – and who knew how many others there were that I couldn't see. They all seemed to be connected by walkie-talkie, or telephone, or some contraption that stuck out of their ears. One of the goons downstairs asked me to take the service elevator upstairs. Apparently the access to the front door was now wired to some kind of electronic set-up, but it looked as though the drawbridge was up. The bigger of the two goons upstairs had to ring the door around twenty-five times, until my Mother's Highness finally answered, an entirely unprecedented move on her part. Her appearance, however, was business as usual: blouse with exotic embroidery, enough make-up for watching the telly, the usual hanging-around-the-house pearls. She didn't even seem as nervous as one would expect her to be. Was it Valium? The sauna? Gonzalito's expert massage technique?

'Ah, Pablo José, come in, come in, dear. This is madness, you know. We are now without a kitchen maid. Your beast of a father fired her this morning – I'll tell you all about that later. And I don't know what is with Eusebia, she refuses to answer the door.' She stepped toward the service hall and raised her voice to call out, 'Eusebia, didn't you hear the doorbell?' Then she turned back to me. 'That moustache is really not very becoming on you, Pablo, José,' she said as she offered up her cheeks for me to kiss. 'You look like a football referee, a big fat football referee . . . You must promise me that you're going to go to a fitness club, darling. And that you'll shave off that awful moustache.'

In the middle of all this, I heard a toilet flush and the sound of water taps from down the service hallway. After a few seconds, Beba appeared, smoothing out her skirt.

'Didn't you hear the doorbell, Eusebia?'

'Of course I heard it: half a dozen times, but I was in the toilet taking a pee.'

'Oh. I've said it to you before and I'll say it again – just tell us you were in the toilet, there's no need to get specific about what you're doing in there. The other day you said the same thing in front of Mrs Mitjans.'

'If you don't want to know, don't ask . . . Anyway, what's the big deal: Mrs Mitjans never takes a pee? God . . . is she a hen or something?'

Part One of the family encounter was my mother's show, and she led me into the living room as quickly as she could. We sat between two polychromatic pantocrators (when she had bought them there was no convincing her that pantocrators were not meant to be displayed in pairs), and I settled in to patiently listen to her version of the events that had transpired over the past day. In short, the long-suffering spouse and mother sitting before me was the victim of a triple conspiracy: that of her obstinate and intolerant husband, that of her obstinate and impertinent cook, and that of her obstinate and insensitive sons – most especially The First, whose obstinacy and insensitivity was made even worse by the fact that he had not even bothered to ring her on the phone. So. Once my mother had told me her side of the story, I figured it was all right for me to start in with my own investigation:

'Mom. Have you spoken recently with a Mr Robellades?'

'Mmm . . . no.'

'Nobody has telephoned asking after Sebastian?'

'I don't know . . . your paranoid father has been in the library day and night answering the telephone himself. See the little light? It's been that way all day long.'

She was pointing to the phone on the end table, and she was referring to the calls to the apartment's 'social' line.

'And you haven't spoken to anyone about the issue I mentioned to you the other day – about Ibarra . . . that rude man who is putting us through all this?'

'No. Just to Gonzalito and Mrs Mitjans. And maybe with one or two other friends. But I haven't breathed a word of it to your father, I promise . . . Oh, yes. Now I remember, yes. A man did call asking after your brother . . . a very strange man . . .'

'Strange how?'

'I don't know, darling. Strange. He kept repeating the same thing over and over again . . . I don't remember what, but it was awfully irritating. He asked after Juan Sebastian and I told him he was up north travelling.'

'Up north travelling? That's all? You didn't say anything about Ibarra?'

'Who?'

'Mom. For God's sake. Ibarra. The rude man.'

'How could I have mentioned him if I can't even remember his name?'

Ugh. Enough. Clearly, the part of Robellades' report that

involved the Ibarra story came straight from my mother. I decided not to press the issue any more – if she noticed some hole in the story, I would have to start making up more lies.

The next phase of the family encounter was with Beba, in the kitchen. As soon as she saw me walk in she wiped her hands on her apron and planted the two kisses she doesn't dare to proffer in the presence of my mother. She was getting ready to make little balls out of the croquette batter sitting on the counter.

'What are you waiting for, to talk to your father? Go, go, start making me those croquettes while I start on your mother's meal. All she eats now is fish that's half-raw and plants . . . seawheat, she calls it . . . how could she want to eat seawheat when she's got home-made croquettes? Plus, without the kitchen maid, she's got me doing double time . . .'

I washed my hands and began sculpting little oblong clumps with the béchamel-and-cod mixture. It never occurred to me that this might be the last time I'd ever make Beba's croquettes for her. She went hunting through the refrigerator and took out a bunch of little bowls with seaweed. Among them I noticed two varieties that were the same as the ones that had garnished the lobsters the night the Blascos had come to dinner.

'Good Lord, how disgusting. Where I come from, they wouldn't feed this slime to the pigs on the farm. Can you tell me why this lady can't just eat what everyone else eats . . . ? Oh, and those boys outside? I have to make them something, don't I?'

She was referring to the gorillas stationed at the front door.

'Don't worry. They're on shifts.'

'And what if one of them has to work the dinner shift?'

'Don't worry about that, Beba. My father will take care of them.'

This comment evidently pushed some button of hers, because she suddenly got all dramatic on me.

'Holy Mary, mother of God, what has happened to this home? You would think, at my age, all I want is a little bit of peace and quiet . . . and look at me now . . . trapped.'

'Beba, stop exaggerating.'

'But that's what we are, trapped . . . Lucky for me that boy outside is such a dear, he even went downstairs to get my medicinal water . . .'

'C'mon, be patient, it's just a few days, that's all.'

She was not convinced by my attempt to minimise the seriousness of the matter. She pursed her lips as she dropped little bunches of seaweed into a mixing bowl and shook her head back and forth.

'No.'

'No what . . . ?'

'Something's not right about all this . . . now I'm getting mad, too. Look, it's been a week and your brother hasn't come by, or called, or breathed! It's as if the earth swallowed him up. Something's happened, I know it . . .'

That was about when the crying fit started. She didn't even try to keep on talking, she just pressed her lips closed and continued, quite doggedly, piling up the bunches of seaweed until the big, fat tears started rolling down her cheeks. I put the croquettes aside, made a vague motion of wiping my hands free of the batter and gave her a squeeze. Her eyes were still all welled up and she resisted surrendering to my hug but finally she let herself go and bawled her eyes out.

'Come on, silly, don't cry. If something really bad

happened, you'd know about it. Plus: Sebastian's tough, with all that judo and tae kwon do, you know him . . . he's liable to crush anyone that breathed on him wrong.'

No good. In addition to soaking my shirt, what Beba really needed right then was a convincing explanation that would assuage her fears as to The First's whereabouts. And since that was what she needed, that was what I gave her. Luckily my extemporaneous talents, while not always brilliant, do tend to work at crucial moments.

'Beba, don't be frightened. Listen: Sebastian can't call because he's in jail . . . Preventive jail.'

I just said it. Blurted it out, just like that – I could smooth it over afterwards. Her first reaction was to quickly extricate herself, look me straight in the eyes and, very alarmed, ask me what had happened. By the time I said something to the effect of "oh, it was nothing, they arrested him by mistake for forty-eight hours and he wasn't allowed to make more than one phone call", she realised that he was at least in one piece. Then I went on to tell her that he'd been arrested in Bilbao, where he had gone to sort out the Ibarra business (I filled her in on the Ibarra details, too). I also told her that he had been arrested for industrial espionage (she said that sounded very ugly but not as bad as murder or larceny), that the accusation was completely bogus and that FH's lawyers would get him out of there in a few days and arraign the judge that had been in charge of it all. I think I convinced her, although I did have to assure her that The First had a private cell, that he was eating well, that he wasn't too cold or too hot and that the guards were very amenable. She still had a knot in her throat, but at least she had an image of The First in an attractive, Lego-type jail, which wasn't quite so tragic. Beba is very sensitive to anything related to either of us. Of course, I warned her that she had to be extremely hush-hush about it, because we didn't want the information to get to my mother, who would just get all upset. I also told her not to mention a word of it to my father, because then he would know that I had disobeyed his orders to keep my mouth shut.

Etcetera.

By the time my mother came into the kitchen, Beba was through with her crying jag and had washed her face clean, and now we were back at work on the croquettes.

'Pablo José, what on earth are you doing in here? I thought you were in the library with your father . . . Eusebia: have you prepared the seaweed salad?'

'No. And you know what I say: whoever wants to eat seawheat can prepare it himself. She can kiss my ass.'

Part three of the visit was with my Father's Highness, in the library. I found him in his element: white shirt, sleeves rolled up, tie loosened, half-smoked cigar in his mouth, no plaster cast or crutches in sight. He looked like his old self: that difficult synthesis of Winston Churchill and Jesús Gil. He was talking on the phone, seated at his rather motley-looking desk, filled with family portraits (including me, at the precise moment of receiving a consecrated host with the expression of an expectant cannibal on my face), blue leather desk accessories, invoices, receipts, reports, catalogues, cards . . . no computer in sight, just an old typewriter on a little cart with wheels. Continental: mother-of-pearl keys, black enamel frame and gold vegetable-dye details. If Mr Microsoft could see him, he'd have a seizure.

The telephone, however, was modern.

'No rush, Santiago, I understand . . . no, no, it's all the same . . . In any event, tell them to look out for the complaint, I'm going to have them put it through right now . . . Yes . . . Listen, I'm going to have to go, I have a visitor.'

The visitor was me, obviously. He gestured for me to sit down, and I did, in one of the two chairs that faced his leather swivel chair. There I was, face to face with the Shirtless General.

'For the past two hours I have been trying to get these people to place the roads in and out of the country under surveillance, and now little Santiago comes and tells me that he can't involve "uniformed agents" if there isn't a complaint report filed. I don't know why but I think this guy is a few cards short of a full deck. All right, then . . . Now, I'd like you to move in here for a few days, Gloria and the children as well. It's easier to protect one house instead of three. And this house is going to become a bunker.'

I didn't bother disagreeing verbally. If you don't happen to like whatever my father has decided for you, there is no use arguing, because it'll be war. And that day, he looked perfectly capable of having four goons immobilise me and hold me captive in his house if he felt like it. Once his Churchill-esque diplomatic efforts fail, my father is incredibly deft at assuming the Jesús Gil alter-ego, and from there, it's straight on into Corleone mode.

'Did you find out anything about the Robellades accident?' I asked, not only to distract his attention but because I was genuinely interested in knowing the answer.

'Well, it was no normal accident. To start with, the driver hadn't had a sip of alcohol, nor had he taken any kind of drug detectable by an autopsy. He was alone, which meant that he could not have been provoked by an argument, nor would he have been trying to show off for a friend . . . or girlfriend. He has not been involved in any kind of accident in the last five years, and his profile doesn't jibe in the least with the kind of guy who goes around drag-racing with other cars at midnight.'

'Maybe yes, maybe no . . . after all, he *was* a private detective . . .'

'Private detectives don't drive at one hundred kilometres an hour with cars on their tail in the middle of a neighbourhood like Les Corts.'

'Unless the roles were reversed, and he was on the other guy's tail.'

'That's exactly it. I think we can assume that he ended up running from someone whom he initially had been following. And in the course of the chase, he fell into the car park pit.'

'But the other car crashed into him nose-first, didn't it?'

'How would you know?'

'I have my methods.'

'It was a red car that hit him, a 1997 Renault, we know this from the paint chips found on the ground. They were driving at more or less the same speed. The most likely story is that the two cars turned too wide for the curve, and that was what caused the crash. An accident. Maybe the men in the Renault were trying to cut him off, or make him stop, but I don't think they would have ever planned to crash into him and then send him down into that pit. That doesn't make sense. So it wouldn't be murder, but it could be homicide. Reason enough to be extremely careful.'

'Could that Renault be the same one that hit you?'

He nodded, though without much conviction, and sat there looking up at the ceiling, pensive. In a wave of weakness, I thought of just telling him everything about the house at Guillamet to see what he thought. But I wasn't ready to go and throw out my thirty-three-year struggle for independence – not then – just because a knot of fear had lodged itself in my throat. "The only one who's going inside Guillamet number 15 is me," I told myself. "And whatever balls I've got." Maybe MH was right after all, when she said she had spent her life surrounded by a bunch of stubborn mules. But the truth is, if a willow may be able stand up to the winds that blow, like the Zen Buddhists would say, then a mule like me can do it just as well, if not better.

'I told Eusebia that Sebastian is in jail. I had to invent something, I had no other choice,' I said so that I wouldn't succumb to the temptation of telling him the Guillamet bit. That was more than enough for the Shirtless General to look down from the ceiling and glare at me with all his might.

'But didn't you tell your mother something else?'

'Yes, but if they end up talking about it, the two versions are entirely compatible. And I had to tell Beba something more dramatic, I don't know . . .'

'Pablo, you know very well that in the end the truth always comes out . . .'

'Shit, Dad. You're lying to them, too . . .'

'I'm not lying. I'm simply not informing them. And I'll thank you to watch your language with me.'

'All right. Let's not argue. I just told you so that you'd know.'

Pause.

'Right. Do you need anything from your flat?' he asked me.

'Anything for what?'

'I want you to move in here tonight. Aren't you going to need a change of clothes, a toothbrush, something? I can send someone over to fetch your things. I suppose you can manage to abstain from getting drunk for one night in your life, but if not, there's plenty of alcohol in the living room bar. Forgive me if I can't offer you any narcotics.'

I ignored the dig and followed his lead:

'I have to go by my flat myself. And I'm going to need at least a couple of hours.'

'A couple of hours to pick up a change of clothes? I can place a call and you'll have everything you need in ten minutes.'

'No. I have to go there myself.'

'Oh, really? And why is that?'

Shit. I always have to go around making up excuses.

'Dad. There are some things a man has to do himself . . .'

'Like looking for a pair of underwear in your top left dresser drawer?'

'Like explaining to the woman who's waiting for you that you can't see her for a few days because you have to hole up in a bunker.'

Pause. Doubt. Did he suspect I was lying to him?

'Well, try not to tell her too much. The less she knows, the better off she'll be.'

'Don't worry, I'll take care of most of it with body language.'

'Listen, Pablo, I don't like to hear that kind of talk, especially if it concerns a woman with whom you are involved. Not in a bar, and most certainly not in my house. Or have you completely abandoned the few manners I tried to instil in you?'

'I think I've still got some left.'

'If you did, you wouldn't be running about with a married woman who happens to live with her husband. Nor would you be parading through the neighbourhood with her. You are exhibiting an incredible disrespect for that man, and for yourself as well. Try, if you might, to avoid doing the same to her, and watch your tongue when you talk about her, at least in my presence.'

I am a brilliant liar, I shouldn't say so but I must. A date, a gentlemanly appointment, is one of the few things that the Grand Master feels is worthy of risking one's life for. A question of honour. Luck was on my side, because he interpreted the simple mention of a woman to be a lover's tryst with Fina. No doubt Lopez had informed him about the two of us gallivanting about the neighbourhood together and his imagination had taken care of the rest, resulting in the perfect excuse to escape for a fair amount of time. In fact, if push came to shove, the excuse could hold up for the entire night.

I got out of there on the double, without even saying goodbye to my mother or Beba, given that I would supposedly be back in a couple of hours.

I took another taxi back to my flat. At the last moment I asked the driver to leave me on the Travessera, not far from where the private gardens are. Neither Lopez nor Antoñito were expecting this detour – I realised this when I saw the Kadett cruise by and stop a block further up the road as they saw me exit the taxi. I walked away from them, toward the tunnel that cuts through one of the buildings and leads into the private gardens. It took me a few seconds to identify Nico among the little group clustered around a bench that was a bit more tucked away than the others.

Everyone's hands went straight into their pockets and all the faces rapidly assumed nice, innocent-boy expressions until Nico signalled that he knew me, at which point they all resumed consuming their respective drugs of choice.

'What do you want, dude?'

'Some coke, if you have any.'

'How much do you want?'

'How much have you got?'

'Dude . . . I don't know . . . come with me down that-away and I'll give you however much you want. I got four grams.'

'Okay. I'll take four.'

Easy sale. Too easy for Nico, probably, because he then felt obliged to specify the price.

'Two hundred fifty, my friend, special price . . .'

'No problemo. And set me up with some hash, too, round it up.'

'Shit, man, you're loaded. You robbed a bank or something?'

'I won a beauty contest.'

'Look at that, you never know what kind of luck'll come your way . . . Come on, I got the goods in the car park.'

We walked down the little path toward the stairs that seemed to sink into the basement beneath the park. When we reached the metal door at the bottom, he pulled out a piece of folded-up cardboard that kept the door from locking, and we walked down another set of stairs. Then we went down half a flight more, through another doorway until we finally reached the massive underground car park. From there we went over to a yellowish early-model Opel Corsa, and in the dark Nico stuck his hand into a little nook in the wall, patted about a bit and then removed four white packets. He gave them to me in one deft, sly movement that didn't really make much sense down there.

'This shit rocks. Uncut.'

'Don't worry, as long as its not lethal, I'm happy. What about the hash?'

He stuck his arm back a few metres further into the

nook and came up with a piece about the size of a woman's high heel.

'This is all I've got.'

I pulled out my wad of bills and gave him a few. He was about to give me the change I had coming, but I stopped him.

'Forget it. So you treat me right when I'm not so flush.'

If I had known that that would be the last time I'd ever see Nico, I'd have given him the whole wad. But I didn't.

I walked out of the car park through the exit that went under the gardens, so that I could return without going outside and through the entire park again.

I had scarcely finished the first line when the telephone rang. It was John. He didn't even bother saying hello, he went straight into the insult routine.

'May I ask where the fuck you've been sticking your nose in, arsehole? I just spoke with Günter on the phone and he told me they're reformatting all their hard drives.

'And . . . ?'

'What do you mean, "and . . ."? The guys at that address you gave him attacked them with a killer virus.'

'What?'

'A virus, goddamnit. You know what a virus is, idiot? They tried to connect via FTP to plant a sniffer on their server and the system went ballistic on them – bounced it back to them in God only knows what kind of aggressive format that's eating the shit out of them. A *scheusal*, says Günter. That is, an ogre, that's what they named it. It spread to all the computers in their place, because they're all hooked up to a local network. They've had to reformat absolutely everything.'

'But aren't they to be the virus experts?'

'Well, they're fucking flipping out, man. Apparently all

their printers started spewing shit all at once, you know? Bing-bing-ffffff. Page after page of some kind of curse written in giant letters. And some kind of insane voice came booming out of their speakers . . . Günter says they got so scared they cut the electricity. Luckily, when the machines rebooted they seemed to work fine . . . no trace of anything in the hard drives and no alterations in their desktops or files. Nothing. But they don't believe it, they're afraid maybe the thing will resuscitate and fuck them up all over again.'

John seemed completely blown away by the whole thing, and he hadn't even been there to see it.

'Did Günter tell you what the printout said, the curse thing?'

'He emailed it to me. Let me read it to you: "Impoverished is he who approaches with impure intentions. He will never reach the heart of the worm, but he will nonetheless be pursued."'

'Yeah. I know it.'

'You know it? Well, you might have told us . . .'

'Listen, tell Günter I'm really sorry, I didn't think anything bad could happen to them.'

'No, no, he's thrilled. They're going to save the ogre on one of their computers so they can study it. They feel like they've caught the genie in his lamp, you know. He says it's got some weird thing that's different from any other virus they've ever seen.'

Every cloud has a silver lining, I thought to myself. But the news made me feel even less inclined to keep making up stories for John. I actually had to pretend someone was at the door so that I could hold him off for a second. When I got back on, I told him that I had to hang up because my upstairs neighbour had called me to tell me about a major water leak that was going to hit my apartment.

'Right. Maybe that was the ogre, too,' John said.

The only reasonable course of action was to do a couple more lines and light a joint. A scheusal, goddamnit. I could just picture my Magnificent Brother trapped in a cage, hanging from some ceiling somewhere, dangling above some lunatic in a pair of massive military boots propped up on a table. I think that was the moment, right there underneath the water in the shower, when I decided what I was going to do. Monday, June 22, midnight: that was the date next to the Jaume Guillamet address in the pencilled-in circle. Sooner or later you have to get on the Death Star.

The next fifteen minutes raced by. Very possibly the combination of cocaine, hash, the remains of Fina's bottle of Cardhu – which I finished off in one gulp – and the several sleepless nights had something to do with that. I was completely awake, focused, but life had become a dream. I arrived at Jaume Guillamet and I staked out behind a lorry that was parked on the side of the street in front of the little garden. At midnight (I imagine it was midnight) the procession began. Someone would arrive (men and women – people of varying ages and appearances kept turning up, always alone), take the red rag from the telephone pole, and ring the doorbell. The front door would swing open, the person would go inside, and after ten seconds the bald dude with the brown robe would emerge, very briefly, to re-tie the red rag to the pole. This happened four or five times, at five-minute intervals.

I was so freaked out that I didn't even notice the two guys that had gotten out of a parked car that had effectively cut off my path to the street, in between the lorry that served as a makeshift parapet and a van closer by.

The car was a navy-blue Peugeot, not a red Renault, but the look on their faces was crystal clear: guaranteed trouble. The guy on the right closed off my most direct escape route via the sidewalk that led toward Travessera, a paradise of traffic and lights, and so I stood as straight up as I could and approached him, sticking a hand in my pocket.

'You, big guy. Are you gonna be nice and let me get by or am I gonna have to beat the shit out of you?'

At first, as I watched him move, I thought he was going to step aside, and in the space of a millisecond I thought of the disadvantage I would face as I walked by him, because I would end up with my back to him. But as things turned out, that wouldn't be an issue, because he had no intention of stepping aside: instead he retreated a pace or two, just enough to transform his leg into a seven-spring catapult and shoot a size forty-five moccasin into my face. The corresponding foot brought the moccasin to life in a very vivid fashion.

The next thing I remember is noticing how the tiled sidewalk of Jaume Guillamet has a sewer drain in the shape of a daisy with four petals. And it's full of powder, brilliant powder, like the twinkling motes of microscopic glitter.

THE PORCELAIN POODLE

When I was a teenager I read a story by Julio Cortázar that was (and I suppose still is) called "The Night Face Up." Basically it's about a guy who supposedly is in some hospital bed, delirious with fever, wavering between consciousness and a dream state in which he is captured by a very dodgy tribe that intends to offer him as a sacrifice to their god. To make a long story short, after several literary stunts that throw off the reader (the usual Cortázar tricks), it turns out that the hospital bit is the dream and the reality to which he awakens is the ritual sacrifice and the dodgy tribe. Well, something like that happened to me that night. By the time I had recovered some modicum of consciousness, I felt as though I were suspended by my feet and hands, and then I was being moved, deposited, moved somewhere else, and when I lost consciousness again, I dreamt that I had arrived at my bed drunk, and that the mattress was moving slightly, as usual. The two things were equally unpleasant, as I associated both with an intense discomfort – dizziness, nausea, but naturally the dream was much more plausible than the reality. When I finally felt that I was being released and allowed to drop onto something soft (in the reality that I thought was a dream), I felt a prick in my arm and shortly thereafter a state of total and complete restfulness put an end to all my pains. That is, until I awoke with this terrible pounding feeling, as if my head had been rammed full of spikes.

When I opened my eyes and tried to sit up, the spike soup suddenly materialised as a sharp blow to the left side of my head. Slowly, my eyes were blinded by a flash and my facial muscles contracted in an attempt to absorb the shock of the hammering inside my brain, and I fell back down on the bed. Much worse than any hangover I have ever experienced. But little by little the flash died down until it was a simple, yellowish fluorescent light shining onto a mirror that hung on the wall facing me. That was when I began to comprehend that my headache most definitely had to do with a certain swelling on my left temple. After another few minutes I was finally able to see things, relatively speaking, and I rose up in bed. I was in my clothes, but someone had removed my shoes, unbuckled my belt, loosened my pants, and unbuttoned my shirt to mid-chest. Aside from the blow to my head, I had no other external pain. I carefully patted my body, but all I found were minor aches and a couple of scratch marks on my wrists.

I wanted to get up and look at myself in that mirror on the wall, to see what I looked like, but I was in no rush to move too fast. For the moment, I decided to check out the room by craning my neck to see what I had behind me. Nothing major: an old hospital bed, high bedside table, a pair of green Skay chairs, a stretcher, a white screen (folded up), a mirror with shelf and washbasin underneath, and a door with a square window in the middle, just about eye level. On the high bedside table were my wallet, my house keys, the Bagheera keys, tobacco, lighter, a pile of money, a woman's high heel and three white papers that seemed to have something hidden in their folds.

Where had I seen a woman's high heel just like that one, somewhere before? In the car park beneath the private gardens, in Nico's hand. From here, I began to retrace the steps, point by point, that had led up to my last hour of consciousness, before I had been attacked by a size forty-five Sebago heading for my left eye at Mach 4 speed. I didn't know how much time had gone by since then. The memory felt like that of something that had occurred three or four days earlier, but I knew that wasn't possible: I ran my hand over my chin and calculated about a day's worth of stubble. I lost consciousness on Monday at midnight, which meant that it was probably Tuesday, probably in the morning.

Tuesday, June 23, the day before the summer solstice. San Juan holiday. Some holiday.

I got up. I was all swollen and my oversized head was killing me, but at least I could walk. The blow to my head, as reflected in the mirror, produced a result that was less spectacular than the pain would suggest: a little reddened dent that widened my face a bit toward the left. Once I had ascertained that I was more or less in one piece, I decided to check out the little window, which promised some kind of view out on to the other side of the door. No such luck: it looked onto a windowless corridor that extended far beyond my field of vision both left and right. The door handle offered no keyhole and I tried to turn it. It gave, but the door was still locked from the outside. I thought about shouting, banging on the door, I don't know, trying to get the attention of someone in the outer world, but instead I chose to take a fifteen-second time-out for reflection. I did have my wallet and all the documents in it. My expired identity card still bore the address of my Magnificent Parents, so if some stranger had found me face down on Jaume Guillamet, I would now be in the Imperial Suite of a luxury hospital and MH would be feeding me chocolate bonbons by now. I also had to rule out the possibility that I was in a public hospital: not even public hospitals have such disgusting rooms, nor is everything so quiet and lonely, nor do they tuck in concussion victims with their cigarettes and cocaine. In other words: a very bad scene. And after thinking about it for a bit I realised that the panorama was even worse than I had first imagined. If those two hyenas who assaulted me with that shoe had put me in the hands of some kind of thug, then wouldn't Lopez have advised my father of this? Clearly he had done nothing of the sort, otherwise my father would have used the red phone and a commando of marines would have already swooped in to rescue me in an F-15 fighter plane complete with minibar.

I tried to remember the last time I had seen my Guardian Angels' white Kadett. It took me about two seconds: on Travessera, a block up from where I had stopped the taxi driver, just before entering the car park labyrinth with Nico. That's where they had lost track of me.

And now I was all alone.

Because of my stupid head.

And also because I was an arsehole.

Plan of action?

I had no other choice but to put together a quick mental pastiche made up of action movie sequences, the scant combat instruction I allowed myself to learn in the military, and all the Bugs Bunny stunts I could remember. Five minutes later, I had a perfect Bugs Bunny strategy, the first part of which involved recovering some of my physical and psychological fitness. To start off with, I was practically pissing my pants – underneath the central pain source in my gut I detected some intense bladder strain. I did my business in the sink and when I was done the world seemed a slightly more comfortable place. After that, I took little sips of water and splashed my face with abundant scoopfuls as well. Then I decided to test the analgesic properties of the cocaine and prepared myself a healthy line, surrendering myself to the notion that I was inhaling a panacea. My next move was to erase all signs of my little tune-up: I dried the visible droplets on the washbasin, put the towel back in its place, rearranged my cocaine supply in the same position as I had found it in. My strategy was to pretend that I was still sleeping so that I might be able to surprise whoever might come in. Before that could happen, of course, I would probably hear footsteps in the hall, so I allowed myself to remain standing in order to do a bit of light exercise to shake off the numbness – you know, the kind of thing healthy people do in the movies. At first I stuck to making big circles with my arms, nothing that would imply violent head movements, but little by little the coke took effect and I was able to test out some more ambitious stretches. I had not put my shoes back on (I would have, but they didn't fit in with the plan) and I even thought to check and see if the soles of my black socks had gotten dirty from walking around shoeless. Stretched out on the bed, the soles of my feet would be visible to whomever entered, and if they were dirty they would most certainly betray my manoeuvring. I thought about wearing them inside-out while I did my exercises, or maybe turning them round so that the heel of the sock covered the top part of my feet, which offered the advantage of returning them to their original position with greater ease . . . But a quick examination of the soles revealed that this was not necessary. Generally, I find it incredibly annoying to make an astute observation only to then realise that it is completely useless, but I was determined to infuse myself with positive energy and so I gave myself a mental pat on the back and tried to boost my morale by congratulating myself for such a tremendous attention to detail.

By the time I heard the faraway voices, the keys jangling, and the footsteps approaching, I stretched out on the bed and pretended to sleep. I realised that I was in reasonably good shape. And just then, I also realised that instead of all that moronic sock strategy, I should have used my time to improvise some kind of powerful weapon. Unfortunately, though, the nature of my mind is more Magilla Gorilla than Terminator.

The footsteps stopped at the door to the room. I thought I could see three pairs of shoes.

'Some piece of work, huh?'

This voice, I could tell, came from the other end of the room. It sounded as though it came from the other side of the window on the door.

'You're telling me. Even with five guards we couldn't lift him up. We had to drag him in on a blanket.'

'Didn't you put him out?'

'They shot him up with sedatives on the street, but after two minutes he was already moving again . . . They had to give him another dose to get him to stop growling and flapping his arms.'

'Well, if he's as stubborn as his brother, he's gonna be a hell of a fight . . . You don't think you overdid it a little with those injections? He's been sleeping for twelve hours . . .'

'No, he woke up already. See? He buttoned his pants.'

I had to interrupt the shower of mental insults I rained

upon myself because one of the guys began to bang away at the door:

'Come on, buddy! Time to wake up!'

With that racket, there was no way I could pretend I didn't hear. First I moved around a bit, but the guy was a real move-it-or-I'm-gonna-hit-you-again type and so I had to fake a sudden bolt-to-attention thing, and opened my eyes wide. Immediately I started making faces as if I was suffering, more or less as I had done when I woke up for real, just exaggerating it a little this time around.

'Open your eyes slowly. That's it. Cover your eyes a little. Can you talk?'

I supposed so, but I thought it would be more useful just to grunt. Finally, they opened the door and the two characters I'd heard talking – one bald, the other skinny – entered the room. Both of them were wearing white robes, which made me think that they had to be veterinarians, at least. They didn't make much of an impression, but on the other side of the room I could see two other guys in blue coveralls, boots and wide belts from which clubs and pistols dangled. These two were normal-sized. I continued with the sick act and one of the veterinarians, the bald one, brought me some water in the glass that had been sitting on the shelf above the washbasin. They were very interested in knowing if I was feeling better, if I wanted more water, if I was allergic to who knows what . . . I uttered various yesses and a few noes with a tweety bird voice and I let them help me up.

'Where am I?' I asked, Hitchcock-style.

'Relax, take deep breaths. Take a few minutes, and as soon as you're feeling better and can walk we'll take you somewhere where everything will be explained to you.'

Pretending that I couldn't walk properly was critical –

I invented an intense ankle pain that prevented me from being able to rest my foot on the floor. The bald guy took off my sock and groped about from the top of my foot to the back of my ankle with the self-importance of a real-life veterinarian.

'Does that hurt?'

'No . . . yes . . . ah, yes . . . that, there.' I made like I was about to put on my shoes but the guy said I'd be better off barefoot until my ankle improved. It was most definitely against my best interests to give up my shoes, but I decided that arguing the point would be unwise. With great effort, I got up on my one good leg, and rested sixty kilos of Pablo on the slender veterinarian. Just then, one of the armed dudes came in to place a pair of handcuffs round my wrists. I began to babble in protest: "but, but why?", "where am I?", etcetera, and then launched into the old violent-struggle routine. I did it with such well-feigned clumsiness that I almost fell forward straight onto the folded screen, but luckily the three guys held on to me.

'Leave him, guard, we don't have to put the handcuffs on him,' said the bald guy.

The guard then made a little bag out of the white tablecloth on the bedside table and gathered up all my things sitting on the table and stuck them inside, and took my shoes as well. Once we left the room – me, still propped up by the slender veterinarian's sternocleido-whatever – I took advantage of the moment to check out the corridor, looking left and then right. To the left I saw a succession of doors that ended at a staircase that led downstairs. In the other direction, about twenty metres to the right, the corridor was cut off by a door with metal bars. There, another guard manned the scene at a little desk. We went toward him, and when he noticed us he rushed to open the door with a key that hung from a little chain. At that moment, the veterinarian crutch-replacement and I were at the head of the pack; the guard carrying my shoes and the white tablecloth with all my things followed behind us, with the bald veterinarian after him and then, finally, the second of the two guards held up the rear.

When we reached the threshold of the door with the metal bars, I knew my moment had arrived. It's difficult to explain what I did next. Right under the doorframe I murmured something and turned slowly (forcing the veterinarian crutch-replacement guy to turn with me, of course), as if I wanted to ask the guard behind us a question. Once we were face to face, I mustered up an expression that made it look as if I was frightened to death of him and he, the poor thing, got so scared by my face that he jerked backwards. From that point on, everything happened very fast: I reached out and grabbed the white tablecloth-satchel with my left hand, and almost simultaneously I wrapped my right arm around the neck of the veterinarian crutch-replacement, who doubled over so that his head might stay attached to the rest of his body. Then I gave him a 150^2 newtons-per-second shove toward the guard who, in turn, fell against the bald veterinarian behind him, and you'll have to imagine the rest because I didn't see anything more. I left them there, yelling amongst themselves, and I made a break for the door.

I turned the corner, running as fast as one can run in socks down a tile floor, and about halfway down the corridor I reached a dark staircase – I picked the ones going upstairs and took the steps three at a time and, two floors further up, trying not to breathe too hard, I stopped for a listen. It wasn't long before the guards reached the stairs ("the stairs," I heard one of them shout), but by then I had already stuck my hand in the satchel and felt about for the high-heel of hash and after taking a fast bite out of it (in the interest of saving at least a little bit), I threw down the remainder of the chunk with all my strength into the open space in between the flights of stairs.

I was in luck: the hash hit the ground with a sharp thud a couple of floors down from where the guards were, and instantly I heard the sound of boots heading downstairs in search of a phantom as I continued upstairs: up, up and away into the darkness, maybe six or seven stories high, ignoring the double doors I passed at the entrance to each floor until, on the very last landing, I had no other choice but to open the door I found before me, and enter a room that was so dark that I could only infer, from the echo of my own movements, that it was some kind of wide, open space. I continued forward, sticking close to the wall.

The wall eventually came to an end, forming a corner with another wall. There, I allowed myself to fall onto the floor to catch my breath. For a few seconds I was nothing but a heart and two lungs, locked in a fierce battle to see which could pound more furiously. Then I began to note the stinging sweat that had seeped into my eyes and, once again, the pain of my throbbing temples. I couldn't see a thing, though it smelled humid, like cardboard, or something, I don't know: I would almost say that the smell in there was like that of dissected animals, not because of any relation the smell actually bore to any existing taxidermy-related fluids but rather because of the relation it bore to the words "dissected animals." I know that's probably a difficult comparison to understand, but it's also pretty difficult to understand the relativity of time and everyone swallows that one just fine. I hadn't heard alarms or anything, and I hopefully guessed that the guards would be scouring each floor for me, one by one until they reached the top. But in any event I did have to get a move-on. From my mouth I removed the bit of hash that I had managed to nick off the chunk Nico had sold me, and I placed it in my shirt pocket. Then I undid the improvised satchel and distributed its contents among my pants pockets, taking a brief break in the process to sniff a bit of coke, my nose stuck against the paper. Then I mixed a bit of the powder with some saliva and applied the paste to my temples in the hope that the cocaine would have some kind of topical effect. After that I tied the tablecloth around my waist – it might come in handy down the road, I thought, feeling as if I was in one of those Roger Wilco adventures, one of those scenarios where you never know what the fuck you're going to need in the next screen.

About ten metres away from me, a thin sliver of light shone at about floor level, the kind of light that shines out from under a closed door. I lit my lighter and moved forward a bit. Bingo: a closed door. I opened it without thinking, really: it was a tiny washroom that looked as though it hadn't been used in years, weakly lit by the glow coming in from a teeny window. I went back out and flicked on the lighter again so I could see a little. It was a broad, diaphanous space, kind of like a big office, but without tables or computers, only dust. Along one of the walls I spotted a door, a fire-door. I walked over and pressed down on the horizontal bar in the middle and it opened. I walked through an extremely thick wall and, a bit further on, I found myself in yet another empty room, visible beyond my flickering lighter. The only difference was that this one was much smaller than the first, and was decorated with English-print wallpaper. You could see from the distribution of the wall plugs, certain marks on the floor and a few areas where the wallpaper subtly changed colour that it had once been a bedroom. From there I went into another corridor and quickly realised that I was in an old, abandoned home whose windows had been boarded up. But all this was part of another building, there was no doubt about it.

From that second room I entered a third, and from the third to a fourth.

Anyway: trying to describe a labyrinth is like trying to photograph a ghost. And in reality, the place wasn't even really a labyrinth – it was a motley bunch of interconnected buildings that occasionally seemed totally normal, occasionally not at all. But nobody had actually planned it specifically to confuse the casual visitor. Even so, it was enough to make me realise that the confusing aspect of a labyrinth is not its geometric complexity but rather the experience it induces, and that interminable darkness induced plenty. I had to summon up every last bit of strength so as to not succumb to the feeling of terror that would no doubt plunge me into an abyss. One thing I did lose, however, was my sense of time, and so I have no way of knowing exactly how long I wandered through those commercial spaces, homes, and staircases, submerged in that eternal, artificial night. The air was still thick with the smell of dissected animals: it was the smell of abandoned, forgotten things. The only things I found, very occasionally, were a few pieces of rickety furniture here and there in the empty rooms, or else small objects that were rather commonplace but chilling nonetheless: a blue porcelain poodle that had been left on a Formica counter; a 1983 calendar with a photograph of some Swiss landscape; the remains of a Bruce Springsteen poster in a bedroom; a roll of toilet paper; a kid-sized toothbrush in a toilet that had been overtaken by spiders – forgotten pieces that provoked the same choked-up feeling as objects recovered from a faraway shipwreck. With *Quest* in mind, I grabbed the porcelain poodle and the toothbrush – the former could double as a respectable flying object that, when broken into fragments, would have useful, sharp edges, and the latter also had a certain useful-object *je ne sais quoi* about it. That was what I was thinking about when suddenly I heard a boom. The boarded-up air began to vibrate with life. Oddly enough, though, I did not get scared – the opposite, in fact, because I quickly realised that it was a firecracker, a blessed firecracker that brought me back to the reality that there was indeed a place, just beyond the walls that surrounded me, where people were getting ready for the San Juan festivities. At least I knew that Barcelona still existed somewhere.

I decided to tempt fate no more and return to the building where I had started my wandering – not just because it was doubtful that the guards looking for me would still be milling about the spot where I had escaped from them, but also because the bathroom of that first office was the only source of natural light I had come across on my search-and-discovery mission. I also remembered the veterinarian's reference to my Magnificent Brother. The First couldn't be very far from here – it seemed implausible that whoever the hell was in charge of this mess would scatter his prisoners all over this labyrinth. Clearly the floor where I had come to was used as a prison by the organisation, or cult, or whatever you'd call the kind of club that would have those low-lifes as members.

Once I made it back to the washroom, I stuck my head out of the little window. Down below, the ventilation shaft grew darker and darker until you could barely make out the black surface at the bottom. Up above, through a green skylight you could see the light from the sky. Aside from suffering from agoraphobia, misanthropy and an aversion to hens, I also have a pretty serious fear of heights, but my need to escape to the outside world was so intense at that moment that I actually considered climbing up toward that greenish light. However, the ventilation shaft most likely ran past the prison zone, so all I had to do to confirm the hypothesis was mentally retrace the steps I had taken since leaving the men in the hall. Once I accepted it as fact, perhaps the most sensible option would not be to climb up the shaft toward the roof, but rather to climb down to the floor in question and try to locate The First. After all, this was not just an escape mission but a rescue effort as well. Plus, as an added bonus, the descent offered thick Uralite pipes that I could cling to on the way down, an option not available on the ride up. Clinging to them for six flights was pretty much out of the question, though, and so I figured I might be able to take the stairs down several floors, and then scale down the shaft for the last (or even last two) floors. Now, the question was how many floors beneath me were empty and on which of them could I gain access to the corresponding toilet without anyone seeing me?

There was only one way to find out: start going downstairs. Taking every possible precaution, I gingerly approached the staircase that I had climbed up when I had fled from the guards. The silence was absolute, as was the darkness. I stuck my head out into the central space and saw electric light on the lowest floor. I dared to descend a flight, peering down into the central opening all the while. Then I leaned in toward the double doors that led into the main space of that floor. I didn't hear a thing, so I opened the door a crack. I looked left and right: all dark, just like the floor above. This seemed encouraging, so I descended to the next floor down. And the next and the next one after that – on and on until I reached the floor immediately above the one with the metal-bar door that opened onto the corridor where I had been locked up initially. Everything was absolutely still – all you could hear was the buzzing of the fluorescent lights: "zzzz." This time, with renewed stealth, I opened the door to the office or apartment space directly above the prison zone.

What I saw, however, was nothing new, at least not in the flickering glow of my lighter. Aside from a parquet floor and a pile of things next to the door (unplugged refrigerator, two dusty chairs, empty coat rack), it was exactly the same as the top floor, just as vacant and dirty, although the strong labyrinth smell was almost imperceptible here – it was almost as if closeness to the inhabited zone of the building had diluted its essence somehow. I went straight to the toilet in the back, opened the shaftway window and confirmed that the black abyss came to an end at the floor just below me. At that point I began working on getting my body out the little window. That was the tough part. After that, I disentangled myself and landed with no problem, but it was pretty damn creepy to feel my bare feet settle down on the ground floor of that foul shaftway, and so I tried to enter the ground-floor toilet as quickly as possible, entering the window head-first, which forced me to land in the toilet in a vertical fashion. The bad thing about that, however, was that everything came falling out of my pockets, resulting in a quarter-gram of cocaine scattered across the floor and a now-broken blue porcelain poodle. I would be able to fix thc poodle a few days later with Krazy Glue, and in fact I am looking at it now as I write this. Crouching down on all-fours to lick a bathroom floor, however, did seem a bit excessive, even for Roger Wilco, and so the quarter-gram of cocaine was lost forever.

Right. So now I was in the toilet of the floor I needed to be on, probably some twenty metres from the guard. Now what?

I heard coughing sounds: that bronchitis-like cough that is something of a brotherly bond between me and my fellow smokers of the world.

I could stay hidden in the toilet, wait until the guy needed to take a piss and as soon as he walked in the door, bop him on the head with the remnants of the porcelain poodle. Of course, the guy could take hours before coming in or, who knew, maybe the guards peed somewhere else, or it maybe was absolutely forbidden for them to abandon their posts. Plus I don't exactly have lots of experience felling goons in a single blow, and I wasn't very confident about my ability to calibrate the minimum impact that was called for: I was sure I would either fall short and thus give him the chance to react, or else crack his head open in one go.

I decided to stick the old moustache out the door for a second to see if I could think up some alternative to the concussion-by-blue-poodle move. The coughs were coming in intervals – the poor guy was clearly trying to expel some very deeply lodged phlegm that wouldn't budge, and so I took advantage of the noisy coughing moments to open the door a crack, to see if it made any creaking noises. As

I did this, I got a bird's-eye view of a flight of stairs going down from the room between the guards, only a few metres away from me. During the next round of coughs I opened the door wider and went out into the light of the hallway. The guard's desk was partially hidden behind the wall and I could only see about half of his body. His arms were bent at the elbow, and his hands were pressed against his ears, like a student cramming for an exam. He was about thirty metres to my left.

From there, the most sensible move was to go down the staircase to my right and see what I found – assuming, of course, that I didn't bump into another sentinel downstairs. At this point, the only thing left to decide was whether to crawl my way out of the washroom right then or wait for another coughing jag and tiptoe my way out. Crawling, in its most conventional form, is not my best mode of movement, for I was likely to drag everything in the vicinity down with me, not unlike a snail. So the tiptoe bit was a better option. But crossing through that door was a tough one. The coughing fits had tapered off, and now I was starting to get nervous. I stuck my nose out again to see what the fuck was going on and I saw the guy lean over to his right. Then I heard noises that sounded kind of like drawers being opened and closed. This, I decided, was my big chance and I left the toilet with bated breath – not very fast, just taking very wide steps in the direction of the stairs. I didn't pick up the pace until I reached the first step, at which point I ran down as quickly as I could to the first landing. I stood there for a second or two, crouching down against the stairs, trying to make out what was on the floor below. The next flight led straight into an open space of about twenty square metres, which gave me the sense that I was going down to some kind of enclosed cell in the middle of a solid edifice of some sort. I could hear the sound of water droplets falling down into a somewhat full bucket: plong, plong, plong . . . The cement floor was completely flooded despite the central drain. I spied a tap sticking out of the wall in front of me, connected to a hose of some sort, and realised that that was the source of the drops – plong, plong, plong – which fell into a large sink attached to the wall. The dominant colour, aside from the tiles running along the lower part of the walls, was a depressing concrete-grey tone, illuminated by the fluorescent light that reflected off the water on the floor. An intense odour of humidity permeated the air, and of all the rooms in that building that reminded me of a jail, this one took the cake: it looked like a Le Corbusier reinterpretation of a medieval torture chamber. The walls were the most interesting thing in the place: there were four doors altogether, two doors on either side, facing one another: metal doors, also grey, with little windows in the middle which served as viewing holes, though these windows were much narrower than the ones on the floor above – they were almost like those little peepholes you see on tanks.

As I went down the stairs, now fully upright, I could feel the dampness penetrate my socks. I approached the first door to my left and peered in through the window. A wooden chair, a foam mattress on the floor, a plastic curtain that hid about a quarter of the room from view, and not much else. The walls were all covered in white tiles from the bottom half down, and all of them had stains – some that were droplets of water, others that were more spattered, others that were more like scrub marks, others that were more faded, and then some long marks that extended across the length of the wall in parallel tracks.

I tried hard not to get too freaked out and went to see

what was behind door number two. This time, the walls and the furniture were the least of it, because the first thing that jumped out at me was a biggish guy in his underwear, sitting in a chair similar to the one in the other cell. He was facing me, head down, hands behind his back. He seemed to be in a half-sleep state, and I could see he was breathing by the way his chest would rise and fall in regular intervals. When I looked closer at his face, even in his semi-hidden position, I could tell that someone had performed quite a bit of bare-fisted cosmetic surgery on him.

Despite that unknown sonofabitch's handiwork, however, I was able to recognise that the person sitting there was Sebastian, my brother.

By the time I had unbolted the door, the seated Christ figure had looked up toward his unexpected visitor and tried to open his eyes.

'Hey, kid,' I said, not so much to piss him off but to make it easier for him to recognise me through his eyelids, which now resembled a pair of ripened figs.

'What . . . what the fuck are you doing here, idiot?'

That was The First. Same as ever.

'Oh, you know: I was just walking by and said to myself, shit, I'm gonna go rescue that fucking pretty-boy brother of mine.'

'Right. And now who's gonna rescue you, jerk?'

In addition to a pair of black eyes that were nothing more than slits, he most definitely had a broken nose, plus there was blood all over his chin and all the way down to his chest. All this fistwork had to have happened days earlier because the blood was all caked up in little strips. His breathing, in short little gulps, had dried out his mouth and as a result he could only speak in raspy, clumsy whispers which were further belaboured by his lip, which was swollen and cut. On the rest of his body I could see bruises here and there beneath the blood that had flowed from his nose, but his body was still in better overall shape than his face.

'Are you calm enough to untie me?'

'I'm actually wondering whether I shouldn't beat you up a little more.'

I let it go, though, because there wasn't much more room on his face to fuck with. I walked around the chair and got to work untying the ropes that kept his hands behind his back. His right ring finger and pinkie were pretty smashed-up; I would have to avoid them if I wanted to keep him from writhing in his chair. Once I undid the rope, his arms moved forward in slow-motion, suggesting some serious pain that seemed most concentrated around his ribcage. I let him be for a moment and left the cell to fetch some water from the sink sticking out of the wall in the other room. I turned on the tap and tasted a bit of the water that came out. Its first-class, bleach-like taste seemed to indicate that it was drinkable. I washed the decapitated, hollow body of the porcelain poodle as best I could, filled it with water, and then brought it to my brother. I placed the poodle to his lips, covering the jagged porcelain edge with my finger, and then repeated the operation various times, going back and forth from my brother to the tap outside the room to refill the poodle. I did this until he was able to stick his tongue out of his mouth and run it over his lips in a wet caress that enabled him to speak a bit clearer.

'How are Gloria and the children . . .'

'Good. Holed up at home, with Mom and Dad and Beba. What about your secretary?'

'She's with them.'

'Them?'

'It's a long story.'

I decided to hold off on that one for the moment.

'Is there any one part of your body that hurts worse than the rest?'

He shook his head.

'Everything kind of . . . aches. Every time they come in and knock me about, they kick the shit out of my bruises but then after a while I get used to it and it stops hurting. Then they leave me alone until I stiffen up again.'

I thought about giving him a bit of coke, but one of his nostrils was almost completely blocked off by his bashed-in bridge, and the other one was completely obstructed by congealed blood.

'Listen. You don't deserve it but I'm gonna wipe up that runny nose you've got. Just stay cool and don't get smart or anything with me. Then we'll see how well you can walk; I'm not planning on carrying you out of here on my shoulders.'

He nodded in agreement. That was when I realised he was trembling from the cold and I figured I ought to take care of that before anything else. I removed my shirt and placed it over his shoulders and he immediately wrapped it around his body, grateful for the warmth it provided. I thought of giving him my socks as well, but they were sopping wet from all the back and forth between the cell and the sink, and that would probably be even worse for him. I did, however, drag the filthy mattress over so that he would have somewhere to prop his feet, and once he seemed to have warmed up a little I told him to tilt his head back so I could inspect his face in the light. I decided not to go anywhere near the left nostril that his broken nose had closed in on, and instead began to pick away at the coagulated blood in the other nostril with my finger, trying to get my nail inside so that I might remove the blackened mass that was blocking the hole. It wasn't easy, and my patient began to complain when I forced his nose skin up and back a little to create some extra space. I needed a very fine instrument with which to dig, and I briefly considered using the tip of my belt buckle. With patience, however, I managed to dislodge a tiny bit of gummy matter, behind which a dark macaroni-sized chunk came popping out, about as thick as a pencil, directly followed by a long, transparent blob of goo with little red vein-like things inside. The First let out an 'aahhh' indicating the relief he felt at being freed of one of his many nagging pains, but there was still something else burbling inside. With firm but gentle pressure, I placed my finger over his left nostril and ordered him to breathe out, hard, through the right. This succeeded in liberating all the dried blood and mucous inside his nostril and finally, I could hear him breathe through his nose. At least one of the passageways was in working order now.

'How is my nose?' he asked, his voice clearer though still little more than a whisper.

'Like a hard cock in profile.'

'Set it straight for me.'

'What?'

'Set it straight. It'll be easier for you than for me, but if you can't handle it just tell me and I'll do it myself. The bone has been sitting like that for a few days now, and if it sets in this position I'm going to have more trouble with it in the long run.'

'It's going to hurt . . .'

'I know.'

I know. After that little comment I didn't want to come off as some kind of sissy, but I still get a chill whenever I think of that cric-cric of those broken nose bones. Technically speaking, it wasn't a difficult operation – all I had to do was take my two forefingers and shift the central nose bone back to the middle of his face and remodel the bridge a little with a bit of help from the toothbrush that I stuck as far as I could up his nostril, kind of like the way you use a shoe tree. I did all of this according to The First's explicit instructions. Every last muscle in my body, from the tips of my toes up to my scalp, remained locked in a state of high tension for the duration of that extemporaneous rhinoplasty. The First simply gritted his teeth throughout the whole thing, even when he saw me faltering and had to cheer me on a bit. Once or twice a tear would suddenly bubble up from his eye and come to rest on the purplish cushion of his eyelids, like a diamond sitting in its velvet case.

When the ordeal was over, his nose was still swollen and ever so slightly inclined toward the left, but it looked a whole lot different now. And when he blew his nose it seemed that he had all but recovered the use of the air passages. This was the moment to avail ourselves of my cocaine and its various virtues. I took out my wad of bills, rolled one up, opened one of the papers with the coke in it, and told him to breathe in.

'What's this?'

'Half sodium bicarbonate, forty per cent random barbiturates and maybe a little bit of third-rate cocaine. But it works.'

'I thought you were only addicted to alcohol and hash . . .'

'And carpenter's glue, too . . . Don't start fucking with

me, Sebastian. Anyway, don't you drink coffee? Well, this is very similar to caffeine. Snort a little of the powder and you'll feel like you've just had a half-litre of espresso. It'll do you good.'

'Thank you, but I don't think I need a cross-addicted loser to give me pharmacology lessons.'

'That's right. What you really need are lessons in how to be a little more street-smart. Lesson one: a man should be friendly and personable with the person who has just reset his fucking nose.'

'Wrong: rule number one is let someone break your nose so that you can protect your moron of a younger brother. Or weren't you wondering why they did this to my face?'

'Let me think: might it have something to do with your insufferable, know-it-all, rich-boy attitude?'

'No. It has something to do with you, motherfucker. I let them practically kill me because I wouldn't give them your name. And then you, all on your little lonesome, came walking into the belly of the beast.'

'Listen, shitface, the one who walked straight into the belly of the beast was you. I was happily intoxicating myself in multiple ways when you got me and the whole family into this mess.'

'I told you to forget about the house on Guillamet. Did I or did I not?'

We were actually screaming at each other, even though it was in very hushed voices. The mention of that godforsaken house did manage to distract me from the predicament.

'Are we in the house on Guillamet?'

'You tell me . . . how did you get in here?'

'I don't know. I was knocked unconscious.'

'Some brave rescue . . .'

'Listen, Mr Virtue, do you want us to do something so we can get out of here or would you rather I tie you back up to that chair and find a way out of here myself? And I should warn you, you smell a hell of a lot worse than I do, and chit-chatting with you hardly appeals to me.'

Silence. He really did smell, an awful combination of sweat and urine. In addition to the blood, his originally white Calvins were sporting various yellowish stains. They must have had him tied up for several days by now. Anyone would have crumbled from the fear and the major humiliation he had been subjected to, but The First is very much The First – even I have to admit he's got balls – pissed on, but balls nonetheless. He agreed to my ultimatum with a sigh of resignation. I relaxed the infuriated look on my face, and passed him the cocaine and the bill. This time he didn't argue and did two lines, one in each nostril. I would even say he had had a bit of practice.

'Help me up, I want some more water.'

I let him lean on me and he stood up on one foot. Aside from a darkening bruise on one shin, his legs were in pretty good shape, though weakened from lack of use. The worst was the pain in his side, although he managed to take the last few steps toward the sink on his own. I told him I thought he'd be better off not washing up for the moment, that it was in his interest to keep looking the way he did and he agreed. Then I tried to stall for time by talking to him as he took little sips of water from the hose.

'So you say they came around every so often to rough you up a bit?'

He nodded.

'How many of them?'

He held up two fingers.

'Armed?'

He nodded again and made a pistol with his thumb and forefinger.

'Well there's only one guard at the exit upstairs, but he's got about a thirty-metre advantage in the hallway to see us coming after him. We'd be better off trying to surprise the two that come into your cell.' Your cell, I specified. 'We hit them with a couple of left hooks, take away their guns and then we'll be better prepared to hit the guy above. You know how to use a gun?'

He indicated that he did. I asked myself where he would have acquired that particular skill and then I remembered that he had been a Magnificent Lieutenant in the Army's Special Operations Unit. I could almost, but not quite, picture him in his custom-made uniform and the little six-point star sewed on to his black beret – not, of course, to be confused with the black beret of Che Guevara.

He finished drinking.

'And you? Do you have any idea how to use a gun?'

'No. But I've seen plenty of movies.'

'Right. So how did you get here without them catching you? Couldn't we take that way out?'

'I slid down a toilet shaftway for eight floors.' The slight exaggeration couldn't hurt, I thought. 'To go back the same way we'd have to go up a bunch of stairs where the guard could catch us pretty easily. Plus, you're in no condition to go shimmying up a set of drainage pipes, nor am I for that matter. I think it'd be easier for us to ambush them up here, you know, prepare a little party for our visitors. One of them might even be able to lend us a disguise, in addition to the weapons. What do you think.'

'You've left out one thing.'

'What thing?'

'I'll tell you as soon as we get control of the first two.'

The First and his little telepathy games. I never could stand them.

We went back into the cell, The First walking very slowly but a little better by now. Once inside, he stood there and began to make a bunch of vaguely Chinese-looking movements. It wasn't tai-chi exactly, but it kind of looked like it.

'And the guys that come in to kick you around, are they the guards? The guys in the blue coveralls and the boots?'

'No, they're dressed normally. In suits. They also work on the outside.'

'Think we can take them on? I mean, are they wimps, kind of?'

'They're in good shape, tough guys who know how to fight.'

Gorillas against hyenas, I thought to myself.

'I know. One of them gave me a little demonstration,' I said, pointing to my temple.

'A shiner?'

'A kick.'

'Not bad . . .'

'Right. If I get the chance, I'll congratulate the guy.'

'Well, knocking you out isn't exactly saying much. You're like a walrus: lots of mass, little mobility.'

'Oh, really. Well you should know that this walrus has his own way of taking care of things.'

'How? By getting your opponent drunk? Listen, instead of wasting time on details, why don't we focus on putting together some kind of basic strategy?'

'Fine: you hit the first guy that comes near you and I'll run out from behind the curtain and beat the shit out of the other one.'

'How do we know that he won't be beating the shit out

of you? You need some technique to be able to knock someone over before he can get to his pistol.'

'You just worry about yourself. Pretend that you can barely speak and let him bend down and put his ear next to your mouth. When you've got him good and close, you whack him hard and I come running out from behind the curtain to nick the other one. I just hope you haven't gotten the Stockholm Syndrome or anything . . .'

'Cut the cracks, if you don't mind, and just try and make sure they don't pop you with a beginner's punch. Cover your head and your crotch at least . . . like this, see? Don't let them knock you off balance; come out sideways, legs open, shift your weight back and forth. Let's see . . .' He jabbed his index finger toward my navel. 'Well, if they get you there, they'll ricochet back. I don't know what kind of offensive moves you're capable of.'

'Don't worry. When I was little I fell into a well and made it out okay. The worst thing that can happen is if the sides are even and then the upstairs guard gets in on the action.'

'He's pretty used to hearing action from down here . . . Try hiding behind the curtain now, let's see if I can see you.'

I tried. Hidden behind the opaque grey plastic curtain was a toilet overflowing with various generations of human shit. The First, jumping around a bit now, warned me that he could see quite a bit of my feet. I corrected the position, he gave me the thumbs-up and I got out from there: I would almost say my Magnificent Brother actually smelled better than that rancid corner.

'Do you have any idea how long they might take?'

'Lately they've been coming around here two or three times a day. The last time was this morning, about three or four hours ago. I've lost track of time, with all the sleeping.'

'So how do you know they came by in the morning, then?'

'In the morning they smell like coffee with milk. In the afternoon, like beer.'

'Not bad for someone who just had his nose bashed in.'

The First kept on jumping up and down.

'They've more or less stopped hitting me. They come in, bored, ask me a few questions, let me taste a bit of food, a sip of water and then they go.'

'What the hell are they waiting for you to tell them?'

'Your name, among other things. They know that I hired someone to stake out the entrance to the place on Jaume Guillamet, but they don't know who. Now they know, of course . . .'

'Hey, speaking of which, did you call your wife to tell her to stick something in an envelope?'

'In an envelope?'

'Yeah. And did you write "Pablo" on a list that included the Jaume Guillamet 15 address?'

'I didn't do anything of the sort. I have no idea what you're talking about.'

'Well, I think your Magnificent Wife may have taken me for a ride.'

'Don't blame her. She must have had her reasons. How long have you been inside here?'

'Since last night. But wait, why did you say that they know you hired me for the Jaume Guillamet business? You haven't told them anything, and neither have I . . .'

'They know. For sure. And now they're going to want to interrogate you, so if they nab us you can just imagine what will go down.'

'Me? Shit, I don't know a fucking thing . . .'

'Maybe so. But they don't know that.'

'Would it be too much to ask who, exactly, "they" are? Or is this one of your telepathy games?'

'See? All this naturally awakens people's curiosity. That's exactly what they're afraid of. The truth is, the less you know the better. And now, if you don't mind, I have to focus on regaining some of my flexibility. Too bad you're out of that decaffeinated cocaine, another dose would come in handy about now.'

I took out the rest of the stash, along with a rolled-up bill and left them on the seat of the chair.

'We've got two grams left. That is, of course, if Sir Sebastian doesn't mind doing low-rent drugs.'

'I don't "do drugs." I medicate. There is a very basic difference between the two.'

He served himself some, bending down to the chair and then repeating the motion as a kind of exercise for his thighs. Then he got busy resting his leg against the wall, raising it high above his head and punishing his thigh muscles once more by hugging his raised calf to his torso until he got the tip of his nose to touch his shin. As difficult to describe as to justify. Once he finished with this little choreography number, he started in with a bunch of fu-fu punches: a sequence of fast, sharp jabs, fu-fu-fu, that curled invisibly in the air and came back as if they'd been shot out by a spring. After a few minutes of these excesses, he was sufficiently warmed up and took off my shirt. It had been ages since I'd last seen The First in underwear: he looked almost exactly the same as he did when he was twenty – a clear-cut case of arrested development. All of him – legs, thorax, arms, back – were a carbon copy of those ads for virtual mayonnaise and crackers for taking easier craps. A damn shame.

'Listen, uh, Bruce Lee, watch out you don't give yourself a hernia. Then we'll be even more fucked.'

'Why don't you worry about yourself, you look like a moose.'

'And you a lobster, dear brother.'

For the next hour, The First dedicated himself more or less exclusively to prancing about like that and I focused my energies on staring up at the ceiling from the mattress on the floor. I would have liked to have slept a bit, but no dice. That decaffeinated cocaine kept you in shape but wouldn't let you sleep a wink, so we had no other choice but to endure one another as best we could. Despite it all, however, between insults we were able to refine our staging and arrive at some kind of agreement as to our plan of attack. Once we heard voices upstairs, we took no more than five seconds to get into position: The First, knocked out on the chair, his arms ostensibly tied behind his back, and me on tiptoes behind the curtain, trying not to breathe too loud.

As soon as I got back there I was already psychologically prepared to crack open whoever's skull I had to crack open, though I was not psychologically prepared to see The First's disfigured face pop in front of mine quite so soon. Contrary to all our plans, he had abandoned his post at the chair and flung open the curtain to reprimand me for something.

'The bolt!'

'What bolt?'

'On the door, idiot, as soon as they come down the stairs they're going to realise that it's open.'

Shit. He was right.

'Get out of here and shut it before they start down. Hide in another cell and as soon as you hear me scream, come running in.'

The best-laid plans . . .

I got out of there as fast as I could, closed the door behind me, bolted it shut and prayed that the slight creaking noise had gone unnoticed among the voices that were moving closer and closer. Then I raced into the facing cell and shut the door.

I heard the footsteps descending the staircase, and then the creaking of the bolt on The First's door. Peeking through the tiny window, I could see the backs of two guys dressed up like insurance agents, both in navy-blue suits. One of them had already entered The First's cell and was handing him a metal tray. The other stood guard at the door. He was saying something to my Magnificent Brother, I couldn't hear what but it sounded like some kind of banter. A couple of seconds went by in which The First was to go through his little deathbed routine, and right away the first guy bent down a bit toward him. The other guy's back was in my way, so I couldn't see exactly what went down, but I heard The First scream and utter a muffled cry and then I saw a metal tray go flying through the air. I couldn't wait any more after that, so I opened the door with a shove and went running through the place yelling like Tarzan. The First's sudden resurrection had sent the guy in the doorway into maximum-alert mode, but my cry indicated that the enemy was attacking from behind as well, and he tried to turn around, fumbling with his shoulder holster in search of something. I didn't give him much time to find it: one hundred and twenty kilos of moose, fuelled by six metres of advance velocity, prevented him from much movement. The impact was tremendous. I rammed into him sideways, protected by the shield formed by my flexed arm. I only regretted the head-banging I got as I smashed into his chin. He, on the other hand, had not planned on suddenly finding himself in the path of a boar-hunting Obelix. For a moment he froze in an expression of pure panic and, milliseconds later, he was toast. Smashed up against the wall at the other end of the cell, about four metres away, he didn't appear to be moving. The majority of my kinetic energy had been transmitted to the body of my unfortunate victim, but I had enough inertia to completely lose my balance, fall uncontrollably and take the seat with me (luckily The First no longer occupied it). I rolled on the floor over and over again for what seemed like an eternity, probably because my mission was to reassume my position as quickly as possible and ensure that the guy couldn't get hold of his gun. At the second tumble, I had already lost my bearings, but I did note that my hand was touching something soft and I realised that it was the guy, who must have slid down from the wall and fallen on the floor. Without seeing very well what he was doing, I patted his jacket in search of his holster, stuck my hand inside and pulled out his gun. Only when I rose up from the floor, as dextrously as I could manage, did I ascertain that the guy was most definitely out of commission, even though he did thrash around a bit, trying to raise his head.

That, however, was only half the job to be done. While I was duking it out with my partner, The First was dealing with the other goon and, from what I could tell, he hadn't found his sweet spot yet. By the time I turned to look at them they were still striking poses at each other. My Magnificent Brother was like a praying mantis in full nuptial dance – it made you want to tattoo a dragon on his back or something. But the suit-and-tied hyena must have had a few tricks of his own, because he refused to give up quite so easily. After a few jabs here and there, the goon did a quick 360° corkscrew spin around the axis of his full height. The neat part of the move, though, was his ability to thrust his leg out at precisely the right moment and ram it into whatever was in its way – specifically, the neck of my Magnificent Brother, who scarcely had time to double over painfully on his bad side so as not to expose his mouth to more abuse. I had a pistol in my hand but no idea of what to do with it. Using it as a battering ram was one idea, but I was afraid it would go off; then we would really be busted. There wasn't much time to think – the blow that The First had just sustained had given the hyena time to take out his own weapon and, from the looks of it, he definitely knew what to do with a pistol. Luckily, though, The First regained his balance and, with a flourish, kicked the goon in the hand and sent the pistol flying. The First was still at a disadvantage, though, because his movements were laboured and his adversary already knew his weak points. The worst part about it, though, was that the dance was so complicated that I couldn't figure out how the hell to break into the action – I got the feeling that I'd only be a nuisance, and so I decided not to intervene. That is, until the hyena landed a fist in The First's side. He'd really hurt him – you could tell from the way he yelped – not very warlike this time around – as he sustained the blow. That was when I took the pistol into the palm of my hand, so as to protect the trigger, and launched into a second lunge attack, this one with special effects and furious growling. I wasn't as lucky this time around: the guy saw me coming out of the corner of his eye and had time to partially move his body mass out of the way, and so we both bore the brunt of the crash against the wall: I smashed into the wall head-on, and he backed into it.

My knee felt as though it had exploded upon contact with the wall and was instantly, almost automatically anaesthetised. I ricocheted onto the floor and remained there. The other guy also took his time recovering, but the rebound favoured him and he ended up tripping his way forward onto his feet. But The First was there waiting for him, with an ingenious compound manoeuvre that consisted of a double fu-fu punch in the solar plexus and, as the guest of honour doubled over onto himself, a precision kick in the back of his neck finished him off and he fell to his knees toward the floor, where he finally ended up like a frog run over by a car.

Miralles Bros: 2. Hyena Club: 0.

The truth is, we didn't have much to celebrate. The First's ribcage had been completely and totally punished, and my knee had all but abandoned me. I could feel the foot and I could feel the thigh, but in between the two, nothing more than a tingling feeling that could have been anything at all.

Our first job was to tie and gag the hyenas. Fortunately, The First performed a very handy Chinese trick which consisted of pressing his thumb and forefinger against the neck. This kept them unconscious as we took off their clothes, tied them up and gagged them. We even recycled the rope they had used to tie my Magnificent Brother to that chair, unbraiding it so that it would go further. I thought I recognised one of the guys, the one I had smashed into the wall, in fact, and my hunch was confirmed when I saw that he wore a pair of black Sebago moccasins. What goes around . . . anyway. I took off his socks and put them in his mouth, taking care not to touch the soggy part with my fingers, and I finished off the procedure by sealing his mouth shut with his own underwear – the tightie-whitie variety – which I wrapped around his head, making sure to position the faint brown stripe in the back just beneath his nostrils.

'May I ask what the fuck you are doing, you psychopath?'

'He should be glad I didn't use the other guy's underwear on him.'

As soon as we had them bound and gagged we took a quick inventory of our spoils. Two suits with Corte Inglés labels, two shirts, two ties, two belts and two pairs of shoes, one of them with laces. We also had two leather wallets with a total of ninety euros between the two, a set of Peugeot car keys, coins, a pack of Camels, a cheap but almost-full lighter, and then the most important items of all: two pistols with their corresponding barrels. Almost all the clothing of one of the guys seemed to fit The First to a t, shoes included. I tried to put on the Sebagos but, aside from the fact that they kind of grossed me out, I couldn't get them on. The First then went to wash up at the sink outside the cell, and I busied myself improvising a sack with the extra pair of trousers, tying up the leg holes and using a belt to close the whole thing up. I put the majority of our booty in there.

When I went out to find him, my Magnificent Brother was still in pretty sorry shape, but minus the blood stains and with the Corte Inglés suit, he already had a different air about him.

'Listen, couldn't we interrogate those two? I don't know why, but I get the feeling we're going to have a tough time finding our way out of this place,' I said.

'That's exactly what we're going to do. Have you got that toothbrush handy, the one you used to straighten my nose? I'm going to scare them a little.'

'Wouldn't you rather scare them with something else? We do have two guns that are in pretty good shape.'

'I've grown fond of that little toothbrush.'

We went back into the cell and closed the door behind us. The hyenas had dragged themselves toward one of the walls, away from the puddles on the floor. The First bent down next to the one who had kicked the hell out of his ribs and said to him in a friendly tone of voice:

'So, you see, I made a little bet with my brother . . . I think that this toothbrush can go all the way up your nose to your brains. See? It's very thin. He says it can't. What do you think?'

The goon didn't say anything, because he was gagged up. But he didn't look all that scared, either.

'We're going to do something here. I'm going to take that thing out of your mouth and then I'm going to ask you a few questions: if you say something interesting maybe I'll call off the bet. What do you say to that?'

The hyena remained implacable as The First untied the undershirt he had used as a gag. The guy sat there for a few seconds, spitting out damp wads of cotton.

'All right. Here's the first question. Now, you see, we aren't from around here and we're looking for the way out. Do you think you can point the way for us?'

'Go to hell, motherfucker,' the guy answered.

The First remained totally calm and stuck the tip of the toothbrush in one of his nostrils. The guy furrowed his brow.

'I still think it'll go all the way in. After all, the brain is a very soft organ . . .'

'I don't think you'll get further than halfway,' I said, in an expert-like voice. 'You'll hit a bone right away.'

The First pushed the toothbrush further up the nostril.

'Half? But look, it's already a quarter of the way in and I haven't even begun to place any pressure on it. It's true, there's bone in there, but if I kind of screw it in as I push . . . Want me to try?'

The question was for the hyena. I suppose that it was already so uncomfortable that he couldn't really talk much. The First realised this and loosened his grip on the toothbrush.

'You're never going to get out of here. And you're going to pay for what you're doing to me,' the guy said, as a little tear cascaded down his nose, though his voice was still as defiant as ever. The First, however, maintained his rich-boy manners.

'I'm sorry, but that's not what I asked you. The difficulty we face regarding our departure is the main topic of the questions that follow. And for the moment, we're still on the first question, or didn't you remember? Where is the way out? Where?'

'Arrgh . . . what do you want, a map? It wouldn't do you any good anyway.'

For someone whose hands and feet were bound up and whose nose was being threatened with impalement by a child-sized toothbrush, the guy sure was holding up well. And The First was starting to lose points: you could tell, because he went on to the next question even though the first was still unanswered.

'Are there guards?'

'Of course there are guards.'

'How many?'

'I don't know . . . lots. And not just guards, either. Agents, too.'

'Excuse me: might someone tell me what exactly an agent is?' I asked, raising my forefinger.

'I'm an agent, idiot,' the guy answered.

I bent down to look for one of the pieces of cutlery that had gone flying off the food tray.

'What should I do?' I asked The First, facetiously. 'Should I serve him the shit in little spoonfuls or should we stick his head in the toilet bowl and let him eat it buffet-style?'

The hyena answered once again.

'Do what you want, moron, if I get out alive I'll remember you. And if not, there are others who will.'

They're so incorrigible, this class of people.

'Listen, motherfucker: don't get too smart with me because I'd be more than glad to slam some sense into you. Know what I mean?'

By now, The First had given up the toothbrush number and was motioning for us to get out of there already.

'Leave him. It's not worth it.'

'Maybe. But I still want him to eat those socks he's got in his mouth.'

'We don't have time. Come on,' said The First, replacing the gag in the guy's mouth. 'The relief guard could come in at any time – these guys have been down here for a while now. Someone might notice they're missing.'

The truth was, the more time we lost the better off the hyena was, and that dude was tough enough to withstand a roughing-up session without spilling any information. And as far as I'm concerned, there's nothing terrifically appealing about shaking down a hulk whose hands and feet are all tied up . . . I don't know, that shit is too much for me.

We left the cell again and walked over to the sink.

'All right. So what do we do? Should we go straight up and flash the guns at the guard, see what he does?' I asked, in full action mode.

'Remember how I said your plan had overlooked one specific detail?'

Shit.

'Let me guess . . . we're in a submarine and we can't escape until we hit the surface and call at the port of Macau. Warm?'

'Cold.'

'Want to give me a clue, or you want to keep me guessing?'

'They've got your girlfriend. She's upstairs. They haven't hurt her, but they do have her sedated so that she won't scream.'

'Right: they found me a girlfriend just so they could kidnap her . . . is she from a good family, at least?'

'Don't be an idiot, damn it, they've got that girl you run around with, that Josephine.'

'Bonaparte's ex?'

'Come on. They saw you running around with her in my car.'

Holy Christ. Fina. I was so dumbfounded that it took me a full few seconds to react.

'But she doesn't have anything to do with this.'

'Right. But they didn't realise that until they got her in here. It was better than capturing you. She didn't have any protection, and you did.'

'Why didn't you tell me when I first got to you?'

'What for? To get you all nervous before it was necessary?'

'Absolutely. I like to get nervous with plenty of time to spare, what's wrong with that? This obsession of yours for withholding information really pisses me off, you know that? So what's the next surprise going to be? You've got an explosive suppository up your arse?'

'For once in your life, why can't you act like a responsible adult? We have to figure out a way to get the three of us out of here.'

Once again, we were screaming at each other in whispers.

'Well, it's your turn to think now. You're the smart one.'

He did.

'Very well: I'm going to go up and get near the guard, pretend to be one of the goons. The tall one is about my height and has the same colour hair. Even his haircut is the same if I part it like he does, and I know a bunch of his tics, he repeats them over and over. I can cover my face and tell him that the prisoner punched me . . . like this, see? You wait, about halfway up the stairs, and back me up with the gun in case something goes wrong. I'll carry mine, too, and make sure to keep it hidden and pointing at the guard the whole time. I've got the advantage that way, I can hit a man in the arm at twenty metres.'

'The boss has everything under control, huh?'

I still couldn't stop thinking about Fina, but there wasn't much time to sit around putting the pieces of that puzzle back together. In any event, the toothbrush once again proved extremely useful: I quickly put it to use on The First's hair. With no mirror to speak of, I had to step in as his temporary hair stylist and wardrobe consultant, fixing the hyena's tie so that it sat just so on the shirt. In exchange for my coiffure and toilette services, my brother tried to give me a brief lesson in pistol-handling techniques. Easy: all you had to do was undo the butterfly-shaped security catch and, if the situation called for it, pull the trigger, always making sure the cannon was facing forward.

The First was good in his role, much as I hate to admit it. I suppose my own histrionic humour is a kind of genetic thing that comes from my mother (my father, in these situations, is more innocent than a packet of Skittles). And so while I staked out the scene crouched down on the steps, he darted upstairs, covering his face with the little white tablecloth and growling curses all the while. It was the first time I had ever heard expressions like "goddamn sonofabitch' and 'I'm gonna shove a pole up his ass" come out of The First's mouth, mixed in with some coughs and grunts for good measure. I even heard him say "that motherfucking cocksucker fucked up my nose" before he disappeared up the stairs. After that I couldn't understand much of what he was saying, but I soon heard the guard engaged in conversation with him, moving his chair and maybe walking over to the ostensibly beaten-up hyena. I guess he caught on to the ruse when he got closer to The First, because I thought I heard someone shout "hey, stop!", which was then followed by sounds of a struggle, groans, and heels banging against the floor. I began to climb the stairs and stuck my head out a bit once I reached the landing.

There was The First, toward the end of the corridor, gripping the guard's inert figure from behind.

'You done already? Shit, man, what do you do to them . . .'

'Don't waste time, come on. Hurry up, we have to tie him up and gag him.'

'Tsss . . . don't yell at me, you're getting me stressed out. I'm dead sick of you and your attitude.'

'Well if you don't approve of my behaviour, I'll let you handle the next guard that crosses our path, you goddamn greasebag.'

'Oh, if it isn't Mister Bruce Lee talking . . . and who, may I ask, was the one who saved you from the other one before? If it wasn't for this little greasebag you would've been eaten alive.'

'Right. Real nice kamikaze interception. It's a miracle you didn't lose all your teeth in the process.'

'Well, even without teeth I'd still be a whole hell of a lot nicer than you, you fucking brat.'

Despite the arguing we managed to tie up the guard before he came to. This time we used his own belt to tie up his hands, and we ripped off a piece of his shirt to tie his ankles together, another bit of shirt to stuff in his mouth, and we added another club and another pistol to our booty, plus something that I had been sorely missing for the past few hours: a pair of boots that fit me. Not that it's terrifically comfortable to go around in someone else's shoes, but it's better than slipping and sliding all over the place in your socks.

'All right, so where is Fina?'

'I don't know, in one of the rooms, I guess. You go look for her while I hide this guy and then I'll go see what I find in the medicine chest.'

That was something, that the place even had a medicine closet of some sort. It must have been in one of the first few rooms because that's where The First went. I walked down the corridor, peering into the window of each door I passed. I went past the room where I had been, recognisable by the screen that was still laying on the floor from when it fell. Finally, when I reached the third room beyond that one I spied a Sleeping Beauty whose face I most definitely recognised. She was wearing a white robe that gave her a vaguely erotic air, kind of like those girls in the phone-sex ads in the newspaper, the ones dressed up in nurse's uniforms.

I went into the room, sat down on the bed next to her and shook her a little to wake her up.

'Fina. It's me, Pablo. Can you hear me?'

She smiled, her eyes still closed.

'Hiiii, how are you . . . what . . . what are you doing . . .'

For the first time in my life I mustered up all my bourgeois weaknesses, put them aside, and punched a woman. Fina. Just like that. Bam-bam: two damn good left hooks. She looked disgruntled.

'I'm going to pick you up now, try to work with me the best you can, all right?' I slung her over my shoulder, Tarzan style, but Fina weighs enough for two Janes and a cheetah, which made carrying her down the hallway slightly difficult, especially given that my knee was incapable of fulfilling its duty as a joint. I made it to the table where the guard had been, and I deposited the Sleeping Beauty there, propping her body against the wall.

In the middle of all this, The First emerged from the medicine closet. I was not amused by the way he looked at Fina. Not one bit.

'I found alcohol, cotton, sedatives, painkillers, syringes, scissors, a scalpel . . . I even found sutures and sterilised needles.'

It was beginning to look like my Magnificent Brother was familiar with Roger Wilco, too . . .

'Listen. I don't know about you, but I'm planning on getting out of this joint and getting good and drunk on the way to the hospital, so I don't know what we need any of that stuff for.'

'Getting out of here?'

'Yes, getting out: leav-ing. Get it?'

'Right.'

'Uh-oh. What now, more telepathy? There has to be some way out, right? We've got three pistols, a club and a porcelain poodle. If that's not enough to get us out of here . . .'

'Get out of here to where? There's a minor army that's been combing the fortress ever since you slipped out, and as soon as the relief guard gets here, they're going to realise that your girlfriend and I have escaped as well.'

'"The Fortress?" Did you say "The Fortress"?'

'Yes, the fortress. We have to hide somewhere safe so we can figure out how to get out. You can barely walk, I can't fight, and your girlfriend is a dead weight if I ever saw one.'

'She's not my girlfriend. She is a friend in *stricto sensu*, got that? And don't just stand there gawking, for God's sake. Don't you know some ancient Chinese secret for waking people up?'

He disappeared into the medicine closet once again and came out with a little white jar that stank of ammonia. He passed it under Fina's nose.

'Pablo . . .'

'Don't worry, you're just under the effects of a sedative. It'll wear off after a while, but you need to make a bit of an effort right now.'

'What . . . what are you doing here?'

'Shit, Fina, can't you see? I'm here to rescue you.'

'And to take chunks out of the walls with your knees,' joked my Magnificent Brother, who suddenly appeared to be bubbling over with good humour and most obliged to dispense it round the group.

Fina then realised that we were not alone and brought her hand up to her mouth, shocked by the meticulous handiwork on The First's face.

The shit-eater couldn't think of anything else but to take Fina's hand and kiss it.

'A pleasure to make your acquaintance. My name is Sebastian. Sebastian Miralles. Brother of Pablo.'

'Well, he's the son of the same parents as me, let's just keep it at that,' I pointed out.

'Delighted to meet you,' Fina replied. 'I'm Josephine. I've heard so much about you.'

'So much? Where would you have heard "so much" about him? Not from me . . .'

'My goodness, your poor face . . .'

'It's nothing, a bit of a bother, that's all. They tied me to a chair and grilled me for a while.'

' . . . I don't remember ever having told you about him . . . are you listening to me?' I asked.

'It must hurt something awful . . .'

'Not at all. It's a question of self-control. A properly trained mind can actually reinterpret pain signals.'

'Fina . . . yoo hoo . . . do you hear me?'

'Yes, yes – what do you want, Pablo, for God's sake? Can't you see I'm talking to your brother . . . and by the way, I'm extremely annoyed with you. How dare you stand me up last night! Two guys got out of a car and shoved a handkerchief in my mouth . . .'

'He stood you up, did he?'

'That's right.'

'Well, don't pay him much mind. He is a bit fond of alcohol, if you know what I mean.'

'A bit? I've seen him drain an entire bottle of vodka in the space of two hours.'

'All right, enough's enough, now.' I had to intervene at this point. 'This is not the time for cocktail conversation.'

The First then announced that he was going to finish packing up our collection of gadgets and left me alone with our rescued princess.

'You never told me you had such a handsome brother.'

Handsome. She said 'handsome.' Not 'good-looking', not 'cute', not 'brilliant' – she said 'handsome', just like in the soap operas.

'Fina, please. His face looks like a roadmap.'

'Maybe so, but he's got good raw material. He's a stud. Under normal circumstances, he'd be a hunk, you can tell. And now that you've got a new lady friend . . . don't think I've forgotten about that . . . Anyway, his big blue eyes are soo incredibly sexy.'

'Right. Just like me.'

'Oh, what do you care . . . Anyway, you do have about forty extra kilos on your frame,' she said. After that, kind of suddenly, a look came over her face, that expression that contemporary males and females get when they need to bring up a delicate subject but don't want to come off sounding embarrassed.

'Listen, I need to ask you something – there wouldn't be any maxi pads, or tampons, or something like that in there, would there? I think I'm about to get my period.'

Never, never would Princess Leia Organa get her period in the middle of a rescue mission, nor would Lady Marian, nor Helen of Troy. But Fina did: Fina had to go and get her period.

'Real nice. You dream about Mr Sexy's blue eyes but you get the fat guy to find you your tampons . . .'

I left her blowing me insipid kisses as I went over to where The First was assembling our goods. I then entered the medicine closet to take a look, but there was nothing in there that even remotely resembled tampons or maxi-pads. I did, however, find a pile of pillowcases in one of the closets. Maybe one of those would work for her. I returned to Fina with the pillowcases under my arm.

'What am I supposed to do with a pillowcase? Make a Ku Klux Klan hat?'

'Shit, Fina, I don't know . . . Before they had Tampax and that sort of thing, women used rags, didn't they? You figure it out . . .'

Anyway. A long time must have gone by until we were finally ready to leave there. Not only did we have to wait until Fina declared herself "presentable", but she also needed an intensive course in weapons-handling, a duty that fell to The First, Magnificent Instructor that he was. His student exhibited an uncommon level of comprehension for her sex and seemed to breeze through the theory part (where the bullets came out, etcetera), but once she actually had to handle the weapon in the more practical phase of the instruction, she clutched it as if it were a jar of honey. Some little scenario. After a while, we were ready: the illustrious commando unit comprising one studly warrior with two pillowcase-saddlebags, Doris Day with a pistol tucked into the belt of her bathrobe, and one Magilla Gorilla who limped along, loaded down with replacement sanitary napkins. Together the three of us advanced beyond the door with the bars on it and into the incipient darkness of that absurd edifice.

'Where are we going?' I asked, for some reason.

'To explore the labyrinth,' said The First.

Lovely. An adventure. The only thing missing was Darth Vader. But, he didn't take long to materialise.

Given that we weren't actually in a real labyrinth, all we had to do was to stick to the areas lit up by emergency exit signs, which eventually led us to a kind of subterranean tunnel that was sort of the backbone of the building. It clearly led to somewhere because there was a truck and an excavator on the side. In other words: the tunnel was massive.

'Holy shit!' was my preliminary evaluation. The First, ever the wise hero, went over to examine a mess of cross-beams and some other construction materials that took up as much space as yet another vehicle sitting behind the excavator. When he returned, he was sporting that annoying, everything's-under-control attitude.

'Our best option is to follow the truck's tyre tracks. It must have to go somewhere to unload all that dirt.'

'Oh, really? You think someone could have removed all that dirt using that little baby truck?'

'They've had plenty of time to do it. Come on, we may have quite a walk ahead of us.'

Clearly it wasn't enough for Captain Thunder to go around making up little mysteries for everyone to solve, now he had to go and start giving out orders. Anyway. I let him take the lead and I held up the rear, behind Fina. We moved forward like that through the tunnel for a while, sticking close to the wall, given the lack of illumination. It was almost completely dark but there was just barely enough light for us to see where we were stepping. My God, it was just like the Temple of Doom, although ours was more the low-rent version – no boa constrictors or subterranean waterfalls or anything. Here and there we would step into little pools of water that had slid down the humid, subterranean walls, which made it downright Arctic in there. I could have done with a windbreaker or something.

Rather quickly, about two or three subterranean city blocks away, we arrived at a point of entry to the tunnel, a sudden widening of the path that broke the monotony of our walk. At first I didn't recognise the place because I was far too taken aback by the structure of semi-buried arches underneath which we could make out a choice selection of human refuse. Coca-Cola bottles (classic dump items), used condoms, an old umbrella, dog-eared magazines . . . But as soon as I spied, among the various bits of garbage, an aerial shot of an enormous pair of tits jerking off a cinnamon-coloured fellow, I realised exactly where we were: in the ruins of the Bóbila, that old abandoned ceramics factory buried beneath the park that was built above it in the eighties. And so, most likely, we were somewhere beneath the street known as Numancia, no doubt quite far below sea level.

I mentioned this to The First. And though I doubt that my Magnificent Brother would have ever been caught jerking off in the Bóbila, arousing himself with stolen girlie magazines, he did venture to guess the location.

'Well, we know there's a way out at Jaume Guillamet 15, and that's about two blocks from where we are now. We might be better off leaving the tunnel and heading onto the next access path to the buildings and trying our luck.'

We didn't have time to ponder our various options. Fina advised us of this by shouting, "Someone's coming from in there!" She rushed to our sides, pointing toward the direction we were going in. Then I heard a "Stop!" come from somewhere far away. The First slung my arm around his neck to help me walk and ordered Fina to start running, as fast as she could down the last exit path we had gone by. I squirmed away from my helper so that I could jump up a bit faster. Fina had already reached the access ramp and was now shouting us on, sticking her head out to check on our progress. Finally we reached her before whomever following us could catch up with us, and we entered at some floor of the car park, as insane as the rest of the place, then Fina ran toward what seemed to be the doors to a lift, and then frantically press the call button. The First disentangled himself from me and told me to continue on by myself. When I turned halfway around to see where the hell he was going, I saw a guard in blue coveralls enter from the tunnel. He stopped very suddenly, surprised by the fact that one of his fugitives had turned around and started running towards him. The guy, moving his arm as if about to throw a javelin, raised his club to slam it into The First, but my Magnificent Brother did something that I am sincerely chagrined that I was not able to record on video for posterity. The long and the short of it is that, following a brief magician-type manoeuvre launched by my brother, the guard found himself with a humungous knee in his balls while my Magnificent Brother was still fully intact and in possession of the guy's club, which he had somehow caught under his left arm. With his right hand, The First pulled the club out in one clean, quick, dry movement to the right and could have easily cracked his opponent's head before the poor slob could utter the long 'uhhhhh' that followed his surprise ball-blasting. The First, however, just nudged him a little and the guy ended up writhing around the floor a bit. That was when a second guard appeared, running toward my brother. But The First didn't even have to touch this one: once the guard saw how his colleague had ended up, he looked at my Magnificent Brother, brandishing that club as if it were a majorette's baton, and he turned halfway around and disappeared back to wherever he had come from.

The First then took advantage of the moment to stride rapidly down the hall toward the lift, where Fina and I were waiting for him, our fingers ready to hit the uppermost floor.

'Excuse me, would you mind signing an autograph?' I said, to lighten the mood a bit.

'Shut up with your nonsense. The guy who came running after the first one had a radio on him. We're in for trouble.'

The lift went up full-speed – you could see the little numbers illuminating the panel – straight to the sixth floor. The building had fourteen floors, but from the sixth floor up you needed a special key to gain access. It appeared that we were being held hostage in a very posh building. For God's sake.

'Don't take out the pistols, if they see we're armed they might get nervous and pelt us with bullets. Josephine, hide yours in your pocket.'

Fina obeyed, dumbfounded. Then, all of a sudden, something that sounded like a red-alert on a combat submarine began ringing through the air – *moook, mooooook* – so freaky it made my skin crawl. By the time we reached the sixth floor we were frantic. The doors opened automatically – *dong, bsss* – and for a moment we remained there, glued to the back wall of the lift. *Mooook, moook*: that alarm wouldn't quit. The First leaned out the door to scope out the scenario, but I already knew that someone was there waiting for us. At the far end of the hall, behind a glass door that revealed what looked like the reception area of an elegant office, I spotted a girl rise up from her chair in an effort to see what all this fuss was about.

'Get out of the lift!' The First said to me and Fina.

We got out. My Magnificent Brother immediately began hacking away at the call button with the butt of the pistol, not stopping until a number of coloured wires emerged from the panel, and he tugged on them until they were rendered completely useless. Then he surveyed his surroundings in search of something (I didn't know what, exactly) and finally settled on a rather innocuous planter containing a little tree, which he uprooted, smashed the clay pot against the floor and shoved one of the shards in front of the door to the other lift, which was parked on our floor. It all happened too fast for me: any decision that can't be made while sipping a beer is generally too fast for me. As such, I let The First, who was used to stressful situations, take control of this one for the moment and instead focused my attention on the fact that behind the glass doors, just beyond a little set of sofas where the reception girl was, a massive picture window revealed both the outside world and the building next door. Twilight was falling now, and we could hear the sound of firecrackers beneath the *moook-moook* of the alarm. The moment seemed to last a lifetime, because all I wanted to do right then was stick my head out that window and see that the world still existed. Once he'd immobilised both lifts, The First came over to us. The girl, frightened by this lunatic advancing toward her, with a face that looked like a map of the Alps, tried to hide behind anything and everything she could as she retreated from him.

'Don't be afraid, we don't want to hurt you,' The First said to her, in an unsuccessful attempt to calm the girl, who now brandished a staple-gun in front of his face. Fina's attempt, however, met with more success.

'Relax, we're friends,' she said. A somewhat absurd comment given the circumstances, but the fact that she was a woman, her mere presence in between two hulks whose appearance would have been the envy of any member of the Hell's Angels, must have held more sway with the girl.

'Don't worry,' Fina insisted. 'We're just trying to get out of here. They're after us.'

The First had moved over to the picture window and I followed suit, pressing my nose against the glass. I could just barely make out the sight of an interior patio and, against the slender strip of summer-solstice sky, the luminous explosion of a rocket soaring through the air. Suddenly the alarm stopped ringing and we heard the sound of footsteps pattering toward us from the area where the lifts were.

'Take cover!' shouted The First, offering no other specifications.

Nobody in my life had ever given me such an instruction, but something about the contextual universe in which we found ourselves told me that he wasn't advising us to protect ourselves from a summertime sunshower, but that we had best find some kind of bullet-proof barrier to place between ourselves and the rest of the world. I wondered if Fina had understood the command or if she was looking for a rainslicker of some sort. I tried to ascertain this, but I couldn't seem to locate her. Then I realised that she was crawling along the floor behind the reception counter, preceded by the staple-gun girl, and then I saw the two of them slink through a double door that looked as though it led into some kind of office. Once I saw the girls' manoeuvre, I decided to barricade myself behind a sofa, imitating my Magnificent Brother. Would a sofa be able to protect me from a shower of bullets?, I asked myself. It was a Chesterton of a difficult-to-describe colour, but I don't suppose the colour was very critical to the sofa's capacity as an improvised bunker. The First, meanwhile, seemed to be following a vaguely different line of thinking.

'Don't move! We're armed!' he shouted, flashing his pistol once again, this time not as a hammer for destroying office fixtures but the more conventional form of firearm usage.

To reinforce his threat, he fired a shot toward the ceiling, producing a sound similar to that of a pellet-gun, which was all but drowned out by the summer solstice firecrackers exploding away outside, beyond the picture window. Nevertheless, I suppose that the chunk of plaster that suddenly crashed down from the ceiling was ominous enough to communicate his intentions.

'Didn't you say not to take out the pistols?' I asked. You never do know what to expect with The First.

'Well now you can, idiot.'

'Listen, you sack of shit . . .'

'Shut up, will you? I'm trying to repel an armed attack.'

'Well, don't worry, you're already repellent enough on your own.'

Just in case I rummaged through my pockets for the pistol and I pulled it out, along with a wad of fifty-euro bills that went fluttering across the floor. If I could have chosen my weapon, I would have preferred to wage battle with the porcelain poodle, but I certainly didn't want the bullets to start flying and end up dead with an unused pistol in my pocket, either. I remembered the basic precaution of pulling the trigger with the gun facing forward and tried to imagine what John Wayne would do in this type of predicament. I had scarcely even worked up my first wad of spit to splatter on the floor when a voice came booming out from the depths of the entrance hall, not far from where the lifts were. It sounded like one of those megaphones that people yell from on the tops of cars that drive around the city during political campaigns. And it was, indeed, a megaphone.

'Surrender your weapons. I repeat: surrender your

weapons and come out with your hands up or we will proceed with the release of gases.'

I am of the opinion that if someone not only threatens you with the word "gases" but, in fact, alludes to the possibility of proceeding with such gases, he or she should be taken very seriously. I didn't know what kind of gases were involved in this threat, but I was sure that they would be fully deleterious to our collective health.

'What do we do now? I get sinusitis from gases, I don't even like pine-scented room freshener.'

'What do you think? Surrender.'

It was a good thing we did. Anyway, the Greenpeace people would have thanked us for it, I guess. The First also took care of the formalities of our armistice, which was a good thing, because protocol is most definitely not my strong suit. He asked me for the pistol and with both weapons in his hands he shouted all right, fine, we surrender, here are the weapons. He slid them across the floor beneath the sofa and raised his two hands from behind the backrest, though not before nudging me first to follow suit. I had a bit of trouble raising both arms because my stiff knee made any and all movements rather difficult, but I managed it somehow.

'Where's the girl? I repeat: where's the girl?'

The megaphone again.

'Over there, inside,' I said. 'She surrenders, too. And whoever touches her, watch out or I'll pop you one. Fina: can you hear me?'

'Yeees. What should I do?'

My Magnificent Brother took over from there.

'Josephine, slide the pistol across the floor and out of the room. Come out with your hands up high.'

Apparently, the guy with the megaphone didn't take too kindly to my brother's initiative.

'Remain silent and with your hands up. I repeat: remain silent and with your hands up. We give the orders here.'

By the time the guy finished repeating himself, Fina had already emerged, with her hands up and her face frozen with fear. Behind her followed the staple-gun girl.

'Am I supposed to surrender, too?' she asked, though it was unclear whether she was addressing me or The First.

'Yes. Stay there, keep quiet and everything will be fine.'

'Silence. I repeat: silence!' shouted the guy with the megaphone, growing testier and testier at the fact that everyone was ignoring him.

As soon as guard number one, complete with helmet and gas mask, collected the three pistols from the floor, some more masked men in blue coveralls began to emerge, all of them pointing rifles (or Uzis, or whatever they were) at us. Predictably, they came around to place a set of handcuffs on each of us, excluding the staple-gun girl, who left as fast as she could once they were able to positively identify her. Before they shackled us, however, they made us line up against the wall, just like when the cops nail you *in flagrante*. The guy with the megaphone must have been the boss of the posse, because he continued to talk into his walkie-talkie and bark orders left and right. Someone tried to body-search Fina and in a sudden burst of rage, the offended lady landed the guy a wallop that knocked off the gas mask hanging from his neck. I had my back to all this, but I did hear the bam and see the mask go flying into the air. Thanks to that, she was able to avoid getting handcuffed, and they simply placed her in line between me and The First.

They herded us into the lift after freeing the car from its temporarily immobilised position. Then they made us walk down a bunch of hallways and then more hallways between the various interconnected buildings. There were people in some of the hallways, too: here and there you could see a guard sitting at a desk, or people dressed in black coveralls similar to those of the staple-gun girl, and even a couple of hyenas with dirty underwear beneath their Corte Inglés suits. The worst part, though, was that one of the guards kept nudging me in the back with the butt of his gun. It was really starting to piss me off. After the umpteenth nudge I stopped cold, making the guy bump into me and I turned around, furious, to face him head-on.

'Listen, why don't you stick your goddamn gun up your balls? Can't you see my leg is busted?'

All that got me was an extra nudge, in the chin this time, plus another one in my gut. The one in my gut was nothing, but the one in my face made me lose it, and I lifted my lame leg and kicked the guy. This was a stupid move on my part: my hands were shackled, and so I fell clumsily to the floor and the guards following us started kicking me until I was able to get up again. Fina, who watched the whole thing, lunged against the first guy she could, grabbed him by the hairs of his head and gave him a free mini-scalping. Luckily The First intervened, and yelled at us to shut up already. In any event, the little number didn't do us a bit of good. The guard continued nudging me with the butt of his gun until we arrived at a rather elegant vestibule and were shoved into another lift. During the ascent I began to wonder what would happen if they decided to interrogate me as they had done with my brother. I promised myself that I would hold out until they rendered me just a bit worse than him. I happen to be particularly fond of my nose but bruises to my honour heal much slower than the physical kind. And if they made me piss myself, well, I'm used to smelling pretty awful, so that part didn't worry me too much.

The floor we got out on, however, much less the office we were led into, didn't look much like torture chambers.

And there, sitting behind a desk in a spectacular, high-backed easy chair, was none other than Darth Vader himself.

THE GAME IS UP

At first glance, the enthroned individual behind the desk reminded me of Mario Vargas Llosa, but with fewer teeth. I suppose it came as something of a surprise, but I was already so surprised that I didn't even flinch. Plus, there was someone else standing next to him: an elegant, thirtysomething lady, a medium-length mane of Head & Shoulders hair, lovely face and eyes like those of a dragon lying in wait.

I was, however, more nonplussed by the manner in which The First and my green-eyed Beatrice stared at each other.

'Well, well . . . The Miralles brothers, reunited at last. And with a lovely young girl, at that,' said the Exorcist.

'Woman,' corrected Fina, who is very sensitive about the way people address her, and who was already a bit peeved at the recent episode with the guards. The guy got up from the table, his eyes fixed squarely on her, and I would have bet my life that he was about to plant a kiss on her hand. Score.

'Excuse me. Woman.'

Fina's scowl slowly softened and she quickly removed her recently smooched hand from sight so that she could shake off the snarl of guard's hairs that were still twisted around her fingers. I would almost say she looked embarrassed by the gaffe.

The Exorcist made like he didn't notice and continued

with his greetings. Now it was my Magnificent Brother's turn: the Exorcist offered his hand to The First who, obviously, couldn't shake it.

'Oh . . . excuse me. I didn't realise you were handcuffed.'

'Don't worry, I can do without the handshake.'

Good for him, damn it. Clearly this guy was the big cheese around here, you could tell from the office. But he simply nodded his head, smiling all the while at The First's snub and then turning to me for the last greeting.

'You and I know each other, don't we? I do hope you had a pleasant dinner with Gloria the other evening. Quail in onion sauce, if I remember correctly . . . And I believe you also know my daughter Eulalia.'

Well, then. That made my little Beatrice both secretary to the Chairman of the Board as well as the niece-granddaughter of a papal nuncio, all in one fell swoop. I tried to hide my shock.

'Yes, we know each other. A divine comedy, Beatrice. Congratulations.'

'Thank you. You weren't so bad yourself . . .'

She said it without even looking at me; she had eyes only for my Magnificent Brother. Then, she went over to him to give him a kiss on the lips. The First didn't fight it, though he glared at her. What a bad scene, I thought, to have a lover and pay her an executive secretary's salary for this.

'It's lovely to see you, but I'm afraid I have to leave now,' she said, not without caressing The First's cheek with the back of her hand. And with that she left the room.

'You'll have to forgive my daughter. We have so many obligations to attend to today. I'm sorry to have ruined your summer solstice party, Pablo . . . may I call you Pablo?'

'I can stand it, I suppose. But I don't believe I ever said

you could speak to me in the familiar,' I said, just to show him that I could be every bit as disagreeable as my Magnificent Brother. The guy laughed a bit, for show.

'Always with your guns cocked, eh . . . Very well, I shan't reproach you for it. But I assure you, we will understand one another when all is said and done. Guard, please remove their handcuffs. They won't be necessary now, will they?' he quipped, turning toward us.

'As far as I'm concerned they will. I plan on wringing your neck as soon as my hands are free,' I answered.

'How kind of you to warn me. Nevertheless, I wouldn't advise you to check the king, not in one move at least. As you can see, I have my rooks very well-situated.'

Immediately he signalled to the guard, indicating that our handcuffs were to be removed. I looked at the two hyenas on either side of the table. They were special – so special that I recognised them: the same two massive hulks that stood guard at the entrance to the restaurant. In addition to them, three of the guards who had brought us here were still with us, plus the loudmouth with the megaphone. Fina, noting that the scene had begun to acquire a more civilised air, dared to ask if there was a ladies' room she might use, and the Exorcist instructed the megaphone guy to get the guards to disperse a bit and added that he would send 'an officer to accompany the lady.' Then he pressed a little intercom button on the table and asked whoever was on the other side to come in, too.

For a few seconds the only thing you could hear were the festival and the fireworks outside, as intensely as you could hear them from any other building in the city.

'The San Juan festivities: a magical night,' our host said, effectively destroying whatever magic the night could have had. I sensed the imminence of a speech on the rape of

Persephone, and I was hungry, thirsty and desperate for this thing to end once and for all. I looked at The First through the corner of my eye and by the scowl on his face I could tell that, for the first time in our lives, we had before us someone that both of us found equally repugnant. Fina, however, seemed utterly tickled by the bit about the 'magical night.' At that moment, two women entered the office, interrupting the dissertation. One was dressed in a guard's uniform and the other in a pair of those black coveralls. Coveralls seemed to be all the rage around here – almost everyone I had seen walking up and down the halls wore them, even though they made them all look like extras in a science fiction movie starring Steve Lawrence and Edye Gormé.

Once Fina had left the room with the female guard ('Won't you excuse me? I'll be back in no time,' she said, absolutely oozing politeness), the Exorcist asked The First and me if we needed anything. Apart from hunger and thirst, I would have killed for a coffee and a joint. I could produce the joint myself if they would give me back the contents of my pockets, which is exactly what I told the guy. The First only wanted water, but his ascetic routine was purely for show, because he certainly didn't deny himself the luxury of firing me one of those long, disapproving glares he loves so very much. The Exorcist then looked up with a 'please' that was directed toward the girl in the black coveralls, to indicate that she was to go and get what we had asked for. Then he asked us to sit down. Both of us accepted the offer and fell down, with relief, upon the two easy chairs facing the desk.

The Exorcist then resumed his position at his black leather throne.

'Did you know that the celebration of the San Juan

summer solstice feast is very probably of Chaldean origins? Some anthropologists have linked it to an ancient religious group that revered the god Bel. It seems that many, many years ago people ate a circular cake in celebration of his memory, a cake with a hole in the middle as a representation of the solar disc . . .'

The last thing I wanted was to attend a lecture, but I didn't much feel like getting on his bad side, at least not until coffee was served. My Magnificent Brother, however, was not able to contain his feelings.

'Listen, Ignacio, your conversations are really scintillating, but if you don't mind, I'd rather return to my prison cell.'

The Exorcist smiled in that sarcastic way of his, displaying his full set of fake pearly whites.

'Oh . . . I'm so inconsiderate. You must be tired, it's been a rough day for you two. What a shame, because this particular evening does inspire such fascinating observations . . . Look outside: the city is on fire.'

As he said it, his hand, which was underneath the table, activated some kind of gadget that intensified the lights somehow. Almost at the exact same time, we heard a mechanical buzzing noise that made us whip around to look at the wall behind us. In reality, it was a huge metallic curtain which was now rising up, up and away to reveal a huge glass cupola through which you could see all of Barcelona dressed up in the night sky, like a cabaret singer in her best sequinned costume. If he was trying to impress us, he was on the right track, but for the moment I was more interested in ascertaining our current location than in marvelling at the pyrotechnics. We were in a very tall building, too tall to see the street it towered over, but all I had to do was look at the rooftops to see that we were on Jaume Guillamet, right next door to number 15. It was maybe eleven o'clock in the evening, and the entire city had to be eating cake and drinking that cheap champagne that all those Registered Windows Users like to call 'cava.' That was exactly what I was thinking when the black coveralled girl reappeared, pushing a little cart that boasted, in addition to what The First and I had requested, a pignoli-nut cake and the aforementioned dark green bottle, though this one didn't hail from San Sadurní but rather from France itself. A more careful examination of the little cart revealed the presence of my booklet of rolling papers and my last bit of hash, both presented on a little silver platter.

Shit.

'I was thinking that we ought to celebrate the evening *comme il faut*,' said the Exorcist. 'A glass of champagne? It is a splendid brut. Of course, one's palate would rather savour something other than sweets, but popular traditions lose all their charm when one doesn't observe them exactly as they are intended. Wouldn't you say so, Pablo?'

'Hmph. I tend to respect only the most basic and necessary of popular traditions.'

'Ahh . . . such as?'

'Breathing.'

He didn't offer the slightest sign of jumping up to the net; all he did was flash those pearly whites in a kind of sportsmanlike gesture. The First, apparently indifferent to the banter, poured some water into a glass and drank it. I did the same as Don Ignacio took advantage of the pause between sets to uncork his Magnificent Bottle. He was still pouring it in a tall flute when The First, who appeared to be familiar with this routine, began to press the issue again.

'All right, Ignacio. If you don't mind getting to the point and telling us what you need to tell us . . .'

The guy returned to his throne with his champagne flute filled to the brim, and took a little sip. Then he closed his eyes, with a theatrical flair, as if he simply adored that horrible bubbly wine that champagne is, when all is said and done. Now it was just the three of us in the room (plus the two heavily-armed mega-hyenas, but they kind of faded into the furniture) and, to be honest, the atmosphere in that space that looked out over the steadily mounting crescendo of the festival outside began to acquire a certain cinematic *je ne sais quoi.* The scenario outside the glass walls was starting to look like a Repsol petrol ad, and I think if I'd had a lyre on hand I might had broken into an ode to the city in flames.

But I had to turn my attention away from the spectacle outside because the Exorcist had finished up his wine-connoisseur bit and had started talking again. This time he heeded The First and tried to get straight to the point.

'I have a proposal in mind for the two of you, but I think we should start out with a round of questions first. I suppose you're both a bit confused . . . Especially you, Pablo. And the better you understand the situation, the better you will be able to evaluate the proposal I am about to make.'

He was looking straight at me as he finished the sentence, but The First was the one who answered him, like a sceptical journalist preparing to nail a politician with some very specific question.

'Very well. Why don't we start with the questions. When are you going to let us out of here?'

'I'd say that depends on the agreement we reach.'

'Very well, then. Let's see: what do you want from us?'

'Complete and total discretion.'

'Okay, we'll be discreet. Can we go now?'

'I'm afraid I'll need some sort of guarantee.'

'You have our word.'

'That won't be enough. Please understand: I don't have anything personal against you. But this doesn't depend on me, you know that.'

I was still on phase one of licking the glue part of the rolling paper, but I didn't want to be left completely out of the loop.

'Excuse me. Can somebody please tell me what we are talking about?' I asked.

The Exorcist momentarily abandoned the circumspect tone he had adopted when speaking to The First and turned to me. In a much more grandiloquent tone, he declared, 'You have entered The Fortress, Mr Miralles. You have crossed the border into a place governed by a different set of laws, a rare privilege for which a high price is usually paid.'

Lovely. The way he said it, it almost came off like a kind of aphorism, but I was beginning to lose patience.

'Listen, Don Ignacio, excuse the honesty but if there is one thing I'm not into it's telepathy. Given that I don't know what the hell this Fortress is that you're talking about, do you think you can tell me in some intelligible manner why we are being detained here?'

He seemed to be flipping through the files of his memory, searching for an appropriately vulgar way to express himself.

'Let's just say that you two know too much. Is that sufficiently intelligible?'

'Now you're talking. But if that's what you're worried about, please know that I don't know a goddamn thing.

In fact, I have wasted the last week of my life on this and still I haven't figured out what the hell is going on.'

'I'm sorry to disagree with you, but you actually know much more than you think you do. You know that Worm exists, you can associate it to a specific address in a specific city, and you know of at least two of the Doors to the Fortress in Barcelona. In addition, you are able to identify various external members of the organisation, including myself, even though I am not exactly external but rather someone whose position in the hierarchy implies a relatively important relationship to Worm. And all that information is sufficient to jeopardise eight hundred years of a most discreet existence. I think you know what I am speaking of: we received your questionnaire on our site. Incidentally, I do hope that the defence virus we sent hasn't caused too great an inconvenience to your German friends. Our technical staff has instructions to take extremely drastic measures in the event of a computer attack.'

A real well-situated pack of raving lunatics. The First, however, was a few steps ahead of me, and insisted that we speed up the conversation.

'All right. You said you had a proposal to make. We're listening.'

The guy reclined a bit in his easy chair and looked at me. Then he turned to The First, and then back to me again, and so on. Finally, when we were as rapt as we could possibly be, he said:

'One of the three of you has to stay here with us. And it has to be Pablo.'

I nearly choked on the puff of smoke in my lungs at that one, so my Magnificent Brother was the first to voice his disagreement.

'What? Forget it . . . Why him?'

The Exorcist displayed a magnanimous gesture of patience.

'Sebastian, please. Be reasonable. You're married, you have two children and a business to oversee. There are too many people who are increasingly aware of your absence with every passing hour. Your father is a powerful man, he has excellent contacts, and he could complicate things considerably for us. That, then, is in nobody's best interests, and I doubt that you'd want your lovely lady friend to remain here with us. Pablo is the only one who can disappear off the face of the Earth without anyone missing him too much: he's certainly done it before. An occasional postcard with a stamp from some exotic place is all we'd need to keep your father happy.'

'Excuse me, but I find myself quite happy on the face of the Earth and I don't intend to leave it. So you'd better think up something else,' I said.

The guy sat there looking at me with an expression on his face that I hadn't seen before.

'I think you might want to try it, Pablo . . . Stay with us. We need men like you.'

It was the first time that anyone who wasn't the proprietor of a bar or restaurant had said something like that to me. And I have to say I felt flattered, though I continued to put up a fight.

'I should warn you that I am extremely poorly suited for membership in a cult. Rules aren't my thing.'

'Cult?' He smiled. 'It never would have occurred to me to think of the Worm as a cult.' He leaned back against his throne. 'If memory serves me right, cults, as they are properly known, fulfil certain requirements that have nothing in common with us. We don't apologise for our way of life, at least not indiscriminately: you could almost say that our mode of action is anti-attraction. Very few people interest us, and the few that actually do find it quite difficult to approach us. You are an exception, for you have overridden the normal procedure. Nor do we have a charismatic leader. I, for example, occupy an important position, but my power isn't personal – I've been elected by a council with a constantly rotating membership. Yes, of course, certain positions carry with them certain privileges, such as this excellent champagne, but the same is true of the board of any multinational company. Our internal members and natives have no other obligation than that of observing the discipline and looking after themselves, and if we have to rely on external employees we are most generous with our remuneration,' he said, with a gesture that indicated the two mega-hyenas, who remained impassive.

'We are most definitely not a cult,' he continued on. 'No more than the Barcelona Football Club, although, like them, we too are a bit more than a mere club. More than a secret society, even. Why, I would almost venture to say that we are a world apart. And this other plane of reality needs thinkers – in the very same way that the world you've lived in up until now needs thinkers, my good friend Pablo.'

'Well you should know that I think as little as possible, and usually only when forced to do so.'

The guy smiled, and an intelligent expression came over his face.

'Don't be modest, now . . . over the past few days we've been following your Invented Reality theory quite closely, and we have been very pleasantly surprised. My goodness, if anything good has come out of this affair it has been the opportunity to meet you. In general, we don't concern ourselves with the Internet beyond what we need to do for internal communication, but after the connection you established with us, under a false name, we thought it convenient to keep tabs on you a bit. Not only did we immediately realise that you were the man Sebastian had hired to investigate our Door, but we also hit upon – almost by accident, mind you – the Metaphysical Club. Isn't that what it's called? At first we simply couldn't believe that the person who wrote those words had absolutely nothing to do with our organisation. They were the very same conclusions: almost literally, the same words that led Geoffrey de Brun to establish The Fortress and withdraw from the world in the Spring of 1254. The difference, perhaps, is that you have eight more centuries to support you and our founder had to make up that distance on his own. Even so, it is quite an exceptional coincidence. I think you could be extremely happy with us, not to mention quite useful to the organisation. We are prepared to offer you whatever it is you need to continue with the work you've begun.'

'I doubt that,' I said. Now The First was the one who didn't understand what the hell we were talking about.

'Why do you doubt it? Try and ask . . .'

'Look, it's not worth it. To start with, I don't have any work to continue. Remember, metaphysicals do very little – in fact, that's exactly why I like the field so much. Nobody pays you but there's also very little work to be done, and what little there is is almost never urgent. In addition, I already told you I'm not good with rules, and I don't care if they're Van Gaal's or those of the Knights of Malta. If you took the time to read my pieces in the Metaphysical Club, you would know that, aside from those eight centuries of accumulated nonsense, I have a habit of doing strictly what I feel like doing: no more, no less. You might call me a free spirit, if you can understand that.'

'What about when your credit runs out? You'll have to excuse me, but I should add that our investigation of you goes beyond the Internet . . . Think, for a moment, of a place where you could do whatever you wanted without ever worrying about money. We don't use money here in the Fortress.'

'Right. Well, since you're so well-informed about me, you must also know that half of my father's money is far more than I'll ever need to keep myself drunk for the next five hundred years. After that, we can talk.'

'Have you seen your father's Last Will and Testament? Perhaps, after all, he isn't going to split his fortune into two equal parts.'

'That's all right, whatever the law says I have coming to me will be fine.'

The guy pretended to blink for a second.

'Shall I take that to mean you do not accept my proposal?'

The First decided to take over the dialogue.

'Of course he doesn't accept.'

'Very well. In that case I have no other choice but to keep the three of you here,' the guy said, as if he really didn't want to have to do it.

The First then snapped back into action.

'Don't be ridiculous, Ignacio. You yourself said we'd be missed. My father will move heaven and earth to find us. Sooner or later he'll find you. You know that.'

'We can always offer him a pair of corpses to cry over. Or, to be exact, three corpses: his two beloved heirs and the lady friend of one of them. A most unfortunate accident: three passengers pressed together inside a two-seater Lotus, high alcohol content in their blood, music playing full-blast . . .'

Just then, I thought of the Opel Corsa, upside-down in the excavation pit where they were digging a car park.

'Robellades' son wasn't even thirty years old. Sir, you are a swine.'

'Who is Robellades?' The First asked, but neither I nor the Exorcist chose to fill him in on the details.

'Before getting rude, you should know that the Robellades incident was a complete accident, and be assured that I am as chagrined about it as you. I am being completely honest, you must believe me. He had gone too far, and we wanted to act accordingly but we had something else in mind entirely. We are not murderers.'

'What about tying this one to a chair and beating the daylights out of him? Was that an accident, too? Or did his face get like that from all the mosquitoes?'

'With your brother, we have had to go a considerable degree further than usual. He is an obstinate man, but we had no idea how very obstinate he could be. We have been extremely careful, however, not to inflict any damage that would take more than a few weeks to heal. Before judging us so harshly, remember that our survival is hanging in the balance, and remember, too, that you were the ones who tried to intimidate one of our employees by inserting a very dangerous object up his nose. A . . . a toothbrush, if I'm not mistaken,' he read from a paper on his desk.

'Well, we only wanted to scare him,' said The First.

'Are you trying to say that psychological torture isn't torture just the same? Not to mention the bones you have broken and the fact that right now a guard is lying in the infirmary with one of his testicles sliced in half. You have no more excuses than we do, Sebastian, and you know it. We have all been trying to avoid the danger that threatens our collective survival. And none of this would have ever happened if you hadn't interfered in our business. You know that Lali is with us voluntarily, just as Gloria is *not* with us voluntarily, and you have no right to meddle with that. You tried to save someone who didn't need saving in the first place. That was your mistake. And I'm not threatening you now, I'm simply offering you the only possibility I can think of to save you. Take it as a sign of my good will: you know I love your wife as if she were my own daughter, and I know that you love my daughter as if she were your own wife.'

Aside from the tongue-twister finale, the Exorcist clearly was in the right when he accused The First of being a meddlesome busybody, I can certainly vouch for that. On the other hand, though, I did think the guy was capable of keeping me and releasing The First and Fina, under the condition that he would axe me if they ever spilled the beans to anyone. In short, it was relatively unimportant if we agreed with him or not. He had all the cards to play and we had none.

I didn't say anything because, for the moment, my pointing out that observation would not help to brighten the mood much. Although, when you got down to it, the Exorcist's solution did seem like a far better option than the three of us getting bumped off on the motorway near Garraf. And in that light, accepting his proposal was really the best option because at least it would allow me to negotiate the conditions.

'All right. Let's suppose, for a moment, that I decide to stay here as your hostage,' I began.

'Forget it,' The First interrupted.

'Shut up for a second, do you mind? I'm speaking to your friend.'

'Very well. Let's suppose,' said the Exorcist. 'But let's begin by referring to you, if we may, not as a hostage but as a guest.'

'Right. Let's suppose I decide to stay here as your guest. Under what conditions would I be living?'

'Whatever conditions you require. We can give you whatever you like, as I said before. What do you think you would need to be comfortable?'

I thought a bit and tried to compose a list of my bare necessities.

'Comfortable, what does that mean to me, comfortable . . . I don't know . . . abundant food . . . a daily bottle of vodka or its equivalent in lower-grade alcohol . . . ten grams a week of hashish . . . female companionship from time to time (for exclusively sexual ends, of course) . . . an Internet connection . . . I guess . . . and no predetermined schedules, I'm allergic to alarm clocks.'

My requirements seemed to amuse him.

'You are an extraordinary man, if I may say so myself. I would be delighted to discuss this further with you, at our leisure. For the moment, however, I can tell you that I am perfectly prepared to accept your conditions, though with one small modification. I can provide you with almost any kind of drug, including alcohol, but as far as female company is concerned, you will have to take care of that on your own. That said, of course, I think you'll find it quite easy in the Fortress to find whomever you might be looking for. Our female population in this enclave totals out at almost two thousand women – internals and natives included – and I'm certain that a considerable number of them would be most interested in your company. Internet connections are a rather rare privilege here on the inside, but given the special circumstances involved in your situation, we can surely provide you with one – always under a certain amount of surveillance, of course. You must understand that we cannot allow you to surf the web indiscriminately. I would venture to say that we would allow you to have access to whatever information you might want, but that your transmissions would be subjected to a process of surveillance. I think that would be technically possible. And in addition, of course, we would provide you with most acceptable health and hygiene conditions, and we would offer you private dwellings that would be ample enough for you to work and rest comfortably. How does that sound to you? Can you think of anything else?'

I thought hard, focusing all the attention I could muster, so as not to leave out anything basic from my list.

'Can I watch television?'

He smiled again. I still couldn't figure out what the hell he found so funny.

'I'm sorry. That I cannot grant you. Unless, of course, you manage to do so via the Internet.'

The First was now looking at me with a you-don't-know-what-you're-getting-into face, but to tell the truth, the place was starting to sound pretty appealing. In fact, I don't think I could have invented a paradise more tailor-made to my desires: there was only one woman in the Garden of Eden, no alcohol, not even a crummy transistor radio – and that's not to mention Yahweh, who was probably like my father only a hell of a lot worse, and omniscient to boot. The only things that concerned me were those 'hygiene and health conditions' (did that mean I was going to have to shower every day?) and the notion that it would be so easy to find female companionship in an environment in which money didn't change hands. The loyal reader will remember how I mistrust all women who don't charge for their services. How on Earth could I possibly be of interest to a Fortress woman? Only for something sordid, that had to be it.

Just then, Fina returned from the ladies' room in the company of her official escort, who appeared only briefly, to open the door for her. She had changed out of her robe and into a pair of black coveralls. Now she looked like one of Charlie's Angels.

'Did I miss anything?'

The Exorcist answered.

'Yes, in fact: a glass of champagne. Would you like one?'

'If it's cold . . .'

'And a slice of cake?'

'With fruit?'

'Pignoli nuts.'

'Well, just a sliver, it's so fattening, you know. I see you're celebrating now,' she replied, and gazed outside. 'Oh, it's so pretty – look, they've lit up Montjüic.'

The Exorcist served Fina her champagne, and then raised his glass to make a toast:

'To your health, Pablo, and to the agreement we have sealed, an agreement that will be as beneficial to us as it will be to you.'

The First rose up from his chair.

'Excuse me, Ignacio, but we haven't made any such agreement. And if you don't mind, I'd like a few words with my brother, alone if possible.'

'Of course. I'm sure you two have some personal issues to sort out. In the meanwhile, perhaps your charming friend and I will finish our champagne together.'

At the Exorcist's bidding, one of the mega-hyenas opened

a sliding door that was almost hidden behind some wood panelling. The First strode confidently over to the door and cocked his head toward it, indicating that I was to follow him.

The room we entered was outfitted with an oval table and twenty or so chairs. Through the metal blinds covering another massive picture window you could see the city lights sparkling down below.

'Are you mad?' said The First.

'Naturally,' I replied.

'They're not exactly proposing a vacation scheme at the Poblet monastery, idiot. They're proposing that you spend the rest of your life inside this place. Do you know what that means?'

'Yes, and so what? If I don't accept it, I will be equally condemned to live the rest of my life on the outside.'

'Do me a favour and drop the jokes, if you don't mind. And stop smoking that shit already, it's making your brain rot. Now. We are going to leave this room and tell Ignacio that we do not accept his proposal.'

'Oh, really? And would you rather he bump us off in your car?'

'Let them try. I can assure you that we'll put up a good fight.'

'Oh, sure. Sven the Terrible has spoken. And Fina? What about her, you're prepared to let her die with her gun cocked? And your kids? How are they ever going to grow up to be good little snobs if you aren't there to teach them?'

He hesitated a moment, and I took advantage of the lull to emphasise my point.

'Think about it for a second: if we refuse to go along with him, there's no way we'll get out of here – all we'll get is death by bloodbath, and a messy one at that. On the other hand, if we accept we'll gain a bit of time, and from the outside you can start moving things to help me escape. Wouldn't it be easier if we only had to worry about getting one of us out of here? That way we can plan the escape slowly and calmly, plus there'll be other people to help us.'

'Very well then. I'll stay and you go with Josephine.'

'But you heard what your friend said: he won't accept anyone but me.'

'We'll see about that.'

I decided to switch tactics.

'Shit, Sebastian – can't you see I want to give it a try?'

That one really got him.

'Try? Try what? Getting yourself stuck in a black hole?'

'All right, all right . . . all your goddamn life you've treated me as if I live in the worst kind of squalor and misery. Why don't you realise once and for all that I adore my little bit of misery.'

'What you are is sick. Very sick.'

'All right. That's fine. But I'm not looking for a cure.'

'All you do is talk shit.'

'Fine, okay. But for once in your life, why don't you listen to my shit, because this time I'm not going to repeat it. I am not interested in your world, or the people in it. Every so often I may grow fond of someone, but almost inevitably it's like the kind of fondness you feel for sea turtles: you can watch them frolic in the sun from the terrace but you never feel they're really with you. Do you know what I mean? I don't need anyone – you do. You need an audience that admires you, little mirrors that reflect that various facets of your grandeur: wife, children, lover, parents, friends, clients, employees, first-class plane tickets, awards, playing Debussy, driving your Lotus, being able to satisfy women sexually. I don't, and do you know why? Because in the majority of cases, admiration is nothing more than a veiled form of envy, and I don't want people to envy me: it makes me sick, it makes me embarrassed, it grosses me out. Get it? And there's something else I'm going to tell you: yes, it is entirely possible that for a while I was sick – sick from loneliness, like a poor little ugly duckling, or else like a fully-erect, smooth-cheeked Neanderthal in a world of Cro-Magnons. I was so sick that I actually travelled around the world trying to find other swans like me. And you know what I found out? There are no swans – oh, maybe one or two for every hundred ducks, and that's as true here as it is in Jakarta. It wasn't easy for me to accept but eventually I got used to the idea. Ever since then I have simply preferred to isolate myself from that world that you all have so poorly created. What do you suggest I do? Replace my beer with a gym membership? Trade in the Metaphysical Club for a sports car? Give up hookers and get myself a wife who sees me as nothing more than a sperm bank and then compensate with a lover who sucks me off now and then? No thanks. I am who I am, I enjoy life in my own way and that is a hell of a lot more than most people can say for themselves.'

My vehemence appeared to have mesmerised The First, who was not used to hearing me speak in that tone of voice. Had I actually spoken my mind? Had I been totally honest with my Magnificent Brother for once in my life? Tough to say: the things we consider to be truths are usually just more lies, only with better spin on them. Let's just say that I said what I felt was appropriate to say to The First at that moment, and I kept at it for a while until I got the sense that he was beginning to understand me somewhat.

When I finished up my little speech, The First had a very serious expression on his face. He pulled out one of the chairs and sat down, resting his arms on the table. He sat there, silent, for about a minute, staring at his intertwined thumbs. I walked around the table and sat down in front of him, in the same position, letting the silence take effect.

'Are you sure?' he asked at last, raising his eyes to meet mine.

'Well, I've been trying to tell you that for a while.'

'All right. But do me one favour.'

'What is it?'

'I am going to propose a modification to the agreement with Ignacio. A year from now, I want us to be able to meet and have a chat alone, just the two of us. And if at that point you've changed your mind, he will have to let me take your place for a year.'

'Real Bugs Bunny, your idea.'

'What?'

'Forget it . . . all right. If he accepts, so do I.'

'What are we going to tell your girlfriend?' he asked.

'Well, for the moment, that we've been kidnapped, that they've demanded a ransom and that Dad has paid up. I suppose the Exorcist will agree to go along with that one. And when I don't leave here with the two of you, just tell her that I have to stay until Dad pays the second half of the ransom. Then I'll write her a conveniently stamped postcard saying that I've left town in search of whatever sounds good. She doesn't know me well enough to see through it, even though she would tell you differently.'

'And Mom and Dad?'

'For now, we'll tell Mom that you've sent me to Bilbao to investigate.'

'Bilbao?'

'She thinks you're in Bilbao.'

'Oh, really. And what, may I ask, am I doing in Bilbao?'

'It'd take too long to explain it all. Now, the person we're going to have a tougher time with is Dad. He's been tailing me for days. But if you do the talking he'll believe anything you can dish up, short of Martians. As far as your wife, you're on your own because I don't even know how much of this she was in on. Speaking of which: sort of odd that your wife and your secretary have the same second last name.'

'I already told you, don't be too hard on Gloria.'

'She sure has talent, I'll say that for her. We hired a private eye and she actually pretended to be the sister of someone who *was*, in fact, her sister . . . Another thing, and forgive me for being dense but I've always had a hell of a time following these plots. Now: if your secretary is, in addition to your wife's half-sister, the daughter of the big boss around here, why did they kidnap her with you?'

'They didn't kidnap her: she just went out of circulation when I did, in case the police were to suddenly get involved. That turned the case into a simple lovers' tryst.'

'But Gloria knew about it . . .'

'Lali is her sister. Gloria never knew her father. Ignacio raised her when her mother died.'

'Jesus, this is like an Almodóvar movie. But wait – I had dinner with your wife at the Vellocino and I didn't perceive the slightest hint of a paterno–filial relationship between her and Ignacio.'

'They must have taken care not to let on.'

'Right. But even so, you're still her husband and, as mental as it sounds, I would even say she loves you . . .'

'That was why she tried to lead them to the person they were really after. She knew they'd get to you sooner or later and wanted to save me the trouble of refusing to confess your name.'

'And Dad . . . why in the hell did they hit him?'

'To put the pressure on me. But they realised pretty quickly that he is not a man to be messed with.'

'Why didn't they leave you alone, then, when they found out that I was the one sniffing around Jaume Guillamet? They've known for days, or it seems so at least.'

'Because I was very careful to give them a bunch of false leads. And I did such a good job of it that when they found you nosing about they figured you might not be the only one doing so and that, in addition to my brother, I was protecting someone else. I imagine they began to suspect Josephine, too. And it was very easy to stick her in a car and bring her here.'

'I'm starting to get dizzy . . .'

'All right then, leave it for now and let's get back to details. We also have to decide what we're going to tell Beba.'

'I told her you were in jail in Bilbao, too, so it won't be too hard to make the version I told her jibe with Mom's.'

'You told Beba I was in jail? You did that?'

'Shit, Sebastian. I'd like to see you try and invent some of the snow jobs I had to come up with to justify the insanity that was going on.'

'Well, for an expert in snow jobs, this one is pretty fucking lame. If you didn't drink so much, maybe you'd be a better liar . . .'

'The only reason you think it's lame is because you're a fucking spoiled brat, that's why, kid.'

'You call me kid once more and I'm going to throw that ashtray in your face. And do me the favour of focusing on what we have to focus on and not getting carried away with your bullshit.'

Anyway. That was the beginning of what would be a very long night, despite the date. I guess you can imagine the rest. But that was pretty much it: the game was up.

EPILOGUE

Everyone knows that the end of one story is merely the beginning of another, very different story.

Today is June 23rd, exactly one year from the days I have described in all these pages. That is, today I am supposed to meet with my Magnificent Brother, although we finally struck an agreement with Ignacio that is far more favourable for me: tonight I have permission to leave and visit the outside world while The First takes my place here. I will have to return before dawn tomorrow, Cinderella style, but I don't need much more than that. One does end up missing those sea turtles, and even I feel the need to stop in at Luigi's bar to get good and wasted, even though I know that tomorrow I will have to come back here.

I still read all my email from the Metaphysical Club and now I have more time than ever to read John's sentences. For the past two months, in fact, we've even had a couple of interns working for us. High philosophy has always been something of a parlour game for idle aristocrats, a delicacy and an indulgence if I may say so myself, and in that sense this the ideal place to occupy myself with being and nothingness – it's even better than the university department where John sleeps off his hangovers, because I don't have to bother myself discussing Heidegger with a bunch of acne-ridden snotnoses. I've actually spent the better part of this past year working on a kind of update of *The*

Stronghold that Ignacio is very concerned about. I'm not sure exactly how I ended up being their scribe but that is how things have turned out. Apparently the Worm World Council has been trying for some time to come up with a document that retains the spirit of the old *Stronghold* without being so scandalously obvious as the original, and Ignacio seems to think that I am the most appropriate person to draft such a document. I don't know . . . he's got this idea that I'm some kind of reincarnation of Geoffrey de Brun – he says it jokingly, but sometimes I catch a glimmer in his eyes that sends a shiver down my spine. Aside from the fact that I'm not particularly interested in being the reincarnation of anyone, I also tried to convince him that writing isn't really my thing, but he insisted so vehemently that I finally warmed up to it. And so we finally sent the definitive version about fifteen days ago and the Council gave it the thumbs-up. I imagine the Metaphysical guys will like it.

Fina, for the record, receives regular postcards from Devil's Lake, South Dakota, where I supposedly teach Spanish to American students and live with that whore who seduced me and to whom I attributed US nationality. In the first letters I received from her – very long, invariably sheathed by a scented, lilac-coloured envelope that matched the paper – she strung me up by the balls. But from what I can tell from her most recent missive – oddly, much shorter and in a sky-blue envelope this time – it seems that good old José María has gotten down to business with her, so much so that they're going to have a couple of human pups. Would Fina know how to do something so complicated? I have prayed to Our Lady of Microsoft so that she doesn't muck anything up in the DNA replication process and I trust that some genetic specialist from the

Social Security Office will explain to her – slowly – exactly what it is she has to do. In any event, I doubt she misses me very much. If there's one thing I know, it's that women are capable of demanding every last bit of attention that one is capable of giving them, but the majority of them undergo a radical change as soon as they achieve their reproductive objective. Give them a couple of pups and they can't be bothered with anything else for years. And the same is true of the husbands, too.

Of course, my family also believes that I am somewhere in Yankee land, we didn't want to go around making up incompatible stories, after all. For my Father's Highness we invented a five-hundred-thousand-euro ransom for his Magnificent Son (we didn't want to get abusive), though I suspect that The First, crafty soul that he is, figured out some way to pocket the cash in the process. No doubt he'll put the money toward a vat of expensive cologne – those little bottles they sell in the department store don't last a minute. I talk to my Father's Highness on the phone every so often and, naturally, the only thing that interests him is my supposed American girlfriend. Beba, on the other hand, smelled a bit of a rat, and made me tell her all about my apartment, the food I eat, and the language academy I work for, so that she could be sure it wasn't some kind of hellhole like in that Sidney Poitier movie. Not to mention the endless speech I had to give her to explain that a person would actually pay me to teach something as easy as Spanish.

As far as everything else, I'm having a pretty good time here. I mean, I can get trashed whenever I want in Jenny G's penthouse and eat at the Vellocino, to cite two establishments the reader is familiar with. And if one wishes to maintain contact with externals, one can play football with guys that charge an arm and a leg to play on a day other than Sunday, and I can even attend training sessions with a Dutch trainer who stopped smoking some time ago. But if you're not into sports, you can hang out with a certain someone who does interviews on TV and another one that plays a cop, and other assorted hotshots you would definitely recognise if you saw them.

But there's more: can you guess who plays the piano as all my evenings come to a close? Well, actually, we use the piano very infrequently – in the long run you end up getting sore from tickling the ivories so much. The worst thing is that lately she won't stop talking about pups – she may be a bohemian, but she is getting on in years, after all. Given, however, that I still find viviparous reproduction to be so retrograde, I adamantly refuse to abandon the cult of latex. That little fox sure knows how to make things difficult for me, though, so who knows? Any day something could go wrong and we'll end up in some kind of mutual mess. I wouldn't put it past us.

Of course, the majority of this brigade that wafts in and out of here only knows part of the whole story about what goes on inside this place – I am an internal, of course, and am always here, just like the rest of the so-called 'natives' and so these pages I have been writing on the sly are no doubt fuelled by the bit of homesickness that still plagues me. That's why I'm glad to be able to leave for a night, even if it's only for one night a year – precisely that night when the most colourful of externals come to celebrate the summer solstice inside this place. Ever since last night at midnight they've been filing in with that little red rag always fluttering in the wind. Sometimes it's hard for me to accept the fact that the outside world still exists, right there behind the walls that encircle the ground floor of our enclave. And

I have to stick my head out on the terrace to hear the sound of firecrackers to remind myself that I am still, in fact, in Barcelona. Naturally I understand that I ought to explain what I mean by such terms as 'natives' and 'internals' and all that other stuff, but The First had a point about something: The Fortress has a way of awakening curiosity in people, and that curiosity is, in fact, the greatest source of danger to people on the outside who venture near here. The more you know, the more you want to know and it's none too wise to go sniffing around – you already know what kind of mess you can get into if you start down that road.

My body and soul are crying out to celebrate the San Juan holiday, and so I will only take another minute to finish explaining that, of course, everything I've written here is completely false. That is to say, true – 'Give a man a mask and he will tell you the truth,' as they say. And for that reason, tonight I will surreptitiously leave here with a diskette containing this text. Despite the care I have taken to change names and places, I know that if I ask Ignacio's permission he will simply say no. So I won't tell him anything. And as far as my readers are concerned: what's the difference if Fina's name isn't really Fina, she's still the same naive girl. And what's the difference if my Magnificent Brother's car is a Maserati instead of a Lotus, or my Magnificent Brother is, in reality, a Magnificent Sister, or if my name is John and not Pablo or if, in fact, I am the same Lady First who appeared in these pages and who finally gave up the bottle and managed to transcribe the insane story that her husband Sebastian and her good-for-nothing brother-in-law got mixed up in.

Still, now that I think about it, lately I've been getting the feeling that Ignacio has something up his sleeve: at times I've even thought that maybe he is the one writing these words. And in that case it would have been an unforgivable gaffe to have supplanted the persona of the president of the Worm World Council for so many pages: the great Pablo Miralles, worthy successor to Geoffrey de Brun.

In any event, everyone knows what a hell of a time I have understanding movie plots, so just in case I got side-tracked and something isn't totally clear, I will be glad to respond to questions directed to pablomiralles@hotmail.com.

I read my email every day.